TRAVELLING COMPANIONS

TRAVELLING COMPANIONS

BY
HENRY JAMES

Short Story Index Reprint Series

BOOKS FOR LIBRARIES PRESS
FREEPORT, NEW YORK

First Published 1919
Reprinted 1972

INTERNATIONAL STANDARD BOOK NUMBER:
0-8369-4111-X

LIBRARY OF CONGRESS CATALOG CARD NUMBER:
75-37552

PRINTED IN THE UNITED STATES OF AMERICA
BY
NEW WORLD BOOK MANUFACTURING CO., INC.
HALLANDALE, FLORIDA 33009

CONTENTS

FOREWORD

To those who associate the name of Henry James with all that is tedious and involved in the art of fiction, the tales in this volume, now collected for the first time, will appear as revelations of simplicity in style. Here we have the author in all his freshness; his principal literary characteristics are ease and precision. For he had not yet forged rules for abstruseness of style, to perplex and weary his reader. In these stories James showed even no remotest sign of ever becoming a by-word for convolutions of English and a mark for the parodist.

Though the author collected in his *Passionate Pilgrim* (1875) a half a dozen of the tales he published in the magazines before his thirty-second year, he overlooked stories which were at least equal to, and in some cases superior to those he then brought together. The seven stories in this volume were written and published exactly at the time of the tales in his *Passionate Pilgrim* (between 1868 and 1874). The issuing of this volume, therefore, is like giving the public a new book by Henry James of the early period. The intellectual and the average man both may read and enjoy it.

It is the tendency of some critics to deprecate what an author has not collected himself. We know that writers often have been the poorest judges of their own work. We are all familiar with the story of Byron who preferred his

Hints from Horace to *Childe Harold*. James was a particularly erring critic when it came to his own writings. This fact is attested to by his rewriting and ruining some of his best early stories. The tales in this volume are not apprentice work. They show the hand of the master. True, there is the influence of Hawthorne and George Eliot in a strong degree and a romanticism is occasionally indulged in from which the later James would have recoiled, but the fiction is solid and above all, entertaining. The author cherished a kindly feeling for these tales all his life, and in the last of his autobiographical works published—*Middle Years*—he tells with gusto how Tennyson highly praised before him one of these tales written just before James went to Europe in the spring of 1869.

James has also left us a record of the affection he entertained for them and also suggests that their origin had as a basis actual experiences. He writes in *Notes of a Son and Brother*, page 436, in speaking of his early tales, published during the period represented by the ones in this volume:

"I of course really and truly cared for them, as we say, more than for aught else whatever—cared for them with that kind of care, infatuated though it may seem, that makes it bliss for the fond votary never to so much as speak of the loved object, makes it a refinement of piety to perform his rites under cover of a perfect freedom of mind as to everything but them. These secrets of imaginative life were in fact more various than I may dream of trying to tell; they referred to actual concretions of existence as well as to the suppositious."

This collection is a resurrecting of literary material whose loss has been and would have continued to be unfortunate for American literature.

ALBERT MORDELL.

Philadelphia,
Feb. 6, 1919.

TRAVELLING COMPANIONS

I

THE most strictly impressive picture in Italy is incontestably the Last Supper of Leonardo at Milan. A part of its immense solemnity is doubtless due to its being one of the first of the great Italian masterworks that you encounter in coming down from the North. Another secondary source of interest resides in the very completeness of its decay. The mind finds a rare delight in filling each of its vacant spaces, effacing its rank defilement, and repairing, as far as possible, its sad disorder. Of the essential power and beauty of the work there can be no better evidence than this fact that, having lost so much, it has yet retained so much. An unquenchable elegance lingers in those vague outlines and incurable scars; enough remains to place you in sympathy with the unfathomable wisdom of the painter. The fresco covers a wall, the reader will remember, at the end of the former refectory of a monastery now suppressed, the precinct of which is occupied by a regiment of cavalry. Horses stamp, soldiers rattle their oaths, in the cloisters which once echoed to the sober tread of monastic sandals and the pious greetings of meek-voiced friars.

It was the middle of August, and summer sat brooding fiercely over the streets of Milan. The great brick-wrought dome of the church of St. Mary of the Graces rose black with the heat against the brazen sky. As my *fiacre* drew up in front of the church, I found another vehicle in possession of the little square of shade which carpeted the glaring pavement before the adjoining convent. I left the two drivers to share this advantage as they could, and made

haste to enter the cooler presence of the Cenacolo. Here I
found the occupants of the *fiacre* without, a young lady
and an elderly man. Here also, besides the official who
takes your tributary franc, sat a long-haired copyist, wooing
back the silent secrets of the great fresco into the cheer-
fulest commonplaces of yellow and blue. The gentleman
was earnestly watching this ingenious operation; the young
lady sat with her eyes fixed on the picture, from which she
failed to move them when I took my place on a line with
her. I, too, however, speedily became as unconscious of
her presence as she of mine, and lost myself in the study
of the work before us. A single glance had assured me
that she was an American.

Since that day, I have seen all the great art treasures of
Italy: I have seen Tintoretto at Venice, Michael Angelo
at Florence and Rome, Correggio at Parma; but I have
looked at no other picture with an emotion equal to that
which rose within me as this great creation of Leonardo
slowly began to dawn upon my intelligence from the tragical twilight of its ruin. A work so nobly conceived can
never utterly die, so long as the half-dozen main lines of
its design remain. Neglect and malice are less cunning than
the genius of the great painter. It has stored away with
masterly skill such a wealth of beauty as only perfect love
and sympathy can fully detect. So, under my eyes, the
restless ghost of the dead fresco returned to its mortal
abode. From the beautiful central image of Christ I perceived its radiation right and left along the sadly broken
line of the disciples. One by one, out of the depths of their
grim dismemberment, the figures trembled into meaning and
life, and the vast, serious beauty of the work stood revealed. What is the ruling force of this magnificent design? Is it art? is it science? is it sentiment? is it knowledge? I am sure I can't say; but in moments of doubt and
depression I find it of excellent use to recall the great picture with all possible distinctness. Of all the works of
man's hands it is the least superficial.

The young lady's companion finished his survey of the
copyist's work and came and stood behind his chair. The

reader will remember that a door has been rudely cut in the wall, a part of it entering the fresco.

"He hasn't got in that door," said the old gentleman, speaking apparently of the copyist.

The young lady was silent. "Well, my dear," he continued. "What do you think of it?"

The young girl gave a sigh. "I see it," she said.

"You see it, eh? Well, I suppose there is nothing more to be done."

The young lady rose slowly, drawing on her glove. As her eyes were still on the fresco, I was able to observe her. Beyond doubt she was American. Her age I fancied to be twenty-two. She was of middle stature, with a charming, slender figure. Her hair was brown, her complexion fresh and clear. She wore a white piqué dress and a black lace shawl, and on her thick dark braids a hat with a purple feather. She was largely characterized by that physical delicacy and that personal elegance (each of them sometimes excessive) which seldom fail to betray my young countrywomen in Europe. The gentleman, who was obviously her father, bore the national stamp as plainly as she. A shrewd, firm, generous face, which told of many dealings with many men, of stocks and shares and current prices,—a face, moreover, in which there lingered the mellow afterglow of a sense of excellent claret. He was bald and grizzled, this perfect American, and he wore a short-bristled white mustache between the two hard wrinkles forming the sides of a triangle of which his mouth was the base and the ridge of his nose, where his eye-glass sat, the apex. In deference perhaps to this exotic growth, he was better dressed than is common with the typical American citizen, in a blue necktie, a white waistcoat, and a pair of gray trousers. As his daughter still lingered, he looked at me with an eye of sagacious conjecture.

"Ah, that beautiful, beautiful, beautiful Christ," said the young lady, in a tone which betrayed her words in spite of its softness. "Oh father, what a picture!"

"Hum!" said her father, "I don't see it."

"I must get a photograph," the young girl rejoined. She

turned away and walked to the farther end of the hall, where the custodian presides at a table of photographs and prints. Meanwhile her father had perceived my Murray.

"English, sir?" he demanded.

"No, I'm an American, like yourself, I fancy."

"Glad to make your acquaintance, sir. From New York?"

"From New York. I have been absent from home, however, for a number of years."

"Residing in this part of the world?"

"No. I have been living in Germany. I have only just come into Italy."

"Ah, so have we. The young lady is my daughter. She is crazy about Italy. We were very nicely fixed at Interlaken, when suddenly she read in some confounded book or other that Italy should be seen in summer. So she dragged me over the mountains into this fiery furnace. I'm actually melting away. I have lost five pounds in three days."

I replied that the heat was indeed intense, but that I agreed with his daughter that Italy should be seen in summer. What could be pleasanter than the temperature of that vast cool hall?

"Ah, yes," said my friend; "I suppose we shall have plenty of this kind of thing. It makes no odds to me, so long as my poor girl has a good time."

"She seems," I remarked, "to be having a pretty good time with the photographs." In fact, she was comparing photographs with a great deal of apparent energy, while the salesman lauded his wares in the Italian manner. We strolled over to the table. The young girl was seemingly in treaty for a large photograph of the head of Christ, in which the blurred and fragmentary character of the original was largely intensified, though much of its exquisite pathetic beauty was also preserved. "They'll not think much of that at home," said the old gentleman.

"So much the worse for them," said his daughter, with an accent of delicate pity. With the photograph in her hand, she walked back to the fresco. Her father engaged in an English dialogue with the custodian. In the course of five minutes, wishing likewise to compare the copy and the original, I returned to the great picture. As I drew near it the young lady turned away. Her eyes then for the first time met my own. They were deep and dark and luminous,—I fancied streaming with tears. I watched her as she returned to the table. Her walk seemed to me peculiarly graceful; light, and rapid, and yet full of decision and dignity. A thrill of delight passed through my heart as I guessed at her moistened lids.

"Sweet fellow-countrywoman," I cried in silence, "you have the divine gift of feeling." And I returned to the fresco with a deepened sense of its virtue. When I turned around, my companions had left the room.

In spite of the great heat, I was prepared thoroughly to "do" Milan. In fact, I rather enjoyed the heat; it seemed to my Northern senses to deepen the Italian, the Southern, the local character of things. On that blazing afternoon, I have not forgotten, I went to the church of St. Ambrose, to the Ambrosian Library, to a dozen minor churches. Every step distilled a richer drop into the wholesome cup of pleasure. From my earliest manhood, beneath a German sky, I had dreamed of this Italian pilgrimage, and, after much waiting and working and planning, I had at last undertaken it in a spirit of fervent devotion. There had been moments in Germany when I fancied myself a clever man; but it now seemed to me that for the first time I really *felt* my intellect. Imagination, panting and exhausted, withdrew from the game; and Observation stepped into her place, trembling and glowing with open-eyed desire.

I had already been twice to the Cathedral, and had wandered through the clustering inner darkness of the high arcades which support those light-defying pinnacles and spires. Towards the close of the afternoon I found myself strolling once more over the great column-planted, altar-studded pavement, with the view of ascending to the roof. On presenting myself at the little door in the right transept, through which you gain admission to the upper regions, I perceived my late fellow-visitors of the fresco preparing apparently for an upward movement, but not without some reluctance on the paternal side. The poor gentleman had been accommodated with a chair, on which he sat fanning himself with his hat and looking painfully apoplectic. The sacristan meanwhile held open the door with an air of invitation. But my corpulent friend, with his thumb in his Murray, balked at the ascent. Recognizing me, his face expressed a sudden sense of vague relief.

"Have you been up, sir?" he inquired, groaningly.

I answered that I was about to ascend; and recalling then the fact, which I possessed rather as information than experience, that young American ladies may not improperly detach themselves on occasion from the parental side, I ventured to declare that, if my friend was unwilling to encounter the fatigue of mounting to the roof in person, I should be most happy, as a fellow-countryman, qualified already perhaps to claim a traveler's acquaintance, to accompany and assist his daughter.

"You're very good, sir," said the poor man; "I confess that I'm about played out. I'd far rather sit here and watch these pretty Italian ladies saying their prayers. Charlotte, what do you say?"

"Of course if you're tired I should be sorry to have you make the effort," said Charlotte. "But I believe the great thing is to see the view from the roof. I'm much obliged to the gentleman."

It was arranged accordingly that we should ascend together. "Good luck to you," cried my friend, "and mind you take good care of her."

Those who have rambled among the marble immensities of the summit of Milan Cathedral will hardly expect me to describe them. It is only when they have been seen as a complete concentric whole that they can be properly appreciated. It was not as a whole that I saw them; a week in Italy had assured me that I have not the architectural *coup̄ d'œil*. In looking back on the scene into which we emerged from the stifling spiral of the ascent, I have chiefly a confused sense of an immense skyward elevation and a fierce blinding efflorescence of fantastic forms of marble. There, reared for the action of the sun, you find a vast marble world. The solid whiteness lies in mighty slabs along the iridescent slopes of nave and transept, like the lonely snow-fields of the higher Alps. It leaps and climbs and shoots and attacks the unsheltered blue with a keen and joyous incision. It meets the pitiless sun with a more than equal glow; the day falters, declines, expires, but the marble shines forever, unmelted and unintermittent. You will know what I mean if you have looked upward from the Piazza at midnight. With confounding frequency, too, on some uttermost point of a pinnacle, its plastic force explodes into satisfied rest in some perfect flower of a figure. A myriad carven statues, known only to the circling air, are poised and niched beyond reach of human vision, the loss of which to mortal eyes is, I suppose, the gain of the Church and the Lord. Among all the jewelled shrines and overwrought tabernacles of Italy, I have seen no such magnificent waste of labor, no such glorious synthesis of cunning secrets. As you wander, sweating and blinking, over the changing levels of the edifice, your eye catches at a hundred points the little profile of a little saint, looking out into the dizzy air, a pair of folded hands praying to the bright immediate heavens, a sandalled monkish foot planted on the edge of the white abyss. And then, besides this mighty world of the great Cathedral itself, you possess the view of all green Lombardy,—vast, lazy Lombardy, resting from its Alpine upheavals.

My companion carried a little white umbrella, with a violet lining. Thus protected from the sun, she climbed and gazed with abundant courage and spirit. Her movements, her glance, her voice, were full of intelligent pleasure. Now that I could observe her closely, I saw that, though perhaps without regular beauty, she was yet, for youth, summer, and Italy, more than pretty enough. Owing to my residence in Germany, among Germans, in a small university town, Americans had come to have for me, in a large degree, the interest of novelty and remoteness. Of the charm of American women, in especial, I had formed a very high estimate, and I was more than ready to be led captive by the far-famed graces of their frankness and freedom. I already felt that in the young girl beside me there was a different quality of womanhood from any that I had recently known; a keenness, a maturity, a conscience, which deeply stirred my curiosity. It was positive, not negative maidenhood.

"You're an American," I said, as we stepped to look at the distance.

"Yes; and you?" In her voice alone the charm faltered. It was high, thin, and nervous.

"Oh, happily, I'm also one."

"I shouldn't have thought so. I should have taken you for a German."

"By education I am a German. I knew you were an American the moment I looked at you."

"I suppose so. It seems that American women are easily recognized. But don't talk about America." She paused and swept her dark eye over the whole immensity of prospect. "This is Italy," she cried, "Italy, Italy!"

"Italy indeed. What do you think of the Leonardo?"

"I fancy there can be only one feeling about it. It must be the saddest and finest of all pictures. But I know nothing of art. I have seen nothing yet but that lovely Raphael in the Brera."

"You have a vast deal before you. You're going southward, I suppose?"

"Yes, we are going directly to Venice. There I shall see Titian."

"Titian and Paul Veronese."

"Yes, I can hardly believe it. Have you ever been in a gondola?"

"No; this is my first visit to Italy."

"Ah, this is all new, then, to you as well."

"Divinely new," said I, with fervor.

She glanced at me, with a smile,—a ray of friendly pleasure in my pleasure. "And you are not disappointed!"

"Not a jot. I'm too good a German."

"I'm too good an American. I live at Araminta, New Jersey!"

We thoroughly "did" the high places of the church, concluding with an ascent into the little gallery of the central spire. The view from this spot is beyond all words, especially the view toward the long mountain line which shuts out the North. The sun was sinking: clear and serene upon their blue foundations, the snow-peaks sat clustered and scattered, and shrouded in silence and light. To the south the long shadows fused and multiplied, and the bosky Lombard flats melted away into perfect Italy. This prospect offers a great emotion to the Northern traveler. A vague, delicious impulse of conquest stirs in his heart. From his dizzy vantage-point, as he looks down at her, beautiful, historic, exposed, he embraces the whole land in the far-reaching range of his desire. "That is Monte Rosa," I said; "that is the Simplon pass; there is the triple glitter of those lovely lakes."

"Poor Monte Rosa," said my companion.

"I'm sure I never thought of Monte Rosa as an object of pity."

"You don't know what she represents. She represents the genius of the North. There she stands, frozen and fixed, resting her head upon that mountain wall, looking over at this lovely southern world and yearning towards it forever in vain."

"It is very well she can't come over. She would melt."

"Very true. She is beautiful, too, in her own way. I mean to fancy that I am her chosen envoy, and that I have come up here to receive her blessing."

I made an attempt to point out a few localities. "Yonder lies Venice, out of sight. In the interval are a dozen divine little towns. I hope to visit them all. I shall ramble all day in their streets and churches, their little museums, and their great palaces. In the evening I shall sit at the door of a café in the little piazza, scanning some lovely civic edifice in the moonlight, and saying, 'Ah! this is Italy!'"

"You gentlemen are certainly very happy. I'm afraid we must go straight to Venice."

"Your father insists upon it?"

"He wishes it. Poor father! in early life he formed the habit of being in a hurry, and he can't break it even now, when, being out of business, he has nothing on earth to do."

"But in America I thought daughters insisted as well as fathers."

The young girl looked at me, half serious, half smiling. "Have you a mother?" she asked; and then, blushing the least bit at her directness and without waiting for an answer, "This is not America," she said. "I should like to think I might become for a while a creature of Italy."

Somehow I felt a certain contagion in her momentary flash of frankness. "I strongly suspect," I said, "that you are American to the depths of your soul, and that you'll never be anything else; I hope not."

In this hope of mine there was perhaps a little impertinence; but my companion looked at me with a gentle smile, which seemed to hint that she forgave it. "You, on the other hand," she said, "are a perfect German, I fancy; and you'll never be anything else."

"I am sure I wish with all my heart," I answered, "to be a good American. I'm open to conversion. Try me."

"Thank you; I haven't the ardor; I'll make you over to my father. We mustn't forget, by the way, that he is waiting for us."

We did forget it, however, awhile longer. We came down from the tower and made our way to the balustrade which edges the front of the edifice, and looked down on the city and the piazza below. Milan had, to my sense, a peculiar charm of temperate gayety,—the softness of the South without its laxity; and I felt as if I could gladly spend a month there. The common life of the streets was beginning to stir and murmur again, with the subsiding heat and the approaching night. There came up into our faces a delicious emanation as from the sweetness of Transalpine life. At the little balconies of the windows, beneath the sloping awnings, with their feet among the crowded flower-pots and their plump bare arms on the iron rails, lazy, dowdy Italian beauties would appear, still drowsy with the broken *siesta*. Beautiful, slim young officers had begun to dot the pavement, glorious with their clanking swords, their brown mustaches, and their legs of azure. In gentle harmony

with these, various ladies of Milan were issuing forth to
enjoy the cool; elegant, romantic, provoking, in short black
dresses and lace mantillas depending from their *chignons,*
with a little cloud of powder artfully enhancing the darkness of their hair and eyes. How it all wasn't Germany!
how it couldn't have been Araminta, New Jersey! "It's
the South, the South," I kept repeating,—"the South in
nature, in man, in manners." It was a brighter world.
"It's the South," I said to my companion. "Don't you feel
it in all your nerves?"

"O, it's very pleasant," she said.

"We must forget all our cares and duties and sorrows.
We must go in for the beautiful. Think of this great trap
for the sunbeams, in this city of yellows and russets and
crimsons, of liquid vowels and glancing smiles being, like
one of our Northern cathedrals, a temple to Morality and
Conscience. It doesn't belong to heaven, but to earth,—
to love and light and pleasure."

My friend was silent a moment. "I'm glad I'm not a
Catholic," she said at last. "Come, we must go down."

We found the interior of the Cathedral delightfully cool
and shadowy. The young lady's father was not at our place
of ingress, and we began to walk through the church in
search of him. We met a number of Milanese ladies, who
charmed us with their sombre elegance and the Spanish romance of their veils. With these pale penitents and postu-
lants my companion had a lingering sisterly sympathy.

"Don't you wish you were a Catholic now?" I asked. "It
would be so pleasant to wear one of those lovely mantillas."

"The mantillas are certainly becoming," she said. "But
who knows what horrible old-world sorrows and fears and
remorses they cover? Look at this person." We were
standing near the great altar. As she spoke, a woman
rose from her knees, and as she drew the folds of her lace
mantle across her bosom, fixed her large dark eyes on us
with a peculiar significant intensity. She was of less than
middle age, with a pale, haggard face, a certain tarnished
elegance of dress, and a remarkable nobleness of gesture and
carriage. She came towards us, with an odd mixture, in

her whole expression, of decency and defiance. "Are you English?" she said in Italian. "You are very pretty. Is he a brother or a lover?"

"He is neither," said I, affecting a tone of rebuke.

"Neither? only a friend! You are very happy to have a friend, Signorina. Ah, you are pretty! You were watching me at my prayers just now; you thought me very curious, apparently. I don't care. You may see me here any day. But I devoutly hope you may never have to pray such bitter, bitter prayers as mine. A thousand excuses." And she went her way.

"What in the world does she mean?" said my companion.

"Monte Rosa," said I, "was the genius of the North. This poor woman is the genius of the Picturesque. She shows us the essential misery that lies behind it. It's not an unwholesome lesson to receive at the outset. Look at her sweeping down the aisle. What a poise of the head! The picturesque is handsome, all the same."

"I do wonder what is her trouble," murmured the young girl. "She has swept away an illusion in the folds of those black garments."

"Well," said I, "here is a solid fact to replace it." My eyes had just lighted upon the object of our search. He sat in a chair, half tilted back against a pillar. His chin rested on his shirt-bosom, and his hands were folded together over his waistcoat, where it most protruded. Shirt and waistcoat rose and fell with visible, audible regularity. I wandered apart and left his daughter to deal with him. When she had fairly aroused him, he thanked me heartily for my care of the young lady, and expressed the wish that we might meet again. "We start to-morrow for Venice," he said. "I want awfully to get a whiff of the sea-breeze and to see if there is anything to be got out of a gondola."

As I expected also to be in Venice before many days, I had little doubt of our meeting. In consideration of this circumstance, my friend proposed that we should exchange cards; which we accordingly did, then and there, before the high altar, above the gorgeous chapel which enshrines the relics of St. Charles Borromeus. It was thus that I learned his name to be Mr. Mark Evans.

"Take a few notes for us!" said Miss Evans, as I shook her hand in farewell.

I spent the evening, after dinner, strolling among the crowded streets of the city, tasting of Milanese humanity. At the door of a café I perceived Mr. Evans seated at a little round table. He seemed to have discovered the merits of absinthe. I wondered where he had left his daughter. She was in her room, I fancied, writing her journal.

The fortnight which followed my departure from Milan was in all respects memorable and delightful. With an interest that hourly deepened as I read, I turned the early pages of the enchanting romance of Italy. I carried out in detail the programme which I had sketched for Miss Evans. Those few brief days, as I look back on them, seem to me the sweetest, fullest, calmest of my life. All personal passions, all restless egotism, all worldly hopes, regrets, and fears were stilled and absorbed in the steady perception of the material present. It exhaled the pure essence of romance. What words can reproduce the picture which these Northern Italian towns project upon a sympathetic retina? They are shabby, deserted, dreary, decayed, unclean. In those August days the southern sun poured into them with a fierceness which might have seemed fatal to any lurking shadow of picturesque mystery. But taking them as cruel time had made them and left them, I found in them an immeasurable instruction and charm. My perception seemed for the first time to live a sturdy creative life of its own. How it fed upon the mouldy crumbs of the festal past! I have always thought the observant faculty a windy impostor, so long as it refuses to pocket pride and doff its bravery and crawl on all-fours, if need be, into the unillumined corners and crannies of life. In these dead cities of Verona, Mantua, Padua, how life had revelled and postured in its strength! How sentiment and passion had blossomed and flowered! How much of history had been performed! What a wealth of mortality had ripened and decayed! I have never elsewhere got so deep an impression of the social secrets of mankind. In England, even, in those verdure-stifled haunts of domestic peace which muffle the sounding chords of British civilization, one has a fainter sense of the possible movement and fruition of individual character. Beyond a certain point you fancy it merged in the general medium of duty, business, and politics. In Italy, in spite of your knowledge of the strenuous public conscience which once inflamed these compact little states, the unapplied, spontaneous moral life of society seems to have been more active and more subtle. I walked about with a volume of Stendhal in my pocket; at every step I gathered some lingering testimony to the exquisite vanity of ambition.

But the great emotion, after all, was to feel myself among scenes in which art had ranged so freely. It had often enough been bad, but it had never ceased to be art. An invincible instinct of beauty had presided at life,—an instinct often ludicrously crude and primitive. Wherever I turned I found a vital principle of grace,—from the smile of a chambermaid to the curve of an arch. My memory reverts with an especial tenderness to certain hours in the dusky, faded saloons of those vacant, ruinous palaces which boast of "collections." The pictures are frequently poor, but the visitor's impression is generally rich. The brick-tiled floors are bare; the doors lack paint; the great windows, curtains; the chairs and tables have lost their gilding and their damask drapery; but the ghost of a graceful aristocracy treads at your side and does the melancholy honors of the abode with a dignity that brooks no sarcasm. You feel that art and piety here have been blind, generous instincts. You are reminded in persuasive accents of the old personal regimen in human affairs. Certain pictures are veiled and curtained *virginibus puerisque*. Through these tarnished halls lean and patient abbés led their youthful virginal pupils. Have you read Stendhal's *Chartreuse de Parme?* There was such a gallery in the palace of the Duchess of San Severino. After a long day of strolling, lounging, and staring, I found a singularly perfect pleasure in sitting at the door of a café in the warm starlight, eating an ice and making an occasional experiment in the way of talk with my neighbors. I recall with peculiar fondness and delight three sweet sessions in the delicious Piazza dei Signori at Verona. The Piazza is small, compact, private almost, accessible only to pedestrians, paved with great slabs which have known none but a gentle human tread. On one side of it rises in elaborate elegance and grace, above its light arched *loggia*, the image-bordered mass of the ancient palace of the Council; facing this stand two sterner, heavier buildings, dedicated to municipal offices and to the lodgment of soldiers. Step through the archway which leads out of the Piazza and you will find a vast quadrangle with a staircase climbing sunward, along the wall, a row of gendarmes sitting in the shade, a group of soldiers cleaning their muskets, a dozen persons of either sex leaning downward from the open windows. At one end of the little square rose into the pale darkness the high slender shaft of a brick campanile; in the centre glittered steadily a colossal white statue of Dante. Behind this statue was the Caffé Dante, where on three successive days I sat till midnight, feeling the scene, learning its sovereign "distinction." But of Verona I shall not pretend to speak. As I drew near Venice I began to feel a soft impatience, an expectant tremor of the heart. The day before reaching it I spent at Vicenza. I wandered all day through the streets, of course, looking at Palladio's palaces and enjoying them in defiance of reason and Ruskin. They seemed to me essentially rich and palatial. In the evening I resorted, as usual, to the city's generous heart, the decayed ex-glorious Piazza. This spot of Vicenza affords you a really soul-stirring premonition of Venice. There is no Byzantine Basilica and no Ducal Palace; but there is an immense impressive hall of council, and a soaring campanile, and there are two discrowned columns telling of defeated Venetian dominion. Here I seated myself before a café door, in a group of gossiping votaries of the Southern night. The tables being mostly occupied, I had some difficulty in finding one. In a short time I perceived a young man walking through the crowd, seeking where he might bestow himself. Passing near me, he stopped and asked me with irresistible grace if he might share my table. I cordially assented: he sat down and ordered a glass of sugar and water. He was of about my own age, apparently, and full of the opulent beauty of the greater number of young Italians. His dress was simple even to shabbiness: he might have been a young prince in disguise, a Haroun-al-Raschid. With small delay we engaged in conversation. My companion was boyish, modest, and gracious; he nevertheless discoursed freely on the things of Vicenza. He was so good as to regret that we had not met earlier in the day; it would have given him such pleasure to accompany me on my tour of the city. He was passionately fond of art: he was in fact an artist. Was I fond of pictures? Was I inclined to purchase? I answered that I had no desire to purchase modern pictures, that in fact I had small means to purchase any. He informed me that he had a beautiful ancient work which, to his great regret, he found himself compelled to sell; a most divine little Correggio. Would I do him the favor to look at it? I had small belief in the value of this unrenowned masterpiece; but I felt a kindness for the young painter. I consented to have him call for me the next morning and take me to his house, where for two hundred years, he assured me, the work had been jealously preserved.

He came punctually, beautiful, smiling, shabby, as before. After a ten minutes' walk we stopped before a gaudy half-palazzo which rejoiced in a vague Palladian air. In the basement, looking on the court, lived my friend; with his mother, he informed me, ѣnd his sister. He ushered me in, through a dark antechamber, into which, through a gaping kitchen door, there gushed a sudden aroma of onions. I found myself in a high, half-darkened saloon. One of the windows was open into the court, from which the light entered verdantly through a row of flowering plants. In an armchair near the window sat a young girl in a dressing-gown, empty-handed, pale, with wonderful eyes, apparently an invalid. At her side stood a large elderly woman in a rusty black silk gown, with an agreeable face, flushed a little, apparently with the expectation of seeing me. The young man introduced them as his mother and his sister. On a table near the window, propped upright in such a way as to catch the light, was a small picture in a heavy frame. I proceeded to examine it. It represented in simple composition a Madonna and Child; the mother facing you, pressing the infant to her bosom, faintly smiling, and looking out of the picture with a solemn sweetness. It was pretty, it was good; but it was not Correggio. There was indeed a certain suggestion of his exquisite touch; but it was a likeness merely, and not the precious reality. One fact, however, struck swiftly home to my consciousness: the face of the Madonna bore a singular resemblance to that of Miss Evans. The lines, the character, the expression, were the same; the faint half-thoughtful smile was hers, the feminine frankness and gentle confidence of the brow, from which the dark hair waved back with the same even abundance. All this, in the Madonna's face, was meant for heaven; and on Miss Evans's in a fair degree, probably, for earth. But the mutual likeness was, nevertheless, perfect, and it quickened my interest in the picture to a point which the intrinsic merit of the work would doubtless have failed to justify; although I confess that I was now not slow to discover a great deal of agreeable painting in it.

"But I doubt of its being a Correggio," said I.

"A Correggio, I give you my word of honor, sir!" cried my young man.

"*Ecco!* my son's word of honor," cried his mother.

"I don't deny," I said, "that it is a very pretty work. It is perhaps Parmigianino."

"O no, sir," the elder insisted, "a true Correggio! We have had it two hundred years! Try another light; you will see. A true Correggio! Isn't it so, my daughter?"

The young man put his arm in mine, played his fingers airily over the picture, and whispered of a dozen beauties.

"O, I grant you," said I, "it's a very pretty picture." As I looked at it I felt the dark eyes of the young girl in the arm-chair fixed upon me with almost unpleasant intensity. I met her gaze for a moment: I found in it a strange union of defiant pride and sad despondent urgency.

"What do you ask for the picture?" I said.

There was a silence.

"Speak, *madre mia*," said the young man.

"La senta!" and the lady played with her broken fan. "We should like you to name a price."

"O, if I named a price, it would not be as for a Correggio. I can't afford to buy Correggios. If this were a real Correggio, you would be rich. You should go to a duke, a prince, not to me."

"We would be rich! Do you hear, my children? We are very poor, sir. You have only to look at us. Look at my poor daughter. She was once beautiful, fresh, gay. A year ago she fell ill: a long story, sir, and a sad one. We have had doctors; they have ordered five thousand things. My daughter gets no better. There it is, sir. We are very poor."

The young girl's look confirmed her mother's story. That she had been beautiful I could easily believe; that she was ill was equally apparent. She was still remarkable indeed for a touching, hungry, unsatisfied grace. She remained silent and motionless, with her eyes fastened upon my face. I again examined the pretended Correggio. It was wonderfully like Miss Evans. The young American rose up in my mind with irresistible vividness and grace. How she seemed to glow with strength, freedom, and joy, beside this sombre, fading, Southern sister! It was a happy thought that, under the benediction of her image, I might cause a ray of healing sunshine to fall at this poor girl's feet.

"Have you ever tried to sell the picture before?"

"Never!" said the old lady, proudly. "My husband had it from his father. If we have made up our minds to part with it now,—most blessed little Madonna!—it is because we have had an intimation from heaven."

"From heaven?"

"From heaven, Signore. My daughter had a dream. She dreamed that a young stranger came to Vicenza, and that he wandered about the streets saying, 'Where, ah where, is my blessed Lady?' Some told him in one church, and some told him in another. He went into all the churches and lifted all the curtains, giving great fees to the sacristans! But he always came out shaking his head and repeating his question, 'Where is my blessed Lady? I have come from over the sea, I have come to Italy to find her!'" The woman delivered herself of this recital with a noble florid unction and a vast redundancy, to my Northern ear, of delightful liquid sounds. As she paused momentarily, her daughter spoke for the first time.

"And then I fancied," said the young girl, "that I heard his voice pausing under my window at night. 'His blessed Lady is here,' I said, 'we must not let him lose her.' So I called my brother and bade him go forth in search of you. I dreamed that he brought you back. We made an altar with candles and lace and flowers, and on it we placed the little picture. The stranger had light hair, light eyes, a flowing beard like you. He kneeled down before the little Madonna and worshipped her. We left him at his devotions and went away. When we came back the candles on the altar were out: the Madonna was gone, too; but in its place there burned a bright pure light. It was a purse of gold!"

"What a very pretty story!" said I. "How many pieces were there in the purse?"

The young man burst into a laugh. "Twenty thousand!" he said.

I made my offer for the picture. It was esteemed generous apparently; I was cordially thanked. As it was inconvenient, however, to take possession of the work at that moment, I agreed to pay down but half the sum, reserving the other half to the time of delivery. When I prepared to take my departure the young girl rose from her chair and enabled me to measure at once her weakness and her beauty. "Will you come back for the picture yourself?" she asked.

"Possibly. I should like to see you again. You must get better."

"O, I shall never get better."

"I can't believe that. I shall perhaps have a dream to tell you!"

"I shall soon be in heaven. I shall send you one."

"Listen to her!" cried the mother. "But she is already an angel."

With a farewell glance at my pictured Madonna I departed. My visit to this little Vicenza household had filled me with a painful, indefinable sadness. So beautiful they all were, so civil, so charming, and yet so mendacious and miserable! As I hurried along in the train toward the briny cincture of Venice, my heart was heavy with the image of that sombre, dying Italian maiden. Her face haunted me. What fatal wrong had she suffered? What hidden sorrow had blasted the freshness of her youth? As I began to smell the nearing Adriatic, my fancy bounded forward to claim asylum in the calmer presence of my bright American friend. I have no space to tell the story of my arrival in Venice and my first impressions. Mr. Evans had not mentioned his hotel. He was not at the Hotel de l'Europe, whither I myself repaired. If he was still in Venice, however, I foresaw that we should not fail to meet. The day succeeding my arrival I spent in a restless fever of curiosity and delight, now lost in the sensuous ease of my gondola, now lingering in charmed devotion before a canvas of Tintoretto or Paul Veronese. I exhausted three gondoliers and saw all Venice in a passionate fury and haste. I wished to probe its fulness and learn at once the best—or the worst. Late in the afternoon I disembarked at the Piazzetta and took my way haltingly and gazingly to the many-domed Basilica,—that shell of silver with a lining of marble. It was that enchanting Venetian hour when the ocean-touching sun sits melting to death, and the whole still air seems to glow with the soft effusion of his golden substance. Within the church, the deep brown shadow-masses, the heavy thick-tinted air, the gorgeous composite darkness, reigned in richer, quainter, more fantastic gloom than my feeble pen can reproduce the likeness of. From those rude concavities of dome and semi-dome, where the multitudinous facets of pictorial mosaic shimmer and twinkle in their own dull brightness; from the vast antiquity of innumerable marbles, incrusting the walls in roughly mated slabs, cracked and polished and triple-tinted with eternal service; from the wavy carpet of compacted stone, where a thousand once-lighted fragments glimmer through the long attrition of idle feet and devoted knees; from sombre gold and mellow alabaster, from porphyry and malachite, from long dead crystal and the sparkle of undying lamps,—there proceeds a dense rich atmosphere of splendor and sanctity which transports the half-stupefied traveller to the age of a simpler and more awful faith. I wandered for half an hour beneath those reverted cups of scintillating darkness, stumbling on the great stony swells of the pavement as I gazed upward at the long mosaic saints who curve gigantically with the curves of dome and ceiling. I had left Europe; I was in the East. An overwhelming sense of the sadness of man's spiritual history took possession of my heart. The clustering picturesque shadows about me seemed to represent the darkness of a past from which he had slowly and painfully struggled. The great mosaic images, hideous, grotesque, inhuman, glimmered like the cruel spectres of early superstitions and terrors. There came over me, too, a poignant conviction of the ludicrous folly of the idle spirit of travel. How with Murray and an opera-glass it strolls and stares where omniscient angels stand diffident and sad! How blunted and stupid are its senses! How trivial and superficial its imaginings! To this builded sepulchre of trembling hope and dread, this monument of mighty passions, I had wandered in search of pictorial effects. O vulgarity! Of course I remained, nevertheless, still curious of effects. Suddenly I perceived a very agreeable one. Kneeling on a low *prie-dieu*, with her hands clasped, a lady was gazing upward at the great mosaic Christ in the dome of the choir. She wore a black lace shawl and a purple hat. She was Miss Evans. Her attitude slightly puzzled me. Was she really at her devotions, or was she only playing at prayer? I walked to a distance, so that she might have time to move before I addressed her. Five minutes afterwards, however, she was in the same position. I walked slowly towards her, and as I approached her attracted her attention. She immediately recognized me and smiled and bowed, without moving from her place.

"I saw you five minutes ago," I said, "but I was afraid of interrupting your prayers."

"O, they were only half-prayers," she said.

"Half-prayers are pretty well for one who only the other day was thanking Heaven that she was not a Catholic."

"Half-prayers are no prayers. I'm not a Catholic yet."

Her father, she told me, had brought her to the church, but had returned on foot to the hotel for his pocket-book. They were to dine at one of the restaurants in the Piazza. Mr. Evans was vastly contented with Venice, and spent his days and nights in gondolas. Awaiting his return, we wandered over the church. Yes, incontestably, Miss Evans resembled my little Vicenza picture. She looked a little pale with the heat and the constant nervous tension of sight-seeing; but she pleased me now as effectually as she had pleased me before. There was an even deeper sweetness in the freedom and breadth of her utterance and carriage. I felt more even than before that she was an example of woman active, not of woman passive. We strolled through the great Basilica in serious, charmed silence. Miss Evans told me that she had been there much: she seemed to know it well. We went into the dark Baptistery and sat down on a bench against the wall, trying to discriminate in the vaulted dimness the harsh mediæval reliefs behind the altar and the mosaic Crucifixion above it.

"Well," said I, "what has Venice done for you?"

"Many things. Tired me a little, saddened me, charmed me."

"How have you spent your time?"

"As people spend it. After breakfast we get into our gondola and remain in it pretty well till bedtime. I believe I know every canal, every canaletto, in Venice. You must have learned already how sweet it is to lean back under the awning to feel beneath you that steady, liquid lapse, to look out at all this bright, sad elegance of ruin. I have been reading two or three of George Sand's novels. Do you know *La Dernière Aldini?* I fancy a romance in every palace."

"The reality of Venice seems to me to exceed all romance. It's romance enough simply to be here."

"Yes; but how brief and transient a romance!"

"Well," said I, "we shall certainly cease to be here, but we shall never cease to have been here. You are not to leave directly, I hope."

"In the course of ten days or a fortnight we go to Florence."

"And then to Rome?"

"To Rome and Naples, and then by sea, probably, to Genoa, and thence to Nice and Paris. We must be at home by the new year. And you?"

"I hope to spend the winter in Italy."

"Are you never coming home again?"

"By no means. I shall probably return in the spring. But I wish you, too, were going to remain."

"You are very good. My father pronounces it impossible. I have only to make the most of it while I'm here."

"Are you going back to Araminta?"

Miss Evans was silent a moment. "O, don't ask!" she said.

"What kind of a place is Araminta?" I asked, maliciously.

Again she was silent. "That is John the Baptist on the cover of the basin," she said, at last, rising to her feet, with a light laugh.

On emerging from the Baptistery we found Mr. Evans, who greeted me cordially and insisted on my coming to dine with them. I think most fondly of our little dinner. We went to the Caffé Quadri and occupied a table beside an open window, looking out into the Piazza, which was beginning to fill with evening loungers and listeners to the great band of music in the centre. Miss Evans took off her hat and sat facing me in friendly silence. Her father sustained the larger burden of conversation. He seemed to feel its weight, however, as the dinner proceeded and when he had attacked his second bottle of wine. Miss Evans then questioned me about my journey from Milan. I told her the whole story, and felt that I infused into it a great deal of color and heat. She sat charming me forward with her steady, listening smile. For the first time in my life I felt the magic of sympathy. After dinner we went down into the Piazza and established ourselves at one of Florian's tables. Night had become perfect; the music was magnificent. At a neighboring table was a group of young Venetian gentlemen, splendid in dress, after the manner of their kind, and glorious with the wondrous physical glory of the Italian race.

"They only need velvet and satin and plumes," I said, "to be subjects for Titian and Paul Veronese."

They sat rolling their dark eyes and kissing their white hands at passing friends, with smiles that were like the moon-flashes on the Adriatic.

"They are beautiful exceedingly," said Miss Evans; "the most beautiful creatures in the world, except——"

"Except, you mean, this other gentleman."

She assented. The person of whom I had spoken was a young man who was just preparing to seat himself at a vacant table. A lady and gentleman, elderly persons, had passed near him and recognized him, and he had uncovered himself and now stood smiling and talking. They were all genuine Anglo-Saxons. The young man was rather short of stature, but firm and compact. His hair was light and crisp, his eye a clear blue, his face and neck violently tanned by exposure to the sun. He wore a pair of small blond whiskers.

"Do you call him beautiful?" demanded Mr. Evans. "He reminds me of myself when I was his age. Indeed, he looks like you, sir."

"He's not beautiful," said Miss Evans, "but he is handsome."

The young man's face was full of decision and spirit; his whole figure had been moulded by action, tempered by effort. He looked simple and keen, upright, downright.

"Is he English?" asked Miss Evans, "or American?"

"He is both," I said, "or either. He is made of that precious clay that is common to the whole English-speaking race."

"He's American."

"Very possibly," said I; and indeed we never learned. I repeat the incident because I think it has a certain value in my recital. Before we separated I expressed the hope that we might meet again on the morrow.

"It's very kind of you to propose it," said Miss Evans; "but you'll thank us for refusing. Take my advice, as for an old Venetian, and spend the coming three days alone. How can you enjoy Tintoretto and Bellini, when you are racking your brains for small talk for me?"

"With you, Miss Evans, I shouldn't talk small. But you shape my programme with a liberal hand. At the end of three days, pray, where will you be?"

They would still be in Venice, Mr. Evans declared. It was a capital hotel, and then those jolly gondolas! I was unable to impeach the wisdom of the young girl's proposition. To be so wise, it seemed to me, was to be extremely charming.

For three days, accordingly, I wandered about alone. I often thought of Miss Evans and I often fancied I should enjoy certain great pictures none the less for that deep associated contemplation and those fine emanations of assent and dissent which I should have known in her society. I wandered far; I penetrated deep, it seemed to me, into the heart of Venetian power. I shook myself free of the sad and sordid present, and embarked on that silent contemplative sea whose irresistible tides expire at the base of the mighty canvases in the Scuola di San Rocco. But on my return to the hither shore, I always found my sweet young countrywoman waiting to receive me. If Miss Evans had been an immense coquette, she could not have proceeded more cunningly than by this injunction of a three days' absence. During this period, in my imagination, she increased tenfold in value. I don't mean to say that there were not hours together when I quite forgot her, and when I had no heart but for Venice and the lessons of Venice, for the sea and sky and the great painters and builders.

But when my mind had executed one of these great passages of appreciation, it turned with a sudden sense of solitude and lassitude to those gentle hopes, those fragrant hints of intimacy, which clustered about the person of my friend. She remained modestly uneclipsed by the women of Titian. She was as deeply a woman as they, and yet so much more of a person; as fit as the broadest and blondest to be loved for herself, yet full of serene superiority as an active friend. To the old, old sentiment what an exquisite modern turn she might give! I so far overruled her advice as that, with her father, we made a trio every evening, after the day's labors, at one of Florian's tables. Mr. Evans drank absinthe and discoursed upon the glories of our common country, of which he declared it was high time I should make the acquaintance. He was not the least of a bore: I relished him vastly. He was in many ways an excellent representative American. Without taste, without culture or polish, he nevertheless produced an impression of substance in character, keenness in perception, and intensity in will, which effectually redeemed him from vulgarity. It often seemed to me, in fact, that his good-humored tolerance and easy morality, his rank self-confidence, his nervous decision and vivacity, his fearlessness of either gods or men, combined in proportions of which the union might have been very fairly termed aristocratic. His voice, I admit, was of the nose, nasal; but possibly, in the matter of utterance, one eccentricity is as good as another. At all events, with his clear, cold gray eye, with that just faintly impudent, more than level poise of his ample chin, with those two hard lines which flanked the bristling wings of his gray moustache, with his general expression of unchallenged security and practical aptitude and incurious scorn of tradition, he impressed the sensitive beholder as a man of incontestable force. He was entertaining, too, partly by wit and partly by position. He was weak only in his love of absinthe. After his first glass he left his chair and strolled about the piazza, looking for possible friends and superbly unconscious of possible enemies. His daughter sat back in her chair, her arms folded, her ungloved hands sustaining them, her prettiness half defined, her voice enhanced and subdued by the gas-tempered starlight. We had infinite talk. Without question, she had an admirable feminine taste: she was worthy to know Venice. I remember telling her so in a sudden explosion of homage. "You are really worthy to know Venice, Miss Evans. We must learn to know it together. Who knows what hidden treasures we may help each other to find?"

II

At the end of my three days' probation, I spent a week constantly with my friends. Our mornings were, of course, devoted to churches and galleries, and in the late afternoon we passed and repassed along the Grand Canal or betook ourselves to the Lido. By this time Miss Evans and I had become thoroughly intimate; we had learned to know Venice together, and the knowledge had helped us to know each other. In my own mind, Charlotte Evans and Venice had played the game most effectively into each other's hands. If my fancy had been called upon to paint her portrait, my fancy would have sketched her with a background of sunset-flushed palace wall, with a faint reflected light from the green lagoon playing up into her face. And if I had wished to sketch a Venetian scene, I should have painted it from an open window, with a woman leaning against the casement,—as I had often seen her lean from a window in her hotel. At the end of a week we went one afternoon to the Lido, timing our departure so as to allow us to return at sunset. We went over in silence, Mr. Evans sitting with reverted head, blowing his cigar-smoke against the dazzling sky, which told so fiercely of sea and summer; his daughter motionless and thickly veiled; I facing them, feeling the broken swerve of our gondola, and watching Venice grow level and rosy beyond the liquid interval. Near the landing-place on the hither side of the Lido is a small *trattoria* for the refreshment of visitors. An arbor outside the door, a horizontal vine checkering still further a dirty table-cloth, a pungent odor of *frittata*, an admiring circle of gondoliers and beggars, are the chief attractions of this suburban house of entertainment,—attractions sufficient, however, to have arrested the inquisitive steps of an elderly American gentleman, in whom Mr. Evans speedily recognized a friend of early years, a comrade in affairs. A hearty greeting ensued. This worthy man had ordered dinner: he besought Mr. Evans at least to sit down and partake of a bottle of wine. My friend vacillated between his duties as a father and the prospect of a rich old-boyish revival of the delectable interests of home; but his daughter graciously came to his assistance. "Sit down with Mr. Munson, talk till you are tired, and then walk over to the beach and find us. We shall not wander beyond call."

She and I accordingly started slowly for a stroll along the barren strand which averts its shining side from Venice and takes the tides of the Adriatic. The Lido has for me a peculiar melancholy charm, and I have often wondered that I should have felt the presence of beauty in a spot so destitute of any exceptional elements of beauty. For beyond the fact that it knows the changing moods and hues of the Adriatic, this narrow strip of sand-stifled verdure has no very rare distinction. In my own country I know many a sandy beach, and many a stunted copse, and many a tremulous ocean line of little less purity and breadth of composition, with far less magical interest. The secret of the Lido is simply your sense of adjacent Venice. It is the salt-sown garden of the city of the sea. Hither came short-paced Venetians for a meagre taste of *terra firma*, or for a wider glimpse of their parent ocean. Along a narrow line in the middle of the island are market-gardens and breeze-twisted orchards, and a hint of hedges and lanes and inland greenery. At one end is a series of low fortifications duly embanked and moated and sentinelled. Still beyond these, half over-drifted with sand and over-clambered with rank grasses and coarse thick shrubbery, are certain quaintly lettered funereal slabs, tombs of former Jews of Venice. Toward these we slowly wandered and sat down in the grass. Between the sand-heaps, which shut out the beach, we saw

in a dozen places the blue agitation of the sea. Over all
the scene there brooded the deep bright sadness of early
autumn. I lay at my companion's feet and wondered
whether I was in love. It seemed to me that I had never
been so happy in my life. They say, I know, that to be in
love is not pure happiness; that in the mood of the uncon-
fessed, unaccepted lover there is an element of poignant
doubt and pain. Should I at once confess myself and taste
of the perfection of bliss? It seemed to me that I cared
very little for the meaning of her reply. I only wanted to
talk of love; I wanted in some manner to enjoy in that atmosphere of romance the woman who was so blessedly fair
and wise. It seemed to me that all the agitation of fancy,
the excited sense of beauty, the fervor and joy and sadness
begotten by my Italian wanderings, had suddenly resolved
themselves into a potent demand for expression. Miss
Evans was sitting on one of the Hebrew tombs, her chin on
her hand, her elbow on her knee, watching the broken
horizon. I was stretched on the grass on my side, leaning
on my elbow and on my hand, with my eyes on her face.
She bent her own eyes and encountered mine; we neither
of us spoke or moved, but exchanged a long steady regard;
after which her eyes returned to the distance. What was her
feeling toward me? Had she any sense of my emotion or
of any answering trouble in her own wonderful heart?
Suppose she should deny me: should I suffer, would I
persist? At any rate, I should have struck a blow for love.
Suppose she were to accept me; would my joy be any
greater than in the mere translation of my heart-beats? Did
I in truth long merely for a bliss which should be of that
hour and that hour alone? I was conscious of an immense
respect for the woman beside me. I was unconscious of
the least desire even to touch the hem of her garment as it
lay on the grass, touching my own. After all, it was but
ten days that I had known her. How little I really knew of
her! how little else than her beauty and her wit! How
little she knew of me, of my vast outlying, unsentimental,
spiritual self! We knew hardly more of each other than
had appeared in this narrow circle of our common impres-

sions of Venice. And yet if into such a circle Love had forced his way, let him take his way! Let him widen the circle! Transcendent Venice! I rose to my feet with a violent movement, and walked ten steps away. I came back and flung myself again on the grass.

"The other day at Vicenza," I said, "I bought a picture."

"Ah? An 'original'?"

"No, a copy."

"From whom?"

"From you!"

She blushed. "What do you mean?"

"It was a little pretended Correggio; a Madonna and Child."

"Is it good?"

"No, it's rather poor."

"Why, then, did you buy it?"

"Because the Madonna looked singularly like you."

"I'm sorry, Mr. Brooke, you hadn't a better reason. I hope the picture was cheap."

"It was quite reason enough. I admire you more than any woman in the world."

She looked at me a moment, blushing again. "You don't know me."

"I have a suspicion of you. It's ground enough for admiration."

"O, don't talk about admiration. I'm tired of it all beforehand."

"Well, then," said I, "I'm in love."

"Not with me, I hope."

"With you, of course. With whom else?"

"Has it only just now occurred to you?"

"It has just occurred to me to say it."

Her blush had deepened a little; but a genuine smile came to its relief. "Poor Mr. Brooke!" she said.

"Poor Mr. Brooke indeed, if you take it in that way."

"You must forgive me if I doubt of your love."

"Why should you doubt?"

"Love, I fancy, doesn't come in just this way."

"It comes as it can. This is surely a very good way."

"I know it's a very pretty way, Mr. Brooke; Venice behind us, the Adriatic before us, these old Hebrew tombs!
Its very prettiness makes me distrust it."

"Do you believe only in the love that is born in darkness
and pain? Poor love! it has trouble enough, first and last.
Allow it a little ease."

"Listen," said Miss Evans, after a pause. "It's not with
me you're in love, but with that painted picture. All this
Italian beauty and delight has thrown you into a romantic
state of mind. You wish to make it perfect. I happen to
be at hand, so you say, 'Go to, I'll fall in love.' And you
fancy me, for the purpose, a dozen fine things that I'm not."

"I fancy you beautiful and good. I'm sorry to find you
so dogmatic."

"You mustn't abuse me, or we shall be getting serious."

"Well," said I, "you can't prevent me from adoring you."

"I should be very sorry to. So long as you 'adore' me,
we're safe! I can tell you better things than that I'm in
love with you."

I looked at her impatiently. "For instance?"

She held out her hand. "I like you immensely. As for
love, I'm in love with Venice."

"Well, I like Venice immensely, but I'm in love with
you."

"In that way I am willing to leave it. Pray don't speak
of it again to-day. But my poor father is probably wandering up to his knees in the sand."

I had been happy before, but I think I was still happier
for the words I had spoken. I had cast them abroad at all
events; my heart was richer by a sense of their possible
fruition. We walked far along the beach. Mr. Evans was
still with his friend.

"What is beyond that horizon?" said my companion.

"Greece, among other things."

"Greece! only think of it! Shall you never go there?"

I stopped short. "If you will believe what I say, Miss
Evans, we may both go there." But for all answer she
repeated her request that I should forbear. Before long,
retracing our steps, we met Mr. Evans, who had parted with

his friend, the latter having returned to Venice. He had arranged to start the next morning for Milan. We went back over the lagoon in the glow of the sunset, in a golden silence which suffered us to hear the far-off ripple in the wake of other gondolas, a golden clearness so perfect that the rosy flush on the marble palaces seemed as light and pure as the life-blood on the forehead of a sleeping child. There is no Venice like the Venice of that magical hour. For that brief period her ancient glory returns. The sky arches over her like a vast imperial canopy crowded with its clustering mysteries of light. Her whole aspect is one of unspotted splendor. No other city takes the crimson evanescence of day with such magnificent effect. The lagoon is sheeted with a carpet of fire. All torpid, pallid hues of marble are transmuted to a golden glow. The dead Venetian tone brightens and quickens into life and lustre, and the spectator's enchanted vision seems to rest on an embodied dream of the great painter who wrought his immortal reveries into the ceilings of the Ducal Palace.

It was not till the second day after this that I again saw Miss Evans. I went to the little church of San Cassiano, to see a famous Tintoretto, to which I had already made several vain attempts to obtain access. At the door in the little bustling *campo* which adjoins the church I found her standing expectant. A little boy, she told me, had gone for the sacristan and his key. Her father, she proceeded to explain, had suddenly been summoned to Milan by a telegram from Mr. Munson, the friend whom he had met at the Lido, who had suddenly been taken ill.

"And so you're going about alone? Do you think that's altogether proper? Why didn't you send for me?" I stood lost in wonder and admiration at the exquisite dignity of her self-support. I had heard of American girls doing such things; but I had yet to see them done.

"Do you think it less proper for me to go about alone than to send for you? Venice has seen so many worse improprieties that she'll forgive me mine."

The little boy arrived with the sacristan and his key, and we were ushered into the presence of Tintoretto's Crucifixion. This great picture is one of the greatest of the Venetian school. Tintoretto, the travelled reader will remember, has painted two masterpieces on this tremendous theme. The larger and more complex work is at the Scuola di San Rocco; the one of which I speak is small, simple, and sublime. It occupies the left side of the narrow choir of the shabby little church which we had entered, and is remarkable as being, with two or three exceptions, the best preserved work of its incomparable author. Never, in the whole range of art, I imagine, has so powerful an effect been produced by means so simple and select; never has the intelligent choice of means to an effect been pursued with such a refinement of perception. The picture offers to our sight the very central essence of the great tragedy which it depicts. There is no swooning Madonna, no consoling Magdalen, no mockery of contrast, no cruelty of an assembled host. We behold the silent summit of Calvary. To the right are the three crosses, that of the Saviour foremost. A ladder pitched against it supports a turbaned executioner, who bends downward to receive the sponge offered him by a comrade. Above the crest of the hill the helmets and spears of a line of soldiery complete the grimness of the scene. The reality of the picture is beyond all words; it is hard to say which is more impressive, the naked horror of the fact represented, or the sensible power of the artist. You breathe a silent prayer of thanks that you, for your part, are without the terrible clairvoyance of genius. We sat and looked at the picture in silence. The sacristan loitered about; but finally, weary of waiting, he retired to the *campo* without. I observed my companion: pale, motionless, oppressed, she evidently felt with poignant sympathy the commanding force of the work. At last I spoke to her; receiving no answer, I repeated my question. She rose to her feet and turned her face upon me, illumined with a vivid ecstasy of pity. Then passing me rapidly, she descended into the aisle of the church, dropped into a chair, and, burying her face in her hands, burst into an agony of sobs. Having allowed time for her feeling to expend itself, I went to her and recommended her not to let the day close

on this painful emotion. "Come with me to the Ducal
Palace," I said; "let us look at the Rape of Europa." But
before departing we went back to our Tintoretto, and gave
it another solemn half-hour. Miss Evans repeated aloud
a dozen verses from St. Mark's Gospel.

"What is it here," I asked, "that has moved you most,
the painter or the subject?"

"I suppose it's the subject. And you?"

"I'm afraid it's the painter."

We went to the Ducal Palace, and immediately made our
way to that transcendent shrine of light and grace, the
room which contains the masterpiece of Paul Veronese, and
the Bacchus and Ariadne of his solemn comrade. I steeped
myself with unprotesting joy in the gorgeous glow and salu-
brity of that radiant scene, wherein, against her bosky
screen of immortal verdure, the rosy-footed, pearl-circled,
nymph-flattered victim of a divine delusion rustles her lustrous satin against the ambrosial hide of bovine Jove. "It
makes one think more agreeably of life," I said to my friend,
"that such visions have blessed the eyes of men of mortal
mould. What has been may be again. We may yet dream
as brightly, and some few of us translate our dreams as
freely."

"This, I think, is the brighter dream of the two," she answered, indicating the Bacchus and Ariadne. Miss Evans,
on the whole, was perhaps right. In Tintoretto's picture
there is no shimmer of drapery, no splendor of flowers and
gems; nothing but the broad, bright glory of deep-toned sea
and sky, and the shining purity and symmetry of deified
human flesh. "What do you think," asked my companion,
"of the painter of that tragedy at San Cassiano being also
the painter of this dazzling idyl; of the great painter of
darkness being also the great painter of light?"

"He was a colorist! Let us thank the great man, and be
colorists too. To understand this Bacchus and Ariadne we
ought to spend a long day on the lagoon, beyond sight of
Venice. Will you come to-morrow to Torcello?" The
proposition seemed to me audacious; I was conscious of
blushing a little as I made it. Miss Evans looked at me

and pondered. She then replied with great calmness that she preferred to wait for her father, the excursion being one that he would probably enjoy. "Will you come, then,—somewhere?" I asked.

Again she pondered. Suddenly her face brightened. "I should very much like to go to Padua. It would bore my poor father to go. I fancy he would thank you for taking me. I should be almost willing," she said with a smile, "to go alone."

It was easily arranged that on the morrow we should go for the day to Padua. Miss Evans was certainly an American to perfection. Nothing remained for me, as the good American which I aspired to be, but implicitly to respect her confidence. To Padua, by an early train, we accordingly went. The day stands out in my memory delightfully curious and rich. Padua is a wonderful little city. Miss Evans was an excellent walker, and, thanks to the broad arcades which cover the footways in the streets, we rambled for hours in perpetual shade. We spent an hour at the famous church of St. Anthony, which boasts one of the richest and holiest shrines in all church-burdened Italy. The whole edifice is nobly and darkly ornate and pictu-resque, but the chapel of its patron saint—a wondrous combination of chiselled gold and silver and alabaster and perpetual flame—splendidly outshines and outshadows the rest. In all Italy, I think, the idea of palpable, material sanctity is nowhere more potently enforced.

"O the Church, the Church!" murmured Miss Evans, as we stood contemplating.

"What a real pity," I said, "that we are not Catholics; that that dazzling monument is not something more to us than a mere splendid show! What a different thing this visiting of churches would be for us, if we occasionally felt the prompting to fall on our knees. I begin to grow ashamed of this perpetual attitude of bald curiosity. What a pleasant thing it must be, in such a church as this, for two good friends to say their prayers together!"

"*Ecco!*" said Miss Evans. Two persons had approached the glittering shrine,—a young woman of the middle class and a man of her own rank, some ten years older, dressed with a good deal of cheap elegance. The woman dropped on her knees; her companion fell back a few steps, and stood gazing idly at the chapel. "Poor girl!" said my friend, "she believes; he doubts."

"He doesn't look like a doubter. He's a vulgar fellow. They're a betrothed pair, I imagine. She is very pretty." She had turned round and flung at her companion a liquid glance of entreaty. He appeared not to observe it; but in a few moments he slowly approached her, and bent a single knee at her side. When presently they rose to their feet, she passed her arm into his with a beautiful, unsuppressed lovingness. As they passed us, looking at us from the clear darkness of their Italian brows, I keenly envied them. "They are better off than we," I said. "Be they husband and wife, or lovers, or simply friends, we, I think, are rather vulgar beside them."

"My dear Mr. Brooke," said Miss Evans, "go by all means and say your prayers." And she walked away to the other side of the church. Whether I obeyed her injunction or not, I feel under no obligation to report. I rejoined her at the beautiful frescoed chapel in the opposite transept. She was sitting listlessly turning over the leaves of her Murray. "I suppose," said said, after a few moments, "that nothing is more vulgar than to make a noise about having been called vulgar. But really, Mr. Brooke, don't call me so again. I have been of late so fondly fancying I am not vulgar."

"My dear Miss Evans, you are——"

"Come, nothing vulgar!"

"You're divine!"

"*A la bonne heure!*" Divinities needn't pray. They are prayed to."

I have no space and little power to enumerate and describe the various curiosities of Padua. I think we saw them all. We left the best, however, for the last, and repaired in the late afternoon, after dining fraternally at a restaurant, to the Chapel of Giotto. This little empty church, standing unshaded and forlorn in the homely market-garden which was once a Roman arena, offers one of the deepest lessons of Italian travel. Its four walls are covered, almost from base to ceiling, with that wonderful series of dramatic paintings which usher in the golden prime of Italian art. I had been so ill-informed as to fancy that to talk about Giotto was to make more or less of a fool of one's self, and that he was the especial property of the mere sentimentalists of criticism. But you no sooner cross the threshold of that little ruinous temple—a mere empty shell, but coated as with the priceless substance of fine pearls and vocal with a murmured eloquence as from the infinite of art—than you perceive with whom you have to deal: a complete painter of the very strongest sort. In one respect, assuredly, Giotto has never been surpassed,—in the art of presenting a story. The amount of dramatic expression compressed into those quaint little scenic squares would equip a thousand later masters. How, beside him, they seem to fumble and grope and trifle! And he, beside them, how direct he seems, how essential, how masculine! What a solid simplicity, what an immediate purity and grace! The exhibition suggested to my friend and me more wise reflections than we had the skill to utter. "Happy, happy art," we said, as we seemed to see it beneath Giotto's hand tremble and thrill and sparkle, almost, with a presentiment of its immense career, "for the next two hundred years what a glorious felicity will be yours!" The chapel door stood open into the sunny corn-field, and the lazy litter of verdure enclosed by the crumbling oval of Roman masonry. A loutish boy who had come with the key lounged on a bench, awaiting tribute, and gazing at us as we gazed. The ample light flooded the inner precinct, and lay hot upon the coarse, pale surface of the painted wall. There seemed an irresistible pathos in such a combination of shabbiness and beauty. I thought of this subsequently at the beautiful Museum at Bologna, where mediocrity is so richly enshrined. Nothing that we had yet seen together had filled us with so deep a sense of enjoyment. We stared, we laughed, we wept almost, we raved with a decent delight. We went over the little compartments one by one: we lingered and returned and compared; we studied; we melted together in unanimous homage. At last the light began to fade and the little saintly figures to grow quaint and terrible in the gathering dusk. The loutish boy had transferred himself significantly to the door-post: we lingered for a farewell glance.

"Mr. Brooke," said my companion, "we ought to learn from all this to be *real;* real even as Giotto is real; to discriminate between genuine and factitious sentiment; between the substantial and the trivial; between the essential and the superfluous; sentiment and sentimentality."

"You speak," said I, "with appalling wisdom and truth. You strike a chill to my heart of hearts."

She spoke unsmiling, with a slightly contracted brow and an apparent sense of effort. She blushed as I gazed at her.

"Well," she said, "I'm extremely glad to have been here. Good, wise Giotto! I should have liked to know you.— Nay, let me pay the boy." I saw the piece she put into his hand; he was stupefied by its magnitude.

"We shall not have done Padua," I said, as we left the garden, "unless we have been to the Caffé Pedrocchi. Come to the Caffé Pedrocchi. We have more than an hour before our train,—time to eat an ice." So we drove to the Caffé Pedrocchi, the most respectable café in the world; a café monumental, scholastic, classical.

We sat down at one of the tables on the cheerful external platform, which is washed by the gentle tide of Paduan life. When we had finished our ices, Miss Evans graciously allowed me a cigar. How it came about I hardly remember, but, prompted by some happy accident of talk, and gently encouraged perhaps by my smoke-wreathed quietude, she lapsed, with an exquisite feminine reserve, into a delicate autobiographical strain. For a moment she became egotistical; but with a modesty, a dignity, a lightness of touch which filled my eyes with admiring tears. She spoke of her home, her family, and the few events of her life. She had lost her mother in her early years; her two sisters had married young; she and her father were equally united by affection and habit. Upon one theme she touched, in regard to which I should be at loss to say whether her treatment told more, by its frankness, of our friendship, or, by its reticence, of her modesty. She spoke of having been engaged, and of having lost her betrothed in the Civil War. She made no story of it; but I felt from her words that she had tasted of sorrow. Having finished my cigar, I was proceeding to light another. She drew out her watch. Our train was to leave at eight o'clock. It was now a quarter past. There was no later evening train.

The reader will understand that I tell the simple truth when I say that our situation was most disagreeable and that we were deeply annoyed. "Of course," said I, "you are utterly disgusted."

She was silent. "I am extremely sorry," she said, at last, just vanquishing a slight tremor in her voice.

"Murray says the hotel is good," I suggested.

She made no answer. Then, rising to her feet, "Let us go immediately," she said. We drove to the principal inn and bespoke our rooms. Out want of luggage provoked, of course, a certain amount of visible surprise. This, however, I fancy, was speedily merged in a more flattering emotion, when my companion, having communed with the chamber-maid, sent her forth with a list of purchases.

We separated early. "I hope," said I, as I bade her good night, "that you will be fairly comfortable."

She had recovered her equanimity. "I have no doubt of it."

"Good night."

"Good night." Thank God, I silently added, for the dignity of American women. Knowing to what suffering a similar accident would have subjected a young girl of the orthodox European training, I felt devoutly grateful that among my own people a woman and her reputation are more indissolubly one. And yet I was unable to detach myself from my Old-World associations effectually enough not to wonder whether, after all, Miss Evans's calmness might not be the simple calmness of despair. The miserable words rose to my lips, "Is she Compromised?" If she were, of course, as far as I was concerned, there was but one possible sequel to our situation.

We met the next morning at breakfast. She assured me that she had slept, but I doubted it. I myself had not closed my eyes,—not from the excitement of vanity. Owing partly, I suppose, to a natural reaction against our continuous talk on the foregoing day, our return to Venice was attended with a good deal of silence. I wondered whether it was a mere fancy that Miss Evans was pensive, appealing, sombre. As we entered the gondola to go from the railway station to the Hotel Danieli, she asked me to request the gondoliers to pass along the Canalezzo rather than through the short cuts of the smaller canals. "I feel as if I were coming home," she said, as we floated beneath the lovely façade of the Ca' Doro. Suddenly she laid her hand on my arm. "It seems to me," she said, "that I should like to stop for Mrs. L——," and she mentioned the wife of the American Consul. "I have promised to show her some jewelry. This is a particularly good time. I shall ask her to come home with me." We stopped accordingly at the American Consulate. Here we found, on inquiry, to my great regret, that the Consul and his wife had gone for a week to the Lake of Como. For a moment my companion meditated. Then, "To the hotel," she said with decision. Our arrival attracted apparently little notice. I went with Miss Evans to the door of her father's sitting-room, where we met a servant, who informed us with inscrutable gravity that Monsieur had returned the evening before, but that he had gone out after breakfast and had not reappeared.

"Poor father," she said. "It was very stupid of me not to have left a note for him." I urged that our absence for the night was not to have been foreseen, and that Mr. Evans had in all likelihood, very plausibly explained it. I withdrew with a handshake and permission to return in the evening.

I went to my hotel and slept, a long, sound, dreamless sleep. In the afternoon I called my gondola, and went over to the Lido. I crossed to the outer shore and sought the spot where a few days before I had lain at the feet of Charlotte Evans. I stretched myself on the grass and fancied her present. To say that I *thought* would be to say at once more and less than the literal truth. I was in a tremulous glow of feeling. I listened to the muffled rupture of the tide, vaguely conscious of my beating heart. Was I or was I not in love? I was able to settle nothing. I wandered musingly further and further from the point. Every now and then, with a deeper pulsation of the heart, I would return to it, but only to start afresh and follow some wire-drawn thread of fancy to a nebulous goal of doubt. That she was a most lovely woman seemed to me of all truths the truest, but it was a hard-featured fact of the sense rather than a radiant mystery of faith. I felt that I was not possessed by a passion; perhaps I was incapable of passion. At last, weary of self-bewilderment, I left the spot and wandered beside the sea. It seemed to speak more musingly than ever of the rapture of motion and freedom. Byond the horizon was Greece, beyond and below was the wondrous Southern world which blooms about the margin of the Midland Sea. To marry, somehow, meant to abjure all this, and in the prime of youth and manhood to sink into obscurity and care. For a moment there stirred in my heart a feeling of anger and pain. Perhaps, after all, I *was* in love!

I went straight across the lagoon to the Hotel Danieli, and as I approached it I became singularly calm and collected. From below I saw Miss Evans alone on her balcony, watching the sunset. She received me with perfect friendly composure. Her father had again gone out, but she had told him of my coming, and he was soon to return. He had not been painfully alarmed at her absence, having learned through a chambermaid, to whom she had happened to mention her intention, that she had gone for the day to Padua.

"And what have you been doing all day?" I asked.

"Writing letters,—long, tiresome, descriptive letters. I have also found a volume of Hawthorne, and have been reading 'Rappacini's Daughter.' You know the scene is laid in Padua." And what had I been doing?

Whether I was in a passion of love or not, I was enough in love to be very illogical. I was disappointed, Heaven knows why! that she should have been able to spend her time in this wholesome fashion. "I have been at the Lido, at the Hebrew tombs, where we sat the other day, thinking of what you told me there."

"What I told you?"

"That you liked me immensely."

She smiled; but now that she smiled, I fancied I saw in the movement of her face an undercurrent of pain. Had the peace of her heart been troubled? "You needn't have gone so far away to think of it."

"It's very possible," I said, "that I shall have to think of it, in days to come, farther away still."

"Other places, Mr. Brooke, will bring other thoughts."

"Possibly. This place has brought that one." At what prompting it was that I continued I hardly know; I *would* tell her that I loved her. "I value it beyond all other thoughts."

"I do like you, Mr. Brooke. Let it rest there."

"It may rest there for you. It can't for me. It begins there! Don't refuse to understand me."

She was silent. Then, bending her eyes on me, "Perhaps," she said, "I understand you too well."

"O, in Heaven's name, don't play at coldness and scepticism!"

She dropped her eyes gravely on a bracelet which she locked and unlocked on her wrist. "I think," she said, without raising them, "you had better leave Venice." I was about to reply, but the door opened and Mr. Evans came in. From his hard, grizzled brow he looked at us in turn; then, greeting me with an extended hand, he spoke to his daughter.

"I have forgotten my cigar-case. Be so good as to fetch it from my dressing-table."

For a moment Miss Evans hesitated and cast upon him a faint protesting glance. Then she lightly left the room.

He stood holding my hand, with a very sensible firmness, with his eyes on mine. Then, laying his other hand heavily on my shoulder, "Mr. Brooke," he said, "I believe you are an honest man."

"I hope so," I answered.

He paused, and I felt his steady gray eyes. "How the devil," he said, "came you to be left at Padua?"

"The explanation is a very simple one. Your daughter must have told you."

"I have thought best to talk very little to my daughter about it."

"Do you regard it, Mr. Evans," I asked, "as a very serious calamity?"

"I regard it as an infernally disagreeable thing. It seems that the whole hotel is talking about it. There is a little beast of an Italian down stairs——"

"Your daughter, I think, was not seriously discomposed."

"My daughter is a d——d proud woman!"

"I can assure you that my esteem for her is quite equal to your own."

"What does that mean, Mr. Brooke?" I was about to answer, but Miss Evans reappeared. Her father, as he took his cigar-case from her, looked at her intently, as if he were on the point of speaking, but the words remained on his lips, and, declaring that he would be back in half an hour, he left the room.

His departure was followed by a long silence.

"Miss Evans," I said, at last, "will you be my wife?"

She looked at me with a certain firm resignation. "Do you *feel* that, Mr. Brooke? Do you know what you ask?"

"Most assuredly."

"Will you rest content with my answer?"

"It depends on what your answer is."

She was silent.

"I should like to know what my father said to you in my absence."

"You had better learn that from him."

"I think I know. Poor father!"

"But you give me no answer," I rejoined, after a pause.

She frowned a little. "Mr. Brooke," she said, "you disappoint me."

"Well, I'm sorry. Don't revenge yourself by disappointing me."

"I fancied that I had answered your proposal; that I had, at least, anticipated it, the other day at the Lido."

"O, that was very good for the other day; but do give me something different now."

"I doubt of your being more in earnest to-day than then."

"It seems to suit you wonderfully well to doubt!"

"I thank you for the honor of your proposal: but I can't be your wife, Mr. Brooke."

"That's the answer with which you ask me to remain satisfied!"

"Let me repeat what I said just now. You had better leave Venice; otherwise, we must leave it."

"Ah, that's easy to say!"

"You mustn't think me unkind or cynical. You have done your duty."

"My duty,—what duty?"

"Come," she said, with a beautiful blush and the least attempt at a smile, "you imagine that I have suffered an injury by my being left with you at Padua. I don't believe in such injuries."

"No more do I."

"Then there is even less wisdom than before in your proposal. But I strongly suspect that if we had not missed the train at Padua, you would not have made it. There is an idea of reparation in it.—O Sir!" And she shook her head with a deepening smile.

"If I had flattered myself that it lay in my power to do you an injury," I replied, "I should now be rarely disenchanted. As little almost as to do you a benefit!"

"You have loaded me with benefits. I thank you from the bottom of my heart. I may be very unreasonable, but if I had doubted of my having to decline your offer three days ago, I should have quite ceased to doubt this evening."

"You are an excessively proud woman. I can tell you that."

"Possibly. But I'm not as proud as you think. I believe in my common sense."

"I wish that for five minutes you had a grain of imagination!"

"If only for the same five minutes you were without it. You have too much, Mr. Brooke. You imagine you love me."

"Poor fool that I am!"

"You imagine that I'm charming. I assure you I'm not in the least. Here in Venice I have not been myself at all. You should see me at home."

"Upon my word, Miss Evans, you remind me of a German philosopher. I have not the least objection to seeing you at home."

"Don't fancy that I think lightly of your offer. But we have been living, Mr. Brooke, in poetry. Marriage is stern prose. Do let me bid you farewell!"

I took up my hat. "I shall go from here to Rome and Naples," I said. "I must leave Florence for the last. I shall write you from Rome and of course see you there."

"I hope not. I had rather not meet you again in Italy. It perverts our dear good old American truth!"

"Do you really propose to bid me a final farewell?"

She hesitated a moment. "When do you return home?"

"Some time in the spring."

"Very well. If a year hence, in America, you are still of your present mind, I shall not decline to see you. I feel very safe! If you are not of your present mind, of course I shall be still more happy. Farewell." She put out her hand; I took it.

"Beautiful, wonderful woman!" I murmured.

"That's rank poetry! Farewell!"

I raised her hand to my lips and released it in silence. At this point Mr. Evans reappeared, considering apparently that his half-hour was up. "Are you going?" he asked.

"Yes. I start to-morrow for Rome."

"The deuce! Daughter, when are we to go?"

She moved her hand over her forehead, and a sort of nervous tremor seemed to pass through her limbs. "O, you must take me home!" she said. "I'm horribly home-sick!" She flung her arms round his neck and buried her head on his shoulder. Mr. Evans with a movement of his head dismissed me.

At the top of the staircase, however, he overtook me. "You made your offer!" And he passed his arm into mine.

"Yes!"

"And she refused you?" I nodded. He looked at me, squeezing my arm. "By Jove, sir, if she had accepted——"

"Well!" said I, stopping.

"Why, it wouldn't in the least have suited me! Not that I don't esteem you. The whole house shall see it." With his arm in mine we passed down stairs, through the hall, to the landing-place, where he called his own gondola and requested me to use it. He bade me farewell with a kindly hand-shake, and the assurance that I was too "nice a fellow not to keep as a friend."

I think, on the whole, that my uppermost feeling was a sense of freedom and relief. It seemed to me on my journey to Florence that I had started afresh, and was regarding things with less of nervous rapture than before, but more of sober insight. Of Miss Evans I forbade myself to think. In my deepest heart I admitted the truth, the partial truth at least, of her assertion of the unreality of my love. The reality I believed would come. The way to hasten its approach was, meanwhile, to study, to watch, to observe,—doubtless even to enjoy. I certainly enjoyed Florence and the three days I spent there. But I shall not attempt to deal with Florence in a parenthesis. I subsequently saw that divine little city under circumstances which peculiarly colored and shaped it. In Rome, to begin with, I spent a week and went down to Naples, dragging the heavy Roman chain which she rivets about your limbs forever. In Naples I discovered the real South— the Southern South,—in art, in nature, in man, and the least bit in woman. A German lady, an old kind friend, had given me a letter to a Neapolitan lady whom she

assured me she held in high esteem. The Signora B——
was at Sorrento, where I presented my letter. It seemed
to me that "esteem" was not exactly the word; but the
Signora B—— was charming. She assured me on my first
visit that she was a "true Neapolitan," and I think, on the
whole, she was right. She told me that I was a true German, but in this she was altogether wrong. I spent four
days in her house; on one of them we went to Capri, where
the Signora had an infant—her only one—at nurse. We
saw the Blue Grotto, the Tiberian ruins, the tarantella
and the infant, and returned late in the evening by moonlight. The Signora sang on the water in a magnificent
contralto. As I looked upward at Northern Italy, it seemed,
in contrast, a cold, dark hyperborean clime, a land of order,
conscience, and virtue. How my heart went out to that
brave, rich, compact little Verona! How there Nature
seemed to have mixed her colors with potent oil, instead of
as here with crystalline water, drawn though it was from
the Neapolitan Bay! But in Naples, too, I pursued my
plan of vigilance and study. I spent long mornings at the
Museum and learned to know Pompeii! I wrote once to
Miss Evans, about the statues in the Museum, without a
word of wooing, but received no answer. It seemed to me
that I returned to Rome a wiser man. It was the middle
of October when I reached it. Unless Mr. Evans had
altered his programme, he would at this moment be passing
down to Naples.

A fortnight elapsed without my hearing of him, during
which I was in the full fever of initiation into Roman
wonders. I had been introduced to an old German archæologist, with whom I spent a series of memorable days in
the exploration of ruins and the study of the classical topog-
raphy. I thought, I lived, I ate and drank, in Latin, and
German Latin at that. But I remember with especial delight certain long lonely rides on the Campagna. The
weather was perfect. Nature seemed only to slumber, ready
to wake far on the hither side of wintry death. From time
to time, after a passionate gallop, I would pull up my
horse on the slope of some pregnant mound and embrace

with the ecstasy of quickened senses the tragical beauty of the scene; strain my ear to the soft low silence, pity the dark dishonored plain, watch the heavens come rolling down in tides of light, and breaking in waves of fire against the massive stillness of temples and tombs. The aspect of all this sunny solitude and haunted vacancy used to fill me with a mingled sense of exaltation and dread. There were moments when my fancy swept that vast funereal desert with passionate curiosity and desire, moments when it felt only its potent sweetness and its high historic charm. But there were other times when the air seemed so heavy with the exhalation of unburied death, so bright with sheeted ghosts, that I turned short about and galloped back to the city. One afternoon after I had indulged in one of these supersensitive flights on the Campagna, I betook myself to St. Peter's. It was shortly before the opening of the recent Council, and the city was filled with foreign ecclesiastics, the increase being of course especially noticeable in the churches. At St. Peter's they were present in vast numbers; great armies encamped in prayer on the marble plains of its pavement: an inexhaustible physiognomical study. Scattered among them were squads of little tonsured neophytes, clad in scarlet, marching and counter-marching, and ducking and flapping, like poor little raw recruits for the heavenly host. I had never before, I think, received an equal impression of the greatness of this church of churches, or, standing beneath the dome, beheld such a vision of erected altitude,—of the builded sublime. I lingered awhile near the brazen image of St. Peter, observing the steady procession of his devotees. Near me stood a lady in mourning, watching with a weary droop of the head the grotesque deposition of kisses. A peasant-woman advanced with the file of the faithful and lifted up her little girl to the well-worn toe. With a sudden movement of impatience the lady turned away, so that I saw her face to face. She was strikingly pale, but as her eyes met mine the blood rushed into her cheeks. This lonely mourner was Miss Evans. I advanced to her with an outstretched hand. Before she spoke I had guessed at the truth.

"You're in sorrow and trouble!"

She nodded, with a look of simple gravity.

"Why in the world haven't you written to me?"

"There was no use. I seem to have sufficed to myself."

"Indeed, you have not sufficed to yourself. You are pale and worn; you looked wretchedly." She stood silent, looking about her with an air of vague unrest. "I have as yet heard nothing," I said. "Can you speak of it?"

"O Mr. Brooke!" she said with a simple sadness that went to my heart. I drew her hand through my arm and led her to the extremity of the left transept of the church. We sat down together, and she told me of her father's death. It had happened ten days before, in consequence of a severe apoplectic stroke. He had been ill but a single day, and had remained unconscious from first to last. The American physician had been extremely kind, and had relieved her of all care and responsibility. His wife had strongly urged her to come and stay in their house, until she should have determined what to do; but she had preferred to remain at her hotel. She had immediately furnished herself with an attendant in the person of a French maid, who had come with her to the church and was now at confession. At first she had wished greatly to leave Rome, but now that the first shock of grief had passed away she found it suited her mood to linger on from day to day. "On the whole," she said, with a sober smile, "I have got through it all rather easily than otherwise. The common cares and necessities of life operate strongly to interrupt and dissipate one's grief. I shall feel my loss more when I get home again." Looking at her while she talked, I found a pitiful difference between her words and her aspect. Her pale face, her wilful smile, her spiritless gestures, spoke most forcibly of loneliness and weakness. Over this gentle weakness and dependence I secretly rejoiced; I felt in my heart an immense uprising of pity,—of the pity that goes hand in hand with love. At its bidding I hastily, vaguely sketched a magnificent scheme of devotion and protection.

"When I think of what you have been through," I said,

"my heart stands still for very tenderness. Have you made any plans?" She shook her head with such a perfection of helplessness that I broke into a sort of rage of compassion: "One of the last things your father said to me was that you are a very proud woman."

She colored faintly. "I may have been! But there is not among the most abject peasants who stand kissing St. Peter's foot a creature more bowed in humility than I."

"How did you expect to make that weary journey home?"

She was silent a moment and her eyes filled with tears. "O don't cross-question me, Mr. Brooke!" she softly cried; "I expected nothing. I was waiting for my stronger self."

"Perhaps your stronger self has come." She rose to her feet as if she had not heard me, and went forward to meet her maid. This was a decent, capable-looking person, with a great deal of apparent deference of manner. As I rejoined them, Miss Evans prepared to bid me farewell. "You haven't yet asked me to come and see you," I said.

"Come, but not too soon?"

"What do you call too soon? This evening?"

"Come to-morrow." She refused to allow me to go with her to her carriage. I followed her, however, at a short interval, and went as usual to my restaurant to dine. I remember that my dinner cost me ten francs,—it usually cost me five. Afterwards, as usual, I adjourned to the Caffè Greco, where I met my German archæologist. He discoursed with even more than his wonted sagacity and eloquence; but at the end of half an hour he rapped his fist on the table and asked me what the deuce was the matter; he would wager I hadn't heard a word of what he said.

I went forth the next morning into the Roman streets, doubting heavily of my being able to exist until evening without seeing Miss Evans. I felt, however, that it was due to her to make the effort. To help myself through the morning, I went into the Borghese Gallery. The great treasure of this collection is a certain masterpiece of Titian. I entered the room in which it hangs by the door facing the picture. The room was empty, save that before the great Titian, beside the easel of an absent copyist, stood a young woman in mourning. This time, in spite of her averted head, I immediately knew her and noiselessly approached her. The picture is one of the finest of its admirable author, rich and simple and brilliant with the true Venetian fire. It unites the charm of an air of latent symbolism with a steadfast splendor and solid perfection of design. Beside a low sculptured well sit two young and beautiful women: one richly clad, and full of mild dignity and repose; the other with unbound hair, naked, ungirdled by a great reverted mantle of Venetian purple, and radiant with the frankest physical sweetness and grace. Between them a little winged cherub bends forward and thrusts his chubby arm into the well. The picture glows with the inscrutable chemistry of the prince of colorists.

"Does it remind you of Venice?" I said, breaking a long silence, during which she had not noticed me.

She turned and her face seemed bright with reflected color. We spoke awhile of common things; she had come alone. "What an emotion, for one who has loved Venice," she said, "to meet a Titian in other lands."

"They call it," I answered,—and as I spoke my heart was in my throat,—"a representation of Sacred and Profane Love. The name perhaps roughly expresses its meaning. The serious, stately woman is the likeness, one may say, of love as an experience,—the gracious, impudent goddess of love as a sentiment; this of the passion that fancies, the other of the passion that knows." And as I spoke I passed my arm, in its strength, around her waist. She let her head sink on my shoulders and looked up into my eyes.

"One may stand for the love I denied," she said; "and the other——"

"The other," I murmured, "for the love which, with this kiss, you accept." I drew her arm into mine, and before the envious eyes that watched us from gilded casements we passed through the gallery and left the palace. We went that afternoon to the Pamfili-Doria Villa. Saying just now that my stay in Florence was peculiarly colored by circumstances, I meant that I was there with my wife.

THE SWEETHEART OF
M. BRISEUX

THE little picture gallery at M—— is a typical *musée de province*—cold, musty, unvisited, and enriched chiefly with miniature works by painters whose maturity was not to be powerful. The floors are tiled in brick, and the windows draped in faded moreen; the very light seems pale and neutral, as if the dismal lack-lustre atmosphere of the pictures were contagious. The subjects represented are of course of the familiar academic sort—the Wisdom of Solomon and the Fureurs d'Oreste; together with a few elegant landscapes exhibiting the last century view of nature, and half a dozen neat portraits of French gentlefolks of that period, in the act, as one may say, of taking the view in question. To me, I confess, the place had a melancholy charm, and I found none of the absurd old paintings too absurd to enjoy. There is always an agreeable finish in the French touch, even when the hand is not a master's. The catalogue, too, was prodigiously queer; a bit of very ancient literature, with comments, in the manner of the celebrated M. La Harpe. I wondered, as I turned its pages, into what measure of reprobation pictures and catalogue together had been compressed by that sole son of M——, who has achieved more than local renown in the arts. Conjecture was pertinent, for it was in these crepuscular halls that this deeply original artist must have heard the first early bird-notes of awakening genius: first, half credulously, as we may suppose, on festal Sundays, with his hand in his father's, gazing rosy and wide-eyed at the classical wrath of Achilles and the sallow flesh-tints of Dido; and later, with his hands in his pockets, an incipient critical frown and the mental vision of an Achilles

53

somehow more in earnest and a Dido more deeply desirable.
It was indeed doubly pertinent, for the little Musée had at
last, after much watching and waiting and bargaining, become possessor of one of Briseux's pictures. I was promptly
informed of the fact by the *concierge,* a person much reduced
by years and chronic catarrh, but still robust enough to dis-
play his æsthetic culture to a foreigner presumably of distinction. He led me solemnly into the presence of the great
work, and placed a chair for me in the proper light. The
famous painter had left his native town early in life, before
making his mark, and an inappreciative family—his father
was a small apothecary with a proper admiration of the
arts, but a horror of artists—had been at no pains to preserve his boyish sketches. The more fools they! The
merest scrawl with his signature now brought hundreds of
francs, and there were those of his blood still in the town
with whom the francs were scarce enough. To obtain a
serious picture had of course been no small affair, and little
M——, though with the yearning heart of a mother, happened to have no scanty maternal savings. Yet the thing
had been managed by subscription, and the picture paid
for. To make the triumph complete, a fortnight after it had
been hung on its nail, M. Briseux succumbs to a fever in
Rome and his pictures rise to the most fantastic prices!
This was the very work which had made the painter famous.
The portrait of a Lady in a Yellow Shawl in the Salon of
1836 had *fait époque.* Every one had heard of the Yellow
Shawl; people talked of it as they did of the Chapeau de
Paille of Rubens or the "Torn Glove" of Titian; or if
they didn't, posterity would! Such was the discursive murmur of the *concierge* as I examined this precious specimen
of Briseux's first manner; and there was a plaintive cadence
in this last assurance, which seemed to denote a too vivid
prevision of the harvest of tributary francs to be reaped by
his successors in office. It would be graceless praise to
say that a glimpse of the picture is worth your franc. It
is a superb performance, and I spent half an hour before
it in such serene enjoyment that I forgot the *concierge* was
a bore.

It is a half-length portrait representing a young woman, not exactly beautiful, yet very far from plain, draped with a singularly simple elegance in a shawl of yellow silk embroidered with fantastic arabesque. She is dark and grave, her dress is dark, the background is of a sober tone, and this brilliant scarf glows splendidly by contrast. It seems indeed to irradiate luminous color, and makes the picture brilliant in spite of its sombre accessories; and yet it leaves their full value to the tenderly glowing flesh portions. The portrait lacks a certain harmonious finish, that masterly interfusion of parts which the painter afterwards practised; the touch is hasty, and here and there a little heavy; but its splendid vivacity and energy, and the almost boyish good faith of some of its more venturesome strokes, make it a capital example of that momentous point in the history of genius when still tender promise blooms—in a night, as it were—into perfect force. It was little wonder that the picture had made a noise: judges of the more penetrating sort must have felt that it contained that invaluable something which an artist gives but once—the prime outgush of his effort—the flower of his originality. As I continued to look, however, I began to wonder whether it did not contain something better still—the reflection of a countenance very nearly as deep and ardent as the artist's talent. In spite of the expressive repose of the figure the brow and mouth wore a look of smothered agitation, the dark gray eye almost glittered, and the flash in the cheek burned ominously. Evidently this was the picture of something more than a yellow shawl. To the analytic eye it was the picture of a mind, or at least of a mood. "Who was the lady?" I asked of my companion.

He shrugged his shoulders, and for an instant looked uncertain. But, as a Frenchman, he produced his hypothesis as follows: "Mon Dieu! a sweetheart of M. Briseux!— *Ces artistes!*"

I left my place and passed into the adjoining rooms, where, as I have said, I found half an hour's diversion. On my return, my chair was occupied by a lady, apparently my only fellow-visitor. I noticed her no further than to see

that, though comely, she was no longer young, that she was
dressed in black, and that she was looking intently at the
picture. Her intentness indeed at last attracted me, and
while I lingered to gather a final impression, I covertly
glanced at her. She was so far from being young that her
hair was white, but with that charming and often premature
brilliancy which belongs to fine brunettes. The *concierge*
hovered near, narrating and expounding, and I fancied that
her brief responses (for she asked no questions) betrayed
an English accent. But I had doubtless no business to fancy
anything, for my companion, as if with a sudden embarrass-
ing sense of being watched, gathered her shawl about her,
rose, and prepared to turn away. I should have immediately retreated, but that with this movement of hers our
eyes met, and in the light of her rapid, just slightly deprecating glance, I read something which helped curiosity
to get the better of politeness. She walked away, and I
stood staring; and as she averted her head it seemed to
me that my rather too manifest surprise had made her
blush. I watched her slowly cross the room and pass into
the next one, looking very vaguely at the pictures; and
then addressed a keenly questioning glance at the Lady with
the Yellow Shawl. Her startlingly vivid eyes answered my
question most distinctly. I was satisfied, and I left the
Musée.

It would perhaps be more correct to say that I was
wholly unsatisfied. I strolled at haphazard through the
little town, and emerged, as a matter of course, on the local
promenade. The promenade at M—— is a most agreeable
spot. It stretches along the top of the old town wall, over
whose sturdy parapet, polished by the peaceful showers of
many generations, you enjoy a view of the pale-hued but
charming Provencal landscape. The middle of the rampart
is adorned with a row of close-clipped lime-trees, with
benches in the spaces between them; and, as you sit in the
shade, the prospect is framed to your vision by the level
parapet and the even limit of the far-projecting branches.
What you see is therefore a long horizontal strip of landscape—a radiant stretch of white rocks and vaporous olives,

scintillating in the southern light. Except a *bonne* or two, with a couple of children grubbing in the gravel, an idle apprentice in a blouse dozing on a bench, and a couple of red-legged soldiers leaning on the wall, I was the only lounger on the rampart, and this was a place to relish solitude. By nature a very sentimental traveler, there is nothing I like better than to light a cigar and lose myself in a meditative perception of local color. I love to ruminate the picturesque, and the scene before me was redolent of it. On this occasion, however, the shady rampart and the shining distance were less interesting than a figure, disembodied but distinct, which soon obtruded itself on my attention. The mute assurance gathered before leaving the Musée had done as much to puzzle as to enlighten me. Was that modest and venerable person, then, the sweetheart of the illustrious Briseux? one of *ces artistes*, as rumor loudly proclaimed him, in the invidious as well as in the most honorable sense of the term. Plainly, she was the original of the portrait. In the days when her complexion would bear it, she had worn the yellow shawl. Time had changed, but not transformed her, as she must have fancied it had, to come and contemplate thus frankly this monument of her early charms. Why had she come? Was it accident, or was it vanity? How did it seem to her to find herself so strangely lifted out of her own possession and made a helpless spectator of her survival to posterity? The more I consulted my impression of her, the more certain I felt that she was no Frenchwoman, but a modest spinster of my own transatlantic race, on whom posterity had as little claim as this musty Musée, which indeed possessed much of that sepulchral chill which clings to such knowledge of us as posterity enjoys. I found it hard to reconcile the lady with herself, and it was with the restlessness of conjecture that I left my place and strolled to the further end of the rampart. Here conjecture paused, amazed at its opportunities; for M. Briseux's sweetheart was seated on a bench under the lime-trees. She was gazing almost as thoughtfully on the distant view as she had done on her portrait; but as I passed, she gave me a glance from which embarrassment seemed to have vanished. I slowly walked the length of the rampart again, and as I went an impulse, born somehow of the delicious mild air, the light-bathed landscape of rock and olive, and of the sense of a sort of fellowship in isolation in the midst of these deeply foreign influences, as well as of a curiosity which was after all but the frank recognition of an obvious fact, was transmuted into a decision sufficiently remarkable in a bashful man. I proceeded gravely to carry it out. I approached my companion and bowed. She acknowledged my bow with a look which, though not exactly mistrustful, seemed to demand an explanation. To give it, I seated myself beside her. Something in her face made explanation easy. I was sure that she was an old maid, and gently but frankly eccentric. Her age left her at liberty to be as frank as she chose, and though I was somewhat her junior, I had gray hairs enough in my mustache to warrant her in smiling at my almost ardent impatience. Her smile, when she perceived that my direct appeal was deeply respectful, broke into a genial laugh which completed our introduction. To her inner sense, as well, evidently, the gray indifference of the historic rampart, the olive-sown landscape, the sweet foreign climate, left the law very much in our own hands; and then moreover, as something in her eyes proclaimed, the well of memory in her soul had been so strongly stirred that it naturally overflowed. I fancy that she looked more like her portrait for that hour or two than she had done in twenty years. At any rate, it had come to seem, before many minutes, a delightful matter of course that I should sit there—a perfect stranger—listening to the story into which her broken responses to my first questions gradually shaped themselves. I should add that I had made a point of appearing a zealous student of the lamented Briseux. This was no more than the truth, and I proved categorically that I knew his works. We were thus pilgrims in the same faith, and licensed to discuss its mysteries. I repeat her story literally, and I surely don't transgress the proper limits of editorial zeal in supplying a single absent clause: she must in those days have been a wonderfully charming girl.

I have been spending the winter (she said) with my niece at Cannes, where I accidentally heard from an English gentleman interested in such matters, that Briseux's "Yellow Shawl" had been purchased by this little Musée. He had stopped to see it on his way from Paris, and, though a famous *connoisseur*, poor man, do you know he never discovered what it took you but a moment to perceive? I didn't enlighten him, in spite of his kindness in explaining, "Bradshaw" in hand, just how I might manage to diverge on my way to Paris and give a day to M——. I contented myself with telling him that I had known M. Briseux thirty years ago, and had chanced to have the first glimpse of his first masterpiece. Even this suggested nothing. But in fact, why should it have suggested anything? As I sat before the picture just now, I felt in all my pulses that I am *not* the person who stands masquerading there with that strangely cynical smile. That poor girl is dead and buried; I should tell no falsehood in saying I'm not she. Yet as I looked at her, time seemed to roll backward and experience to repeat itself. Before me stood a pale young man in a ragged coat, with glowing dark eyes, brushing away at a great canvas, with gestures more like those of inspiration than any I have ever seen. I seemed to see myself—to be myself—muffled in that famous shawl, *posing* there for hours in a sort of fever that made me unconscious of fatigue. I've often wondered whether, during those memorable hours, I was more or less myself than usual, and whether the singular episode they brought forth was an act of folly or of transcendent reason. Perhaps you can tell me.

It was in Paris, in my twenty-first year. I had come abroad with Mrs. Staines, an old and valued friend of my mother's, who during the last days of her life, a year before, had consigned me appealingly to this lady's protection. But for Mrs. Staines, indeed, I should have been homeless. My brother had recently married, but not happily, and experiment had shown me that under his roof I was an indifferent peacemaker. Mrs. Staines was what is called a very superior person—a person with an aquiline nose, who wore gloves in the house, and gave you her ear to kiss.

My mother, who considered her the wisest of women, had written her every week since their schooldays a crossed letter beginning "My dearest Lucretia"; but it was my poor mother's nature to like being patronized and bullied. Mrs. Staines would send her by return of mail a budget of advice adapted to her "station"—this being a considerate mode of allusion to the fact that she had married a very poor clergyman. Mrs. Staines received me, however, with such substantial kindness, that I should have had little grace to complain that the manner of it was frigid. When I knew her better I forgave her frigidity, for it was that of a disappointed woman. She was ambitious, and her ambitions had failed. She had married a very clever man, a rising young lawyer, of political tendencies, who promised to become famous. She would have enjoyed above all things being the wife of a legal luminary, and she would have insisted on his expanding to the first magnitude. She believed herself born, I think, to be the lawful Egeria of a cabinet minister. A cabinet minister poor Mr. Staines might have become if he had lived; but he broke down at thirty-five from overwork, and a year later his wife had to do double mourning. As time went on she transferred her hopes to her only boy; but here her disappointment lay the heavier on her heart that maternal pride had bidden it be forever dumb. He would never tread in his father's steps, nor redeem his father's pledges. His genius—if genius it was—was bent in quite another way, and he was to be, not a useful, but an ornamental member of society. Extremely ornamental he seemed likely to become, and his mother found partial comfort as he grew older. He did his duty apparently in growing up so very handsome that, whatever else he might do, he would be praised less for that than for his good looks. They were those of a decorous young Apollo. When I first saw him, as he was leaving college, he might well have passed for an incipient great man. He had in perfection the *air* of distinction, and he carried it out in gesture and manner. Never was a handsomer, graver, better-bred young man. He was tall, slender, and fair, with the finest blond hair curling close about his shapely head; a blue eye, as

clear and cold as a winter's morning; a set of teeth so handsome that his infrequent smile might have seemed almost
a matter of modesty; and a general expression of discretion
and maturity which seemed to protest against the imputation of foppishness. After a while, probably, you would
have found him too imperturbably neat and polite, and have
liked him better if his manner had been sometimes at fault
and his cravat occasionally awry. Me, I confess, he vastly
impressed from the first, and I secretly worshipped him. I
had never seen so fine a gentleman, and I doubted if the
world contained such another. My experience of the world
was small, and I had lived among what Harold Staines
would have considered very shabby people—several of
whom wore ill-brushed hats. I was, therefore, not sorry
to find that I appreciated merit of the most refined sort;
and in fact, ignorant though I was, my judgment was not at
fault. Harold was perfectly honorable and amiable, and
his only fault was that he looked wiser than he could reasonably be expected to be. In the evening especially, in a
white cravat, leaning in a doorway, and overtopping the
crowd by his whole handsome head, he seemed some inscrutable young diplomatist whose skepticism hadn't undermined his courtesy.

He had, through his mother, expectation of property
sufficient to support him in ample ease; but though he had
elegant tastes, idleness was not one of them, and he agreed
with his mother that he ought to choose a profession. Then
it was that she fully measured her disappointment. There
had been nothing in her family but judges and bishops, and
anything else was of questionable respectability. There
was a great deal of talk on the matter between them; for
superficially at least they were a most united pair, and if
Harold had not asked her opinion from conviction he would
have done so from politeness. In reality, I believe, there
was but one person in the world whose opinion he greatly
cared for—and that person was not Mrs. Staines; nor had
it yet come to pass that he pretended for a while it was I.
It was so far from being Mrs. Staines that one day, after
a long talk, I found her leaving him in tears; and tears with

this superior woman were an event of portentous rarity. Harold on the same day was not at home at dinner, and I thought the next day held his handsome head even higher than usual. I asked no questions, but a little later my curiosity was satisfied. Mrs. Staines informed me, with an air of dignity which evidently cost her some effort and seemed intended to deprecate criticism, that Harold had determined to be an—artist. "It's not the career I should have preferred," she said, "but my son has talent—and respectability—which will make it honorable." That Harold would do anything more for the profession of the brush than Raphael and Rembrandt had done, I was perhaps not prepared to affirm; but I answered that I was very glad, and that I wished him all success. Indeed, I was not surprised, for Mrs. Staines had what in any one else would have been called a mania for pictures and bronzes, old snuff-boxes and candlesticks. He had not apparently used his pencil very freely; but he had recently procured—indeed, I think he had himself designed—a "sketching apparatus" of the most lavish ingenuity. He was now going to use it in earnest, and I remember reflecting with a good deal of satisfaction that the great white umbrella which formed its principal feature was large enough to protect his handsome complexion from the sun.

It was at this time I came to Mrs. Staines to stay indefinitely—with doubts and fears so few that I must have been either very ignorant or very confident. I had indeed an ample measure of the blessed simplicity of youth; but if I judged my situation imperfectly, I did so at any rate with a conscience. I was stoutly determined to receive no favors that I couldn't repay, and to be as quietly useful and gracefully agreeable as I could modestly devise occasion for. I was a homeless girl, but I was not a poor relation. My fortune was slender, but I was ready to go out into the world and seek a better, rather than fall into an attitude of irresponsive dependence. Mrs. Staines thought at first that I was dull and amiable, and that as a companion I would do no great credit to anything but her benevolence. Later, for a time, as I gave proofs of some sagacity and per-

haps of some decision, I think she fancied me a schemer
and—Heaven forgive her!—a hypocrite. But at last, evidently—although to the end, I believe, she continued to
compliment my shrewdness at the expense of that feminine
sweetness by which I should have preferred to commend
myself—she decided that I was a person of the best intentions, and—here comes my story—that I would make a
suitable wife for her son.

To this unexpectedly flattering conclusion, of course, she
was slow in coming; it was the result of the winter we
passed together after Harold had "turned his attention," as
his mother always publicly phrased it, "to art." He had
declared that we must immediately go abroad that he might
study the works of the masters. His mother, I believe,
suggested that he might begin with the rudiments nearer
home. But apparently he had mastered the rudiments, for
she was overruled and we went to Rome. I don't know how
many of the secrets of the masters Harold learned; but we
passed a delightful winter. He began his studies with the
solemn promptitude which he used in all things, and devoted a great deal of time to copying from the antique in
the Vatican and the Capitol. He worked slowly, but with
extraordinary precision and neatness, and finished his draw-
ings with exquisite care. He was openly very little of a
dogmatist, but on coming to know him you found that he
had various principles of which he was extremely tenacious.
Several of these related to the proportions of the human
body, as ascertained by himself. They constituted, he
affirmed, an infallible method for learning to draw. If
other artists didn't know it, so much the worse for them.
He applied this rare method persistently all winter, and
carried away from Rome a huge portfolio full of neatly
shaded statues and statuesque *contadini*. At first he had
gone into a painter's studio with several other pupils, but
he took no fancy to either his teacher or his companions,
and came home one day in disgust, declaring that he had
washed his hands of them. As he never talked about disagreeable things, he said nothing as to what had vexed
him; but I guessed that he had received some mortal offence,

and I was not surprised that he shouldn't care to frater-
nize with the common herd of art-students. They had
long, untidy hair, and smoked bad tobacco; they lay no
one knew where, and borrowed money and took liberties.
Mr. Staines certainly was not a man to refuse a needy friend
a napoleon, but he couldn't forgive a liberty. He took none
with himself! We became very good friends, and it was
especially for this that I liked him. Nothing is truer than
that in the long run we like our opposites; they're a change
and a rest from ourselves. I confess that my good intentions
sometimes clashed with a fatal light-headedness, of which
a fair share of trouble had not cured me. In moments of
irritation I had a trick of giving the reins to my "sarcasm;" so at least my partners in quadrilles had often called
it. At my leisure I was sure to repent, and frank public
amends followed fast on the heels of offence. Then I believe I was called generous—not only by my partners in
quadrilles. But I had a secret admiration for people who
were just, from the first and always, and whose demeanor
seemed to shape itself with a sort of harmonious unity, like
the outline of a beautiful statue. Harold Staines was a finished gentleman, as we used to say in those days, and I
admired him the more that I still had ringing in my ears
that eternal refrain of my schoolroom days—"My child,
my child, when will you ever learn to be a lady?" He
seemed to me an embodiment of the serene amenities of
life, and I didn't know how very great a personage I thought
him until I once overheard a young man in a crowd at St.
Peter's call him *that confounded prig*. Then I came to the
conclusion that it was a very coarse and vulgar world, and
that Mr. Staines was too good for it.

This impression was not removed by—I hardly know
what to call it—the gallant propriety of his conduct toward
me. He had treated me at first with polite condescension,
as a very young and rather humble person, whose presence
in the house rested on his mother's somewhat eccentric
benevolence, rather than on any very obvious merits of her
own. But later, as my native merit, whatever it was, got
the better of my shyness, he approached me, especially in

company, with a sort of ceremonious consideration which seemed to give notice to the world that if his mother and he treated me as their equal—why, I *was* their equal. At last, one fine day in Rome, I learned that I had the honor to please him. It had seemed to me so little of a matter of course that I should captivate Mr. Staines, that for a moment I was actually disappointed, and felt disposed to tell him that I had expected more of his taste. But as I grew used to the idea, I found no fault with it, and I felt prodigiously honored. I didn't take him for a man of genius, but his admiration pleased me more than if it had come in chorus from a dozen of the men of genius whom I had had pointed out to me at archæological picnics. They somehow were covered with the world's rust and haunted with the world's errors, and certainly on any vital question could not be trusted to make their poor wives the same answers two days running. Besides, they were dreadfully ugly. Harold was consistency itself, and his superior manner and fine blond beauty seemed a natural result of his spiritual serenity. The way he declared himself was very characteristic, and to some girls might have seemed prosaic. To my mind it had a peculiar dignity. I had asked him, a week before, as we stood on the platform before the Lateran, some question about the Claudian aqueduct, which he had been unable to answer at the moment, although on coming to Rome he had laid in a huge provision of books of reference which he consulted with unfailing diligence. "I'll look it up," he said gravely; but I thought no more about it, and a few days afterwards, when he asked me to ride with him on the Campagna, I never supposed I was to be treated to an archæological lecture. It was worthy of a wiser listener. He led the way to a swelling mound, overlooking the long stretch of the aqueduct, and poured forth the result of his researches. This was surely not a trivial compliment; and it seemed to me a finer sort of homage than if he had offered me a fifty-franc bouquet or put his horse at a six-foot wall. He told me the number of the arches, and very possibly of the stones; his story bristled with learning. I listened respectfully and stared hard at the long ragged ruin, as if it had suddenly become intensely interesting. But it was Mr. Staines who was interesting: all honor to the man who kept his polite promises so handsomely! I said nothing when he paused, and after a few minutes was going to turn away my horse. Then he laid his hand on the bridle, and, in the same tone, as if he were still talking of the aqueduct, informed me of the state of his affections. I, in my unsuspectingness, had enslaved them, and it was proper that I should know he adored me. Proper! I have always remembered the word, though I was far from thinking then that it clashed with his eloquence. It often occurred to me afterwards as the key-note of his character. In a moment more, he formally offered himself.

Don't be surprised at these details: to be just I must be perfectly frank, and if I consented to tell you my story, it is because I fancied I should find profit in hearing it myself. As I speak my words come back to me. I left Rome engaged to Mr. Staines, subject to his mother's approval. He might dispense with it, I told him, but I could not, and as yet I had no reason to expect it. She would, of course, wish him to marry a woman of more consequence. Mine of late had risen in her eyes, but she could hardly regard me as yet as a possible daughter-in-law. With time I hoped to satisfy her and to receive her blessing. Then I would ask for no further delay. We journeyed slowly up from Rome along the Mediterranean, stopping often for several days to allow Harold to sketch. He depicted mountains and villages with the same diligence as the statues in the Vatican, and presumably with the same success. As his winter's practice had given him great facility, he would dash off a magnificent landscape in a single morning. I always thought it strange that, being very sober in his speech and manner, he should be extremely fond of color in art. Such at least was the fact, and these rapid watercolors were a wonderful medley. Crimson and azure, orange and emerald—nothing less would satisfy him. But, for that matter, nature in those regions has a dazzling brightness. So at least it had for a lively girl of twenty, just engaged. So it had for a certain time afterwards. I'll not deny, the lustrous sea and sky began vaguely to reflect my own occasionally sombre mood. How to explain to you the process of my feeling at this time is more than I can say; how especially to make you believe that I was neither perverse nor capricious. I give it up; I can only assure you that I observed my emotions, even before I understood them, with painful surprise. I was not disillusioned, but an end had suddenly come to my elation. It was as if my heart had had wings, which had been suddenly clipped. I have never been especially fond of my own possessions, and I have learned that if I wish to admire a thing in peace, I must remain at a respectful distance. My happiness in Harold's affection reached its climax too suddenly, and before I knew it I found myself wondering, questioning, and doubting. It was no fault of his, certainly, and he had promised me nothing that he was not ready to bestow. He was all attention and decorous devotion. If there was a fault, it was mine, for having judged like the very young and uninformed person I was. Since my engagement I felt five years older, and the first use I made of my maturity —cruel as it may seem—was to turn round and look keenly at my lover and revise my judgment. His rigid urbanity was still extremely impressive, but at times I could have fancied that I was listening to a musical symphony, of which only certain brief, unresonant notes were audible. Was this all, and were there no others? It occurred to me more than once, with a kind of dull dismay, in the midst of my placid expectancy, that Harold's grave notes were the beginning and the end of his character. If the human heart were a less incurable skeptic, I might have been divinely happy. I sat by my lover's side while he worked, gazing at the loveliest landscape in the world, and admiring the imperturbable audacity with which he attacked it. Sooner than I expected, these rather silent interviews, as romantic certainly as scenery could make them, received Mrs. Staines's sanction. She had guessed our secret, and disapproved of nothing but its secrecy. She was satisfied with her son's choice, and declared with great emphasis that she was not ambitious. She was kindness itself (though, as you see, she indulged in no needless flattery), and I wondered that I could ever have thought her stern. From this time forward she talked to me a great deal about her son; too much, I might have thought, if I had cared less for the theme. I have said I was not perverse. Do I judge myself too tenderly? Before long I found something oppressive—something almost irritating—in the frequency and complacency of Mrs. Staines's maternal disquisitions. One day, when she had been reminding me at greater length than usual of what a prize I had drawn, I abruptly changed the subject in the midst of a sentence, and left her staring at my petulance. She was on the point, I think, of administering a reprimand, but she suppressed it and contented herself with approaching the topic more cautiously in future. Here is another reminiscence. One morning (it was near Spezia, I think) Harold had been sketching under a tree, not far from the inn, and I sitting by and reading aloud from Shelley, whom one might feel a kindness for there if nowhere else. We had had a little difference of opinion about one of the poems—the beautiful "Stanzas Written in Dejection near Naples," which you probably remember. Harold pronounced them childish. I thought the term ill-chosen, and remember saying, to reinforce my opinion, that though I was no judge of painting, I pretended to be of poetry. He told me (I have not forgotten his words) that "I lacked cultivation in each department," and I believe I replied that I would rather lack cultivation than imagination. For a pair of lovers it was a very pretty quarrel as it stood. Shortly afterwards he discovered that he had left one of his brushes at the inn, and went off in search of it. He had trouble in finding it, and was absent for some time. His verdict on poor Shelley rang in my ears as I sat looking out on the blue iridescence of the sea, and murmuring the lines in which the poet has so wonderfully suggested it. Then I went and sat down on Harold's stool to see how he had rendered this enchanting effect. The picture was nearly finished, but unfortunately I had too little cultivation to enjoy it. The blue sea, however, seemed in all conscience blue enough. While I was comparing it with the far-fading azure of the original, I heard a voice behind me, and turning, saw two gentlemen from the inn, one of whom had been my neighbor the evening before at dinner. He was a foreigner, but he spoke English. On recognizing me he advanced gallantly, ushering his companion, and immediately fell into ecstasies over my picture. I informed him without delay that the picture was not mine; it was the work of Mr. Staines. Nothing daunted, he declared that it was pretty enough to be mine, and that I must have given suggestions; but his companion, a less superficial character apparently, and extremely near-sighted, after examining it minutely with his nose close to the paper, exclaimed with an annoying smile, "Monsieur Staines? Surprising! I should have sworn it was the work of a *jeune fille*."

The compliment was doubtful, and not calculated to restore my equanimity. As a *jeune fille* I suppose I ought to have been gratified, but as a betrothed I should have preferred Harold to paint like a man. I don't know how long after this it was that I allowed myself to wonder, by way of harmless conjecture, how a woman might feel who should find herself married to an ineffective mediocrity. Then I remembered—as if the case were my own—that I had never heard any one talk about his pictures, and that when I had seen them handed about before company by his mother, the buzz of admiration usual on such occasions seemed rather heavy-winged. But I quickly reminded myself that it was not because he painted better or worse that I cared for him, but because personally and morally he was the pink of perfection. This being settled, I fell to wondering whether one mightn't grow weary of perfection— whether (Heaven forgive me!) I was not already the least bit out of patience with Harold's. I could fancy him a trifle too absolute, too imperturbable, too prolific in cut-and-dried opinions. Had he settled everything, then, in his mind? Yes, he had certainly made the most of his time, and I could only admire his diligence. From the moment that I observed that he wasted no time in moods, or reveries, or intellectual pleasantry of any sort, I decided without appeal that he was not a man of genius; and yet, to listen to him at times, you would have vowed at least that he might be. He dealt out his opinions as if they were celestial manna, and nothing was more common than for him to say, "You remember, a month ago, I told you so-and-so!" meaning that he had laid down the law on some point and expected me to engrave it on my heart. It often happened that I had forgotten the lesson, and was obliged to ask him to repeat it; but it left me more unsatisfied than before. Harold would settle his shirt collar as if he considered that he had exhausted the subject, and I would take refuge in a silence which from day to day covered more treacherous conjectures. Nevertheless (strange as you may think it), I believe I should have decided that, Harold being a paragon, my doubts were immoral, if Mrs. Staines, after his cause might have been supposed to be gained, had not persisted in pleading it in season and out. I don't know whether she suspected my secret falterings, but she seemed to wish to secure me beyond relapse. I was so very modest a match for her son, that if I had been more worldly-wise, her enthusiasm might have alarmed me. Later I understood it; then I only understood that there was a general flavor of insinuation in her talk which made me vaguely uneasy. I did the poor lady injustice, and if I had been quicker-witted (and possibly harder-hearted) we might have become sworn allies. She judged her son less with a mother's tenderness than with a mother's zeal, and foresaw the world's verdict—which I won't anticipate! She perceived that he must depend upon a clever wife to float him into success; he would never prosper on his own merits. She did me the honor to believe me socially a sufficiently buoyant body for this arduous purpose, and must have felt it a thousand pities that she couldn't directly speak her mind. A thousand pities indeed! My answer would have been to the point, and would have saved us all a vast deal of pain. Meanwhile, trying half to convince and half to entangle me, she did everything to hasten our marriage.

If there had been anything less than the happiness of a lifetime at stake, I think I should have felt that I owed Harold a sort of reparation for thinking him too great a man, and should still have offered him an affection none the less genuine for being transposed into a minor key. But it was hard for a girl who had dreamed blissfully of a grandly sentimental union, to find herself suddenly face to face with a sternly rational one. When, therefore, Harold mentioned a certain day as the latest for which he thought it proper to wait, I found it impossible to assent, and asked for another month's delay. What I wished to wait for I could hardly have told. Possibly for the first glow of illusion to return; possibly for the last uneasy throb which told that illusion was ebbing away. Harold received this request very gravely, and inquired whether I doubted of his affection.

"No," I said, "I believe it's greater than I deserve."

"Why then," he asked, "should you wait?"

"Suppose I were to doubt of my own?"

He looked as if I had said something in very bad taste and I was almost frightened at his sense of security. But he at last consented to the delay. Perhaps on reflection he was alarmed, for the grave politeness with which he discharged his attentions took a still more formal turn, as if to remind me at every hour of the day that his was not a sentiment to be trifled with. To trifle, Heaven knows, was far enough from my thoughts; for I was fast losing my spirits, and I woke up one morning with the conviction that I was decidedly not happy.

We were to be married in Paris, where Harold had determined to spend six months in order that he might try his fortune again in the studio of a painter whom he especially esteemed—a certain Monsieur Martinet, an old man, and belonging, I believe, to a rather antiquated school of art. During our first days in Paris I went with Harold a great deal to the Louvre, where he was a very profitable companion. He had the history of the schools at his fingers' ends, and, as the phrase is, he knew what he liked. We had a fatal habit of not liking the same things; but I pretended to no critical insight, and desired nothing better than to agree with him. I listened devoutly to everything that could be said for Guido and Caravaggio. One day we were

standing before the inscrutable "Joconde" of Leonardo, a
picture disagreeable to most women. I had been expressing
my great aversion to the lady's countenance, which Harold
on this occasion seemed to share. I was surprised therefore,
when, after a pause, he said quietly, "I believe I'll copy
her."

I hardly knew why I should have smiled, but I did, apparently to his annoyance. "She must be very difficult," I
said. "Try something easier."

"I want something difficult," he answered sternly.

"Truly?" I said. "You mean what you say?"

"Why not?"

"Why then copy a portrait when you can copy an original?"

"What original?"

"Your betrothed! Paint my portrait. I promise to be
difficult enough. Indeed, I'm surprised you should never
have proposed it." In fact the idea had just occurred to
me; but I embraced it with a sort of relief. It seemed to
me that it would somehow test my lover, and that if he succeeded, I might believe in him irremissibly. He stared a
moment as if he had hardly understood me, and I completed
my thought. "Paint my portrait, and the day you finish
it I'll fix our wedding day."

The proposal was after all not very terrible, and before
long he seemed to relish it. The next day he told me that
he had composed his figure mentally, and that we might
begin immediately. Circumstances favored us, for he had
for the time undisturbed all of M. Martinet's studio. This
gentleman had gone into the country to paint a portrait,
and Harold just then was his only pupil. Our first sitting
took place without delay. At his request I brought with me
a number of draperies, among which was the yellow shawl
you have just been admiring. We wore such things then,
just as we played on the harp and read "Corinne." I
tried on my scarfs and veils, one after the other, but Harold was satisfied with none. The yellow shawl, in especial,
he pronounced a meretricious ornament, and decided that
I should be represented in a plain dark dress, with as few

accessories as possible. He quoted with a bow the verse about beauty when unadorned, and began his work.

After the first day or two it progressed slowly, and I felt at moments as if I had saddled him with a cruel burden. He expressed no irritation, but he often looked puzzléd and wearied, and sometimes would lay aside his brushes, fold his arms, and stand gazing at his work with a sort of vacant scowl which tried my patience. "Frown at me," I said more than once; "don't frown at that blameless sheet of canvas. Don't spare me, though I confess it's not my fault if I'm hard to paint." Thus admonished, he would turn toward me without smiling, often shading his eyes with his hand, and would walk slowly round the room, examining me at a distance. Then coming back to his easel, he would make half a dozen strokes and pause again, as if his impetus had already expired. For some time I was miserable; it seemed to me that I had been wonderfully wise to withhold my hand till the picture was finished. He begged I would not look at it, but I knew it was standing still. At last, one morning, after gazing at his work for some time in silence, he laid down his palette gravely, but with no further sign of discomposure than that he gently wiped his forehead with his pocket-handkerchief. "You make me nervous," he suddenly declared.

I fancied there was a tremor in his voice, and I began to pity him. I left my place and laid my hand on his arm. "If it wearies you," I said, "give it up."

He turned away and for some time made no answer. I knew what he was thinking about, and I suppose he knew that I knew it, and was hesitating to ask me seriously whether in giving up his picture he gave up something more. He decided apparently to give up nothing, but grasped his palette, and, with the short incisive gesture habitual to him, motioned me back to my seat. "I'll bother no longer over the drawing," he said; "I'll begin to paint." With his colors he was more prosperous, for the next day he told me that we were progressing fast.

We generally went together to the studio, but it happened one day that he was to be occupied during the early

morning at the other end of Paris, and he arranged to meet
me there. I was punctual, but he had not arrived, and I
found myself face to face with my reluctant image. Opportunity served too well, and I looked at it in spite of his
prohibition, meaning of course to confess my fault. It
brought me less pleasure than faults are reputed to bring.
The picture, as yet very slight and crude, was unpromising
and unflattering. I chiefly distinguished a long white face
with staring black eyes, and a terribly angular pair of arms.
Was it in this unlovely form that I had impressed myself
on Harold's vision? Absorbed by the question, it was some
moments before I perceived that I was not alone. I heard
a sound, looked round, and discovered a stranger, a young
man, gazing over my shoulder at Harold's canvas. His
gaze was intense and not expressive of pleasure, and some
moments passed before he perceived that I had noticed him.
He reminded me strongly of certain dishevelled copyists
whom I had seen at work in the Louvre, and as I supposed
he had some lawful errand in the studio, I contented myself
with thinking that he hadn't the best manners in the world,
and walked to the other end of the room. At last, as he
continued to betray no definite intentions, I ventured to
look at him again. He was young—twenty-five at most—
and excessively shabby. I remember, among other details,
that he had a black cravat wound two or three times round
his neck, without any visible linen. He was short, thin, pale
and hungry-looking. As I turned toward him, he passed his
hand through his hair, as if to do what he could to make
himself presentable, and called my attention to his prodigious shock of thick black curls— a real *coiffure de rapin.*
His face would have been meagre and vulgar, if from beneath their umbrageous locks there had not glanced an extraordinary pair of eyes—eyes really of fire. They were not
tender nor appealing, but they glittered with a sort of
feverish intelligence and penetration, and stamped their
possessor not, as the French say, the first comer. He
almost glared at me and stopped my words short.

"That's your portrait?" he asked, with a toss of his head.
I assented with dignity.

"It's bad, bad, bad!" he cried. "Excuse my frankness, but it's really too bad. It's a waste of colors, of money, of time."

His frankness certainly was extreme; but his words had an accent of ardent conviction which doesn't belong to commonplace impertinence. "I don't know who you are, that I should value your opinion," I said.

"Who I am? I'm an artist, mademoiselle. If I had money to buy visiting-cards, I would present you with one. But I haven't even money to buy colors—hardly to buy bread. I've talent—I've imagination—too much!—I've ideas—I've promise—I've a future; and yet the machine won't work—for want of fuel! I have to roam about with my hands in my pockets—to keep them warm—for want of the very tools of my trade. I've been a fool—an ignoble fool; I've thrown precious hours to the dogs and made enemies of precious friends. Six months ago I quarreled with the père Martinet, who believed in me and would have been glad to keep me. *Il faut que jeunesse se passe!* Mine has passed at a rattling pace, ill-mounted though it was; we have parted company forever. Now I only ask to do a man's work with a man's will. Meanwhile the père Martinet, justly provoked, has used his tongue so well that not a colorman in Paris will trust me. There's a situation! And yet what could I do with ten francs' worth of paint? I want a room and light and a model, and a dozen yards of satin tumbling about her feet. Bah! I shall have to want! There are things I want more. Behold the force of circumstances. I've come back with my pride in my pocket to make it up with the venerable author of the 'Apotheosis of Molière,' and ask him to lend me a louis."

I arrested this vehement effusion by informing him that M. Martinet was out of town, and that for the present the studio was—private. But he seemed too much irritated to take my hint. "That's not his work?" he went on, turning to the portrait. "Martinet is bad, but is not as bad as that. *Quel genre!* You deserve, mademoiselle, to be better treated; you're an excellent model. Excuse me, once for all; I know I'm atrociously impudent. But I'm an artist, and I find it pitiful to see a fine great canvas besmeared in such a fashion as that! There ought to be a society for the protection of such things."

I was at loss what to reply to this extraordinary explosion of contempt. Strange to say—it's the literal truth—I was neither annoyed nor disgusted; I simply felt myself growing extremely curious. This impudent little Bohemian was forcing me somehow to respect his opinion; he spoke with penetratng authority. Don't say that I was willing to be convinced; if you had been there, you would have let him speak. It would have been, of course, the part of propriety to request him in a chilling voice to leave the room, or to ring for the *concierge,* or to flee in horror. I did none of these things: I went back to the picture, and tried hard to see something in it which would make me passionately contradict him. But it seemed to exhale a mortal chill, and all I could say was: "Bad—bad? How bad?"

"Ridiculously bad; impossibly bad! You're an angel of charity, mademoiselle, not to see it!"

"Is it weak—cold—ignorant?"

"Weak, cold, ignorant, stiff, empty, hopeless! And, on top of all, pretentious—oh, pretentious as the *façade* of the Madeleine!"

I endeavored to force a skeptical smile. "After all, monsieur, I'm not bound to believe you."

"Evidently!" And he rubbed his forehead and looked gloomily round the room. "But one thing I can tell you" —fixing me suddenly with his extraordinary eyes, which seemed to expand and glow with the vividness of prevision —"the day will come when people will fight for the honor of having believed me, and of having been the first. 'I discovered him—I always said so. But for me you'd have let the poor devil starve!' You'll hear the chorus! So now's your chance, mademoiselle! Here I stand, a man of genius if there ever was one, without a sou, without a friend, without a ray of reputation. Believe in me now, and you'll be the first, by many a day. You'd find it easier, you'll say, if I had a little more modesty. I assure

you I don't go about blowing my trumpet in this fashion
every day. This morning I'm in a kind of fever, and
I've reached a crisis. I must do something—even make
an ass of myself! I can't go on devouring my own heart.
You see for these three months I've been *à sec*. I haven't
dined every day. Perhaps a sinking at the stomach is pro-
pitious to inspiration: certainly, week by week, my brain
has grown clearer, my imagination more restless, my de-
sires more boundless, my visions more splendid! Within
the last fortnight my last doubt has vanished, and I feel
as strong as the sun in heaven! I roam about the streets
and lounge in the public gardens for want of a better refuge,
and everything I look at—the very sunshine in the gutter,
the chimney-pots against the sky—seems a picture, a subject, an opportunity! I hang over the balustrade that runs
before the pictures at the Louvre, and Titian and Correggio
seem to turn pale, like people when you've guessed their
secret. I don't know who the author of this masterpiece
may be, but I fancy he would have more talent if he weren't
so sure of his dinner. Do you know how I learned to look
at things and use my eyes? By staring at the *charcutier's*
windows when my pockets were empty. It's a great lesson
to learn even the shape of a sausage and the color of a
ham. This gentleman, it's easy to see, hasn't noticed such
matters. He goes by the sense of taste. *Voilà le monde!*
I—I—I—"—and he slapped his forehead with a kind of
dramatic fury—"here as you see me—ragged, helpless, hopeless, with my soul aching with ambition and my fingers
itching for a brush—and *he*, standing up here after a good
breakfast, in this perfect light, among pictures and tapes-
tries and carvings, with you in your blooming beauty for
a model, and painting that—sign-board."

His violence was startling; I didn't know what might
come next, and I took up my bonnet and mantle. He
immediately protested with ardor. "A moment's reflection,
mademoiselle, will tell you that, with the appearance I present, I don't talk about your beauty *pour vous faire la
cour*. I repeat with all respect, you're a model to make
a painter's fortune. I doubt if you've many attitudes or

much flexibility; but for once—the portrait of Mlle. X.—
you're perfect."

"I'm obliged to you for your—information," I answered
gravely. "You see my artist is chosen. I expect him here
at any moment, and I won't answer for his listening to you
as patiently as I have done."

"He's coming?" cried my visitor. *"Quelle chance!* I
shall be charmed to meet him. I shall vastly enjoy seeing
the human head from which that conception issued. I see
him already: I construct the author from the work. He's
tall and blond, with eyes very much the color of his own
china-blue there. He wears straw-colored whiskers, and
doubtless he paints in straw-colored gloves. In short. he's
un homme magnifique!"

This was sarcasm run mad; but I listened to it and
resented it as little as I enjoyed it. My companion seemed
to possess a sort of demonic veracity of which the influence
was irresistible. I questioned his sincerity so little that, if
I offered him charity, it was with no intention of testing it.
"I dare say you've immense talent," I said, "but you've
horrible manners. Nevertheless, I believe you will perceive
that there is no reason why our conversation should continue; and I should pay you a poor compliment in thinking
that you need to be bribed to withdraw. But since M.
Martinet isn't here to lend you a louis, let me act for him."
And I laid the piece of gold on the table.

He looked at it hard for a moment and then at me, and
I wondered whether he thought the gift too meagre. "I
won't go so far as to say that I'm proud," he answered at
last. "But from a lady, *ma foi!* it's beggarly—it's humil-
iating. Excuse me then if I refuse; I mean to ask for
something else. To do me justice, remember that I speak
to you not as a man, but as an artist. Bestow your charity
on the artist, and if it costs you an effort, remember that
that is the charity which is of most account with heaven.
Keep your louis; go and stand as you've been standing for
this picture, in the same light and the same attitude, and
then 'et me look at you for three little minutes." As he
spoke he drew from his pocket a ragged note-book and the

stump of a pencil. "The few scrawls I shall make here will be your alms."

He spoke of effort, but it is a fact that I made little to comply. While I resumed my familiar attitude in front of Harold's canvas, he walked rapidly across the room and stooped over a chair upon which a mass of draperies had been carelessly tossed. In a moment I saw what had attracted him. He had caught a glimpse of the famous yellow scarf, glowing splendidly beneath a pile of darker stuffs. He pulled out the beautiful golden-hued tissue with furious alacrity, held it up before him and broke into an ecstasy of admiration. "What a tone—what a glow—what a texture! In Heaven's name, put it on!" And without further ceremony he tossed it over my shoulders. I need hardly tell you that I obeyed but a natural instinct in gathering it into picturesque folds. He rushed away, and stood gazing and clapping his hands. "The harmony is perfect—the effect sublime! You possess that thing and you bury it out of sight? Wear it, wear it, I entreat you—and your portrait —but ah!" and he glared angrily askance at the picture: "you'll never wear it there!"

"We thought of using it, but it was given up."

"Given up? *Quelle horreur!* He hadn't the pluck to attack it! Oh, if I could just take a brush at it and rub it in for him!" And, as if possessed by an uncontrollable impulse, he seized poor Harold's palette. But I made haste to stop his hand. He flung down the brushes, buried his face in his hands, and pressed back, I could fancy, the tears of baffled eagerness. "You'll think me crazy!" he cried.

He was not crazy, to my sense; but he was a raging, aimless force, which I suddenly comprehended that I might use. I seemed to measure the full proportions of Harold's inefficiency, and to foresee the pitiful result of his undertaking. He wouldn't succumb, but he would doggedly finish his task and present me, in evidence of his claim, with a dreadful monument of his pretentious incapacity. Twenty strokes from this master-hand would make a difference; ten minutes' work would carry the picture forward. I thrust the palette into the young man's grasp

again and looked at him solemnly. "Paint away for your
life," I said; "but promise me this: to succeed!"

He waved his hand in the air, despatched me with a
glance to my place, and let himself loose on the canvas;
there are no other words for his tremulous eagerness. A
quarter of an hour passed in silence. As I watched his
motions grow every moment broader and more sweeping,
I could fancy myself listening to some ardent pianist, plung-
ing deeper into a passionate symphony and devouring the
key-board with outstretched arms. Flushed and dishevelled,
consuming me almost with his ardent stare, daubing,
murmuring, panting, he seemed indeed to be painting for
life.

At last I heard a tread in the vestibule. I knew it was
Harold's, and I hurried to look at the picture. How would
he take it? I confess I was prepared for the worst. The picture spoke for itself. Harold's work had disappeared with
magical rapidity, and even my unskilled eye perceived that
a graceful and expressive figure had been powerfully
sketched in. As Harold appeared, I turned to meet him.
He seemed surprised at not finding me alone, and I laid
my finger gravely on my lips and led him to the front of
the canvas. The position of things was so singular that
for some moments it baffled his comprehension. My companion finished what he was immediately concerned with;
then with an obsequious bow laid down his brushes. "It
was a loan, monsieur," he said. "I return it with interest."
Harold flushed to his eyes, and sat down in silence. I had
expected him to be irritated; but this was more than
irritation. At last: "Explain this extraordinary performance," he said in a low voice.

I felt pain, and yet somehow I felt no regret. The situation was tense, as the phrase is, and yet I almost relished
it. "This gentleman is a great artist," I said boldly.
"Look for yourself. Your picture was lost; he has redeemed
it."

Harold looked at the intruder slowly from head to foot.
"Who is this person?" he demanded, as if he had not
heard me.

The young man understood no English, but he apparently guessed at the question. "My name is Pierre Briseux; let *that*" (pointing to his work) "denote my profession. If you're affronted, monsieur, don't visit your displeasure on mademoiselle; I alone am responsible. You had got into a tight place; I wished to help you out of it; *sympathie de confrère!* I've done you no injury. I've made you a present of half a masterpiece. If I could only trust you not to spoil it!"

Harold's face betrayed his invincible disgust, and I saw that my offence was mortal. He had been wounded in his tenderest part, and his self-control was rapidly ebbing. His lips trembled, but he was too angry even to speak. Suddenly he seized a heavy brush which stood in a pot of dusky varnish, and I thought for a moment he was going to fling it at Briseux. He balanced it an instant, and then tossed it full in the face of the picture. I raised my hands to my face as if I felt the blow. Briseux, at least, felt it sorely.

"*Malheureux!*" he cried. "Are you blind as well? Don't you know a good thing when you see it? That's what I call a waste of material. *Allons*, you're very angry; let me explain. In meddling with your picture I certainly took a great liberty. My misery is my excuse. You have money, materials, models—everything but talent. No, no, you're no painter; it's impossible! There isn't an intelligent line on your canvas. I, on the other hand, am a born painter. I've talent and nothing more. I came here to see M. Martinet; learning he was absent, I staid for very envy! I looked at your work, and found it a botch; at your empty stool and idle palette, and found them an immense temptation; at mademoiselle, and found her a perfect model. I persuaded, frightened, convinced her, and out of charity she gave me a five minutes' sitting. Once the brush in my hand, I felt the divine afflatus; I hoped for a miracle—that you'd never come back, that you'd be run over in the street, or have an attack of apoplexy. If you had only let me go on, I should have served you up a great work, monsieur—a work to which, in spite of your natural irritation, you wouldn't have dared to do a violence. You'd have been afraid of it. That's the sort of thing I meant to paint. If you could only believe me, you'd not regret it. Give me a start, and ten years hence I shall see you buying my pictures, and not thinking them dear. Oh, I thought I had my foot in the stirrup; I dreamed I was in the saddle and riding hard. But I've turned a somersault!"

I doubt that Harold, in his resentment, either understood M. Briseux's words or appreciated his sketch. He simply felt that he had been the victim of a monstrous aggression, in which I, in some painfully inexplicable way, had been half dupe and half accomplice. I was watching his anger and weighing its ominous significance. His cold fury, and the expression it threw into his face and gestures, told me more about him than weeks of placid love-making had done, and, following close upon my vivid sense of his incapacity, seemed suddenly to cut the knot that bound us together, and over which my timid fingers had been fumbling. "Put on your bonnet," he said to me; "get a carriage and go home."

I can't describe his tone. It contained an assumption of my confusion and compliance, which made me feel that I ought to lose no time in undeceiving him. Nevertheless I felt cruelly perplexed, and almost afraid of his displeasure. Mechanically I took up my bonnet. As I held it in my hand, my eyes met those of our terrible companion, who was evidently trying to read the riddle of my relations with Harold. Planted there with his trembling lips, his glittering, searching eyes, an indefinable something in his whole person that told of joyous impulse arrested, but pausing only for a more triumphant effort, he seemed a strangely eloquent embodiment of youthful genius. I don't know whether he read in my glance a ray of sympathy, but his lips formed a soundless "*Restez, madame,*" which quickened the beating of my heart. The feeling that then invaded it I despair of making you understand; yet it must help in your eyes to excuse me, and it was so profound that often in memory it seems more real and poignant than

the things of the present. Poor little Briseux, ugly, shabby,
disreputable, seemed to me some appealing messenger from
the mysterious immensity of life; and Harold, beside him,
comely, elegant, imposing, justly indignant, seemed to me
simply his narrow, personal, ineffectual self. This was a
wider generalization than the feminine heart is used to. I
flung my bonnet on the floor and burst into tears.

"This is not an exhibition for a stranger," said Harold
grimly. "Be so good as to follow me."

"You must excuse me; I can't follow you; I can't explain. I have something more to say to M. Briseux. He's
less of a stranger than you think."

"I'm to leave you here?" stammered Harold.

"It's the simplest way."

"With that dirty little Frenchman?"

"What should I care for his being clean? It's his genius
that interests me."

Harold stared in dark amazement. "Art you insane?
Do you know what you're doing?"

"An act, I believe, of real charity."

"Charity begins at home. It's an act of desperate folly.
Must I *command* you to leave?"

"You've done that already. I can't obey you. If I were
to do so, I should pretend what isn't true; and, let me say
it, it's to undeceive you that I refuse."

"I don't understand you," cried Harold, "nor to what
spell this meddlesome little beggar has subjected you!
But I'm not a man to be trifled with, you know, and this
is my last request; my last, do you understand? If you
prefer the society of this abandoned person, you're welcome, but you forfeit mine forever. It's a choice! You
give up the man who has offered you an honorable affection,
a name, a fortune, who has trusted and cherished you, who
stands ready to make you a devoted husband. What you
get the Lord knows!"

I had sunk into a chair. I listened in silence, and for
some time answered nothing. His words were vividly true.
He offered me much, and I gave up everything. He had
played an honorable part, and I was playing a very

strange one. I asked myself sternly whether I was ready to rise and take his arm and let him lead me blindfold through life. When I raised my eyes Briseux stood before me, and from the expression of his face I could have fancied he had guessed at the meaning of Harold's words. "I'll make you immortal," he murmured; "I'll delight mankind—and I'll begin my own career!"

An ineffable prevision of the truth which after the lapse of years has brought about our meeting here seemed to raise me as if on wings, and made decision easy. We women are so habitually condemned by fate to act simply in what is called the domestic sphere, that there is something intoxicating in the opportunity to exert a far-reaching influence outside of it. To feel the charms of such an opportunity, one must perhaps be of a reprehensibly fanciful turn. Such at any rate was my mood for that hour. I seemed to be the end of an electric chain, of which the rest was throbbing away through time. I seemed to hold in my hand an immeasurable gift. "We had better part on the spot," I said to Harold. "I've foreseen our parting for weeks, only it has come more abruptly. Forgive the abruptness. To myself the pretext seems better than to you; perhaps some day you'll appreciate it. A single question," I added. "Could you ever have finished my portrait?"

He looked at me askance for some moments, with a strange mistrust, as if I had suddenly developed some monstrous and sinister slyness; then catching his breath with a little groan—almost a shudder—he marched out of the room.

Briseux clasped his hands in ecstasy. "You're magnificent!" he cried. "If you could only look so for three hours!"

"To business," I said sternly. "If you don't paint a perfect picture, you're the most shameless of impostors."

He had but a single sitting, but it was a long one; though how many hours it lasted, I doubt that either of us could have told. He painted till dusk, and then we had lamps. Before I left him I looked at the picture for the last and only time before seeing it to-day. It seemed to me as perfect as it seemed this morning, and I felt that my choice was justified and that Briseux's fortune was made. It gave me all the strength I needed for the immediate future. He was evidently of the same opinion and profoundly absorbed in it. When I bade him farewell, in very few words, he answered me almost absently. I had served his purpose and had already passed into that dusky limbo of unhonored victims, the experience—intellectual and other —of genius. I left him the yellow shawl, that he might finish this part of his work at his leisure, and, as for the picture, I told him to keep it, for that I should have little pleasure in seeing it again. Then he stared a moment, but the next he was painting hard.

I had the next morning what under other circumstances I might call an explanation with Mr. Staines, an explanation in which I explained nothing to his satisfaction but that he had been hideously wronged, and that I was a demon of inconstancy. He wrapped himself in an icy silence, and, I think, expected some graceful effusion of humility. I may not have been humble, but I was considerate, and I perceived, for my reward, that the sore point with him was not that he had lost me, but that I had ventured to judge him. Mrs. Staines's manner, on the other hand, puzzled me, so strange a mixture was it of half-disguised elation and undisguised sarcasm. At last I guessed her meaning. Harold, after all, had had an escape; instead of being the shrewd, practical girl she had thought me, I was a terribly romantic one! Perhaps she was right; I was romantic enough to make no further claim on her hospitality, and with as little delay as possible I returned home. A month later I received an enclosure of half a dozen cuttings from newspapers, scrawled boldly across with the signature of Pierre Briseux. The Paris *salon* had opened and the critics had spoken. They had not neglected the portrait of Mademoiselle X——. The picture was an immense success, and M. Briseux was famous. There were a few protesting voices, but it was evident that his career had begun. For Mademoiselle X—— herself, I believe, there were none but compliments, several of which took the form of gallant

conjecture as to her real identity. Mademoiselle X——
was an assumed name, and according to more than one voice
the lady was an imperious Russian princess with a distate
for vulgar publicity. You know the rest of M. Briseux's
history. Since then he has painted real princesses by the
dozen. He has delighted mankind rarely. As for his having made me immortal, I feel as if it were almost true. It
must be an eternity since the thing happened—so very
unreservedly I've described it!

PROFESSOR FARGO

I

THE little town of P—— is off the railway, and reached by a coach drive of twenty-five miles, which the primitive condition of the road makes a trial to the flesh, and the dulness of the landscape a weariness to the spirit. It was therefore not balm to my bruises, physical or intellectual, to find, on my arrival, that the gentleman for whose sake I had undertaken the journey had just posted off in a light buggy for a three days' holiday. After venting my disappointment in a variety of profitless expletives, I decided that the only course worthy of the elastic philosophy of a commercial traveller was to take a room at the local tavern and await his return. P—— was obviously not an exhilarating place of residence, but I had outweathered darker hours, and I reflected that having, as the phrase is, a bone to pick with my correspondent, a little accumulated irritation would arm me for the combat. Moreover, I had been rattling about for three months by rail; I was mortally tired, and the prospect of spending a few days beyond earshot of the steam whistle was not unwelcome. A certain audible, rural hush seemed to hang over the little town, and there was nothing apparently to prevent my giving it the whole of my attention. I lounged awhile in the tavern porch, but my presence seemed only to deepen the spell of silence on that customary group of jaundiced ruminants who were tilting their chairs hard by. I measured thrice, in its length, the dusty plank sidewalk of the main street, counted the hollyhocks in the front yards, and read the names on the little glass door plates; and finally, in despair, I visited the cemetery. Although we were at the end of September, the day was hot, and this youthful institution boasted but a scanty growth of funereal umbrage. No weeping willow, no dusky cypress offered a friendly shelter to the meditative visitor. The yellow grass and white tombstones glared in the hot light, and though I felt very little merrier than a graveyard ghost, I staid hardly longer than one who should have mistaken his hour. But I am fond of reading country epitaphs, and I promised myself to come back when the sun was lower. On my way back to the inn I found myself, on a lately opened cross street, face to face with the town hall, and pausing approached its threshold with hopes of entertainment scarcely less ardent than those which, during a journey abroad, had guided my steps toward some old civic palace of France or Italy. There was, of course, no liveried minion to check my advance, and I made my way unchallenged into the large, bare room which occupied the body of the edifice. It was the accustomed theatre of town meetings, caucuses, and other solemn services, but it seemed just now to have been claimed for profaner uses. An itinerant lecturer, of a boisterous type, was unpacking his budget and preparing his *mise en scène*. This seemed to consist simply of a small table and three chairs in a row, and of a dingy specimen of our national standard, to whose awkward festoons, suspended against the blank wall at the rear of the platform, the orator in person was endeavoring to impart a more artistic grace. Another personage on the floor was engaged in scrawling the date of the performance, in red chalk, upon a number of printed handbills. He silently thrust one of these documents at me as I passed, and I saw with some elation that I had a resource for my evening. The latter half of the page consisted of extracts from village newspapers, setting forth the merits of the entertainments. The headings alone, as I remember them, ran somewhat in this fashion:

A MESSAGE FROM THE SPIRIT WORLD.
THE HIGHER MATHEMATICS MADE EASY TO
LADIES AND CHILDREN.
A NEW REVELATION! A NEW SCIENCE!
GREAT MORAL AND SCIENTIFIC COMBINATION.

PROFESSOR FARGO, THE INFALLIBLE WAKING MEDIUM AND
MAGICIAN, CLAIRVOYANT, PROPHET, AND SEER!
COLONEL GIFFORD, THE FAMOUS LIGHTNING CALCULATOR
AND MATHEMATICAL REFORMER!

This was the substance of the program, but there were
a great many incidental *fioriture* which I have forgotten.
By the time I had mastered them, however, for the occasion,
the individual who was repairing the tattered flag, turned
round, perceived me, and showed me a countenance which
could belong only to an "infallible waking medium." It
was not, indeed, that Professor Fargo had the abstracted
and emaciated aspect which tradition attributes to prophets
and visionaries. On the contrary, the fleshly element in his
composition seemed, superficially, to enjoy a luxurious
preponderance over the spiritual. He was tall and corpulent, and wore an air of aggressive robustness. A mass of
reddish hair was tossed back from his forehead in a leonine
fashion, and a lustrous auburn beard diffused itself complacently over an expansive but by no means immaculate
shirt front. He was dressed in a black evening suit, of a
tarnished elegance, and it was in keeping with the festal
pattern of his garments, that on the right forefinger of a
large, fat hand, he should wear an immense turquoise ring.
His intimate connection with the conjuring class was
stamped upon his whole person; but to a superficial glance
he might have seemed a representative of its grosser accom-
plishments. You could have fancied him, in spangled flesh-
ings, looking down the lion's mouth, or cracking the ring-
master's whip at the circus, while Mlle. Josephine jumped
through the hoops. It was his eyes, when you fairly met
them, that proved him an artist on a higher line. They
were eyes which had peeped into stranger places than even
lions' mouths. Their pretension, I know, was to pierce
the veil of futurity; but if this was founded, I could only
say that the vision of Ezekiel and Jeremiah was but another
name for consummate Yankee shrewdness. They were, in
a single word, the most impudent pair of eyes I ever beheld,
and it was the especial sign of their impudence that they

seemed somehow to undertake to persuade you of the disinterested benevolence. Being of a fine reddish brown color, it was probable that several young women that evening would pronounce them magnificent. Perceiving, apparently, that I had not the rustic physiognomy of a citizen of P——, Professor Fargo deemed my patronage worth securing. He advanced to the cope of the platform with his hands in his pockets, and gave me a familiar nod.

"Mind you come to-night, young man!" he said, jocosely imperious.

"Very likely I shall," I answered. "Anything in the world to help me through an evening at P——."

"Oh, you won't want your money back," the Professor rejoined. "Mine is a first-class entertainment; none of your shuffling break-downs. We are perfect, my friends and I, in our respective parts. If you are fond of a good, stiff, intellectual problem, we'll give you something to think about." The Professor spoke very slowly and benignantly, and his full, sonorous voice rolled away through the empty hall. He evidently liked to hear it himself; he balanced himself on his toes and surveyed the scene of his impending exploits. "I don't blow my own trumpet," he went on; "I'm a modest man; you'll see for yourself what I can do. But I should like to direct your attention to my friend the Colonel. *He's* a rare old gentleman to find in a traveling show! The most remarkable old gentleman, perhaps, that ever addressed a promiscuous audience. You needn't be afraid of the higher mathematics; it's all made as pretty as a game of billiards. It's his own daughter does the sums. We don't put her down in the bills, for motives of delicacy; but I'll tell you for your private satisfaction that she is an exquisite young creature of seventeen."

It was not every day that I found myself in familiar conversation with a prophet, and the opportunity for obtaining a glimpse of the inner mechanism of the profession was too precious to be neglected. I questioned the Professor about his travels, his expenses, his profits, and the mingled emotions of the itinerant showman's lot; and then, taking the bull by the horns, I asked him whether, between ourselves, an accomplished medium had not to be also a tolerable conjurer? He leaned his head on one side and stood stroking his beard, and looking at me between lids shrewdly half closed. Then he gave a little dry chuckle, which expressed, at my choice, compassion either for my disbelief in his miracles or for my faith in his urbanity.

"I confess frankly," I said, "that I'm a skeptic. I don't believe in messages from the spirit world. I don't believe that even the depressing prospect of immortality is capable of converting people who talked plain sense here on earth into the authors of the inflated platitudes which people of your profession pretend to transmit from them. I don't believe people who have expressed themselves for a lifetime in excellent English can ever be content with conversation by raps on the dinner table. I don't believe that you know anything more about the future world than you do about the penal code of China. My impression is that you don't believe so yourself. I can hardly expect you, of course, to take the wind out of your own sails. What I should vastly like you to do is, to tell me *viva voce,* in so many words, that your intentions are pure and your miracles genuine."

The Professor remained silent, still caressing his prophetic beard. At last, in a benevolent drawl, "Have you got any dear friend in the spirit land?" he asked.

"I don't know what you call the spirit land," I answered. "Several of my friends have died."

"Would you like to see 'em?" the Professor promptly demanded.

"No, I confess I shouldn't."

The Professor shook his head.

"You've not a rich nature," he rejoined blandly.

"It depends on what you call rich. I possess on some points a wealth of curiosity. It would gratify me peculiarly to have you say outright, standing there on your own platform, that you're an honest man."

It seemed to give him pleasure to trifle with my longing for this sensation. "I'll give you leave," he said, for all answer, "to tie my hands into the tightest knot you can in-

vent—and then I'll make your great-grandfather come in
and stop the clock. You know I couldn't stop a clock,
perched up on a mantel shelf five feet high, with my
heels."

"I don't know," said I. "I fancy you're very clever."

"Cleverness has nothing to do with it. I've great magnetism."

"You'd magnetize my great-grandfather down from
heaven?"

"Yes, sir, if I could establish communication. You'll see
to-night what I can do. I'll satisfy you. If I don't I shall
be happy to give you a private sitting. I'm also a healing
medium. You don't happen to have a toothache? I'd set
you down there and pull it right out, as I'd pull off your
boot."

In compliment to this possibility, I could only make
him my bow. His, at least, was a "rich nature." I bade
him farewell, with the assurance that, skeptic as I was,
I would applaud him impartially in the evening. I had
reached the top of the hall, on my way out, when I heard
him give a low, mellifluous whistle. I turned round, and
he beckoned to me to return. I walked back, and he leaned
forward from the platform, uplifting his stout forefinger.
"I simply desire to remark," he said, "that I'm an honest
man!"

On my return to the hotel I found that my impatience
for the Professor's further elucidation of his honesty made
the interval look long. Fortune, however, assisted me to
traverse it at an elastic pace. Rummaging idly on a book-
shelf in the tavern parlor, I found, amid a pile of farmers'
almanacs and Methodist tracts, a tattered volume of "Don
Quixote." I repaired to my room, tilted back my chair,
and communed deliciously with the ingenious hidalgo.
Here was "magnetism" superior even to that of Professor
Fargo. It proved so effective that I lost all note of time,
and, at last on looking at my watch, perceived that dinner
must have been over for an hour. Of "service" at this un-
sophisticated hostelry there was but a rigidly democratic
measure, and if I chose to cultivate a too elegant absence

of eagerness for beefsteak pie and huckleberry pudding, the young lady in long tight ringlets and short sleeves, who administered these delicacies in the dining-room, was altogether too haughty a spirit to urge them on my attention. So I sat alone and ate them cold. After dinner I returned for an hour to La Mancha, and then strolled forth, according to my morning's vow, to see the headstones in the cemetery cast longer shadows. I was disappointed in the epitaphs; they were posterior to the age of theological *naïveté*. The cemetery covered the two opposed sides of a hill, and on walking up to the ridge and looking over it, I discovered that I was not the only visitor. Two persons had chosen the spot for a quiet talk. One of them was a young girl, dressed in black, and seated on a headstone, with her face turned toward me. In spite of her attitude, however, she seemed not to perceive me, wrapt as she was in attention to her companion—a tall, stout fellow, standing before her, with his back to me. They were at too great a distance for me to hear their talk, and indeed in a few minutes I began to fancy they were not speaking. Nevertheless, the young girl's eyes remained fixed on the man's face; he was holding her spellbound by an influence best known to himself. She was very pretty. Her hat was off, and she was holding it in her lap; her lips were parted, and her eyes fixed intently on her companion's face. Suddenly she gave a bright, quick smile, made a rapid gesture in the air, and laid her forefinger on her lips. The movement, and the manner of it, told her story. She was deaf and dumb, and the man had been talking to her with his fingers. I would willingly have looked at her longer, but I turned away in delicacy, and walked in another direction. As I was leaving the cemetery, however, I saw her advancing with her companion to take the path which led to the gate. The man's face was now turned to me, and I straightway recognized it, in spite of the high peaked white hat which surmounted it. It was natural enough, I suppose, to find Professor Fargo in a graveyard; as the simplest expedient for ascertaining what goes on beyond the tomb might seem to be to get as close as possible to the hither cope of it.

Besides, if he was to treat the townsfolk to messages from their buried relatives, it was not amiss to "get up" a few names and dates by the perusal of the local epitaphs. As he passed me, however, and flourished his hand in the air by way of salutation, there was a fine absence in his glance of any admission that he had been caught cheating. This, too, was natural enough; what surprised me was that such a vulgar fellow should be mated with so charming a companion. She gave me as she passed the trustfully unshrinking glance of those poor mortals who are obliged to listen, as one may say, with their eyes. Her dress was scanty and simple, but there was delicacy in her mobile features. Who was she, and how had *he* got hold of her? After all, it was none of my business; but as they passed on, walking rather briskly, and I strolled after them, watching the Professor's ponderous tread and the gliding footfall of the young girl, I began to wonder whether he might not be right—might not, in truth, have that about him which would induce the most venerable of my ancestors to revert from eternity and stop the clock.

II

His handbills had done their office, and the Town Hall, when I entered it that evening, was filled with a solemnly expectant auditory. P—— was evidently for the evening a cluster of empty houses. While my companions scanned the stage for the shadow of coming events, I found ample pastime in perusing the social physiognomy of the town. A shadow presently appeared in the person of a stout young countryman, armed with an accordion, from which he extracted an ingenious variety of lamentable sounds. Soon after this mysterious prelude, the Professor marshalled out his forces. They consisted, first and foremost, of himself, his leonine *chevelure,* his black dress suit, and his turquoise ring, and then of an old gentleman who walked in gravely and stiffly, without the Professor's portentous salaam to the audience, bearing on his arm a young girl in black. The Professor managed somehow, by pushing about the chairs, turning up the lamps, and giving a twist to the patriotic drapery in the background, to make his audience feel his presence very intimately. His assistants rested themselves tranquilly against the wall. It took me but a short time to discover that the young girl was none other than the companion of the Professor's tour of inspection in the cemetery, and then I remembered that he had spoken in the morning of the gentleman who performed the mathematical miracles being assisted by his daughter. The young girl's infirmity, and her pretty face, promised to impart a picturesque interest to this portion of the exhibition; but meanwhile I inferred from certain ill-suppressed murmurs, and a good deal of vigorous pantomime among the female spectators, that she was found wanting in the more immediate picturesqueness demanded of a young lady attached to a show. Her plain black dress found no favor; the admission fee had justified the expectation of a good deal of trimming and several bracelets. She, however, poor girl, sat indifferent in her place, leaning her head back rather wearily against the wall, and looking as if, were she disposed, she might count without trouble all the queer bonnets among her judges. Her father sat upright beside her, with a cane between his knees and his two hands crossed on the knob. He was a man of sixty-five—tall, lean, pale, and serious. The lamp hanging above his head deepened the shadows on his face, and transformed it into a sort of pictorial mask. He was very bald, and his forehead, which was high and handsome, wore in the lamplight the gleam of old ivory. The sockets of his eyes were in deep shadow, and out of them his pupils gazed straight before him, with the glow of smouldering fire. His high-arched nose cast a long shadow over his mouth and chin, and two intensified wrinkles, beside his mustache, made him look strangely tragic. With his tragic look, moreover, he seemed strangely familiar. His daughter and the Professor I regarded as old friends; but where had I met this striking specimen of antique melancholy? Though his gaze seemed fixed, I imagined it was covertly wandering over the audience. At last it appeared to me that it met mine, and that its sombre glow emitted a spark of recognition of my extra-provincial and inferentially more discriminating character. The next moment I identified him—he was Don Quixote in the flesh; Don Quixote, with his sallow Spanish coloring, his high-browed, gentlemanly visage, his wrinkles, his mustache, and his sadness.

Professor Fargo's lecture was very bad. I had expected he would talk a good deal of nonsense, but I had imagined it would be cleverer nonsense. Very possibly there was a deeper cleverness in it than I perceived, and that, in his extreme shrewdness, he was giving his audience exactly what they preferred. It is an ascertained fact, I believe, that rural assemblies have a relish for the respectably ponderous, and an honest pride in the fact that they cannot be bored. The Professor, I suppose, felt the pulse of his listeners, and detected treasures of latent sympathy in their solemn, irresponsive silence. I should have said the performance was falling dead, but the Professor probably would have claimed that this was the rapture of attention and awe. He certainly kept very meagrely the promise of his grandiloquent program, and gave us a pound of precept to a grain of example. His miracles were exclusively miracles of rhetoric. He discoursed upon the earth life and the summer land, and related surprising anecdotes of his intimacy with the inhabitants of the latter region; but to my disappointment, the evening passed away without his really bringing us face to face with a ghost. A number of "prominent citizens" were induced to step upon the platform and be magnetized, but the sturdy agricultural temperament of P—— showed no great pliancy under the Professor's manual blandishments. The attempt was generally a failure—the only brilliant feature being the fine impudence with which the operator lodged the responsibility of the *fiasco* upon what he called his victim's low development. With three or four young girls the thing was a trifle better. One of them closed her eyes and shivered; another had a fearful access of nervous giggling; another burst into tears, and was restored to her companions with an admonitory wink. As every one knew every one else and every one else's family history, some sensation was probably produced by half a dozen happy guesses as to the Christian names and last maladies of certain defunct town worthies. Another deputation of the prominent citizens ascended the platform and wrote the names of departed friends on small bits of paper, which they threw into a hat. The Professor then folded his arms and clutched his beard, as if he were invoking inspiration. At last he approached the young girl, who sat in the background, took her hand, and led her forward. She picked the papers out of the hat and held them up one by one, for the Professor to look at. "There is no possible collusion," he said with a flourish, as he presented her to the audience. "The young lady is a deaf mute!" On a gesture of her companion she passed the paper to one of the contemplative gray heads who represented the scientific curiosity of P——, and he verified the Professor's guess. The Professor risked an "Abijah" or a "Melinda," and it turned out generally to be an Ezekiel or a Hepzibah. Three several times, however, the performer's genius triumphed; whereupon, the audience not being up to the mark, he gave himself a vigorous round of applause. He concluded with the admission that the spirits were shy before such a crowd, but that he would do much better for the ladies and gentlemen individually, if they would call on him at the hotel.

It was all terribly vulgar rubbish, and I was glad when it was over. While it lasted, the old gentleman behind continued to sit motionless, seeming neither to see, to hear, nor to understand. I wondered what he thought of it, and just what it cost his self-respect to give it the sanction of his presence. It seemed, indeed, as if mentally he were not present; as if by an intense effort he had succeeded in making consciousness a blank, and was awaiting his own turn in a kind of trance. Once only he moved—when the Professor came and took his daughter by the hand. He gave an imperceptible start, controlled himself, then, dropping his hand a little, closed his eyes and kept them closed until she returned to his side. There was an intermission, during which the Professor walked about the platform, shaking his mane and wiping his forehead, and surveying the audience with an air of lofty benevolence, as if, having sown the seed, he was expecting to see it germinate on the spot. At last he rapped on the table and introduced the old gentleman—Colonel Gifford, the Great Mathematical Magician and Lightning Calculator; after which he retreated in turn to the background—if a gentleman with tossing mane and flowing beard, that turquoise ring, and generally expansive and importunate presence, could be said to be, under any circumstances, in the background. The old gentleman came forward and made his bow, and the young girl placed herself beside him, simply, unaffectedly, with her hands hanging and crossed in front of her—with all the childish grace and serenity of Mignon in "Wilhelm Meister," as we see her grouped with the old harper. Colonel Gifford's performance gave me an exquisite pleasure, which I am bound to confess was quite independent of its intrinsic merits. These, I am afraid, were at once too numerous and too scanty to have made it a popular success. It was a very ingenious piece of scientific contrivance, but it was meagrely adapted to tickle the ears of the groundlings. If one had read it—the substance of it—in a handsomely printed pamphlet, under the lamp, of a wet evening when no one was likely to call, one would have been charmed at once with the quaint vivacity of the author's mode of statement, and with the unexpected agility of one's own intellect. But in spite of an obvious effort to commend himself to understandings more familiar with the rule of thumb than with the differential calculus, Colonel Gifford remained benignantly but formidably unintelligible. He had devised—so far as I understood it—an extension of the multiplication table to enormous factors, by which he expected to effect a revolution in the whole science of accounts. There was the theory, which rather lost itself, thanks to his discursive fervor in the mists of the higher mathematics, and there was the practice, which, thanks to his daughter's coöperation, was much more gracefully concrete. The interesting thing to me was the speaker's personality, not his system. Although evidently a very positive old man, he had a singularly simple,

unpretentious tone. His intensity of faith in the supreme
importance of his doctrine gave his manner a sort of rever-
ential hush. The echoes of Professor Fargo's windy ver-
biage increased the charms of his mild sincerity. He spoke
in a feeble, tremulous voice, which every now and then
quavered upward with excitement, and then subsided into
a weary, plaintive cadence. He was an old gentleman of a
single idea, but his one idea was a religion. It was impossible not to feel a kindness for him, and imagine that he
excited among his auditors something of the vague good
will—half pity and half reverence—that uncorrupted souls
entertained for those neat, keen-eyed, elderly people who
are rumored to have strange ways and say strange things—
to be "cracked," in short, like a fine bit of porcelain which
will hold together only so long as you don't push it about.
But it was upon the young girl, when once she had given
them a taste of her capacity, that they bestowed their frankest admiration. Now that she stood forward in the bright
light, I could observe the character of her prettiness. It
was no brilliant beauty, but a sort of meagre, attenuated,
angular grace, the delicacy and fragility of the characteristic
American type. Her chest was flat, her neck extremely thin,
her visage narrow, and her forehead high and prominent.
But her fair hair encircled her head in such fleecy tresses,
her cheeks had such a pale pink flush, her eyes such an appealing innocence, her attitude such a quaint unconscious
felicity, that one watched her with a kind of upstart belief
that to such a stainless little spirit the working of miracles
might be really possible. A couple of blackboards were
hung against the wall, on one of which the old man rapidly
chalked a problem—choosing one, of course, on the level of
the brighter minds in the audience. The young girl glanced
at it, and before we could count ten dashed off a great bold
answer on the other tablet. The brighter minds were then
invited to verify, and the young lady was invariably found
to have hit the mark. She was in fact a little arithmetical
fairy, and her father made her perform a series of gymnas-
tics among numbers as brilliant in their way as the vocal
flourishes and roulades of an accomplished singer. Com-

municating with her altogether by the blackboard, he drew
from her a host of examples of the beauty of his system of
transcendent multiplication. A person present was requested to furnish two enormous numbers, one to multiply
the other. The old man wrote them out. After standing
an instant meditative and just touching her forehead with
her forefinger, she chalked down the prodigious result. Her
father then performed rapidly, on the blackboard, the
operation according to his own system (which she had em-
ployed mentally), and finally satisfied every one by repeating it in the round-about fashion actually in use. This was
all Colonel Gifford's witchcraft. It sounds very ponderous,
but it was really very charming, and I had an agreeable sense
of titillation in the finer parts of my intellectual mechanism.
I felt more like a thinking creature. I had never supposed
I was coming to P—— to take a lesson in culture.

It seemed on the morrow as if, at any rate, I was to take
a lesson in patience. It was a Sunday, and I awoke to hear
the rain pattering against my window panes. A rainy Sunday at P—— was a prospect to depress the most elastic
mind. But as I stepped into my slippers, I bethought myself of my unfinished volume of "Don Quixote," and promised myself to borrow from Sancho Panza a philosophic
proverb or so applicable to my situation. "Don Quixote"
consoled me, as it turned out, in an unexpected fashion. On
descending to the dining-room of the inn, while I mentally
balanced the contending claims of muddy coffee and sour
green tea, I found that my last evening's friends were also
enjoying the hospitality of the establishment. It was the
only inn in the place, and it would already have occurred
to a more investigating mind that we were fellow-lodgers.
The Professor, happily, was absent; and it seemed only
reasonable that a ghost-seer should lie in bed late of a
morning. The melancholy old mathematician was seated at
the breakast table cutting his dry toast into geometrical
figures. He gave me a formal bow as I entered, and proceeded to dip his sodden polygons into his tea. The young
girl was at the window, leaning her forehead against the
pane, and looking out into the sea of yellow mud in the

village street. I had not been in the room a couple of minutes when, seeming in spite of her deafness to feel that I
was near, she turned straight round and looked at me. She
wore no trace of fatigue from her public labors, but was the
same clear-eyed, noiseless little sprite as before. I observed
that, by daylight, her black dress was very shabby, and her
father's frock coat, buttoned with military precision up to
his chin, had long since exchanged its original lustre for the
melancholy brilliancy imparted by desperate brushing. I
was afraid that Professor Fargo was either a niggardly *impresario*, or that the great "moral and scientific combination" was not always as remunerative as it seemed to have
been at P——. While I was making these reflections the
Professor entered, with an exhilaration of manner which I
conceived to be a tribute to unwonted success.

"Well, sir," he cried, as his eyes fell upon me, "what do
you say to it now? I hope we did things handsomely, eh?
I hope you call that a solid entertainment. This young
man, you must know, is one of the scoffers," he went on,
turning to the Colonel. "He came yesterday and bearded
the lion in his den. He snaps his fingers at spirits, suspects
me of foul play, and would like me to admit, in my private
character, that you and I are a couple of sharpers. I hope
we satisfied you!"

The Colonel went on dipping his toast into his tea, looking grave and saying nothing. "Poor man!" I said to myself; "he despises his colleague—and so do I. I beg your
pardon," I cried with warmth; "I would like nothing of
the kind. I was extremely interested in this gentleman's
exhibition;" and I made the Colonel a bow. "It seemed to
me remarkable for its perfect good faith and truthfulness."

"Many thanks for the compliment," said the Professor.
"As much as to say the Colonel's an apostle, and I'm a
rascal. Have it as you please; if so, I'm a hardened one!"
he declared with a great slap on his pocket; "and anyhow,
you know, it's all one concern," and the Professor betook
himself to the window where Miss Gifford was standing.
She had not looked round at him on his entrance, as she had
done at me. The Colonel, in response to my compliment,

looked across at me with mild benignity, and I assured him afresh of my admiration. He listened silently, stirring his tea; his face betrayed an odd mixture of confidence and deprecation; as if he thought it just possible that I might be laughing at him, but that if I was not, it was extremely delightful. I continued to insist on its being distinctly *his* half of the performance that had pleased me; so that, gradually convinced of my respectful sympathy, he seemed tacitly to intimate that, if we were only alone and he knew me a little better, it would do him a world of good to talk it all over. I determined to give him a chance at the earliest moment. The Professor, meanwhile, waiting for his breakfast, remained at the window experimenting in the deaf and dumb alphabet with the young girl. It took him, as an amateur, a long time to form his sentences, but he went on bravely, brandishing his large, plump knuckles before her face. She seemed very patient of his slowness, and stood watching his gestures with the same intense earnestness I had caught a glimpse of in the cemetery. Most of my female friends enjoy an unimpeded use of their tongues, and I was unable from experience to appreciate his situation; but I could easily fancy what a delightful sense of intimacy there must be in this noiseless exchange of long looks with a pretty creature toward whom all *tendresse* of attitude might be conveniently attributed to compassion. Before long the Colonel pushed away his cup, turned about, folded his arms, and fixed his eyes with a frown on the Professor. It seemed to me that I read in his glance a complete revelation of moral torture. The stress of fortune had made them associates, but the Colonel jealously guarded the limits of their private intimacy. The Professor, with all his audacity, suffered himself to be reminded of them. He suddenly pulled out his watch and clamored for his coffee, and was soon seated at a repast which indicated that the prophetic temperament requires a generous diet. The young girl roamed about the room, looking idly at this and that, as if she were used to doing nothing. When she met my eye, she smiled brightly, after a moment's gravity, as if she were also used to saying to people, mentally, "Yes, I know

I'm a strange little creature, but you must not be afraid of me." The Professor had hardly got that array of innumerable little dishes, of the form and dimension of soap-trays, with which one is served in the rural hostelries of New England, well under contribution, before a young lady was introduced who had come to request him to raise a ghost—a resolute young lady, with several ringlets and a huge ancestral umbrella, whose matutinal appetite for the supernatural had not been quenched by the raw autumnal storm. She produced very frankly a "tin-type" of a florid young man, actually deceased, and demanded to be confronted with his ghost. The day was beginning well for the Professor. He gallantly requested her to be seated, and promised her every satisfaction. While he was hastily despatching his breakfast, the Colonel's daughter made acquaintance with her bereaved sister. She drew the young man's portrait gently out of her hand, examined it, and then shook her head with a little grimace of displeasure. The young woman laughed good-naturedly, and screamed into her ear that she didn't believe she was a bit deaf and dumb. At the announcement the Colonel, who, after eyeing her while she stated her credulous errand with solemn compassion, had turned away to the window, as if to spare himself the spectacle of his colleague's unblushing pretensions, turned back again and eyed her coldly from head to foot. "I recommend you, madam," he said sternly, "to reserve your suspicions for an occasion in which they may be more pertinent."

Later in the morning I found him still in the dining-room with his daughter. Professor Fargo, he said, was in the parlor, raising ghosts by the dozen; and after a little pause he gave an angry laugh, as if his suppressed irritation were causing him more than usual discomfort. He was walking up and down, with slow, restless steps, and smoking a frugal pipe. I took the liberty of offering him a good cigar, and while he puffed it gratefully, the need to justify himself for his odd partnership slowly gathered force. "It would be a satisfaction for me to tell you, sir," he said at last, looking at me with eyes that fairly glittered with the pleasure of hearing himself speak the words, "that my connection with Professor Fargo implies no—no——" and he paused for a moment—"no intellectual approval of his extraordinary pretensions. This, of course, is between ourselves. You're a stranger to me, and it's doubtless the height of indiscretion in me to take you into my confidence. My subsistence depends on my not quarrelling with my companion. If you were to repeat to him that I went about undermining the faith, the extremely retributive faith, as you see" (and he nodded toward the parlor door), "of his audiences, he would of course dissolve our partnership and I should be adrift again, trying to get my heavy boat in tow. I should perhaps feel like an honest man again, but meanwhile, probably, I should starve. Misfortune," he added bitterly, "makes strange bedfellows; and I have been unfortunate!"

There was so much melancholy meaning in this declaration that I asked him frankly who and what he was. He puffed his cigar vigorously for some moments without replying, and at last turned his fine old furrowed visage upon me through a cloud of smoke. "I'm a fanatic. I feed on illusions and cherish ambitions which will never butter my bread. Don't be afraid; I won't buttonhole *you;* but I have a head full of schemes which I believe the world would be the happier for giving a little quiet attention to. I'm an inventor; and like all inventors whose devices are of value, I believe that my particular contrivance would be the salvation of a misguided world. I have looked a good deal into many things, but my latest hobby is the system of computation of which I tried to give a sketch last night. I'm afraid you didn't understand a word of it, but I assure you it's a very beautiful thing. If it could only get a fair hearing and be thoroughly propagated and adopted, it would save our toiling human race a prodigious deal of ungrateful labor. In America alone, I have calculated, it would save the business community about 23,000 hours in the course of ten years. If time is money, they are worth saving. But there I go! You oughtn't ask me to talk about myself. Myself is my ideas!"

A little judicious questioning, however, drew from him

a number of facts of a more immediately personal kind. His colonelship, he intimated, was held by the inglorious tenure of militia service, and was only put forward to help him to make a figure on Professor Fargo's platform. It was part of the general humbuggery of the attempt to *bribe* people to listen to wholesome truths—truths the neglect of which was its own chastisement. "I have always had a passion for scientific research, and I have squandered my substance in experiments which the world called fruitless. They were curious, they were beautiful, they were divine! But they wouldn't turn any one's mill or grind any one's corn, and I was treated like a mediæval alchemist, astray in the modern world. Chemistry, physics, mathematics, philology, medicine—I've dug deep in them all. Each, in turn, has been a passion to which I've given my days and my nights. But apparently I haven't the art of finding favor for my ideas—of sweetening the draught so that people will drink it. So here I am, after all my vigils and ventures, an obscure old man, ruined in fortune, broken down in health and sadly diminished in hope, trying hard to keep afloat by rowing in the same boat as a gentleman who turns tables and raises ghosts. I'm a proud man, sir, and a devotee of the exact sciences. You may imagine what I suffer. I little fancied ten years ago that I was ever going to make capital, on a mountebank's booth, of the pathetic infirmity of my daughter."

The young girl, while her father talked, sat gazing at him in wistful surprise. I inferred from it that this expansive mood was rare; she wondered what long story he was telling. As he mentioned her, I gave her a sudden glance. Perceiving it, she blushed slightly and turned away. The movement seemed at variance with what I had supposed to be her characteristic indifference to observation. "I have a good reason," he said, "for treating her with more than the tenderness which such an infirmity usually commands. At the time of my marriage, and for some time after, I was performing a series of curious chemical researches. My wife was a wonderfully pretty little creature. She used to come tripping and rustling about my laboratory, asking questions

of the most comical ignorance, peeping and rummaging
everywhere, raising the lids of jars, and making faces at the
bad smells. One day while she was in the room I stepped
out on the balcony to examine something which I had placed
to dry in the sun. Suddenly I heard a terrific explosion;
it smashed the window-glass into atoms. Rushing in, I
found my wife in a swoon on the floor. A compound which
I had placed to heat on a furnace had been left too long; I
had underestimated its activity. My wife was not visibly
injured, but when she came to her senses again, she found
she had lost her hearing. It never returned. Shortly afterwards my daughter was born—born the poor deaf creature
you see. I lost my wife and I gave up chemistry. As I
advanced in life, I became convinced that my ruling passion
was mathematics. I've gone into them very deeply; I considered them the noblest acquisition of the human mind,
and I don't hesitate to say that I have profound and original views on the subject. If you have a head for such
things, I could open great vistas to you. But I'm afraid
you haven't! Ay, it's a desperately weak-witted generation.
The world has a horror of concentrated thought; it wants
the pill to be sugared; it wants everything to be made easy;
it prefers the brazen foolery that you and I sat through last
night to the divine harmonies of the infinite science of numbers. That's why I'm a beggar, droning out my dreary
petition and pushing forth my little girl to catch the cop-
pers. That's why I've had to strike a partnership with a
vulgar charlatan. I was a long time coming to it, but I'm
well in for it now. I won't tell you how, from rebuff to
rebuff, from failure to failure, through hope deferred and
justice denied, I have finally come to this. It would overtax
both your sympathy and your credulity. You wouldn't
believe the stories I could relate of the impenetrable stupid-
ity of mankind, of the leaden empire of Routine. I squandered my property, I confess it, but not in the vulgar way.
It was a carnival of high research, a long debauch of experiment. When I had melted down my last cent in the consuming crucible, I thought the world might be willing to
pay me something for my results. The world had better

uses for its money than the purchase of sovereign truth! I
became a solicitor; I went from door to door, offering people a choice of twenty superb formulated schemes, the
paltriest of which contained the germs of a peaceful revolution. The poor unpatented visions are at this hour all in
a bundle upstairs in my trunk. In the midst of my troubles
I had the ineffable pleasure of finding that my little girl
was a genius. I don't know why it should have been a
pleasure; her poor father's genius stood there before me as
a warning. But it was a delight to find that her little imprisoned, soundless mind was not a blank. She had in-
herited my passion for numbers. My folly had taken a
precious faculty from her; it was but just I should give her
another. She was in good hands for becoming perfect. Her
gift is a rare one among women, but she is not of the common feminine stuff. She's very simple—strangely simple in
some ways. She has never been talked to by women about
petticoats, nor by men about love. She doesn't reason; her
skill at figures is a kind of intuition. One day it came
into my head that I might lecture for a livelihood. I had
listened to windy orators, in crowded halls, who had less to
say than I. So I lectured, sometimes to twenty people,
sometimes to five, once to no one at all. One morning, some
six months ago, I was waited upon by my friend there. He
told me frankly that he had a show which didn't draw as
powerfully as it deserved, and proposed that, as I also
seemed unable to catch the public ear, we should combine
our forces and carry popularity by storm. His entertainment, alone, was rather thin; mine also seemed to lack the
desirable consistency; but a mixture of the two might pro-
duce an effective compound. I had but five dollars in my
pocket. I disliked the man, and I believe in spiritualism
about as much as I believe that the sun goes round the
earth. But we must live, and I made a bargain. It was
a very poor bargain, but it keeps us alive. I took a few
hints from the Professor, and brightened up my lucky for-
mulas a little. Still, we have terribly thin houses. I
couldn't play the mountebank; it's a faculty I lack. At
last the Professor bethought himself that I possessed the

golden goose. From the mountebank's point of view a pretty little deaf and dumb daughter, who could work miracles on the blackboard, was a treasure to a practical mind. The idea of dragging my poor child and her pathetic idiosyncrasies before the world was extremely repulsive to me; but the Professor laid the case before the little maid herself, and at the end of a fortnight she informed him that she was ready to make her curtsey on the platform as a 'lightning calculator.' I consented to let her try, and you see that she succeeded. She draws, not powerfully, but sufficiently, and we manage to keep afloat."

Half an hour later the Professor returned from his morning's labors—flushed, dishevelled, rubbing his hands, evidently in high good humor. The Colonel immediately became silent and grave, asked no questions, and, when dinner was served shortly afterwards, refused everything and sat with a melancholy frown and his eyes fixed on his plate. His comrade was plainly a terrible thorn in his side. I was curious, on the other hand, to know how the Colonel affected the Professor, and I soon discovered that the latter was by no means his exuberant impudent self within the radius of his colleague's pregnant silence. If there was little love lost between them, the ranting charlatan was at least held in check by an indefinable respect for his companion's probity. He was a fool, doubtless, with his careful statements and his incapacity to take a humorous view of human credulity; but, somehow, he was a venerable fool, and the Professor, as a social personage, without the inspiration of a lecture-room more or less irritatingly interspaced, and with that pale, grave old mathematician sitting by like a marble monument to Veracity, lacked the courage to ventilate his peculiar pretensions. On this occasion, however, he swallowed the Colonel's tacit protest with a wry face. I don't know what he had brought to pass in the darkened parlor; whatever it was, it had agreeably stimulated his confidence in his resources. We had been joined, moreover, at dinner by half a dozen travelers of less oppressively skeptical mould than the Colonel, and under these circumstances it

was peculiarly trying to have to veil one's brighter genius.
There was undischarged thunder in the air.

The rain ceased in the afternoon, and the sun leaped
out and set the thousand puddles of the village street a-flash-
ing. I found the Colonel sitting under the tavern porch
with a village urchin between his knees, to whom he seemed
to be imparting the rudiments of mathematical science.
The little boy had a bulging forehead, a prodigious number
of freckles, and the general aspect of a juvenile Newton.
Being present at the Colonel's lecture, he had been fired
with a laudable curiosity to know more, and learning that
Professor Fargo imparted information *à domicile,* had ventured to believe that his colleague did likewise. The child's
father, a great, gaunt, brown-faced farmer, with a yellow
tuft on his chin, stood by, blushing at the audacity of his
son and heir, but grinning delightedly at his brightness.
The poor Colonel, whose meed of recognition had as yet been
so meagre, was vastly tickled by this expression of infantine
sympathy, and discoursed to the little prodigy with the most
condescending benevolence. Certainly, as the boy grows up,
the most vivid of his childish memories will be that of the
old man with glowing eyes and a softened voice coming from
under his white mustache—the voice which held him stock-
still for a whole half hour, and assured him afterwards that
he was a little Trojan. When the lesson was over, I proposed a walk to the Colonel, and we wandered away out of
the village. The afternoon, as it waned, became glorious;
the heavy clouds, broken and dispersed, sailed through the
glowing sky like high-prowed galleys, draped in purple and
silver. I, on my side, shall never forget the Colonel's excited talk, nor how at last, as we sat on a rocky ridge looking off to the sunset, he fairly unburdened his conscience.

"Yes, sir!" he said; "it's a base concession to the ignoble
need of keeping body and soul together. Sometimes I feel
as if I couldn't stand it another hour—as if it were better
to break with the impudent rascal and sink or swim as fate
decrees, than get a hearing for the truth at such a cost. It's
all very well holding my tongue and insisting that I, at least,
make no claims for the man's vile frauds; my connection

with him is itself a sanction, and my presence at his damnable mummeries an outrage to the purity of truth. You see I have the misfortune to believe in something, to *know* something, and to think it makes a difference whether people feed, intellectually, on poisoned garbage or on the ripe, sweet fruit of true science! I shut my eyes every night, and lock my jaws, and clench my teeth, but I can't help hearing the man's windy rubbish. It's a tissue of scandalous lies, from beginning to end. I know them all by heart by this time, and I verily believe I could stand up and rattle them off myself. They ring in my ears all day, and I have horrible dreams at night of crouching under a table with a long cloth, and tapping on the top of it. The Professor stands outside swearing to the audience that it's the ghost of Archimedes. Then I begin to suffocate, and overturn the table, and appear before a thousand people as the accomplice of the impostor. There are times when the value of my own unheeded message to mankind seems so vast, so immeasurable, that I am ready to believe that any means are lawful which may enable me to utter it; that if one's ship is to set sail for the golden islands, even a flaunting buccaneer may tow it into the open sea. In such moods, when I sit there against the wall, in the shade, closing my eyes and trying not to hear—I really *don't* hear! My mind is a myriad miles away—floating, soaring on the wings of invention. But all of a sudden the odiousness of my position comes over me, and I can't believe my senses that it's verily I who sit there—I to whom a grain of scientific truth is more precious than a mountain of gold!"

He was silent a long time, and I myself hardly knew what consolation to offer him. The most friendly part was simply to let him expend his bitterness to the last drop. "But that's not the worst," he resumed after a while. "The worst is that I hate the greasy rascal to come near my daughter, and that, living and travelling together as we do, he's never far off. At first he used to engage a small child beforehand to hold up his little folded papers for him; but a few weeks ago it came into his head that it would give the affair an even greater air of innocence, if he could make use of my

poor girl. It does, I believe, and it tells, and I've been
brought so low that I sit by night after night and endure
it. She, on her side, dreams of no harm, and takes the Professor for an oracle and his lecture for a masterpiece. I
have never undeceived her, for I have no desire to teach
her that there are such things as falsity and impurity. Except that our perpetual railway journeys give her bad head-
aches, she supposes that we lead a life of pure felicity. But
some fine day our enterprising friend will be wanting to put
her into a pink dress and a garland of artificial flowers, and
then, with God's help, we shall part company!"

My silence, in reply to this last burst of confidence, im-
plied the most deferential assent; but I was privately wondering whether "the little maid" was so perfectly ignorant of
evil as the old man supposed. I remembered the episode at
the cemetery the day before, and doubted greatly whether
her father had countenanced it. With his sentiments touching the Professor, this was most unlikely. The young girl,
then, had a secret, and it gave me real discomfort to think
this coarse fellow should keep the key of it. I feared that
the poor Colonel was yoked to his colleague more cruelly
than he knew. On my return to the inn this impression was
vividly confirmed. Dusk had fallen when we entered the
public room, and in the gray light which pervaded it two
figures at one of the windows escaped immediate recognition.
But in a moment one of them advanced, and in the sonorous
accents of Professor Fargo hoped that we had enjoyed
our expedition. The Colonel started and stared, and left me
to answer. He sat down heavily on the sofa; in a moment
his daughter came over and sat beside him, placing her
hand gently on his knee. But he let it lie, and remained
motionless, resting his hot head on his cane. The Professor withdrew promptly, but with a swagger which suggested to my sense that he could now afford to treat his
vanity to a dose of revenge for the old man's contempt.

Later in the evening I came down stairs again, and as I
passed along the hall heard Professor Fargo perorating
vigorously in the bar-room. Evidently he had an audience,
and the scene was probably curious. Drawing near, I found

this gifted man erect on the floor, addressing an assemblage of the convivial spirits of P——. In an extended hand he brandished a glass of smoking whiskey and water; with the other he caressed his rounded periods. He had evidently been drinking freely, and I perceived that even the prophetic vision was liable to obfuscation. It had been a brilliant day for him; fortune smiled, and he felt strong. A dozen rustic loafers, of various degrees of inveteracy, were listening to him with a speechless solemnity, which may have been partly faith, but was certainly partly rum. In a corner, out of the way, sat the Colonel, with an unfinished glass before him. The Professor waved his hand as I appeared, with magnificent hospitality, and resumed his discourse.

"Let me say, gentlemen," he cried, "that it's not my peculiar influence with the departed that I chiefly value; for, after all, you know, a ghost is but a ghost. It can't do much any way. You can't touch it, half the time you can't see it. If it happens to be the spirit of a pretty girl, you know, this makes you kind of mad. The great thing now is to be able to exercise a mysterious influence over living organisms. You can do it with your eye, you can do it with your voice, you can do it with certain motions of your hand—as thus, you perceive; you can do it with nothing at all by just setting your mind on it. That is, of course, some people can do it; not very many—certain rich, powerful sympathetic natures that you now and then come across. It's called magnetism. Various works have been written on the subject, and various explanations offered, but they don't amount to much. All you can say is that it's just magnetism, and that you've either got it or you haven't got it. Now the Lord has seen fit to bestow it on me. It's a great responsibility, but I try to make a noble use of it. I can do all sorts of things. I can find out things. I can make people confess. I can make 'em sick and I can make 'em well. I can make 'em in love—what do you say to that? I can take 'em out of love again, and make 'em swear they wouldn't marry the loved object, not if they were paid for it. How it is I do it I confess I can't tell you. I just say to myself, 'Come now, Professor, we'll fix this one or that one.' It's a free gift. It's magnetism, in short. Some folks call it animal magnetism, but I call it spiritual magnetism."

There was a profound silence; the air seemed charged with that whimsical retention of speech which is such a common form of American sociability. I looked askance at the Colonel; it seemed to me that he was paler than usual, and that his eyes were really fierce. Professor Fargo turned about to the bar to replenish his glass, and the old man slowly rose and came out into the middle of the room. He looked round at the company; he evidently meant to say something. He stood silent for some moments, and I saw that he was in a tremor of excitement. "You've listened to what this gentleman has been saying?" he began. "I won't say, Have you understood it? It's not to be understood. Some of you, perhaps, saw me last night sitting on the platform while Professor Fargo said his say. You know that we are partners—that for convenience's sake we work together. I wish to say that you are not therefore to believe that I assent to the doctrines he has just promulgated. 'Doctrines' is a flattering name for them. I speak in the name of science. Science recognizes no such thing as 'spiritual magnetism'; no such thing as mysterious fascinations; no such thing as spirit-rappings and ghost-raising. I owe it to my conscience to say so. I can't remain there and see you all sit mum when this gentleman concludes such a monstrous piece of talk. I have it on my conscience to assure you that no intelligent man, woman, or child need fear to be made to do anything against his own will by the supernatural operation of the will of Professor Fargo."

If there had been silence on the conclusion of Professor Fargo's harangue, what shall I say of the audible absence of commentary which followed the Colonel's remarks? There was an intense curiosity—I felt it myself—to see what a clever fellow like the Professor would do. The Colonel stood there wiping his forehead, as if, having thrown down the gauntlet, he were prepared to defend it. The Professor looked at him with his head on one side, and a smile which was an excellent imitation of genial tolerance. "My dear sir," he cried, "I'm glad you've eased your mind. I knew you wanted to; I hope you feel better. With your leave, we won't go into the philosophy of the dispute. It was George Washington, I believe, who said that people should wash their dirty linen at home. You don't endorse my views—you're welcome. If you weren't a very polite old gentleman, I know you'd like to say that, in a single word, they're the views of a quack. Now, in a single word, I deny it. You deny the existence of the magnetic power; I reply that I personally possess it, and that if you'll give me a little more time, I'll force you to say that there's something in it. I'll force you to say I can do something. These gentlemen here can't witness the consummation, but at least they can hear my promise. I promise you evidence. You go by facts: I'll give you facts. I'd like just to have you remark before our friends here, that you'll take account of them!"

The Colonel stood still, wiping his forehead. He had even less prevision than I of the character of the Professor's projected facts, but of course he could make but one answer. He bowed gravely to the Professor and to the company. "I shall never refuse," he said, "to examine serious evidence. Whatever," he added, after a moment, "it might cost my prejudices."

III

The Colonel's incorruptible conservatism had done me good mentally, and his personal situation had deeply interested me. As I bade him farewell the next day—the "Combination" had been heralded in a neighboring town—I wished him heartily that what was so painfully crooked in the latter might be straightened out in time. He shook his head sadly, and answered that his time was up.

He was often in my thoughts for the next six weeks, but I got no tidings of him. Meanwhile I too was leading an ambulant life, and travelling from town to town in a cause which demanded a good deal of ready-made eloquence. I didn't exactly pretend that the regeneration of society depended on its acceptance of my wares, but I devoted a good deal of fellow feeling to the Colonel's experience as an uncredited solicitor. At the beginning of the winter I found myself in New York. One evening, as I wandered along a certain avenue, undedicated to gentility, I perceived, in the flare of a gas-lamp, on a placard beside a doorway, the name and attributes of Professor Fargo. I immediately stopped and read the manifesto. It was even more grandiloquent than the yellow hand-bill at P——; for to overtop concurrence in the metropolis one must mount upon very high stilts indeed. The "Combination" still subsisted, and Colonel Gifford brought up the rear. I observed with interest that his daughter now figured in an independent and extremely ornamental paragraph. Above the door was a blue lamp, and beneath the lamp the inscription "Excelsior Hall." No one was going in, but as I stood there a young man in a white overcoat, with his hat on his nose, came out and planted himself viciously, with a tell-tale yawn, in the doorway. The poor Colonel had lost an auditor; I was determined he should have a substitute. Paying my fee and making my way into the room, I found that the situation was indeed one in which units rated high. There were not more than twenty people present, and the appearance of this meagre group was not in striking harmony with the statement of the placard without, that Professor Fargo's entertainment was thronged with the intellect and fashion of the metropolis. The professor was on the platform, unfolding his budget of miracles; behind him, as at P——, sat the Colonel and his daughter. The Professor was evidently depressed by the preponderance of empty benches, and carried off his revelations with an indifferent grace. Disappointment made him brutal. He was heavy, vulgar, slipshod; he stumbled in his periods, and bungled more than once in his guesses when the folded papers with the names were put into the hat. His brow wore a vicious, sullen look, which seemed to deepen the expression of melancholy patience in his companions. I trembled for my friends. The Colonel had told me that his bargain with his impresario was a poor one, and I was sure that if, when the "Combination" was in a run of luck, as it had been at P——, his dividend was scanty, he was paying a heavy share of the penalty for the present eclipse of fortune. I sat down near the door, where the hall was shrouded in a thrifty dimness, so that I had no fear of being recognized. The Professor evidently was reckless—a fact which rather puzzled me in so shrewd a man. When he had brought his own performance to an unapplauded close, instead of making his customary speech on behalf of his coadjutor, he dropped into a chair and gaped in the face of his audience. But the Colonel, after a pause, threw himself into the breach—or rather lowered himself into it with stately gravity—and addressed his humble listeners (half of whom were asleep) as if they had been the flower of the Intellect and Fashion. But if his manner was the old one, his discourse was new. He had too many ideas to repeat himself, and, although those which he now attempted to expound were still above the level of my frivolous apprehension, this unbargained abundance of inspiration half convinced me that his claim to original genius was just. If there had been something grotesquely sad in his appeal to the irresponsive intellect of P——, it was almost intolerably dismal to sit there and see him grappling with the dusky void of Excelsior Hall. The sleepers waked up, or turned over, at least, when Miss Gifford came forward. She wore, as yet, neither a pink dress nor an artificial garland, but it seemed to me that I detected here and there an embryonic hint of these ornaments—a ruffle round her neck, a colored sash over her black dress, a curl or two more in her hair. But her manner was as childish, as simple and serene as ever; the empty benches had no weary meaning for her.

I confess that in spite of my personal interest in my friend, the entertainment seemed wofully long; more than once I was on the point of departing, and awaiting the conclusion in the street. But I had not the heart to inflict upon the poor Colonel the sight of a retreating spectator. When at last my twenty companions had shuffled away, I made my way to the platform and renewed acquaintance with the trio. The Professor nodded with uncompromising familiarity, the Colonel seemed cordially glad to see me, and his daughter, as I made her my bow, gazed at me with even more than usual of her clear-eyed frankness. She seemed to wonder what my reappearance meant for them. It meant, to begin with, that I went the next day to see the Colonel at his lodging. It was a terribly modest little lodging, but he did me the honors with a grace which showed that he had an old habit of hospitality. He admitted frankly that the "Combination" had lately been doing a very poor business, but he made the admission with a gloomy stoicism which showed me that he had been looking the event full in the face, and had assented to it helplessly. They had gone their round in the country, with varying success. They had the misfortune to have a circus keeping just in advance of them, and beside the gorgeous pictorial placards of this establishment, their own superior promises, even when swimming in a deluge of exclamation points, seemed pitifully vague. "What are my daughter and I," said the Colonel, "after the educated elephant and the female trapezist? What even is the Professor, after the great American clown?" Their profits, however, had been kept fairly above the minimum, and victory would still have hovered about their banners if they had been content to invoke her in the smaller towns. The Professor, however, in spite of remonstrance, had suddenly steered for New York, and what New York was doing for them I had seen the night before. The last half dozen performances had not paid for the room and the gas. The Colonel told me that he was bound by contract for five more lectures, but that when these were delivered he would dissolve the partnership. The Professor, in insisting on coming to the city, had shown a signal want of shrewdness; and when his shrewdness failed him, what had you left? What to attempt himself, the Colonel couldn't imagine. "At the worst," he said, "my daughter can go into an asylum, and I can go into the poor-house." On my asking him whether his colleague had yet established, according to his vow, the verities of "spiritual magnetism," he stared in surprise and seemed quite to have forgotten the Professor's engagement to convert him. "Oh, I've let him off," he said, shaking his head. "He was tipsy when he made the promise, and I expect to hear no more about it."

I was very busy, and the pensive old man was gloomy company; but his characters and his fortunes had such a melancholy interest that I found time to pay him several visits. He evidently was thankful to be diverted from his sombre self-consciousness and his paternal anxiety, and, when once he was aroused from the dogged resignation in which he seemed plunged, enjoyed vastly the chance to expiate on his multitudinous and irrealizable theories. Most of the time his meaning was a cloud bank to me, but I listened, assented, applauded; I felt the charm of pure intellectual passion. I incline to believe that he had excogitated some extremely valuable ideas. We took long walks through the crowded streets. The Colonel was indefatigable, in spite of his leanness and pallor. He strode along with great steps, talking so loud, half the time, in his high, quavering voice, that even the eager pedestrians in the lower latitudes of Broadway slackened pace to glance back at him. He declared that the crowded streets gave him a strange exhilaration, and the mighty human hum of the great city quickened his heart-beats almost to pain. More than once he stopped short, on the edge of a curbstone or in the middle of a crossing, and laying his hand on my arm, with a deeper glow beneath his white eyebrows, broke into a kind of rhapsody of transcendental thought. "It's for all these millions I would work, if they would let me!" he cried. "It's to the life of great cities my schemes are addressed. It's to make millions wiser and better that I stand pleading my cause so long after I have earned my rest." One day he seemed taciturn and preoccupied. He talked much less than usual, noticed nothing, and walked with his eyes on the pavement. I imagined that, in a phrase with which he had made me familiar, he had caught the tail of an idea and was holding it fast, in spite of its slippery contortions. As we neared his lodging at the end of our walk, he stopped abruptly in the middle of the street, and I had to give him a violent pull to rescue him from a rattling butcher's cart. When we reached the pavement he stopped again, grasped me by the

hand, and fixed his eyes on me with a very extraordinary
exaltation. We were at the top of the shabby cross- street in
which he had found a shelter. A row of squalid tenements
faced us, and half a dozen little Irish ragamuffins were
sprawling beneath our feet, between their doorways and the
gutter. "Eureka! Eureka!" he cried. "I've found it—I've
found it!" And on my asking him what he had found,"Something science has groped for, for ages—the solution of the in-
calculable! Perhaps, too, my fortune; certainly my immortality! Quick, quick! Before it vanishes I must get at my
pen." And he hurried me along to his dingy little dwelling.
On the doorstep he paused. "I can't tell you now," he cried.
"I must fling it down in black and white. But for heaven's
sake, come to-night to the lecture, and in the first flush of
apprehension I think I can knock off a statement!" To the
lecture I promised to come. At the same moment I raised
my eyes and beheld in the window of the Colonel's apartment the ominous visage of Professor Fargo. I had been
kindled by the Colonel's ardor, but somehow I was suddenly
chilled by the presence of the Professor. I feared that, be
the brilliancy of my friend's sudden illumination what it
might, the shock of meeting his unloved *confrère* under his
own roof would loosen his grasp of his idea. I found a pretext for keeping him standing a moment, and observed that
the Professor disappeared. The next moment the door
opened and he stepped forth. He had put on his hat, I
suppose, hastily; it was cocked toward one side with a
jauntiness which seemed the climax of his habitual swagger.
He was evidently in better spirits than when I listened to
him at Excelsior Hall; but neither the Professor's smiles nor
his frowns were those of an honest man. He bestowed on
my companion and me one of the most expansive of the
former, gave his hat a cock in the opposite direction, and
was about to pass on. But suddenly bethinking himself,
he paused and drew from his pocket a small yellow ticket,
which he presented to me. It was admission to Excelsior
Hall.

"If you can use this to-night," he said, "I think you'll
see something out of the common." This intimation, ac-

companied with a wink of extreme suggestiveness, seemed to indicate that the Professor also, by a singular coincidence, had had a flash of artistic inspiration. But giving me no further clue, he rapidly went his way. As I shook hands in farewell with the Colonel, I saw that the light of the old man's new inspiration had gone out in angry wonderment over the Professor's errand with his daughter.

I can hardly define the vague apprehensiveness which led me to make that evening a peculiarly prompt appearance at Excelsior Hall. There was no one there when I arrived, and for half an hour the solitude remained unbroken. At last a shabby little man came in and sat down on the last bench, in the shade. We remained a while staring at the white wall behind the three empty chairs of the performers and listening to the gasburners, which were hissing with an expressiveness which, under the circumstances, was most distressing. At last my companion left his place and strolled down the aisle. He stopped before the platform, turned about, surveyed the capacity of the room, and muttered something between a groan and an imprecation. Then he came back toward me and stopped. He had a dirty shirt-front, a scrubby beard, a small, wrathful black eye, and a nose unmistakably Judaic.

"If you don't want to sit and be lectured at all alone," he said, "I guess you'd better go."

I expressed a hope that some one would turn up yet, and said that I preferred to remain, in any event, as I had a particular interest in the performance.

"A particular interest?" he cried; "that's about what I've got. I've got the rent of my room to collect. This thing has been going on here for three weeks now, and I haven't seen the first dollar of *my* profits. It's been going down hill steady, and I think the Professor, and the Colonel, and the deaf and dumb young woman had better shut up shop. They ain't appreciated; they'd better try some other line. There's mighty little to this thing, anyway; it ain't what I call an attractive exhibition. I've got an offer for the premises for a month from the Canadian Giantess, and I mean to ask the present company to pay me down and vacate."

It looked, certainly, as if the "Combination" would have some difficulty in meeting its engagements. The Professor's head emerged inquiringly from a door behind the stage and disappeared, after a brief communion with the vacuity of the scene. In a few minutes, however, the customary trio came forth and seated itself gravely on the platform. The Professor thrust his thumbs into his waistcoat and drummed on the floor with his toes, as if it cost his shrewdness a painful effort to play any longer at expectation. The Colonel sat stiff and solemn, with his eyes on the ground. The young girl gazed forth upon the ungrateful void with her characteristically irresponsible tranquillity. For myself, after listening some ten minutes more for an advancing tread, I leaned my elbows on the back of the bench before me and buried my head; I couldn't bear any longer to look at the Colonel. At last I heard a scramble behind me, and looking round, saw my little Jew erecting himself on his feet on a bench.

"Gentlemen!" he cried out, "I don't address the young woman; I'm told she can't hear. I suppose the man with the biggest audience has a right to speak. The amount of money in this hall to-night is just thirty cents—unless, indeed, my friend here is on the free list. Now it stands to reason that you can't pay your night's expenses out of thirty cents. I think we might as well turn down some of this gas; we can still see to settle our little account. To have it paid will gratify me considerably more than anything you can do there. I don't judge your entertainment; I've no doubt it's a very smart thing. But it's very evident it don't suit this city. It's too intellectual. I've got something else in view—I don't mind telling you it's the Canadian Giantess. It is going to open to-morrow with a matinée, and I want to put some props under that platform. So you'd better pay this young man his money back, and go home to supper. But before you leave, I'll trouble you for the sum of ninety-three dollars and eighty-seven cents."

The Professor stroked his beard; the Colonel didn't move.

The little Jew descended from his perch and approached the platform with his bill in his hand. In a moment I followed him.

"We're a failure," said the Professor, at last. "Very well! I'm not discouraged; I'm a practical man. I've got an idea in my head by which, six months hence, I expect to fill the Academy of Music." Then, after a pause, turning to his companion, "Colonel, do you happen to have ninety-three dollars and eighty-seven cents?"

The Colonel slowly raised his eyes and looked at him; I shall never forget the look.

"Seriously speaking," the Professor went on, daunted but for an instant, "you're liable for half the debt. But I'll assume your share on a certain condition. I have in my head the plan of another entertainment. Our friend here is right; we have been too intellectual. Very good!" and he nodded at the empty benches. "I've learned the lesson. Henceforth I'm going to be sensational. My great sensation"—and he paused a moment to engage again the eye of the Colonel, who presently looked vaguely up at him—"is this young lady!" and he thrust out a hand toward Miss Gifford. "Allow me to exhibit your daughter for a month, in my own way and according to my own notions, and I assume your debt."

The young girl dropped her eyes on the ground, but kept her place. She had evidently been schooled. The Colonel slowly got up, glaring and trembling with indignation. I wished to cut the knot, and I interrupted his answer. "Your inducement is null," I said to the Professor. "I assume the Colonel's debt. It shall be paid this moment."

Professor Fargo gave an honestly gleeful grin; this was better even than the Colonel's assent. "You refuse your consent then," he demanded of the old man, "to your daughter's appearance under my exclusive management."

"Utterly!" cried the Colonel.

"You are aware, I suppose, that she's of age?"

The Colonel stared at me with a groan. "What under heaven is the fellow coming to?"

"To this!" responded the Professor; and he fixed his eye

for a moment on the young girl. She immediately looked up at him, rose, advanced, and stood before him. Her face betrayed no painful consciousness of what she was doing, and I have often wondered how far, in her strangely simple mood and nature, her consciousness on this occasion was a guilty one. I never ascertained. This was the most unerring stroke I had seen the Professor perform. The poor child fixed her charming eyes on his gross, flushed face, and awaited his commands. She was fascinated; she had no will of her own. "You'll be so good as to choose," the Professor went on, addressing her in spite of her deafness, "between your father and me. He says we're to part. I say you're to follow me. What do you say?"

For all answer, after caressing him a moment with her gentle gaze, she dropped before him on her knees. The Colonel sprang toward her with a sort of howl of rage and grief, but she jumped up, retreated, and tripped down the steps of the platform into the room. She rapidly made her way to the door. There she paused and looked back at us. Her father stood staring after her in helpless bewilderment. The Professor disappeared into the little ante-room behind the stage, and came back in a moment jamming his hat over his eyes and carrying the young girl's shawl. He reached the edge of the platform, and then, stopping, shook the forefinger with the turquoise ring at the Colonel.

"What do you say now?" he cried. "Is spiritual magnetism a humbug?"

The little Jew rushed after him, shrieking and brandishing the unpaid bill; but the Professor cleared at half a dozen strides the interval which divided him from the door, caught the young girl round the waist, and made a triumphant escape. Half an hour later the Colonel and I left the little Jew staring distractedly at his unretributed gas-burners.

I walked home with the old man, and, having led him into his shabby refuge, suffered him to make his way alone, with groans, and tears, and imprecations, into his daughter's empty room. At last he came tottering out again; it seemed as if he were going mad. I brought him away by force, and he passed the night in my own quarters. He had spoken shortly before of the prospect of an asylum for his daughter, but it became evident that the asylum would have to be for him.

I sometimes go to see him. He spends his days covering little square sheets of paper with algebraic signs, but I am assured by his superintendent, who understands the matter, that they represent no coherent mathematical operation. I never treated myself to the "sensation" of attending Professor Fargo's new entertainment.

AT ISELLA

M Y story begins properly, I suppose, with my journey, and my journey began properly at Lucerne. It had been on the point of beginning a number of times before. About the middle of August I actually started. I had been putting it off from day to day in deference to the opinion of several discreet friends, who solemnly assured me that a man of my make would never outweather the rage of an Italian August. But ever since deciding to winter in Italy, instead of subsiding unimaginatively upon Paris, I had had a standing quarrel with Switzerland. What was Switzerland after all? Little else but brute Nature surely, of which at home we have enough and to spare. What we seek in Europe is Nature refined and transmuted to art. In Switzerland, what a pale historic coloring; what a penury of relics and monuments! I pined for a cathedral or a gallery. Instead of dutifully conning my Swiss Bädeker, I had fretfully deflavored my Murray's North Italy. Lucerne indeed is a charming little city, and I had learned to know it well. I had watched the tumbling Reuss, blue from the melting pinnacles which know the blue of heaven, come rushing and swirling beneath those quaintly timbered bridges, vaulted with mystical paintings in the manner of Holbein, and through the severed mass of the white, compact town. I had frequented the great, bald, half-handsome, half-hideous church of the Jesuit, and listened in the twilight to the seraphic choir which breathes through its mighty organ-tubes. I had taken the most reckless pleasure in the fact that this was Catholic Switzerland. I had strolled and restrolled across the narrow market-place at Altorf, and kept my countenance in the presence of that ludicrous plaster-cast of the *genius loci* and his cross-bow. I had peregrinated further to the little hamlet of Bürglen, and peeped into the frescoed chapel which commemorates the hero's natal scene. I had also investigated that sordid lake-side sanctuary, with its threshold lapped by the waves and its walls defiled by cockneys, which consecrates the spot at which the great mountaineer, leaping from among his custodians in Gesler's boat, spurned the stout skiff with his invincible heel. I had contemplated from the deck of the steamer the images of the immortal trio, authors of the oath of liberation, which adorned the pier at Brunnen. I had sojourned at that compact little State of Gersau, sandwiched between the lake and the great wall of the Righi, and securely niched somewhere in history as the smallest and most perpetual of republics. The traveler's impatience hereabouts is quickened by his nearness to one of the greatest of the Alpine highways. Here he may catch a balmy side-wind, stirred from the ranks of southward-trooping pilgrims. The Saint Gothard route begins at Lucerne, where you take your place in the diligence and register your luggage. I used to fancy that a great wave of Southern life rolled down this mighty channel to expire visibly in the blue lake, and ripple to its green shores. I used to imagine great gusts of warm wind hovering about the coach office at Fluelen, scented with oleander and myrtle. I used to buy at Fluelen, to the great peril of my digestion, certain villanous peaches and plums, offered by little girls at the steamboat landing, and of which it was currently whispered that they had ripened on those further Italian slopes.

One fine morning I marked my luggage *Milan!* with a great imaginative flourish which may have had something to do with my subsequent difficulty in recovering it in the Lombard capital, banished it for a fortnight from sight and mind, and embarked on the steamboat at Lucerne with the interval's equipment in a knapsack. It is noteworthy how readily, on leaving Switzerland, I made my peace with it. What a pleasure-giving land it is, in truth! Besides the massive glory of its mountains, how it heaps up the measure of delight with the unbargained grace of town and tower, of remembered name and deed! As we passed away from Lucerne, my eyes lingered with a fresher fondness than before upon an admirable bit of the civic picturesque—a great line of mellow-stuccoed dwellings, with verdurous water-steps and grated basements, rising squarely from the rushing cobalt of the Reuss. It was a palpable foretaste of Venice. I am not ashamed to say how soon I began to look out for premonitions of Italy. It was better to begin too soon than too late; so, to miss nothing, I began to note "sensations" at Altorf, the historic heart of Helvetia. I remember here certain formal burgher mansions, standing back from the dusty highroad beyond spacious, well-swept courts, into which the wayfarer glances through immense gates of antique wrought iron. I had a notion that deserted Italian palazzos took the lingering sunbeams at somewhat such an angle, with just that coarse glare. I wondered of course who lived in them, and how they lived, and what was society in Altorf; longing plaintively, in the manner of roaming Americans, for a few stray crumbs from the native social board; with my fancy vainly beating its wings against the great blank wall, behind which, in travel-haunted Europe, all gentle private interests nestle away from intrusion. Here, as everywhere, I was struck with the mere surface-relation of the Western tourist to the soil he treads. He filters and trickles through the dense social body in every possible direction, and issues forth at last the same virginal water drop. "Go your way," these antique houses seemed to say, from their quiet courts and gardens; "the road is yours and welcome, but the land is ours. You may pass and stare and wonder, but you may never know us." The Western tourist consoles himself, of course, by the reflection that the gentry of Altorf and other ancient burghs gain more from the imagination possibly than they might bestow upon it.

I confess that so long as I remained in the land, as I did for the rest of the afternoon—a pure afternoon of late summer, charged with mellow shadows from the teeming verdure of the narrow lowland, beyond which to-morrow and Italy seemed merged in a vague bright identity—I felt that I was not fairly under way. The land terminates at Amstaeg, where I lay that night. Early the next morning I attacked the mighty slopes. Just beyond Amstaeg, if I am not mistaken, a narrow granite bridge spans the last mountain-plunge of the Reuss; and just here the great white road begins the long toil of its ascent. To my sense, these mighty Alpine highways have a grand poetry of their own. I lack, doubtless, that stout stomach for pure loneliness which leads your genuine mountaineer to pronounce them a desecration of the mountain stillness. As if the mountain stillness were not inviolable! Gleaming here and there against the dark sides of the gorges, unrolling their measured bands further and higher, doubling and stretching and spanning, but always climbing, they break it only to the anxious eye. The Saint Gothard road is immensely long drawn, and, if the truth be told, somewhat monotonous. As you follow it to its uppermost reaches, the landscape takes on a darker local color. Far below the wayside, the yellow Reuss tumbles and leaps and foams over a perfect torture-bed of broken rock. The higher slopes lie naked and raw, or coated with slabs of gray. The valley lifts and narrows and darkens into the scenic mountain pass of the fancy. I was haunted as I walked by an old steel plate in a French book that I used to look at as a child lying on my stomach on the parlor floor. Under it was written "Saint Gothard." I remember distinctly the cold, gray mood which this picture used to generate; the same tone of feeling is produced by the actual scene. Coming at last to the Devil's Bridge, I recognized the source of the steel plate of my infancy. You have no impulse here to linger fondly. You hurry away after a moment's halt, with an impression fierce and chaotic as the place itself. A great torrent of wind, sweeping from a sudden outlet and snatching uproar and spray from the mad torrent of water leaping in liquid thunderbolts beneath; a giddy, deafened, deluged stare, with my two hands to my hat, and a rapid shuddering retreat—these are my chief impressions of the Devil's Bridge. If, on leaving Amstaeg in the morning, I had been asked whither I was bending my steps, "To Italy!" I would have answered, with a grand absence of detail. The radiance of this broad fact had quenched the possible side-lights of reflection. As I ap-

proached the summit of the pass, it became a profoundly
solemn thought that I might, by pushing on with energy,
lay my weary limbs on an Italian bed. There was something
so delightful in the mere protracted, suspended sense of approach, that it seemed a pity to bring it to so abrupt a close.
And then suppose, metaphysical soul of mine, that Italy
should not, in vulgar parlance, altogether come up to time?
Why not prolong awhile the possible bliss of ignorance—of
illusion? Something short of the summit of the Saint Gothard pass, the great road of the Furca diverges to the right,
passes the Rhône Glacier, enters the Rhône Valley, and con-
ducts you to Brieg and the foot of the Simplon. Reaching
in due course this divergence of the Furca road, I tarried
awhile beneath the mountain sky, debating whether or not
delay would add to pleasure. I opened my Bädeker and
read that within a couple of hours' walk from my halting-
place was the *Albergo di San Gothardo, vaste et sombre
auberge Italienne*. To think of being at that distance from
a vast, sombre Italian inn! On the other hand, there were
some very pretty things said of the Simplon. I tossed up a
napoleon; the head fell uppermost. I trudged away to the
right. The road to the Furca lies across one of those high
desolate plateaux which represent the hard prose of mountain scenery. Naked and stern it lay before me, rock and
grass without a shrub, without a tree, without a grace—like
the dr 'ied of some gigantic river of prehistoric times.

The stunted hamlet of Realp, beside the road dwarfed
by the huge scale of things, seemed litttle more than a
cluster of naked, sun-blackened bowlders. It contained an
inn, however, and the inn contained the usual Alpine larder
of cold veal and cheese, and, as I remember, a very affable
maid-servant, who spoke excellent lowland French, and confessed in the course of an after-dinner conversation that
the winters in Realp were *un peu tristes*. This conversation
took place as I sat resting outside the door in the late afternoon, watching the bright, hard light of the scene grow gray
and cold beneath a clear sky, and wondering to find
humanity lodged in such an exaltation of desolation.

The road of the Furca, as I discovered the next morning,

is a road and little else. Its massive bareness, however, gives it an incontestable grandeur. The broad, serpentine terrace uncoils its slanting *cordons* with a multiplicity of curves and angles and patient reaches of circumvention, which give it the air of some wanton revelry of engineering genius. Finally, after a brief level of repose, it plunges down to the Rhône Glacier. I had the good fortune to see this great spectacle on the finest day of the year. Its perfect beauty is best revealed beneath the scorching glare of an untempered sun. The sky was without a cloud—the air incredibly lucid. The glacier dropped its billowy sheet—a soundless tumult of whiteness, a torrent of rolling marble—straight from the blue of heaven to the glassy margin of the road. It seems to gather into its bosom the whole diffused light of the world, so that round about it all objects lose their color. The rocks and hills stand sullen and neutral; the lustre of the sky is turned to blackness. At the little hotel near the glacier I waited for the coach to Brieg, and started thitherward in the early afternoon, sole occupant of the *coupé*.

Let me not, however, forget to commemorate the French priest whom we took in at one of the squalid villages of the dreary Haut-Valais, through which on that bright afternoon we rattled so superbly. It was a Sunday, and throughout this long dark chain of wayside hamlets the peasants were straddling stolidly about the little central *place* in the hideous festal accoutrements of the rustic Swiss. He came forth from the tavern, gently cleaving the staring crowd, accompanied by two brother ecclesiastics. These were portly, elderly men; he was young and pale and priestly in the last degree. They had a little scene of adieux at the coach door. They whispered gently, gently holding each other's hands and looking lovingly into each other's eyes, and then the two elders saluted their comrade on each cheek, and, as we departed, blew after him just the least little sacramental kiss. It was all, dramatically speaking, delightfully low in tone. Before we reached Brieg the young priest had gained a friend to console him for those he had lost. He proved to be a most amiable person; full of homely frankness and appealing innocence of mundane things; and invested withal with a most pathetic air of sitting there as a mere passive object of transmission—a simple priestly particle in the great ecclesiastical body, transposed by the logic of an inscrutable *thither!* and *thus!* On learning that I was an American, he treated me so implicitly as a travelled man of the world, that he almost persuaded me for the time I was one. He was on pins and needles with his sense of the possible hazards of travel. He asked questions the most innocently *saugrenues.* He was convinced on general grounds that our driver was drunk, and that he would surely overturn us into the Rhône. He seemed possessed at the same time with a sort of schoolboy relish for the profane humor of things. Whenever the coach made a lurch toward the river-bank or swung too broadly round a turn, he would grasp my arm and whisper that our hour had come; and then, before our pace was quite readjusted, he would fall to nursing his elbows and snickering gently to himself. It seemed altogether a larger possibility than any he had been prepared for that on his complaining of the cold I should offer him the use of my overcoat. Of this and of other personal belongings he ventured to inquire the price, and indeed seemed oppressed with the sudden expensiveness of the world. But now that he was fairly launched he was moving in earnest. He was to reach Brieg, if possible, in time for the night diligence over the Simplon, which was to deposit him at the Hospice on the summit.

By a very early hour the next morning I had climbed apace with the sun. Brieg was far below me in the valley. I had measured an endless number of the giant elbows of the road, and from the bosky flank of the mountain I looked down at nestling gulfs of greenness, cool with shade; at surging billows of forest crested with the early brightness; at slopes in light and cliffs in shadow; at all the heaving mountain zone which belongs to the verdant nearness of earth; and then straight across to the sacred pinnacles which take their tone from heaven.

If weather could bless an enterprise, mine was blessed beyond words. It seemed to me that Nature had taken an interest in my little project and was determined to do the thing handsomely. As I mounted higher, the light flung its dazzling presence on all things. The air stood still to take it; the green glittered within the green, the blue burned beyond it; the dew on the forests gathered to dry into massive crystals, and beyond the brilliant void of space the clear snow-fields stood out like planes of marble inserted in a field of lapis-lazuli. The Swiss side of the Simplon has the beauty of a boundless luxury of green; the view remains gentle even in its immensity. The ascent is gradual and slow, and only when you reach the summit do you get a sense of proper mountain grimness. On this favoring day of mine the snowy horrors of the opposite Aletsch Glacier seemed fairly to twinkle with serenity. It seemed to me when I reached the Hospice that I had been winding for hours along the inner hollow of some mighty cup of verdure toward a rim of chiselled silver crowned with topaz. At the Hospice I made bold to ask leave to rest. It stands on the bare topmost plateau of the pass, bare itself as the spot it consecrates, and stern as the courage of the pious brothers who administer its charities. It broods upon the scene with the true, bold, convent look, with ragged yellow walls and grated windows, striving to close in human weakness from blast and avalanche as in valleys and cities to close it in from temptation and pollution. A few St. Bernard dogs were dozing outside in the chilly sunshine. I climbed the great stone steps which lift the threshold above the snow-land, and tinkled the bell of appeal. Here for a couple of hours I was made welcome to the cold, hard fare of the convent. There was to my mind a solemn and pleasant fitness in my thus entering church-burdened Italy through the portal of the church, for from the convent door to the plain of Lombardy it was all to be downhill work. I seemed to feel on my head the hands of especial benediction, and to hear in my ears the premonition of countless future hours to be passed in the light of altar-candles. The inner face of the Hospice is well-nigh as cold and bare as the face it turns defiant to the Alpine snows. Huge stone corridors and ungarnished rooms, in which poor unacclimatized friars must

sit aching and itching with chilblains in high midsummer;
everywhere that peculiar perfume of churchiness—the *odeur
de sacristie* and essence of incense—which impart throughout the world an especial pungency to Catholicism. Having the good fortune, as it happened, to be invited to dine
with the Prior, I found myself in fine priestly company.
A dozen of us sat about the board in the greasy, brick-
paved refectory, lined with sombre cupboards of ponderous
crockery, all in stole and cassock but myself. Several of
the brothers were *in transitu* from below. Among them I
had the pleasure of greeting my companion in the *coupé* to
Brieg, slightly sobered perhaps by his relapse into the clerical ranks, but still timidly gracious and joyous. The
Prior himself, however, especially interested me, so every
inch was he a prior—a priest dominant and militant. He
was still young, and familiar, I should say, with the passions
of youth; tall and powerful in frame, stout-necked and
small-headed, with a brave beak of a nose and closely
placed, fine, but sinister eyes. The simple, childish cut
of his black cassock, with its little linen band across his
great pectoral expanse as he sat at meat, seemed to denote
a fantastical, ironical humility. Was it a mere fancy of
a romantic Yankee tourist that he was more evil than
gentle? Heaven grant, I mused as I glanced at him, that
his fierce and massive manhood be guided by the Lord's
example. What was such a man as that doing up there
on a lonely mountain top, watching the snow clouds from
closed windows and doling out restorative cognac to frost-
bitten wagoners? He ought to be down in the hard, dense
world, fighting and sinning for his mother Church. But
he was one who could bide his time. Unless I'm scribbling
nonsense, it will come. In deference probably to the eso-
teric character of a portion of the company, our conversation at dinner was not rigidly clerical. In fact, when my
attention wandered back to its theme, I found the good
brothers were talking of Alexandre Dumas with a delightful
air of protest and hearsay, and a spice of priestly malice.
The great romancer, I believe, had among his many fictions
somewhere promulgated an inordinate fiction touching the

manners and customs of the Hospice. The game being
started, each of them said his say and cast his pebble,
weighted always with an "*on dit*," and I was amazed to
find they were so well qualified to reprobate the author
of "Monte Cristo." When we had dined my young Frenchman came and took me by the arm and led me in great
triumph over the whole convent, delighted to have something
to show me—me who had come from America and had lent
him my overcoat. When at last I had under his auspices
made my farewell obeisance to the Prior, and started on
my downward course, he bore me company along the road.
But before we lost sight of the Hospice he gave me his
fraternal blessing. "*Allons!*" he was pleased to say, "the
next time I shall know an American"; and he gathered up
his gentle petticoat, and, as I looked behind, I saw his
black stockings frolicking back over the stones by a short
cut to the monastery.

I should like to be able to tell the veracious tale of that
divine afternoon. I should like to be able to trace the soft
stages by which those rugged heights melt over into a
Southern difference. Now at last in good earnest I began
to watch for the *symptoms* of Italy. Now that the long
slope began to tend downward unbroken, it was not absurd
to fancy a few adventurous tendrils of Southern growth
might have crept and clambered upward. At a short distance beyond the Hospice stands the little village of Simplon,
where I believe the coach stops for dinner; the uttermost
outpost, I deemed it, of the lower world, perched there like
an empty shell, with its murmur not yet quenched, tossed
upward and stranded by some climbing Southern wave.
The little inn at the Italian end of the street, painted in a
bright Italian medley of pink and blue, must have been
decorated by a hand which had learned its cunning in the
land of the fresco. The Italian slope of the Simplon road
commands a range of scenery wholly different from the
Swiss. The latter winds like a thread through the blue
immensity; the former bores its way beneath crag and
cliff, through gorge and mountain crevice. But though
its channel narrows and darkens, Italy nears and nears none

the less. You suspect it first in—what shall I say?—the growing warmth of the air, a fancied elegance of leaf and twig; a little while yet, and they will curl and wanton to your heart's content. The famous Gorge of Gando, at this stage of the road, renews the sombre horrors of the Via Mala. The hills close together above your head, and the daylight filters down their corrugated sides from three inches of blue. The mad torrent of the Dauria, roaring through the straitened vale, fills it forever with a sounding din, as—to compare poetry to prose—a railway train a tunnel. Emerging from the Gorge of Gando, you fairly breathe Italian air. The gusts of a mild climate come wandering along the road to meet you. Lo! suddenly, by the still wayside, I came upon a sensation: a little house painted a hot salmon color, with a withered pine-twig over the door in token of entertainment, and above this inscribed in square chirography—literally in Italics—*Osteria!* I stopped devotedly to quaff a glass of sour wine to Italy gained. The place seemed wrapped in a desolation of stillness, save that as I stood and thumped the doorpost, the piping cry of a baby rose from the loft above and tickled the mountain echoes. Anon came clattering down the stairs a nursing mother of peasants; she gave me her only wine, out of her own bottle, out of her only glass. While she stood to wait on me, the terrible cry of her infant became so painful that I bade her go and fetch him before he strangled; and in a moment she reappeared, holding him in her arms, pacified and utterly naked. Standing there with the little unswaddled child on her breast, and smiling simply from her glowing brow, she made a picture which, in coming weeks, I saw imitated more or less vividly over many an altar and in many a palace. Onward still, through its long-drawn evolutions, the valley keeps darkly together, as if to hold its own to the last against the glittering breadth of level Lombardy. In truth, I had gained my desire. If Italy meant stifling heat, this was the essence of Italy. The afternoon was waning, and the early shadows of the valley deepening into a dead summer night. But the hotter the better, and the more Italian! At last, at a turn in the road, glimpsed the

first houses of a shallow village, pressed against the mountain wall. It was Italy—the Dogana Isella! so I quickened my jaded steps. I met a young officer strolling
along the road in sky-blue trousers, with a moustache *à la*
Victor Emanuel, puffing a cigarette, and yawning with the
sensuous *ennui* of Isella—the first of that swarming company of warriors whose cerulean presence, in many a rich
street-scene, in later hours touched up so brightly the foreground of the picture. A few steps more brought me to
the Dogana, and to my first glimpse of those massive and
shadowy arcades so delightfully native to the South. Here
it was my privilege to hear for the first time the music of
an Italian throat vibrate upon Italian air. "Nothing to
declare—*niente?*" asked the dark-eyed functionary, emerging from the arcade. "*Niente*" seemed to me delicious;
I would have told a fib for the sake of repeating the word.
Just beyond stood the inn, which seemed to me somehow
not as the inns of Switzerland. Perched something aloft
against the hillside, a vague light tendency to break out
into balconies and terraces and trellises seemed to enhance
its simple façade. Its open windows had an air of being
familiar with Southern nights; with balmy dialogues, possibly, passing between languid ladies leaning on the iron
rails, and lounging gentlemen, star-gazing from the road
beneath at their mistresses' eyes. Heaven grant it should
not be fastidiously neat, scrubbed and furbished and *frotté*
like those prosy taverns on the Swiss lakes! Heaven was
generous. I was ushered into a room whereof the ceiling
was frescoed with flowers and gems and cherubs, but whose
brick-tiled floor would have been vastly amended by the
touch of a wet cloth and broom. After repairing my
toilet within the limits of my resources, I proceeded to
order supper. The host, I remember, I decreed to have
been the *chef de cuisine* of some princely house of Lombardy. He wore a grizzled moustache and a red velvet
cap, with little gold ear-rings. I could see him, under
proper inspiration, whip a towel round his waist, turn back
his sleeves, and elaborate a masterly pasticcio. "I shall

take the liberty," he said, "of causing monsieur to be served at the same time with a lady."

"With a lady—an English lady?" I asked.

"An Italian lady. She arrived an hour ago." And mine host paused a moment and honored me with a genial smile. "She is alone—she is young—she is pretty."

Stolid child of the North that I was, surely my smile of response was no match for his! But, nevertheless, in my heart I felt that fortune was kind. I went forth to stroll down the road while my repast was being served, and while daylight still lingered, to reach forward as far as possible into the beckoning land beyond. Opposite the inn the mountain stream, still untamed, murmured and tumbled between the stout parapet which edged the road and the wall of rock which enclosed the gorge. I felt indefinably curious, expectant, impatient. Here was Italy, at last; but what next? Was I to eat my supper and go contentedly to bed? Was there nothing I could see, or do, or feel? I had been deeply moved, but I was primed for a deeper emotion still. Would it come? Along the road toward Domo d'Ossola the evening shadows deepened and settled, and filled the future with mystery. The future would take care of itself; but ah, for an intenser present! I stopped and gazed wistfully along the broad dim highway. At this moment I perceived beyond me, leaning against the parapet, the figure of a woman, alone and in meditation. Her two elbows rested on the stone coping, her two hands were laid against her ears to deaden the din of the stream, and her face, between them, was bent over upon the waters. She seemed young and comely. She was bare-headed; a black organdy shawl was gathered round her shoulders; her dress, of a light black material, was covered with a multitude of little puffs and flounces, trimmed and adorned with crimson silk. There was an air of intense meditation in her attitude; I passed near her without her perceiving me. I observed her black-brown tresses, braided by a cunning hand, but slightly disarranged by travel, and the crumpled disorder of her half-fantastic dress. She was a lady and an Italian; she was alone, young, and pretty; was she possibly

my destined companion? A few yards beyond the spot at
which she stood, I retraced my steps; she had now turned
round. As I approached her she looked at me from a pair
of dark expressive eyes. Just a hint of suspicion and defiance I fancied that at this moment they expressed. "Who
are you, what are you, roaming so close to me?" they seemed
to murmur. We were alone in this narrow pass, I a new
comer, she a daughter of the land; moreover, her glance
had almost audibly challenged me; instinctively, therefore,
and with all the deference I was master of, I bowed. She
continued to gaze for an instant; then suddenly she perceived, I think, that I was utterly a foreigner and presumably a gentleman, and hereupon, briefly but graciously, she
returned my salute. I went my way and reached the hotel.
As I passed in, I saw the fair stranger come slowly along
the road as if also to enter the inn. In the little dining-
room I found mine host of the velvet cap bestowing the
finishing touches upon a small table set *en tête-à-tête* for
two. I had heard, I had read, of the gracious loquacity of
the Italian race and their sweet familiarities of discourse.
Here was a chance to test the quality of the matter. The
landlord, having poised two fantastically folded napkins
directly *vis-à-vis,* glanced at me with a twinkle in his eye
which seemed to bespeak recognition of this cunning ar-
rangement.

"*A propos,*" I said, "this lady with whom I am to dine?
Does she wear a black dress with red flounces?"

"Precisely, Signore. You have already had a glimpse
of her? A pretty woman, isn't it so?"

"Extremely pretty. Who is the lady?"

"Ah!" And the landlord turned back his head and
thrust out his chin, with just the least play of his shoulders.
"That's the question! A lady of that age, with that face
and those red flounces, who travels alone—not even a maid
—you may well ask who she is! She arrived here an hour
ago in a carriage from Domo d'Ossola, where, her vetturino
told me, she had arrived only just before by the common
coach from Arona. But though she travels by the common
vehicle, she is not a common person; one may see that

with half an eye. She comes in great haste, but ignorant
of the ways and means. She wishes to go by the diligence
to Brieg. She ought to have waited at Domo, where she
could have found a good seat. She didn't even take the
precaution of engaging one at the office there. When the
diligence stops here, she will have to fare as she can. She
is pretty enough indeed to fare very well—or very ill;
isn't it so, Signore?" demanded the worthy Bonifazio, as
I believe he was named. "Ah, but behold her strolling
along the road, bare-headed, in those red flounces! What
is one to say? After dusk, with the dozen officers in gar-
rison here watching the frontier! Watching the ladies who
come and go, *per Dio!* Many of them, saving your presence, Signore, are your own compatriots. You'll not deny
that some of them are a little free—a little bold. What
will you have? Out of their own country! What else were
the use of travel? But this one; eh! she's not out of her
own country yet. Italians are Italians, Signore, up to the
frontier—eh! eh!" And the Signor Bonifazio indulged in
a laugh the most *goguenard*. "Nevertheless, I have not kept
an inn these twenty years without learning to know the
sheep from the goats. This is an honorable lady, Signore;
it is for that reason that I have offered to you to sup with
her. The other sort! one can always sup with them!"

It seemed to me that my host's fluent commentary was
no meagre foretaste of Italian frankness. I approached the
window. The fair object of our conversation stood at the
foot of the stone staircase which ascended to the inn door,
with the toe of her shoe resting upon the first step. She was
looking fixedly and pensively up the road toward Switzerland. Her hand clasped the knob of the iron balustrade
and her slight fingers played an impatient measure. She
had begun to interest me. Her dark eyes, intent upon the
distant turn of the road, seemed to expand with a vague
expectancy. Whom was she looking for? Of what romance
of Italy was she the heroine? The *maître d'hôtel* appeared
at the head of the steps, and with a flourish of his napkin
announced that the Signora was served. She started a little
and then lightly shrugged her shoulders. As the same mo-

ment I caught her eye as I stood gazing from the window.
With a just visible deepening of her color, she slowly ascended the steps. I was suddenly seized with a sense of
being dingy, travel-stained, unpresentable to a woman so
charming. I hastily retreated to my room, and, surveying myself in my dressing-glass, objurgated fortune that
I lacked the wherewithal to amend my attire. But I could
at least change my cravat. I had no sooner replaced my
black neck-tie by a blue one than it occurred to me that the
Signora would observe the difference; but what then? It
would hardly offend her. With a timid hope that it might
faintly gratify her as my only feasible tribute to the honor
of her presence, I returned to the dining-room. She was
seated and had languidly addressed herself to the contents
of her soup-plate. The worthy Bonifazio had adorned our
little table with four lighted candles and a centre-piece
of Alpine flowers. As I installed myself opposite my companion, after having greeted her and received a murmured
response, it seemed to me that I was sitting down to one
of those factitious repasts which are served upon the French
stage, when the table has been moved close to the footlights,
and the ravishing young widow and the romantic young
artist begin to manipulate the very *nodus* of the comedy.
Was the Signora a widow? Our attendant, with his crimson cap, his well-salted discourse, his light-handed gestures,
and his smile from behind the scenes, might have passed
for a classic *valet de théâtre*. I had the appetite of a man
who had been walking since sunrise, but I found ample
occasion, while I plied my knife and fork, to inspect the
Signora. She merely pretended to eat; and to appeal, perhaps, from the overflattering intentness of my vision, she
opened an idle conversation with Bonifazio. I listened ad-
miringly, while the glancing shuttle of Italian speech passed
rapidly from lip to lip. It was evident, frequently, that
she remained quite heedless of what he said, losing herself
forever in a kind of fretful intensity of thought. The repast was long and multifarious, and as he time and again
removed her plate with its contents untouched, mine host
would catch my eye and roll up his own with an air of mock

commiseration, turning back his thumb at the same moment
toward the region of his heart. *"Un coup de tête,"* he took
occasion to murmur as he reached over me to put down a
dish. But the more I looked at the fair unknown, the more
I came to suspect that the source of her unrest lay deeper
than in the petulance of wounded vanity. Her face wore
to my eye the dignity of a deep resolution—a resolution
taken in tears and ecstasy. She was some twenty-eight
years of age, I imagined; though at moments a painful
gravity resting upon her brow gave her the air of a woman
who in youth has anticipated old age. How beautiful she
was by natural gift I am unable to say; for at this especial
hour of her destiny, her face was too serious to be fair and
too interesting to be plain. She was pale, worn, and weary-
looking; but in the midst of her weariness there flickered
a fierce impatience of delay and forced repose. She was a
gentle creature, turned brave and adventurous by the stress
of fate. It burned bright in her soft, grave eyes, this longing for the larger freedom of the tarrying morrow. A dozen
chance gestures indicated the torment of her spirit—the
constant rapping of her knife against the table, her bread
crumbed to pieces but uneaten, the frequent change from
posture to posture of her full and flexible figure, shifting
through that broad range of attitude—the very gamut of
gracefulness—familiar to Italian women.

The repast advanced without my finding a voice to address her. Her secret puzzled me, whatever it was, but I
confess that I was afraid of it. A *coup de tête!* Heaven
only knew how direful a *coup!* My mind was flooded by
the memory of the rich capacity of the historic womanhood
of Italy. I thought of Lucrezia Borgia, of Bianca Capello,
of the heroines of Stendhal. My fair friend seemed invested
with an atmosphere of candid passion, which placed her
quite apart from the ladies of my own land. The gallant
soul of the Signor Bonifazio, however, had little sufferance
for this pedantic view of things. Shocked by my apparent
indifference to the privilege of my rare position, he thrust
me by the shoulders into the conversation. The Signora

eyed me for a moment not ungraciously, and then, "Do you understand Italian?" she asked.

I had come to Italy with an ear quite unattuned, of course, to the spoken tongue; but the mellow cadence of the Signora's voice rang in upon my senses like music. "I understand *you*," I said.

She looked at me gravely, with the air of a woman used to receive compliments without any great flutter of vanity. "Are you English?" she abruptly asked.

"English is my tongue."

"Have you come from Switzerland?"

"He has walked from Brieg!" proclaimed our host.

"Ah, you happy men, who can walk—who can run—who needn't wait for coaches and conductors!" The Signora uttered these words with a smile of acute though transient irony. They were followed by a silence. Bonifazio, seeing the ice was broken, retired with a flourish of his napkin and a contraction of his eyelids as much in the nature of a wink as his respect for me, for the Signora, and for himself allowed. What was the motive of the Signora's impatience? I had a presentiment that I should learn. The Italians are confidential; of this I had already received sufficient assurance; and my companion, with her lucid eye and her fine pliable lips, was a bright example of the eloquent genius of her race. She sat idly pressing with her fork the crimson substance out of a plateful of figs, without raising them to her lips.

"You are going over into Switzerland," I said, "and you are in haste."

She eyed me a minute suspiciously. "Yes, I'm in haste!"

"I, who have just begun to feel the charm of Italy," I rejoined, "can hardly understand being in haste to leave it."

"The charm of Italy!" cried the Signora, with a slightly cynical laugh. "Foreigners have a great deal to say about it."

"But you, a good Italian, certainly know what we mean."

She shrugged her shoulders—an operation she performed more gracefully than any woman I ever saw, unless it be Mlle. Madeleine Brohan of the Théâtre Français. "For me it has no charm! I have been unhappy here. Happiness for me is *there!*" And with a superb nod of her head she indicated the Transalpine world. Then, as if she had spoken a thought too freely, she rose suddenly from her chair and walked away to the window. She stepped out on the narrow balcony, looked intently for an instant up and down the road and at the band of sky above it, and then turned back into the room. I sat in my place, divided between my sense of the supreme sweetness of figs and my wonder at my companion's mystery. "It's a fine night!" she said. And with a little jerk of impatience she flung herself into an arm-chair near the table. She leaned back, with her skirt making a great wave around her and her arms folded. I went on eating figs. There was a long silence. "You've eaten at least a dozen figs. You'll be ill!" said the Signora at last.

This was friendly in its frankness. "Ah, if you only knew how I enjoy them!" I cried, laughing. "They are the first I ever tasted. And this the first Asti wine. We don't have either in the North. If figs and Asti wine are for anything in your happiness, Signora," I added, "you had better not cross the Alps. See, the figs are all gone. Do you think it would hurt me to have any more?"

"Truly," cried the Signora, "I don't know what you English are made of!"

"You think us very coarse, and given up altogether to eating and drinking?" She gave another shrug tempered by a smile. "To begin with, I am not an Englishman. And in the second place, you'd not call me coarse if you knew—if you only knew what I feel this evening. Eh! such thick-coming fancies!"

"What are your fancies?" she demanded, with a certain curiosity gleaming in her dark eye.

"I *must* finish this Asti!" This I proceeded to do. I am very glad I did, moreover, as I borrowed from its mild and luscious force something of the courage with which I came to express myself. "I don't know how it is that I'm talking Italian at such a rate. Somehow the words come to me. I know it only from books. I have never talked it."

"You speak as well," the Signora graciously affirmed, "as if you had lived six months in the country."

"Half an hour in your society," said I, "is as profitable as six months elsewhere."

"Bravo!" she responded. "An Italian himself couldn't say it better."

Sitting before me in the vague candlelight, beautiful, pale, dark-browed, sad, the Signora seemed to me an incorporate image of her native land. I had come to pay it my devotions. Why not perform them at her feet? "I have come on a pilgrimage," I said. "To understand what I mean, you must have lived, as I have lived, in a land beyond the seas, barren of romance and grace. This Italy of yours, on whose threshold I stand, is the home of history, of beauty, of the arts—of all that makes life splendid and sweet. Italy, for us dull strangers, is a magic word. We cross ourselves when we pronounce it. We are brought up to think that when we have earned leisure and rest—at some bright hour, when fortune smiles—we may go forth and cross oceans and mountains and see on Italian soil the primal substance— the Platonic 'idea'—of our consoling dreams and our richest fancies. I have been brought up in these thoughts. The happy hour has come to me—Heaven be praised!—while I am still young and strong and sensitive. Here I sit for the first time in the enchanted air in which love and faith and art and knowledge are warranted to become deeper passions than in my own chilly clime. I begin to behold the promise of my dreams. It's Italy. How can I tell you what that means to one of us? Only see already how fluent and tender of speech I've become. The air has a perfume; everything that enters my soul, at every sense, is a suggestion, a promise, a performance. But the best thing of all is that I have met *you, bella donna!* If I were to tell you how you seem to me, you would think me either insincere or impertinent. *Ecco!*"

She listened to me without changing her attitude or without removing her fathomless eyes from my own. Their blue-black depths, indeed, seemed to me the two wells of poetic unity, from which I drew my somewhat transcendental allocution. She was puzzled, I think, and a little amused, but not offended. Anything from an *Inglese!* But it was doubtless grateful to feel these rolling waves of sentiment break softly at her feet, chained as she was, like Andromeda, to the rock of a lonely passion. With an admirable absence of *minauderie*, "How is it that I seem to you, Signore?" she asked.

I left my place and came round and stood in front of her. "Ever since I could use my wits," I said, "I have done little else than fancy dramas and romances and love-tales, and lodge them in Italy. You seem to me as the heroine of all my stories."

There was perhaps a slight movement of coquetry in her reply: "Your stories must have been very dull, Signore," and she gave a sad smile.

"Nay, in future," I said, "my heroines shall be more like you than ever. Where do you come from?" I seated myself in the chair she had quitted. "But it's none of my business," I added. "From anywhere. In Milan or Venice, in Bologna or Florence, Rome or Naples, every grave old palazzo I pass, I shall fancy your home. I'm going the whole length of Italy. My soul, what things I shall see!"

"You please me, Signore. I say to you what I wouldn't say to another. I came from Florence. Shall you surely go there?"

"I have reasons," I said, "for going there more than elsewhere. In Florence"—and I hesitated, with a momentary horror at my perfect unreserve—"in Florence I am to meet my—my *promessa sposa*."

The Signora's face was instantly irradiated by a generous smile. "Ah!" she said, as if now for the first time she really understood me.

"As I say, she has been spending the summer at the Baths of Lucca. She comes to Florence with her mother in the middle of September."

"Do you love her?"

"Passionately."

"Is she pretty?"

"Extremely. But not like you. Very fair, with blue eyes."

"How long since you have seen her?"

"A year."

"And when are you to be married?"

"In November, probably, in Rome."

She covered me for a moment with a glance of the largest sympathy. "Ah, what happiness!" she cried abruptly.

"After our marriage," I said, "we shall go down to Naples. Do you know Naples?"

Instead of answering, she simply gazed at me, and her beautiful eyes seemed to grow larger and more liquid. Suddenly, while I sat in the benignant shadow of her vision, I saw the tears rise to her lids. Her face was convulsed and she burst into sobs. I remember that in my amazement and regret I suddenly lost my Italian. "Dearest lady," I cried in my mother tongue, "forgive me that I have troubled you. Share with me at least the sorrow that I have aroused." In an instant, however, she had brushed away her tears and her face had recovered its pale composure. She tried even to smile.

"What will you think of me?" she asked. "What do you think of me already?"

"I think you are an extremely interesting woman. You are in trouble. If there is anything I can do for you, pray say the word."

She gave me her hand. I was on the point of raising it to my lips. "No—*à l'Anglaise*," she said, and she lightly shook my own. "I like you—you're an honest man—you don't try to make love to me. I should like to write a note to your *promessa sposa* to tell her she may trust you. You can't help me. I have committed myself to God and the Holy Virgin. They will help me. Besides, it's only a little longer. Eh, it's a long story, Signore! What is said in your country of a woman who travels alone at night without even a servant?"

"Nothing is said. It's very common."

"Ah! women must be very happy there, or very un-

happy! Is it never supposed of a woman that she has a
lover? That is worst of all."

"Fewer things are 'supposed' of women there than here.
They live more in the broad daylight of life. They make
their own law."

"They must be very good then—or very bad. So that
a man of fancy like you, with a taste for romance, has to
come to poor Italy, where he can suppose at leisure! But
we are not all romance, I assure you. With me, I promise
you, it's no light-minded *coup de tête*." And the Signora
enforced her candid assurance with an almost imperious
nod. "I know what I'm doing. Eh! I'm an old woman.
I've waited and waited. But now my hour has come!
Ah, the heavenly freedom of it! Ah, the peace—the joy!
Just God, I thank thee!" And sitting back in her chair,
she folded her hands on her bosom and closed her eyes in
a kind of ecstasy. Opening them suddenly, she perceived,
I suppose, my somewhat intent and dilated countenance.
Breaking then into a loud, excited laugh, "How you stare
at me!" she cried. "You think I've at least poisoned my
husband. No, he's safe and sound and strong! On the
contrary, I've forgiven him. I forgive him with all my
heart, with all my soul; there! I call upon you to witness
it. I bear him no rancor. I wish never to think of him
again; only let me never see him—never hear of him! Let
him never come near me: I shall never trouble him! Hark!"
She had interrupted herself and pressed her hand with a
startled air upon my arm. I listened, and in a moment my
ear caught the sound of rolling wheels on the hard highroad.
With a great effort at self-composure, apparently, she laid
her finger on her lips. "If it should be he—if it should
be he!" she murmured. "Heaven preserve me! Do go
to the window and see."

I complied, and perceived a two-horse vehicle advancing
rapidly from the Italian quarter. "It's a carriage of some
sort from Italy," I said. "But what—whom do you fear?"

She rose to her feet. "That my husband should overtake me," and she gave a half-frantic glance round the room,
like a hunted stag at bay. "If it should be he, protect

me! Do something, say something—anything! Say I'm not fit to go back to him. He wants me because he thinks me good. Say I'm not good—to your knowledge. Oh, Signore—Holy Virgin!" Recovering herself, she sank into a chair, and sat stiff and superb, listening to the deepening sound of the wheels. The vehicle approached, reached the inn, passed it, and went on to the Dogana.

"You're safe," I said. "It's not a posting-chaise, but a common wagon with merchandise."

With a hushed sigh of relief she passed her hand over her brow, and then looking at me: "I have lived these three days in constant terror. I believe in my soul he has come in pursuit of me; my hope is in my having gained time through his being absent when I started. My nerves are broken. I have neither slept nor eaten, nor till now have I spoken. But I *must* speak! I'm frank; it's good to take a friend when you find one."

I confess that to have been thus freely admitted by the fair fugitive into the whirling circle of her destiny was one of the keenest emotions of my life. "I know neither the motive of your flight nor the goal of your journey," I answered; "but if I may help you and speed you, I will joyfully turn back from the threshold of Italy and give you whatever furtherance my company may yield. To go with you," I added, smiling, "will be to remain in Italy, I assure you."

She acknowledged my offer with a glance more potent than words. "I'm going to a friend," she said, after a silence. "To accept your offer would be to make friendship cheap. He is lying ill at Geneva; otherwise I shouldn't be *thus!* But my head is on fire. This room is close; it smells of supper. Do me the favor to accompany me into the air."

She gathered her shawl about her shoulders, I offered her my arm, and we passed into the entry toward the door. In the doorway stood mine host, with his napkin under his arm. He drew himself up as we approached, and, as if to deprecate a possible imputation of scandal, honored us with a bow of the most ceremonious homage. We de-

scended the steps and strolled along the road toward the
Swiss frontier. A vague remnant of daylight seemed to
linger imprisoned in the narrow gorge. We passed the
Dogana and left the village behind us. My thoughts reverted as we went, to the aching blank of my fancy as I
entered Isella an hour before. It seemed to palpitate now
with a month's experience. Beyond the village a narrow
bridge spans the stream and leads to a path which climbs
the opposite hillside. We diverged from the road and lingered on the bridge while the sounding torrent gushed
beneath us, flashing in the light of the few stars which
sparkled in our narrow strip of sky, like diamonds tacked
upon a band of velvet. I remained silent, thinking a passive silence the most graceful tribute to the Signora's generous intentions. "I will tell you all!" she said at last.
"Do you think me pretty? But you needn't answer. The
less you think so, the more you'll say it. I *was* pretty! I
don't pretend to be so now. I have suffered too much. I
have a miserable fear that when *he* sees me, after these
three years, he'll notice the loss of my beauty. But, *pove-
rino!* he is perhaps too ill to notice anything. He is young
—a year younger than I—twenty-seven. He is a painter;
he has a most beautiful talent. He loved me four years
ago, before my marriage. He was a friend of my poor
brother, who was fatally wounded at the battle of Mentana,
where he fought with Garibaldi. My brother, Giuseppino,
was brought home with his wound; he died in a week.
Ernesto came to make a drawing of his face before we lost
it forever. It was not the first time I had seen him,
but it was the first time we understood each other. I was
sitting by poor Giuseppino's bedside, crying—crying! He,
too, cried while he drew and made great blisters on the
paper. I know where to look for them still. They loved
each other devotedly. I, too, had loved my brother! for
my mother was dead, and my father was not a mother—
not even a father! Judge for yourself! We placed together the love which each of us had borne for Giuseppino,
and it made a great love for each other. It was a misfortune; but how could we help it? He had nothing but

his talent, which as yet was immature. I had nothing at
all but the poor little glory of my father's being a Marchese,
without a *soldo*, and my prettiness! But you see what has
become of that! My father was furious to have given his
only son to that scoundrel of a Garibaldi, for he is of that
way of thinking. You should have heard the scene he
made me when poor Ernesto in despair asked leave to marry
me. My husband, whom I had never seen or at least never
noticed, was at that time in treaty for my hand. By his
origin he was little better than a peasant, but he had made
a fortune in trade, and he was very well pleased to marry a
marchesina. It's not every man who is willing to take a
penniless girl; it was the first chance and perhaps the best.
So I was given over blindfold, bound hand and foot, to that
brute. Eh! what I hadn't brought in cash I had to pay
down in patience. If I were to tell you what I've suffered
these three years, it would bring tears to your eyes—
Inglese as you are. But they are things which can't be
told. He is a peasant, with the soul of a peasant—the
taste, the manner, the vices of a peasant. It was my
great crime that I was proud. I had much to be proud
of. If I had only been a woman of his own sort! to pay
him in his own coin! Ernesto, of course, had been altogether suppressed. He proposed to me to escape with him
before my marriage, and I confess to you that I would
have done it if I could. I tried in vain; I was too well
watched. I implored him then to go away till better days;
and he at last consented to go to Paris and pursue his
studies. A week after my marriage he came to bid me
farewell. My husband had taken me to Naples, to make
me believe I was not wretched. Ernesto followed me, and I
contrived to see him. It lasted three minutes by the clock:
I have not seen him since. In three years I have had five
letters from him; they are here in my dress. I am sure of
his love; I don't need to have him write, to tell me. I have
answered him twice. These letters—seven in all, in three
years!—are all my husband has to reproach me with. He
is furious at not having more. He knows of course that
I love another; he knows that to bear such things a woman

must borrow strength somewhere. I have had faith, but it has not been all faith! My husband has none; nothing is sacred to him, not the Blessed Virgin herself. If you were to hear the things he says about the Holy Father! I have waited and waited. I confess it, I have hoped at times that my husband would die. But he has the health of a peasant. He used to strike me—to starve me—to lock me up without light or fire. I appealed to my father, but, I'm sorry to say it, my father is a coward! Heaven forgive me! I'm saying dreadful things here! But, ah, Signore, let me breathe at last! I've waited and waited, as I say, for this hour! Heaven knows I have been good. Though I stand here now, I have not trifled with my duties. It's not coquetry! I determined to endure as long as I could, and then to break—to break forever! A month ago strength and courage left me; or rather, they came to me! I wrote to Ernesto that I would come to him. He answered that he would come down to meet me—if possible at Milan. Just afterwards he wrote me in a little scrawl in pencil that he had been taken ill in Geneva, and that if I could I must come alone, before he got worse. Here I am then, alone, pursued, frantic with ignorance and dread. Heaven only keep him till I come. I shall do the rest! Exactly how I left home, I can't tell you. It has been like a dream! My husband—God be praised!—was obliged to make a short absence on business, of which I took advantage. My great trouble was getting a little money. I never have any. I sold a few trinkets for a few francs—hardly enough! The people saw I was too frightened to make a stand, so that they cheated me. But if I can only come to the end! I'm certain that my husband has pursued me. Once I get to Switzerland, we can hide. Meanwhile I'm in a fever. I've lost my head. I began very well, but all this delay has so vexed and confused me. I hadn't even the wit to secure a place in the coach at Domo d'Ossola. But I shall go, if I have to sit on the roof—to crouch upon the doorstep. If I had only a little more money, so that I needn't wait for coaches. To overtake me my husband, for once in his life, won't count his *lire!*"

I listened with a kind of awe to this torrent of passionate confidence. I had got more even than I had bargained for. The current of her utterance seemed to gather volume as it came, and she poured out her tragic story with a sort of rapturous freedom. She had unburdened at last her heavy heart. As she spoke, the hot breath of her eloquence seemed to pass far beyond my single attentive sense, and mingle joyously with the free air of the night. Her tale, in a measure, might be untrue or imperfect; but her passion, her haste, her sincerity, were imperiously real. I felt, as I had never felt it, the truth of the poet's claim for his touch of nature. I became conscious of a hurrying share in my companion's dread. I seemed to hear in the trembling torrent the sound of rapid wheels. I expected every moment to see the glare of lights along the road, before the inn, then a strong arm locked about her waist, and, in the ray of a lantern from the carriage window, to catch the mute agony of her solemn eyes. My heart beat fast; I was part and parcel of a romance! Come! the *dénouement* shouldn't fail by any prosy fault of mine.

"How I've talked!" cried the Signora, after a brief pause. "And how you stare at me! Eh! don't be afraid. I've said all, and it has done me good. You'll laugh with your *promessa sposa* about that crazy creature who was flying from her husband. The idea of people not being happy in marriage, you'll say to her!"

"I thank you with all my heart," I said, "for having trusted me as you have. But I'm almost sorry you have taken the time. You oughtn't to be lingering here while your husband is making the dust fly."

"That's easy to say, Signore; but I can't walk to Brieg, like you. A carriage costs a hundred and fifty francs. I have only just enough to pay my place in the coach."

I drew out my portemonnaie and emptied it in my hand; it contained a hundred and seventy-five francs. *"Ecco!"* I said, holding them out to her.

She glanced at them an instant, and then, with a movement which effectually rounded and completed my impression of her simple and passionate sincerity, seized with both her hands my own hand as it held them. "Ah, the Blessed Virgin be praised!" she cried. "Ah, you're an angel from heaven! Quick, quick! A carriage, a carriage!"

She thrust the money into her pocket, and, without waiting for an answer, hurried back to the road, and moved swiftly toward the inn. I overtook her as she reached the doorstep, where our host was enjoying a pipe in the cool. "A carriage!" she cried. "I must be off. Quick, without delay! I have the money; you shall be well paid. Don't tell me you haven't one. There must be one here. Find one, prepare it, lose not a moment. Do you think I can lie tossing here all night? I shall put together my things, and give you ten minutes! You, sir, see that they hurry!" And she rapidly entered the house.

Bonifazio stared, somewhat aghast at the suddenness and the energy of her requisition. Fearing that he might not be equal to the occasion, I determined to take him by his gallantry. "Come, my friend," I said, "don't stand scratching your head, but *act*. I know you admire the Signora. You don't want to see so charming a woman in trouble. You don't wish to have a scandal in your inn. It is of the first importance that she should leave in ten minutes. Stir up your hostler."

A wise grin illumined his face. "Ah," said he, "it's as bad as that. I had my notions. I'll do what I can." He exerted himself to such good purpose that in the incredibly short period of twenty minutes a small closed carriage was drawn by a couple of stout horses to the door. Going in to summon the fair fugitive, I found her in the dining-room, where, fretting with impatience, and hooded and shawled, she had suffered a rather bungling chambermaid to attempt the insertion of a couple of necessary pins. She swept past me on her exit as if she had equally forgotten my face and her obligations, and entered the carriage with passionate adjurations of haste. I followed her and watched her take her place; but she seemed not even to see me. My hour was over. I had added an impulse to her straining purpose; its hurrying current had left me alone on the brink. I could not resist the influence of a poignant regret at having dropped from her consciousness. Learning from a peasant who was lounging near at hand that an easy footpath wound along the side of the mountain and struck the highroad at the end of half an hour's walk, I immediately discovered and followed it. I saw beneath me in the dimness as I went the white highroad, with the carriage slowly beginning its ascent. Descending at last from the slope, I met the vehicle well on its way up the mountain, and motioned to the driver to stop. The poor Signora, haunted with the fear of interruption, thrust her pale face from the window. Seeing me, she stared an instant almost vacantly, and then passing her hand over her face broke into a glorious smile. Flinging open the carriage door from within, she held out her two hands in farewell.

"Give me your blessing," she cried, "and take mine! I had almost forgotten you. Love is selfish, Signore. But I should have remembered you later and cried with gratitude. My Ernesto will write to you. Give me your card—write me your address, there in the carriage lamp. No? As you please, then. Think of me kindly. And the young girl you marry—use her well—love her if only a little—it will be enough. We ask but a little, but we need that. Addio!" and she raised her two hands to her lips, seemed for an instant to exhale her whole soul upon her finger tips, and flung into the air a magnificent Italian kiss.

I returned along the winding footpath more slowly, a wiser, possibly a sadder man than a couple of hours before. I had entered Italy, I had tasted of sentiment, I had assisted at a drama. It was a good beginning. I found Bonifazio finishing his pipe before the inn. "Well, well, Signore," he cried, "what does it all mean?"

"Aren't you enough of an Italian to guess?" I asked.

"Eh, eh, it's better to be an Inglese and to be told," cried Bonifazio with a twinkle.

"You must sleep to-night with an ear open," I said. "A personage will arrive post-haste from Domo. Stop him if you can."

Bonifazio scratched his head. "If a late supper or an early breakfast will stop him!" he murmured. I looked

deep into his little round eye, expecting to read there the
recipe for the infusion of a sleeping potion into *café au lait*.
My room that night was close and hot, and my bed
none of the best. I tossed about in a broken sleep. I
dreamed that I was lying ill in a poor tavern at Naples,
waiting, waiting with an aching heart, for the arrival from
the Baths of Lucca of a certain young lady, who had been
forced by her mother, Mrs. B. of Philadelphia, into a cruel
marriage with a wealthy Tuscan *contadino*. At last I
seemed to hear a great noise without and a step on the
stairs; through the opened door rushed in my *promessa
sposa*. Her blue eyes were bright with tears, and she wore
a flounced black dress trimmed with crimson silk. The
next moment she was kneeling at my bedside crying,
"Ernesto, Ernesto!" At this point I awoke into the early
morning. The noise of horses and wheels and voices came
up from outside. I sprang from my bed and stepped to
my open window. The huge, high-piled, yellow diligence
from Domo d'Ossola had halted before the inn. The door
of the *coupé* was open; from the aperture half emerged
the Personage. "A peasant," she had called him, but he
was well *dicrotti*, though he *hud* counted his *lire* and taken
the diligence. He struck me as of an odd type for an Italian: dark sandy hair, a little sandy moustache, waxed at
the ends, and sandy whiskers *à l'Anglaise*. He had a
broad face, a large nose, and a small keen eye, without
any visible brows. He wore a yellow silk handkerchief
tied as a nightcap about his head, and in spite of the heat
he was very much muffled. On the steps stood Bonifazio,
cap in hand, smiling and obsequious.

"Is there a lady here?" demanded the gentleman from
the *coupé*. "A lady alone—good-looking—with little luggage?"

"No lady, Signore," said Bonifazio. "Alas! I have an
empty house. If *eccellenza* would like to descend——"

"Have you had a lady—yesterday, last night? Don't
lie."

"We had three, *eccellenza*, a week ago—three Scotch

ladies going to Baveno. Nay, three days since we had a *prima donna* on her way to Milan."

"Damn your Scotch *prima donna!*" said the other. "Have you had my wife?"

"The wife of *eccellenza?* Save the ladies I mention, we have had neither wife nor maid. Would *eccellenza* like a cup of coffee?"

"*Sangue di Dio!*" was *eccellenza's* sole response. The *coupé* door closed with a slam, the conductor mounted, the six horses started and the great mountain coach rolled away.

GUEST'S CONFESSION

I

"ARRIVE half past eight. Sick. Meet me."

The telegrammatic brevity of my step-brother's missive gave that melancholy turn to my thoughts which was the usual result of his communications. He was to have come on the Friday; what had made him start off on Wednesday? The terms on which we stood were a perpetual source of irritation. We were utterly unlike in temper and taste and opinions, and yet, having a number of common interests, we were obliged, after a fashion, to compromise with each other's idiosyncrasies. In fact, the concessions were all on my side. He was altogether too much my superior in all that makes the man who counts in the world for me not to feel it, and it cost me less to let him take his way than to make a stand for my dignity. What I did through indolence and in some degree, I confess, through pusillanimity, I had a fancy to make it appear (by dint of much whistling, as it were, and easy thrusting of my hands into my pockets) that I did through a sort of generous condescension. Edgar cared little enough upon what recipe I compounded a salve for my vanity, so long as he held his own course; and I am afraid I played the slumbering giant to altogether empty benches. There had been, indeed, a vague tacit understanding that he was to treat me, in form, as a man with a mind of his own, and there was occasionally something most incisively sarcastic in his observance of the treaty. What made matters the worse for me, and the better for him, was an absurd physical disparity; for Musgrave was like nothing so much as Falstaff's description of Shallow,—a man made after supper of a cheese-paring. He was a miserable invalid, and was perpetually concerned with his stomach, his lungs, and his liver, and as he was both doctor and patient in one, they kept him very busy. His head was grotesquely large for his diminutive figure, his eye fixed and salient, and his complexion liable to flush with an air of indignation and suspicion. He practised a most resolute little strut on a most attenuated pair of little legs. For myself, I was tall, happily; for I was broad enough, if I had been shorter, to have perhaps incurred that invidious monosyllabic epithet which haunted Lord Byron. As compared with Edgar, I was at least fairly good-looking; a stoutish, blondish, indolent, amiable, rather gorgeous young fellow might have served as my personal formula. My patrimony, being double that of my step-brother (for we were related by my mother), was largely lavished on the adornment of this fine person. I dressed in fact, as I recollect, with a sort of barbaric splendor, and I may very well have passed for one of the social pillars of a small watering-place.

L—— was in those days just struggling into fame, and but that it savored overmuch of the fresh paint lately lavished upon the various wooden barracks in which visitors were to be accommodated, it yielded a pleasant mixture of rurality and society. The vile taste and the sovereign virtue of the spring were fairly established, and Edgar was not the man to forego the chance of trying the waters and abusing them. Having heard that the hotel was crowded, he wished to secure a room at least a week beforehand; the upshot of which was, that I came down on the 19th of July with the mission to retain and occupy his apartment till the 26th. I passed, with people in general, and with Edgar in particular, for so very idle a person that it seemed almost a duty to saddle me with some wholesome errand. Edgar had, first and always, his health to attend to, and then that neat little property and those everlasting accounts, which he was never weary of contemplating, verifying, and overhauling. I had made up my mind to make over his room to him, remain a day or two for civility's sake and then leave him to his cups. Meanwhile, on the

24th, it occurred to me that I ought really to see something of the place. The weather had been too hot for going about, and, as yet, I had hardly left the piazza of the hotel. Towards afternoon the clouds gathered, the sun was obscured, and it seemed possible even for a large, lazy man to take a walk. I went along beside the river, under the trees, rejoicing much in the midsummer prettiness of all the land and in the sultry afternoon stillness. I was discomposed and irritated, and all for no better reason than that Edgar was coming. What was Edgar that his comings and goings should affect me? Was I, after all, so excessively his younger brother? I would turn over a new leaf! I almost wished things would come to a crisis between us, and that in the glow of exasperation I might say or do something unpardonable. But there was small chance of my quarrelling with Edgar for vanity's sake. Somehow, I didn't believe in my own egotism, but I had an indefeasible respect for his. I was fatally good-natured, and I should continue to do his desire until I began to do that of some one else. If I might only fall in love and exchange my master for a mistress, for some charming goddess of unreason who would declare that Mr. Musgrave was simply intolerable and that was an end of it!

So, meditating vaguely, I arrived at the little Episcopal chapel, which stands on the margin of the village where the latter begins to melt away into the large river-side landscape. The door was slightly ajar: there came through it into the hot outer stillness the low sound of an organ,— the rehearsal, evidently, of the organist or of some gentle amateur. I was warm with walking, and this glimpse of the cool musical dimness within prompted me to enter and rest and listen. The body of the church was empty; but a feeble glow of color was diffused through the little yellow and crimson windows upon the pews and the cushioned pulpit. The organ was erected in a small gallery facing the chancel, into which the ascent was by a short stairway directly from the church. The sound of my tread was apparently covered by the music, for the player continued without heeding me, hidden as she was behind a little blue silk curtain on the edge of the gallery. Yes, that gentle, tentative, unprofessional touch came from a feminine hand. Uncertain as it was, however, it wrought upon my musical sensibilities with a sort of provoking force. The air was familiar, and, before I knew it, I had begun to furnish the vocal accompaniment,—first gently, then boldly. Standing with my face to the organ, I awaited the effect of my venture. The only perceptible result was that, for a moment, the music faltered and the curtains were stirred. I saw nothing, but I had been seen, and, reassured apparently by my aspect, the organist resumed the chant. Slightly mystified, I felt urged to sing my best, the more so that, as I continued, the player seemed to borrow confidence and emulation from my voice. The notes rolled out bravely, and the little vault resounded. Suddenly there seemed to come to the musician, in the ardor of success, a full accession of vigor and skill. The last chords were struck with a kind of triumphant intensity, and their cadence was marked by a clear soprano voice. Just at the close, however, voice and music were swallowed up in the roll of a huge thunder-clap. At the same instant, the storm-drops began to strike the chapel-windows, and we were sheeted in a summer rain. The rain was a bore; but, at least, I should have a look at the organist, concerning whom my curiosity had suddenly grown great. The thunder-claps followed each other with such violence that it was vain to continue to play. I waited, in the confident belief that that charming voice—half a dozen notes had betrayed it—denoted a charming woman. After the lapse of some moments, which seemed to indicate a graceful and appealing hesitancy, a female figure appeared at the top of the little stairway and began to descend. I walked slowly down the aisle. The stormy darkness had rapidly increased, and at this moment, with a huge burst of thunder, following a blinding flash, a momentary midnight fell upon our refuge. When things had become visible again, I beheld the fair musician at the foot of the steps, gazing at me with all the frankness of agitation. The little chapel was rattling to its foundations.

"Do you think there is any danger?" asked my companion.

I made haste to assure her there was none. "The chapel has nothing in the nature of a spire, and even if it had, the fact of our being in a holy place ought to insure us against injury."

She looked at me wonderingly, as if to see whether I was in jest. To satisfy her, I smiled as graciously as I might. Whereupon, gathering confidence, "I think we have each of us," she said, "so little right to be here that we can hardly claim the benefit of sanctuary."

"Are you too an interloper?" I asked.

She hesitated a moment. "I'm not an Episcopalian," she replied; "I'm a good Unitarian."

"Well, I'm a poor Episcopalian. It's six of one and half a dozen of the other." There came another long, many-sheeted flash and an immediate wild reverberation. My companion, as she stood before me, was vividly illumined from head to feet. It was as if some fierce natural power had designed to interpose her image on my soul forever, in this merciless electric glare. As I saw her then, I have never ceased to see her since. I have called her fair, but the word needs explanation. Singularly pleasing as she was, it was with a charm that was all her own. Not the charm of beauty, but of a certain intense expressiveness, which seems to have given beauty the go-by in the very interest of grace. Slender, meagre, without redundancy of outline or brilliancy of color, she was a person you might never have noticed, but would certainly never forget. What there was was so charming, what there was might be so interesting! There was none of the idleness of conscious beauty in her clear gray eyes; they seemed charged with the impatience of a restless mind. Her glance and smile, her step and gesture, were as light and distinct as a whispered secret. She was nervous, curious, zealous, slightly imperious, and delicately elegant withal; without which, possibly, she might have seemed a trifle too positive. There is a certain sweet unreason in a picturesque toilet. She was dressed in a modish adjustment of muslins and lace, which denoted the woman who may have fancied that even less beauty might yet please. While I drew my conclusions,—they were eminently flattering,—my companion was buttoning her gloves and looking anxiously at the dripping windows. Wishing, as far as I might, to beguile her impatience, I proceeded to apologize for the liberty I had taken in singing to her music. "My best excuse," I said, "is your admirable playing, and my own most sensitive ear!"

"You might have frightened me away," she answered. "But you sang too well for that, better than I played. In fact, I was afraid to stop, I thought you might be one of the—the hierarchy."

"A bishop!"

"A bishop,—a dean,—a deacon,—or something of that sort."

"The sexton, perhaps."

"Before the sexton I should have succumbed. I take it his business would have been to eject me as a meddlesome heretic. I came in for no better reason than that the church door was ajar."

"As a church door ought always to be."

She looked at me a moment. "No; see what comes of it."

"No great harm, it seems to me."

"O, that's very well for us! But a church shouldn't be made a place of convenience."

I wished, in the interest of our growing intimacy, to make a point. "If it is not a place of convenience," I ventured to propound, deprecating offence with a smile, "what is it?"

It was an observation I afterwards made, that in cases when many women drop their eyes and look prettily silly or prudishly alarmed, this young lady's lucid glance would become more unaffectedly direct and searching. "Indeed," she answered, "you *are* but an indifferent Episcopalian! I came in because the door was open, because I was warm with my walk, and because, I confess, I have an especial fondness for going into churches on week-days. One does it in Europe, you know; and it reminds me of Europe."

I cast a glance over the naked tabernacle, with the counterfeit graining scarcely dry on its beams and planks, and a strong aroma of turpentine and putty representing the odor of sanctity. She followed my glance; our eyes met, and we laughed. From this moment we talked with a freedom tempered less by the sanctity of the spot than by a certain luxury of deference with which I felt prompted to anticipate possible mistrust. The rain continued to descend with such steady good-will that it seemed needful to accept our situation frankly and conjure away the spirit of awkwardness. We spoke of L——, of the people there, of the hot weather, of music. She had as yet seen little of the place, having been confined to her apartments by domestic reasons. I wondered what her domestic reasons were. She had come forth at last to call upon a friend at one of the boarding-houses which adorned this suburb of the village. Her friend being out, but likely soon to return, she had sought entertainment in a stroll along the road, and so had wandered into the chapel. Our interview lasted half an hour. As it drew to a close, I fancied there had grown up between us some delicate bond, begotten of our mutual urbanity. I might have been indiscreet; as it was, I took my pleasure in tracing the gradual evanescence of my companion's sense of peril. As the moments elapsed, she sat down on the bench with an air of perfect equanimity, and looked patiently at the trickling windows. The still small voice of some familiar spirit of the Lord, haunting the dedicated vault, seemed to have audibly blessed our meeting. At last the rain abated and suddenly stopped, and through a great rift in the clouds there leaped a giant sunbeam and smote the trickling windows. Through little gaudy lozenges the chapel was flooded with prismatic light. "The storm is over," said my companion. She spoke without rising, as if she had been cheated of the sense of haste. Was it calculated civility, or was it momentary self-oblivion? Whatever it was, it lasted but a moment. We were on our feet and moving toward the door. As we stood in the porch, honest gallantry demanded its rights.

"I never knew before," I said, "the possible blessings of a summer rain."

She proceeded a few steps before she answered. Then glancing at the shining sky, already blue and free, "In ten minutes," she said, "there will be no trace of it!"

"Does that mean," I frankly demanded, "that we are not to meet again as friends?"

"Are we to meet again at all?"

"I count upon it."

"Certainly, then, not as enemies!" As she walked away, I imprecated those restrictions of modern civilization which forbade me to stand and gaze at her.

Who was she? What was she?—questions the more intense as, in the absence of any further evidence than my rapid personal impression, they were so provokingly vain. They occupied me, however, during the couple of hours which were to elapse before my step-brother's arrival. When his train became due, I went through the form, as usual, of feeling desperately like treating myself to the luxury of neglecting his summons and leaving him to shift for himself; as if I had not the most distinct prevision of the inevitable event,—of my being at the station half an hour too early, of my calling his hack and making his bargain and taking charge of his precious little hand-bag, full of medicine-bottles, and his ridiculous bundle of umbrellas and canes. Somehow, this evening, I felt unwontedly loath and indocile; but I contented myself with this bold flight of the imagination.

It is hard to describe fairly my poor step-brother's peculiar turn of mind, to give an adequate impression of his want of social charm, to put it mildly, without accusing him of wilful malevolence. He was simply the most consistent and incorruptible of egotists. He was perpetually affirming and defining and insuring himself, insisting upon a personal right or righting a personal wrong. And above all, he was a man of conscience. He asked no odds, and he gave none. He made honesty something unlovely, but he was rigidly honest. He demanded simply his dues, and he collected them to the last farthing. These things gave him a portentous solemnity. He smiled perhaps once a month, and made a joke once in six. There are jokes of his making which, to this day, give me a shiver when I think of them. But I soon perceived, as he descended from the train, that there would be no joke that evening. Something had happened. His face was hard and sombre, and his eye bright and fierce. "A carriage," he said, giving me his hand stiffly. And when we were seated and driving away, "First of all," he demanded, "are there any mosquitoes? A single mosquito would finish me. And is my room habitable, on the shady side, away from the stairs, with a view, with a hair-mattress?" I assured him that mosquitoes were unknown, and that his room was the best, and his mattress the softest in the house. Was he tired? how had he been?

"Don't ask me. I'm in an extremely critical state. Tired? Tired is a word for well people! When I'm tired I shall go to bed and die. Thank God, so long as I have any work to do, I can hold up my head! I haven't slept in a week. It's singular, but I'm never so well disposed for my duties as when I haven't slept! But be so good, for the present, as to ask me no questions. I shall immediately take a bath and drink some arrow-root; I have brought a package in my bag, I suppose I can get them to make it. I'll speak about it at the office. No, I think, on the whole, I'll make it in my room; I have a little machine for boiling water. I think I shall drink half a glass of the spring to-night, just to make a beginning."

All this was said with as profound a gravity as if he were dictating his will. But I saw that he was at a sort of white-heat exasperation, and I knew that in time I should learn where the shoe pinched. Meanwhile, I attempted to say something cheerful and frivolous, and offered some information as to who was at the hotel and who was expected; "No one you know or care about, I think."

"Very likely not. I'm in no mood for gossip."

"You seem nervous," I ventured to say.

"Nervous? Call it frantic! I'm not blessed with your apathetic temperament, nor with your elegant indifference

to money-matters. Do you know what's the matter with
me? I've lost twenty thousand dollars."

I, of course, demanded particulars; but, for the present,
I had to content myself with the naked fact. "It's a
mighty serious matter," said Edgar. "I can't talk of it
further till I have bathed and changed my linen. The ther-
mometer has been at ninety-one in my rooms in town.
I've had this pretty piece of news to keep me cool."

I left him to his bath, his toilet, and his arrow-root
and strolled about pondering the mystery of his disaster.
Truly, if Edgar had lost money, shrewdness was out of
tune. Destiny must have got up early to outwit my step-
brother. And yet his misfortune gave him a sort of unwonted grace, and I believe I wondered for five minutes
whether there was a chance of his being relaxed and softened
by it. I had, indeed, a momentary vision of lending him
money, and taking a handsome revenge as a good-natured
creditor. But Edgar would never borrow. He would
either recover his money or grimly do without it. On going
back to his room I found him dressed and refreshed, screw-
ing a little portable kettle upon his gas-burner.

"You can never get them to bring you water that really
boils," he said. "They don't know what it means. You're
altogether wrong about the mosquitoes; I'm sure I heard
one, and by the sound, he's a monster. But I have a net
folded up in my trunk, and a hook and ring which I mean
to drive into the ceiling."

"I'll put up your net. Meanwhile, tell me about your
twenty thousand dollars."

He was silent awhile, but at last he spoke in a voice
forcibly attuned to composure. "You're immensely tickled,
I suppose, to find me losing money! That comes of worry-
ing too much and handling my funds too often. Yes, I
have worried too much." He paused, and then, suddenly, he
broke out into a kind of fury. "I hate waste, I hate shift-
lessness, I hate nasty mismanagement! I hate to see money
bring in less than it may. My imagination loves a good
investment. I respect my property, I respect other
people's. But your own honesty is all you'll find in this

world, and it will go no farther than you're there to carry
it. You've always thought me hard and suspicious and
grasping. No, you never said so; should I have cared if
you had? With your means, it's all very well to be a fine
gentleman, to skip the items and glance at the total. But,
being poor and sick, I have to be close. I wasn't close
enough. What do you think of my having been cheated?
—cheated under my very nose? I hope I'm genteel enough
now!"

"I should like to see the man!" I cried.

"You shall see him. All the world shall see him. I've
been looking into the matter. It has been beautifully done.
If I were to be a rascal, I should like to be just such a
one."

"Who is your rascal?"

"His name is John Guest."

I had heard the name, but had never seen the man.

"No, you don't know him," Edgar went on. "No one
knows him but I. But I know him well. He had things
in his hands for a week, while I was debating a transfer of
my New Jersey property. In a week this is how he mixed
matters."

"Perhaps, if you had given him time," I suggested, "he
meant to get them straight again."

"O, I shall give him time. I mean he shall get 'em
straight, or I shall twist him so crooked his best friend
won't know him."

"Did you never suspect his honesty?"

"Do you suspect mine?"

"But you have legal redress?"

"It's no thanks to him. He had fixed things to a charm,
he had done his best to cut me off and cover his escape.
But I've got him, and he shall disgorge!"

I hardly know why it was; but the implacable firmness
of my brother's position produced in my mind a sort of
fantastic reaction in favor of Mr. John Guest. I felt a
sudden gush of the most inconsequent pity. "Poor man!"
I exclaimed. But to repair my weakness, I plunged into a
series of sympathetic questions and listened attentively to

Edgar's statement of his wrongs. As he set forth the case, I found myself taking a whimsical interest in Mr. Guest's own side of it, wondering whether he suspected suspicion, whether he dreaded conviction, whether he had an easy conscience, and how he was getting through the hot weather. I asked Edgar how lately he had discovered his loss and whether he had since communicated with the criminal.

"Three days ago, three nights ago, rather; for I haven't slept a wink since. I have spoken of the matter to no one; for the present I need no one's help, I can help myself. I haven't seen the man more than three or four times; our dealings have generally been by letter. The last person you'd suspect. He's as great a dandy as you yourself, and in better taste, too. I was told ten days ago, at his office, that he had gone out of town. I suppose I'm paying for his champagne at Newport."

II

On my proposing, half an hour later, to relieve him of my society and allow him to prepare for rest, Edgar declared that our talk had put an end to sleep and that he must take a turn in the open air. On descending to the piazza, we found it in the deserted condition into which it usually lapsed about ten o'clock; either from a wholesome desire on the part of our fellow-lodgers to keep classic country hours, or from the soporific influences of excessive leisure. Here and there the warm darkness was relieved by the red tip of a cigar in suggestive proximity to a light corsage. I observed, as we strolled along, a lady of striking appearance, seated in the zone of light projected from a window, in conversation with a gentleman. "Really, I'm afraid you'll take cold," I heard her say as we passed. "Let me tie my handkerchief round your neck." And she gave it a playful twist. She was a pretty woman, of middle age, with great freshness of toilet and complexion, and a picturesque abundance of blond hair, upon which was coquettishly poised a fantastic little hat, decorated with an immense pink rose. Her companion was a seemingly affable man, with a bald head, a white waistcoat, and a rather florid air of distinction. When we passed them a second time, they had risen and the lady was preparing to enter the house. Her companion went with her to the door; she left him with a great deal of coquettish by-play, and he turned back to the piazza. At this moment his glance fell upon my step-brother. He started, I thought, and then, replacing his hat with an odd, nervous decision, came towards him with a smile. "Mr. Musgrave!" he said.

Edgar stopped short, and for a moment seemed to lack words to reply. At last he uttered a deep, harsh note: "Mr. Guest!"

In an instant I felt that I was in the presence of a "situation." Edgar's words had the sound of the "click" upon the limb of the entrapped fox. A scene was imminent; the actors were only awaiting their cues. Mr. Guest made a half-offer of his hand, but, perceiving no response in Edgar's, he gracefully dipped it into his pocket. "You must have just come!" he murmured.

"A couple of hours ago."

Mr. Guest glanced at me, as if to include me in the operation of his urbanity, and his glance stirred in my soul an impulse of that kindness which we feel for a man about to be executed. It's no more than human to wish to shake hands with him. "Introduce me, Edgar," I said.

"My step-brother," said Edgar, curtly. "This is Mr. Guest, of whom we have been talking."

I put out my hand; he took it with cordiality. "Really," he declared, "this is a most unexpected—a—circumstance."

"Altogether so to me," said Edgar.

"You've come for the waters, I suppose," our friend went on. "I'm sorry your health continues—a—unsatisfactory."

Edgar, I perceived, was in a state of extreme nervous exacerbation, the result partly of mere surprise and partly of keen disappointment. His plans had been checked. He had determined to do thus and so, and he must now extemporize a policy. Well, as poor, pompous Mr. Guest wished it, so he should have it! "I shall never be strong," said Edgar.

"Well, well," responded Mr. Guest, "a man of your parts may make a little strength serve a great purpose."

My step-brother was silent a moment, relishing secretly, I think, the beautiful pertinence of this observation. "I suppose I can defend my rights," he rejoined.

"Exactly! What more does a man need?" and he appealed to me with an insinuating smile. His smile was singularly frank and agreeable, and his glance full of a sort of conciliating gallantry. I noted in his face, however, by the gaslight, a haggard, jaded look which lent force to what he went on to say. "I have been feeling lately as if I hadn't even strength for that. The hot weather, an overdose of this abominable water, one thing and another, the inevitable premonitions of—a—mortality, have quite pulled me down. Since my arrival here, ten days ago, I have really been quite—a—the invalid. I've actually been in bed. A most unprecedented occurrence!"

"I hope you're better," I ventured to say.

"Yes, I think I'm myself again,—thanks to capital nursing. I think I'm myself again!" He repeated his words mechanically, with a sort of exaggerated gayety, and began to wipe his forehead with his handkerchief. Edgar was watching him narrowly, with an eye whose keenness it was impossible to veil; and I think Edgar's eye partly caused his disquiet. "The last thing I did, by the way, before my indisposition, was to write you ten lines, Mr. Musgrave, on—a little matter of business."

"I got your letter," said Edgar grimly.

Mr. Guest was silent a moment. "And I hope my arrangements have met your approval?"

"We shall talk of that," said Edgar.

At this point, I confess, my interest in the situation had become painful. I felt sick. I'm not a man of ready-made resolution, as my story will abundantly prove. I am discountenanced and bullied by disagreeable things. Poor Mr. Guest was so infallibly booked for exposure that I instinctively retreated. Taking advantage of his allusion to business, I turned away and walked to the other end of the piazza. This genial gentleman, then, was embodied fraud! this sayer of civil things was a doer of monstrously shabby ones! that irreproachable white waistcoat carried so sadly spotted a conscience! Whom had he involved in his dishonor? Had he a wife, children, friends? Who was that so prosperously pretty woman, with her flattering solicitude for his health? I stood for some time reflecting how guilt is not the vulgar bugaboo we fancy it,—that it has organs, senses, affections, passions, for all the world like those of innocence. Indeed, from my cursory observation of my friend, I had rarely seen innocence so handsomely featured. Where, then, was the line which severed rectitude from error? Was manhood a baser thing than I had fancied, or was sin a thing less base? As I mused thus, my disgust ebbed away, and the return of the wave brought an immense curiosity to see what it had come to betwixt guilt and justice. Had Edgar launched his thunder? I retraced my steps and rejoined my companions. Edgar's thunder was apparently still in the clouds; but there had been a premonitory flash of lightning. Guest stood before him, paler than before, staring defiantly, and stammering out some fierce denial. "I don't understand you," he said. "If you mean what you seem to mean, you mean rank insult."

"I mean the truth," said Edgar. "It's a pity the truth should be insulting."

Guest glared a moment, like a man intently taking thought for self-defence. But he was piteously unmasked. His genial smile had taken flight and left mere vulgar confusion. "This is between ourselves, sir," he cried, angrily turning to me.

"A thousand pardons," I said, and passed along. I began to be doubtful as to the issue of the quarrel. Edgar had right on his side, but, under the circumstances, he might not have force. Guest was altogether the stouter, bigger, weightier person. I turned and observed them from a distance. Edgar's thunderbolt had fallen and his victim stood stunned. He was leaning against the balustrade of the piazza, with his chin on his breast and his eyes sullenly fixed on his adversary, demoralized and convicted. His hat had dropped upon the floor. Edgar seemed to have made a proposal; with a passionate gesture he repeated it. Guest slowly stooped and picked up his hat, and Edgar led the way toward the house. A series of small sitting-rooms opened by long windows upon the piazza. These were for the most part lighted and empty. Edgar selected one of them, and, stopping before the window, beckoned to me to come to him. Guest, as I advanced, bestowed upon me a scowl of concentrated protest. I felt, for my own part, as if I were horribly indelicate. Between Edgar and him it was a question of morals, but between him and myself it was, of course, but one of manners. "Be so good as to walk in," said Edgar, turning to me with a smile of unprecedented suavity. I might have resisted his dictation; I couldn't his petition.

"In God's name, what do you mean to do?" demanded Guest.

"My duty!" said Edgar. "Go in."

We passed into the room. The door of the corridor was open; Guest closed it with a passionate kick. Edgar shut the long window and dropped the curtain. In the same fury of mortification, Guest turned out one of the two burners of the chandelier. There was still light enough, however, for me to see him more distinctly than on the piazza. He was tallish and stoutish, and yet sleek and jaunty. His fine blue eye was a trifle weak, perhaps, and his handsome grizzled beard was something too foppishly trimmed; but, on the whole, he was a most comely man. He was dressed with the punctilious elegance of a man who loved luxury and appreciated his own good points. A little moss-rose-bud figured in the lappet of his dark-blue coat. His whole person seemed redolent of what are called the "feelings of a gentleman." Confronted and contrasted with him under the lamp, my step-brother seemed wofully mean and gro-tesque; though for a conflict of forces that lay beneath the surface, he was visibly the better equipped of the two. He seemed to tremble and quiver with inexorable purpose. I felt that he would heed no admonitory word of mine, that I could not in the least hope to blunt the edge of his re-

sentiment, and that I must on the instant decide either to
stand by him or leave him. But while I stood thus ungraciously gazing at poor Guest, the instant passed. Curiosity and a mingled sympathy with each—to say nothing
of a touch of that relish for a fight inherent in the truly
masculine bosom—sealed my lips and arrested my steps.
And yet my heart paid this graceful culprit the compliment
of beating very violently on his behalf.

"I wish you to repeat before my brother," said Edgar,
"the three succinct denials to which you have just treated
me."

Guest looked at the ceiling with a trembling lip. Then
dropping upon the sofa, he began to inspect his handsome
finger-nails mechanically, in the manner of one who hears
in some horrible hush of all nature the nearing foosteps
of doom. "Come, repeat them!" cried Edgar. "It's really
delicious. You never wrote to Stevens that you had my assent in writing to the sale of the bonds. You never showed
Stevens my telegram from Boston, and assured him that my
'Do as you think best' was a permission to raise money on
them. If it's not forgery sir, it's next door to it, and a
very flimsy partition between."

Guest leaned back on the sofa, with his hands grasping
his knees. "You might have let things stand a week or
so," he said, with unnatural mildness. "You might have
had common patience. Good God, there's a gentlemanly
way of doing things! A man doesn't begin to roar for a
pinch. I would have got things square again."

"O, it would have been a pity to spoil them! It was
such a pretty piece of knavery! Give the devil his due!"

"I would have rearranged matters," Guest went on. "It
was just a temporary convenience. I supposed I was deal-
ing with a man of common courtesy. But what are you to
say to a gentleman who says, 'Sir, I trust you,' and then
looks through the keyhole?"

"Upon my word, when I hear you scuttling through the
window," cried Edgar, "I think it's time I should break
down the door. For God's sake, don't nauseate me with
any more lies! You know as well as you sit there, that you

had neither chance nor means nor desire to redeem your
fraud. You'd cut the bridge behind you! You thought
you'd been knowing enough to eat your cake and have it,
to lose your virtue and keep your reputation, to sink half
my property through a trap-door and then stand whistling
and looking t' other way while I scratched my head and
wondered what the devil was in it! Sit down there and
write me your note for twenty thousand dollars at twenty
days."

Guest was silent a moment. "Propose something reasonable," he said, with the same tragic gentleness.

"I shall let the law reason about it."

Guest gave a little start and fixed his eyes on the ground.
"The law wouldn't help you," he answered, without looking up.

"Indeed! do you think it would help *you?* Stoddard and
Hale will help me. I spoke to them this morning."

Guest sprang to his feet. "Good heavens! I hope you
mentioned no names."

"Only one!" said Edgar.

Guest wiped his forehead and actually tried to smile.
"That was your own, of course! Well, sir, I hope they ad-
vised you to—a—temper justice with mercy."

"They are not parsons, Mr. Guest; they are lawyers.
They accept the case."

Guest dropped on the sofa, buried his face in his hands,
and burst into tears. "O my soul!" he cried. His soul,
poor man! was a rough term for name and fame and comfort and all that made his universe. It was a pitiful sight.

"Look here, Edgar," I said. "Don't press things too
hard. I'm not a parson either——"

"No, you've not that excuse for your sentimentality!"
Edgar broke out. "Here it is, of course! Here come folly
and fear and ignorance maundering against the primary
laws of life! Is rascality alone of all things in the world
to be handled without gloves? Didn't he press me hard?
He's danced his dance,—let him pay the piper! Am I a
child, a woman, a fool, to stand and haggle with a swindler?
Am I to go to the wall to make room for impudent fraud?

Not while I have eyes to know black from white! I'm a decent man. I'm this or I'm nothing. For twenty years I've done my best for order and thrift and honesty. I've never yielded an inch to the detestable sharp practice that meets one nowadays at every turn. I've hated fraud as I hate all bad economy; I've no more patience with it than a bull with a red rag. Fraud is fraud; it's waste, it's wantonness, it's chaos; and I shall never give it the go-by. When I catch it, I shall hold it fast, and call all honest men to see how vile and drivelling a thing it is!"

Guest sat rigidly fixed, with his eyes on the carpet. "Do you expect to get your money?" he finally demanded.

"My money be hanged! I expect to let people know how they may be served if they intrust their affairs to you! A man's property, sir, is a man's person. It's as if you had given be a blow in the chest!"

Guest came towards him and took him by the button-hole. "Now see here," he said, with the same desperate calmness. "You call yourself a practical man. Don't go on like one of those d—d long-haired reformers. You're off the track. Don't attempt too much. Don't make me confoundedly uncomfortable out of pure fantasticality. Come, sir, you're a man of the world." And he patted him gently on the shoulder. "Give me a chance. I confess to not having been quite square. There! My very dear sir, let me get on my legs again."

"O, you confess!" cried Edgar. "That's a vast comfort. You'll never do it again! Not if I know it. But other people, eh? Suppose I had been a decent widow with six children, and not a penny but that! You'd confess again, I suppose. Would your confession butter their bread! Let your confession be public!"

"My confession *is* public!" and Guest, with averted eyes, jerked his head towards me.

"O, my step-brother! Why, he's the most private creature in the world. Cheat him and he'll thank you! David, I retain you as a witness that Mr. Guest has confessed."

"Nothing will serve you then? You mean to prosecute?"

"I mean to prosecute."

The poor man's face flushed crimson, and the great sweat-drops trickled from his temples. "O you blundering brute!" he cried. "Do you know what you mean when you say that? Do we live in a civilized world?"

"Not altogether," said Edgar. "But I shall help it along."

"Have you lived among decent people? Have you known women whom it was an honor to please? Have you cared for name and fame and love? Have you had a dear daughter?"

"If I had a dear daughter," cried Edgar, flinching the least bit at this outbreak, "I trust my dear daughter would have kept me honest! Not the sin, then, but the detection unfits a man for ladies' society!—Did you kiss your daughter the day you juggled away my bonds?"

"If it will avail with you, I didn't. Consider her feelings. My fault has been that I have been too tender a father,—that I have loved the poor girl better than my own literal integrity. I became embarrassed because I hadn't the heart to tell her that she must spend less money. As if to the wisest sweetest girl in the world a whisper wouldn't have sufficed! As if five minutes of her divine advice wouldn't have set me straight again! But the stress of my embarrassment was such——"

"Embarrassment!" Edgar broke in. "That may mean anything. In the case of an honest man it may be a motive for leniency; in that of a knave it's a ground for increased suspicion."

Guest, I felt, was a good-natured sinner. Just as he lacked rectitude of purpose, he lacked rigidity of temper, and he found in the mysteries of his own heart no clew to my step-brother's monstrous implacability. Looking at him from head to foot with a certain dignity,—a reminiscence of his former pomposity,—"I do you the honor, sir," he said, "to believe you are insane."

"Stuff and nonsense! you believe nothing of the sort," cried Edgar.

I saw that Guest's opposition was acting upon him as a lively irritant. "Isn't it possible," I asked, "to adopt some compromise? You're not as forgiving a man under the circumstances as I should be."

"In these things," retorted Edgar, without ceremony, "a forgiving man is a fool."

"Well, take a fool's suggestion. You can perhaps get satisfaction without taking your victim into court.—Let Mr. Guest write his confession."

Guest had not directly looked at me since we entered the room. At these words he slowly turned and gave me a sombre stare by which the brilliancy of my suggestion seemed somewhat obscured. But my interference was kindly meant, and his reception of it seemed rather ungrateful. At best, however, I could be but a thorn in his side. I had done nothing to earn my sport. Edgar hereupon flourished his hand as if to indicate the superfluity of my advice. "All in good time, if you please. If I'm insane, there's a method in my madness!" He paused, and his eyes glittered with an intensity which might indeed, for the moment, have seemed to be that of a disordered brain. I wondered what was coming. "Do me the favor to get down on your knees." Guest jerked himself up as if he had received a galvanic shock. "Yes, I know what I say,—on your knees. Did you never say your prayers? You can't get out of a tight place without being squeezed. I won't take less. I sha'n't feel like an honest man till I've seen you there at my feet."

There was in the contrast between the inflated self-complacency of Edgar's face as he made this speech, and the blank horror of the other's as he received it, something so poignantly grotesque that it acted upon my nerves like a mistimed joke, and I burst into irrepressible laughter. Guest walked away to the window with some muttered imprecation, pushed aside the curtain, and stood looking out. Then, with a sudden turn, he marched back and stood before my brother. He was drenched with perspiration. "A moment," said Edgar. "You're very hot. Take off your coat." Guest, to my amazement, took it off and flung it upon the floor. "Your shirt-sleeves will serve as a kind of sackcloth and ashes. Fold your hands, so. Now, beg my pardon."

It was a revolting sight,—this man of ripe maturity and massive comeliness on his two knees, his pale face bent upon his breast, his body trembling with the effort to keep his shameful balance; and above him Edgar, with his hands behind his back, solemn and ugly as a miniature idol, with his glittering eyes fixed in a sort of rapture on the opposite wall. I walked away to the window. There was a perfect stillness, broken only by Guest's hard breathing. I have no notion how long it lasted; when I turned back into the room he was still speechless and fixed, as if he were ashamed to rise. Edgar pointed to a blotting-book and inkstand which stood on a small table against the wall. "See if there is pen and paper!" I obeyed and made a clatter at the table, to cover our companion's retreat. When I had laid out a sheet of paper he was on his feet again. "Sit down and write," Edgar went on. Guest picked up his coat and busied himself mechanically with brushing off the particles of dust. Then he put it on and sat down at the table.

"I dictate," Edgar began. "I hereby, at the command of Edgar Musgrave, Esq., whom I have grossly wronged, declare myself a swindler." At these words, Guest laid down the pen and sank back in his chair, emitting long groans, like a man with a violent toothache. But he had taken that first step which costs, and after a moment's rest he started afresh. "I have on my bended knees, in the presence of Mr. Musgrave and his step-brother, expressed my contrition; in consideration of which Mr. Musgrave forfeits his incontestable right to publish his injury in a court of justice. Furthermore, I solemnly declare myself his debtor in the sum of twenty thousand dollars; which, on his remission of the interest, and under pain of exposure in a contrary event, I pledge myself to repay at the earliest possible moment. I thank Mr. Musgrave for his generosity."

Edgar spoke very slowly, and the scratching of Guest's pen kept pace with his words. "Now sign and date," he said; and the other, with a great heroic dash, consummated this amazing document. He then pushed it away, and rose and bestowed upon us a look which I long remembered. As outraged human soul was abroad in the world, with which henceforth I felt I should have somehow to reckon.

Edgar possessed himself of the paper and read it coolly to the end, without blushing. Happy Edgar! Guest watched him fold it and put it into his great morocco pocket-book. "I suppose," said Guest, "that this is the end of your generosity."

"I have nothing further to remark," said Edgar.

"Have *you*, by chance, anything to remark, Mr. Step-brother?" Guest demanded, turning to me, with a fierce-ness which showed how my presence galled him.

I had been, to my own sense, so abjectly passive during the whole scene that, to reinstate myself as a responsible creature, I attempted to utter an original sentiment. "I pity you," I said.

But I had not been happy in my choice. "Faugh, you great hulking brute!" Guest roared, for an answer.

The scene at this point might have passed into another phase, had it not been interrupted by the opening of the door from the corridor. "A lady," announced a servant, flinging it back.

The lady revealed herself as the friend with whom Guest had been in conversation on the piazza. She was appar-ently not a person to mind the trifle of her friend's being accompanied by two unknown gentlemen, and she advanced, shawled as if for departure, and smiling re-proachfully. "Ah, you ungrateful creature," she cried, "you've lost my rosebud!"

Guest came up smiling, as they say. "Your own hands fastened it!—Where is my daughter?"

"She's coming. We've been looking for you, high and low. What on earth have you been doing here? Business? You've no business with business. You came here to rest. Excuse me, gentlemen! My carriage has been waiting this ten minutes. Give me your arm."

It seemed to me time we should disembarrass the poor

man of our presence. I opened the window and stepped out upon the piazza. Just as Edgar had followed me, a young lady hastily entered the room.

"My dearest father!" she exclaimed.

Looking at her unseen from without, I recognized with amazement my charming friend of the Episcopal chapel, the woman to whom—I felt it now with a sort of convulsion —I had dedicated a sentiment.

III

My discovery gave me that night much to think of, and I thought of it more than I slept. My foremost feeling was one of blank dismay as if Misfortune, whom I had been used to regard as a good-natured sort of goddess, who came on with an easy stride, letting off signals of warning to those who stood in her path, should have blinded her lantern and muffled her steps in order to steal a march on poor me,—of all men in the world! It seemed a hideous practical joke. "If I had known,—if I had only known!" I kept restlessly repeating. But toward morning, "Say I had known," I asked myself, "could I have acted otherwise? I might have protested by my absence; but would I not thus have surrendered poor Guest to the vengeance of a very Shylock? Had not that suggestion of mine diverted the current of Edgar's wrath and saved his adversary from the last dishonor? Without it, Edgar would have held his course and demanded his pound of flesh!" Say what I would, however, I stood confronted with this acutely uncomfortable fact, that by lending a hand at that revolting interview, I had struck a roundabout blow at the woman to whom I owed a signally sweet impression. Well, my blow would never reach her, and I would devise some kindness that should! So I consoled myself, and in the midst of my regret I found a still further compensation in the thought that chance, rough-handed though it had been, had forged between us a stouter bond than any I had ventured to dream of as I waxed sentimental a few hours before. Her father's being a rascal threw her image into

more eloquent relief. If she suspected it, she had all the
interest of sorrow; if not, she wore the tender grace of
danger.

The result of my meditations was that I determined to
defer indefinitely my departure from L——. Edgar informed me, in the course of the following day, that Guest
had gone by the early train to New York, and that his
daughter had left the hotel (where my not having met her
before was apparently the result of her constant attendance
on her father during his illness) and taken up her residence
with the lady in whose company we had seen her. Mrs.
Beck, Edgar had learned this lady's name to be; and I
fancied it was upon her that Miss Guest had made her
morning call. To begin with, therefore, I knew where to
look for her. "That's the charming girl," I said to Edgar,
"whom you might have plunged into disgrace."

"How do you know she's charming?" he asked.

"I judge by her face."

"Humph! Judge her father by his face and *he's* charming."

I was on the point of assuring my step-brother that no
such thing could be said of him; but in fact he had suddenly assumed a singularly fresh and jovial air. "I don't
know what it is," he said, "but I feel like a trump; I
haven't stood so firm on my legs in a twelvemonth. I
wonder whether the waters have already begun to act.
Really, I'm elated. Suppose, in the afternoon of my life,
I were to turn out a sound man. It winds me up, sir. I
shall take another glass before dinner."

To do Miss Guest a kindness, I reflected, I must see her
again. How to compass an interview and irradiate my
benevolence, it was not easy to determine. Sooner or later,
of course, the chances of watering-place life would serve
me. Meanwhile, I felt most agreeably that here was something more finely romantic than that feverish dream of my
youth, treating Edgar some fine day to the snub direct. Assuredly, I was not in love; I had cherished a youthful passion, and I knew the signs and symptoms; but I was in
a state of mind that really gave something of the same

zest to consciousness. For a couple of days I watched and waited for my friend in those few public resorts in which the little world of L—— used most to congregate,— the drive, the walk, the post office, and the vicinage of the spring. At last, as she was nowhere visible, I betook myself to the little Episcopal chapel, and strolled along the road, past a scattered cluster of decent boarding-houses, in one of which I imagined her hidden. But most of them had a shady strip of garden stretching toward the river, and thitherward, of course, rather than upon the public road, their inmates were likely to turn their faces. A happy accident at last came to my aid. After three or four days at the hotel, Edgar began to complain that the music in the evening kept him awake and to wonder whether he might find tolerable private lodgings. He was more and more interested in the waters. I offered, with alacrity, to make inquiries for him, and as a first step, I returned to the little colony of riverside boarding-houses. I began with one I had made especial note of,—the smallest, neatest, and most secluded. The mistress of the establishment was at a neighbor's, and I was requested to await her return. I stepped out of the long parlor window, and began hopefully to explore the garden. My hopes were brightly rewarded. In a shady summer-house, on a sort of rustic embankment, overlooking the stream, I encountered Miss Guest and her coquettish duenna. She looked at me for a moment with a dubious air, as if to satisfy herself that she was distinctly expected to recognize me, and then, as I stood proclaiming my hopes in an appealing smile, she bade me a frank good-morning. We talked, I lingered, and at last, when the proper moment came for my going my way again, I sat down and paid a call in form.

"I see you know my name," Miss Guest said, with the peculiar—the almost boyish—directness which seemed to be her most striking feature; "I can't imagine how you learned it, but if you'll be so good as to tell me your own, I'll introduce you to Mrs. Beck. You must learn that she's my deputed chaperon, my she-dragon, and that I'm not to know you unless she knows you first and approves."

Mrs. Beck poised a gold eye-glass upon her pretty
retroussé nose,—not sorry, I think, to hold it there a moment with a plump white hand and acquit herself of one
of her most effective manœuvres,—and glanced at me with
mock severity. "He's a harmless-looking young man, my
dear," she declared, "and I don't think your father would
object." And with this odd sanction I became intimate
with Miss Guest,—intimate as, by the soft operation of
summer and rural juxtaposition, an American youth is free
to become with an American maid. I had told my friends,
of course, the purpose of my visit, and learned, with complete satisfaction, that there was no chance for Mr. Musgrave, as they occupied the only three comfortable rooms
in the house,—two as bedrooms, the third as a common parlor. Heaven forbid that I should introduce Edgar *dans
cette galère.* I inquired elsewhere, but saw nothing I could
recommend, and, on making my report to him, found him
quite out of conceit of his project. A lady had just been
telling him horrors of the local dietary and making him feel
that he was vastly well off with the heavy bread and cold
gravy of the hotel. It was then too, I think, he first mentioned the symptoms of that relapse which subsequently
occurred. He would run no risks.

I had prepared Miss Guest, I fancy, to regard another
visit as a matter of course. I paid several in rapid succession; for, under the circumstances, it would have been
a pity to be shy. Her father, she told me, expected to be
occupied for three or four weeks in New York, so that for
the present I was at ease on that score. If I was to please,
I must go bravely to work. So I burned my ships behind
me, and blundered into gallantry with an ardor over which,
in my absence, the two ladies must have mingled their
smiles. I don't suppose I passed for an especially knowing fellow; but I kept my friends from wearying of each
other (for such other chance acquaintances as the place
afforded they seemed to have little inclination), and by my
services as a retailer of the local gossip, a reader of light
literature, an explorer and suggester of drives and strolls,
and, more particularly, as an oarsman in certain happy

rowing-parties on the placid river whose slow, safe current made such a pretty affectation of Mrs. Beck's little shrieks and shudders, I very fairly earned my welcome. That detestable scene at the hotel used to seem a sort of horrid fable as I sat in the sacred rural stillness, in that peaceful streamside nook, learning what a divinely honest girl she was, this daughter of the man whose dishonesty I had so complacently attested. I wasted many an hour in wondering on what terms she stood with her father's rankling secret, with his poor pompous peccability in general, if not with Edgar's particular grievance. I used to fancy that certain momentary snatches of revery in the midst of our gayety, and even more, certain effusions of wilful and excessive gayety at our duller moments, portended some vague torment in her filial heart. She would quit her place and wander apart for a while, leaving me to gossip it out with Mrs. Beck, as if she were oppressed by the constant need of seeming interested in us. But she would come back with a face that told so few tales that I always ended by keeping my compassion in the case from myself, and being reminded afresh, by my lively indisposition to be thus grossly lumped, as it were, with the duenna, of how much I was interested in the damsel. In truth, the romance of the matter apart, Miss Guest was a lovely girl. I had read her dimly in the little chapel, but I had read her aright. Felicity in freedom, that was her great charm. I have never known a woman so simply and sincerely original, so finely framed to enlist the imagination and hold expectation in suspense, and yet leave the judgment in such blissful quietude. She had a genius for frankness; this was her only coquetry and her only cleverness, and a woman could not have acquitted herself more naturally of the trying and ungracious *rôle* of being expected to be startling. It was the pure personal accent of Miss Guest's walk and conversation that gave them this charm; everything she did and said was gilded by a ray of conviction; and to a respectful admirer who had not penetrated to the sources of spiritual motive in her being, this sweet, natural, various emphasis of conduct was ineffably provoking. Her creed, as I guessed it, might have been resumed in the simple notion that a man should do his best; and nature had treated her, I fancied, to some brighter vision of uttermost manhood than illumined most honest fellows' consciences. Frank as she was, I imagined she had a remote reserve of holiest contempt. She made me feel deplorably ignorant and idle and unambitious, a foolish, boyish spendthrift of time and strength and means; and I speedily came to believe that to win her perfect favor was a matter of something more than undoing a stupid wrong,—doing, namely, some very pretty piece of right. And she was poor Mr. Guest's daughter, withal! Truly, fate was a master of irony.

I ought in justice to say that I had Mrs. Beck more particularly to thank for my welcome, and for the easy terms on which I had become an *habitué* of the little summer-house by the river. How could I know how much or how little the younger lady meant by her smiles and hand-shakes, by laughing at my jokes and consenting to be rowed about in my boat? Mrs. Beck made no secret of her relish for the society of a decently agreeable man, or of her deeming some such pastime the indispensable spice of life; and in Mr. Guest's absence, I was graciously admitted to competition. The precise nature of their mutual senti-ments—Mr. Guest's and hers—I was slightly puzzled to divine, and in so far as my conjectures seemed plausible, I confess they served as but a scanty offset to my knowledge of the gentleman's foibles. This lady was, to my sense, a very artificial charmer, and I think that a goodly portion of my admiration for Miss Guest rested upon a little private theory that for her father's sake she thus heroically ac-cepted a companion whom she must have relished but little. Mrs. Beck's great point was her "preservation." It was rather too great a point for my taste, and partook too much of the nature of a physiological curiosity. Her age really mattered little, for with as many years as you pleased one way or the other, she was still a triumph of juvenility. Plump, rosy, dimpled, frizzled, with rings on her fingers and rosettes on her toes, she used to seem to me a sort of fantastic vagary or humorous experiment of time. Or, she might have been fancied a strayed shepherdess from some rococo Arcadia, which had melted into tradition during some profane excursion of her own, so that she found herself saddled in our prosy modern world with this absurdly perpetual prime. All this was true, at least of her pretty face and figure; but there was another Mrs. Beck, visible chiefly to the moral eye, who seemed to me excessively wrinkled and faded and world-wise, and whom I used to fancy I could hear shaking about in this enamelled envelope, like a dried nut in its shell. Mrs. Beck's morality was not Arcadian; or if it was, it was that of a shepherdess with a keen eye to the state of the wool and the mutton market, and a lively perception of the possible advantages of judicious partnership. She had no design, I suppose, of proposing to me a consolidation of our sentimental and pecuniary interests, but she performed her duties of duenna with such conscientious precision that she shared my society most impartially with Miss Guest. I never had the good fortune of finding myself alone with this young lady. She might have managed it, I fancied, if she had wished, and the little care she took about it was a sign of that indifference which stirs the susceptible heart to effort. "It's really detestable," I at last ventured to seize the chance to declare, "that you and I should never be alone."

Miss Guest looked at me with an air of surprise. "Your remark is startling," she said, "unless you have some excellent reason for demanding this interesting seclusion."

My reason was not ready just yet, but it speedily ripened. A happy incident combined at once to bring it to maturity and to operate a diversion for Mrs. Beck. One morning there appeared a certain Mr. Crawford out of the West, a worthy bachelor who introduced himself to Mrs. Beck and claimed cousinship. I was present at the moment, and I could not but admire the skill with which the lady gauged her aspiring kinsman before saying yea or nay to his claims. I think the large diamond in his shirt-front decided her; what he may have lacked in elegant culture was supplied by this massive ornament. Better and

brighter than his diamond, however, was his frank Western
bonhomie, his simple friendliness, and a certain half-boyish
modesty which made him give a humorous twist to any expression of the finer sentiments. He was a tall, lean gentleman, on the right side of forty, yellow-haired, with a somewhat arid complexion, and an irrepressible tendency to cock
back his hat and chew his toothpick, and a spasmodic
liability, spasmodically repressed when in a sedentary posture, to a centrifugal movement of the heels. He had a
clear blue eye, in which simplicity and shrewdness con-
tended and mingled in so lively a fashion that his glance
was the oddest dramatic twinkle. He was a genial sceptic.
If he disbelieved much that he saw, he believed everything
he fancied, and for a man who had seen much of the
rougher and baser side of life, he was able to fancy some
very gracious things of men, to say nothing of women. He
took his place as a very convenient fourth in our little
party, and without obtruding his eccentricities, or being too
often reminded of a story, like many cooler humorists, he
treated us to a hundred anecdotes of his adventurous ascent
of the ladder of fortune. The upshot of his history was
that he was now owner of a silver mine in Arizona, and
that he proposed in his own words to "lay off and choose."
Of the nature of his choice he modestly waived specifica-
tion; it of course had reference to the sex of which Mrs.
Beck was an ornament. He lounged about meanwhile with
his hands in his pockets, watching the flies buzz with that
air of ecstatically suspended resolve proper to a man who
has sunk a shaft deep into the very stuff that dreams are
made of. But in spite of shyness he exhaled an atmosphere
of regretful celibacy which might have relaxed the conjugal
piety of a more tenderly mourning widow than Mrs. Beck.
His bachelor days were evidently numbered, and unless I
was vastly mistaken, it lay in this lady's discretion to determine the residuary figure. The two were just nearly
enough akin to save a deal of time in courtship.

Crawford had never beheld so finished a piece of lady-
hood, and it pleased and puzzled him and quickened his
honest grin very much as a remarkably neat mechanical

toy might have done. Plain people who have lived close to frank nature often think more of a fine crisp muslin rose than of a group of dewy petals of garden growth. Before ten days were past, he had begun to fumble tenderly with the stem of this unfading flower. Mr. Crawford's *petits soins* had something too much of the ring of the small change of the Arizona silver-mine, consisting largely as they did of rather rudimentary nosegays compounded by amateur florists from the local front-yards, of huge bundles of "New York candy" from the village store, and of an infinite variety of birch-bark and bead-work trinkets. He was no simpleton, and it occurred to me, indeed, that if these offerings were not the tokens and pledges of a sentiment, they were the offset and substitute of a sentiment; but if they were profuse for that, they were scanty for this. Mrs. Beck, for her part, seemed minded to spin the thread of decision excessively fine. A silver-mine was all very well, but a lover fresh from the diggings was to be put on probation. Crawford lodged at the hotel, and our comings and goings were often made together. He indulged in many a dry compliment to his cousin, and, indeed, declared that she was a magnificent little woman. It was with surprise, therefore, that I learned that his admiration was divided. "I've never seen one just like her," he said; "one so out and out a woman,—smiles and tears and everything else! But Clara comes out with her notions, and a man may know what to expect. I guess I can afford a wife with a notion or so! Short of the moon, I can give her what she wants." And I seemed to hear his hands producing in his pockets that Arizonian tinkle which served with him as the prelude to renewed utterance. He went on, "And tells me I musn't make love to my grandmother. That's a very pretty way of confessing to thirty-five. She's a bit of coquette, is Clara!" I handled the honest fellow's illusions as tenderly as I could, and at last he eyed me askance with a knowing air. "You praise my cousin," he said, "because you think I want you to. On the contrary, I want you to say something against her. If there is anything, I want to know it." I declared I knew nothing in the world; whereupon Crawford, after a silence, heaved an impatient sigh.

"Really," said I, laughing, "one would think you were disappointed."

"I wanted to draw you out," he cried; "but you're too confoundedly polite. I suppose Mrs. Beck's to be my fate; it's borne in on me. I'm being roped in fast. But I only want a little backing to hang off awhile. Look here," he added suddenly, "let's be frank!" and he stopped and laid his hand on my arm. "That other young lady isn't so pretty as Mrs. Beck, but it seems to me I'd kind of trust her further. You didn't know I'd noticed her. Well, I've taken her in little by little, just as she gives herself out. Jerusalem! there's a woman. But you know it, sir, if I'm not mistaken; and that's where the shoe pinches. First come, first served. I want to act on the square. Before I settle down to Mrs. Beck, I want to know distinctly whether you put in a claim to Miss Guest."

The question was unexpected and found me but half prepared. "A claim?" I said "Well, yes, call it a claim!"

"Any way," he rejoined, "I've no chance. She'd never look at me. But I want to have her put out of my own head, so that I can concentrate on Mrs. B. If you're not in love with her, my boy, let me tell you you ought to be! If you are, I've nothing to do but to wish you success. If you're not, upon my word, I don't know but what I would go in! She could but refuse me. Modesty is all very well; but after all, it's the handsomest thing you can do by a woman to offer yourself. As a compliment alone, it would serve. And really, a compliment with a round million isn't so bad as gallantry goes hereabouts. You're young and smart and good-looking, and Mrs. Beck tells me you're rich. If you succeed, you'll have more than your share of good things. But Fortune has her favorites, and they're not always such nice young men. If you're in love well and good! If you're not,—by Jove, I am!"

This admonition was peremptory. My companion's face in the clear starlight betrayed his sagacious sincerity. I felt a sudden satisfaction in being summoned to take my

stand. I performed a rapid operation in sentimental arith-
metic, combined my factors, and established my total. It
exceeded expectation. "Your frankness does you honor,"
I said, "and I'm sorry I can't make a kinder return. But
——I'm madly in love!"

IV

My situation, as I defined it to Crawford, was not
purely delightful. Close upon my perception of the state
of my heart followed an oppressive sense of the vanity of
my pretensions. I had cut the ground from under my feet;
to offer myself to Miss Guest would be to add insult to
injury. I may truly say, therefore, that, for a couple of
days, this manifest passion of mine rather saddened than
exalted me. For a dismal forty-eight hours I left the two
ladies unvisited. I even thought of paying a supreme
tribute to delicacy and taking a summary departure. Some
day, possibly, Miss Guest would learn with grief and scorn
what her father had to thank me for; and then later, as
resentment melted into milder conjecture, she would read
the riddle of my present conduct and do me justice,—guess
that I had loved her, and that, to punish myself, I had re-
nounced her forever. This fantastic magnaminity was followed by a wholesome reaction. I was punished enough,
surely, in my regret and shame; and I wished now not to
suffer, but to act. Viewing the matter reasonably, she need
never learn my secret; if by some cruel accident she should,
the favor I had earned would cover that I had forfeited.
I stayed, then, and tried to earn this precious favor; but
I encountered an obstacle more serious, I fancied, than
even her passionate contempt would have been,—her serene
and benevolent indifference. Looking back at these momentous days, I get an impression of a period of vague
sentimental ferment and trouble, rather than of definite
utterance and action; though I believe that by a singular
law governing human conduct in certain cases, the very
modesty and humility of my passion expressed itself in a
sort of florid and hyperbolical gallantry; so that, in so far

as my claims were inadmissible, they might pass, partly as a kind of compensatory homage, and partly as a jest. Miss Guest refused to pay me the compliment of even being discomposed, and pretended to accept my addresses as an elaborate device for her amusement. There was a perpetual assurance in her tone of her not regarding me as a serious, much less as a dangerous, man. She could not have contrived a more effective irritant to my resolution; and I confess there were certain impatient moods when I took a brutal glee in the thought that it was not so very long since, on a notable occasion, my presence had told. In so far as I *was* serious, Miss Guest frankly offered to accept me as a friend, and laughingly intimated, indeed, that with a little matronly tuition of her dispensing, I might put myself into condition to please some simple maiden in her flower. I was an excellent, honest fellow; but I was excessively young and—as she really wished to befriend me, she would risk the admonition—I was decidedly frivolous. I lacked "character." I was fairly clever, but I was more clever than wise. I liked overmuch to listen to my own tongue. I had done nothing; I was idle; I had, by my own confession, never made an effort; I was too rich and too indolent; in my very good-nature there was nothing moral, no hint of principle; in short, I was—boyish. I must forgive a woman upon whom life had forced the fatal habit of discrimination. I suffered this genial scepticism to expend itself freely, for her candor was an enchantment. It was all true enough. I had been indolent and unambitious; I had made no effort; I had lived in vulgar ignorance and ease; I had in a certain frivolous fashion tried life at first hand, but my shallow gains had been in proportion to my small hazards. But I was neither so young nor so idle as she chose to fancy, and I could at any rate prove I was constant. Like a legendary suitor of old, I might even slay my dragon. A monstrous accident stood between us, and to dissipate its evil influence would be a fairly heroic feat.

Mr. Guest's absence was prolonged from day to day, and Laura's tone of allusion to her father tended indeed to make a sort of invincible chimera of her possible discovery of the truth. This fond filial reference only brought out the more brightly her unlikeness to him. I could as little fancy her doing an act she would need to conceal as I could fancy her arresting exposure by a concession to dishonor. If I was a friend, I insisted on being a familiar one; and while Mrs. Beck and her cousin floated away on perilous waters, we dabbled in the placid shallows of disinterested sentiment. For myself, I sent many a longing glance toward the open sea, but Laura remained firm in her preference for the shore. I encouraged her to speak of her father, for I wished to hear all the good that could be told of him. It sometimes seemed to me that she talked of him with a kind of vehement tenderness designed to obscure, as it were, her inner vision. Better—had she said to herself?—that she should talk fond nonsense about him than that she should harbor untender suspicions. I could easily believe that the poor man was a most lovable fellow, and could imagine how, as Laura judged him in spite of herself, the sweet allowances of a mother had grown up within the daughter. One afternoon Mrs. Beck brought forth her photograph-book, to show to her cousin. Suddenly, as he was turning it over, she stayed his hand and snatched one of the pictures from its place. He tried to recover it and a little tussle followed, in the course of which she escaped, ran to Miss Guest, and thrust the photograph into her hand. "You keep it," she cried; "he's not to see it." There was a great crying out from Crawford about Mrs. Beck's inconstancy and his *right* to see the picture, which was cut short by Laura's saying with some gravity that it was too childish a romp for a man of forty and a woman of—thirty! Mrs. Beck allowed us no time to relish the irony of this attributive figure; she caused herself to be pursued to the other end of the garden, where the amorous frolic was resumed over the following pages of the album. "Who is it?" I asked. Miss Guest, after a pause, handed me the card.

"Your father!" I cried precipitately.

"Ah, you've seen him?" she asked.

"I know him by his likeness to you."

"You prevent my asking you, as I meant, if he doesn't look like a dear good man. I do wish he'd drop his stupid business and come back."

I took occasion hereupon to ascertain whether she suspected his embarrassments. She confessed to a painful impression that something was wrong. He had been out of spirits for many days before his return to town; nothing indeed but mental distress could have affected his health, for he had a perfect constitution. "If it comes to that," she went on, after a long silence, and looking at me with an almost intimate confidence, "I wish he would give up business altogether. All the business in the world, for a man of his open, joyous temper, doesn't pay for an hour's depression. I can't bear to sit by and see him embittered and spoiled by this muddle of stocks and shares. Nature made him a happy man; I insist on keeping him so. We are quite rich enough, and we need nothing more. He tries to persuade me that I have expensive tastes, but I've never spent money but to please him. I have a lovely little dream which I mean to lay before him when he comes back; it's very cheap, like all dreams, and more practicable than most. He's to give up business and take me abroad. We're to settle down quietly somewhere in Germany, in Italy, I don't care where, and I'm to study music seriously. I'm never to marry; but as he grows to be an old man, he's to sit by a window, with his cigar, looking out on the Arno or the Rhine, while I play Beethoven and Rossini."

"It's a very pretty programme," I answered, "though I can't subscribe to certain details. But do you know," I added, touched by a forcible appeal to sympathy in her tone, "although you refuse to believe me anything better than an ingenuous fool, this liberal concession to my interest in your situation is almost a proof of respect."

She blushed a little, to my great satisfaction. "I surely respect you," she said, "if you come to that! Otherwise we should hardly be sitting here so simply. And I think, too," she went on, "that I speak to you of my father with peculiar freedom, because—because, somehow, you remind me of him." She looked at me as she spoke with such penetrating candor that it was my turn to blush. "You are genial, and gentle, and essentially honest, like him; and like him," she added with a half-smile, "you're addicted to saying a little more than it would be fair to expect you to stand to. You ought to be very good friends. You'll find he has your own *jeunesse de cœur.*"

I murmured what I might about the happiness of making his acquaintance; and then, to give the conversation a turn, and really to test the force of this sympathetic movement of hers, I boldly mentioned my fancy that he was an admirer of Mrs. Beck. She gave me a silent glance, almost of gratitude, as if she needed to unburden her heart. But she did so in few words. "He does admire her," she said. "It's my duty, it's my pleasure, to respect his illusions. But I confess to you that I hope this one will fade." She rose from her seat and we joined our companions; but I fancied, for a week afterwards, that she treated me with a certain gracious implication of deference. Had I ceased to seem boyish? I struck a truce with urgency and almost relished the idea of being patient.

A day or two later, Mr. Guest's "illusions" were put before me in a pathetic light. It was a Sunday; the ladies were at church, and Crawford and I sat smoking on the piazza. "I don't know how things are going with you," he said; "you're either perfectly successful or desperately resigned. But unless it's rather plainer sailing than in my case, I don't envy you. I don't know where I am, anyway! She will and she won't. She may take back her word once too often, I can tell her that! You see, she has two strings to her bow. She likes my money, but she doesn't like *me.* Now, it's all very well for a woman to relish a fortune, but I'm not prepared to have my wife despise—my *person!*" said Crawford with feeling. "The alternative, you know, is Mr. Guest, that girl's father. I suppose he's handsome, and a wit, and a dandy; though I must say an old dandy, to my taste, is an old fool. She tells me a dozen times an hour that he's a fascinating man. I suppose if I were to leave her alone for a week, I might seem a fascinating man. I wish to heaven she wasn't so confoundedly taking. I can't give her up; she amuses me too much. There was once a little actress in Galveston, but Clara beats that girl! If I could only have gone in for some simple wholesome girl who doesn't need to count on her fingers to know the state of her heart!"

That evening as we were gathered in the garden, poor Crawford approached Laura Guest with an air of desperate gallantry, as if from a desire to rest from the petty torment of Mrs. Beck's sentimental mutations. Laura liked him, and her manner to him had always been admirable in its almost sisterly frankness and absence of provoking arts; yet I found myself almost wondering, as they now strolled about the garden together, whether there was any danger of this sturdy architect of his own fortunes putting out my pipe. Mrs. Beck, however, left me no chance for selfish meditation. Her artless and pointless prattle never lacked a purpose; before you knew it she was, in vulgar parlance, "pumping" you, trying to pick your pocket of your poor little receipt for prosperity. She took an intense delight in imaginatively bettering her condition, and one was forced to carry bricks for her castles in the air.

"You needn't be afraid of my cousin," she said, laughing, as I followed his red cigar-tip along the garden paths. "He admires Laura altogether too much to make love to her. There's modesty! Don't you think it's rather touching in a man with a million of dollars? I don't mind telling you that he has made love to me, that being no case for modesty. I suppose you'll say that my speaking of it is. But what's the use of being an aged widow, if one can't tell the truth?"

"There's comfort in being an aged widow," I answered gallantly, "when one has two offers a month."

"I don't know what you know about my offers; but even two swallows don't make a summer! However, since you've mentioned the subject, tell me frankly what you think of poor Crawford. Is he at all presentable? You see I like him, I esteem him, and I'm afraid of being blinded by my feelings. Is he so dreadfully rough? You see I like downright simple manliness and all that; but a little polish does no harm, even on fine gold. I do wish you'd take hold of my poor cousin and teach him a few of the amenities of life. I'm very fond of the amenities of life; it's very frivolous and wicked, I suppose, but I can't help it. I have the misfortune to be sensitive to ugly things. Can one really accept a man who wears a green cravat? Of course you can make him take it off; but you'll be knowing all the while that he pines for it, that he would put it on if he could. Now that's a symbol of that dear, kind, simple fellow,—a heart of gold, but a green cravat! I've never heard a word of wisdom about that matter yet. People talk about the sympathy of souls being the foundation of happiness in marriage. It's pure nonsense. It's not the great things, but the little, that we dispute about, and the chances are terribly against the people who have a different taste in colors."

It seemed to me that, thus ardently invoked, I might hazard the observation, "Mr. Guest would never wear a green cravat."

"What do you know about Mr. Guest's cravats?"

"I've seen his photograph, you know."

"Well, you do him justice. You should see him in the life. He looks like a duke. I never saw a duke, but that's my notion of a duke. Distinction, you know; perfect manners and tact and wit. If I'm right about it's being perfection in small things that assures one's happiness, I might—well, in two words, I might be very happy with Mr. Guest!"

"It's Crawford and soul, then," I proposed, smiling, "or Guest and manner!"

She looked at me a moment, and then with a toss of her head and a tap of her fan, "You wretch!" she cried, "you want to make me say something very ridiculous. I'll not pretend I'm not worldly. I'm excessively wordly. I always make a point of letting people know it. Of course I know very well my cousin's rich, and that so long as he's good he's none the worse for that. But in my quiet little way I'm a critic, and I look at things from a high ground. I compare a rich man who is simply a good fellow to a perfect gentleman who has simply a nice little fortune. Mr. Guest has a nice property, a very nice property. I shouldn't have to make over my old bonnets. You may ask me if I'm not afraid of Laura. But you'll marry Laura and carry her off!"

I found nothing to reply for some moments to this little essay in "criticism"; and suddenly Mrs. Beck, fancying perhaps that she was indiscreetly committing herself, put an end to our interview. "I'm really very kind," she cried, "to be talking so graciously about a lover who leaves me alone for a month and never even drops me a line. It's not such good manners after all. If you're not jealous of Mr. Crawford, I am of Miss Guest. We'll go down and separate them."

Miss Guest's repose and dignity were decidedly overshadowed. I brought her the next afternoon a letter from the post office, superscribed in a hand I knew, and wandered away while she sat in the garden and read it. When I came back she looked strangely sad. I sat down near her and drew figures in the ground with the end of her parasol, hoping that she would do me the honor to communicate her trouble. At last she rose in silence, as if to return to the house. I begged her to remain. "You're in distress," I said, speaking as calmly and coldly as I could, "and I hoped it might occur to you that there is infinite sympathy close at hand. Instead of going to your own room to cry, why not stay here and talk of it with me?"

She gave me a brilliant, searching gaze; I met it steadily and felt that I was turning pale with the effort not to obey the passionate impulse of self-denunciation. She began slowly to walk away from the house, and I felt that a point was gained. "It's your father, of course," I said. It was all I could say. She silently handed me his unfolded letter. It ran as follows:—

MY DEAREST DAUGHTER:—I have sold the house and everything in it, except your piano and books, of course at a painful sacrifice. But I needed ready money. Forgive your poor blundering, cruel father. My old luck has left me; but only *trust me,* and we shall be happy again."

Her eyes, fortunately, were wandering while I read; for I felt myself blushing to my ears.

"It's not the loss of the house," she said at last; "though of course we were fond of it. I grew up there,—my mother died there. It's the trouble it indicates. Poor dear father! Why does he talk of 'luck'? I detest the word. Why does he talk of forgiving him and trusting him? There's a wretched tone about it all. If he would only come back and let me look at him!"

"Nothing is more common in business," I answered, "than a temporary embarrassment demanding ready money. Of course it must be met at a sacrifice. One throws a little something overboard to lighten the ship, and the ship sails ahead. As for the loss of the house, nothing could be better for going to Italy, you know. You've no excuse left for staying here. If your father will forgive me the interest I take in his affairs, I strongly recommend his leaving business and its sordid cares. Let him go abroad and forget it all."

Laura walked along in silence, and I led the way out of the garden into the road. We followed it slowly till we reached the little chapel. The sexton was just leaving it, shouldering the broom with which he had been sweeping it for the morrow's services. I hailed him and gained his permission to go in and try the organ, assuring him that we were experts. Laura said that she felt in no mood for music; but she entered and sat down in one of the pews. I climbed into the gallery and attacked the little instrument. We had had no music since our first meeting, and I felt an irresistible need to recall the circumstances of that meeting. I played in a simple fashion, respectably enough, and fancied, at all events, that by my harmonious fingers I could best express myself. I played for an hour, in silence, choosing what I would, without comment or response from my companion. The summer twilight overtook us; when it was getting too dark to see the keys, I rejoined Miss Guest.

She rose and came into the aisle. "You play very well," she said, simply; "better than I supposed."

Her praise was sweet; but sweeter still was a fancy of mine that I perceived in the light gloom just the glimmer of a tear. "In this place," I said, "your playing once moved me greatly. Try and remember the scene distinctly."

"It's easily remembered," she answered, with an air of surprise.

"Believe, then, that when we parted, I was already in love with you."

She turned away abruptly. "Ah, my poor music!"

The next day, on my arrival, I was met by Mrs. Beck, whose pretty forehead seemed clouded with annoyance. With her own fair hand she buttonholed me. "You apparently," she said, "have the happiness to be in Miss Guest's confidence. What on earth is going on in New York? Laura received an hour ago a letter from her father. I found her sitting with it in her hand as cheerful as a Quakeress in meeting. 'Something's wrong, my dear,' I said; 'I don't know what. In any case, be assured of my sympathy.' She gave me the most extraordinary stare. 'You'll be interested to know,' she said, 'that my father has lost half his property.' Interested to know! I verily believe the child meant an impertinence. What is Mr. Guest's property to me? Has he been speculating? Stupid man!" she cried, with vehemence.

I made a brief answer. I discovered Miss Guest sitting by the river, in pale contemplation of household disaster. I asked no questions. She told me of her own accord that her father was to return immediately, "to make up a month's sleep," she added, glancing at his letter. We spoke of other matters, but before I left her, I returned to this one. "I wish you to tell your father this," I said. "That there is a certain gentleman here, who is idle, indolent, ignorant, frivolous, selfish. That he has certain funds for which he is without present use. That he places them at Mr. Guest's absolute disposal in the hope that they may partially relieve his embarrassment." I looked at Laura as

I spoke and watched her startled blush deepen to crimson. She was about to reply; but before she could speak, "Don't forget to add," I went on, "that he hopes his personal faults will not prejudice Mr. Guest's acceptance of his offer, for it is prompted by the love he bears his daughter."

"You must excuse me," Laura said, after a pause. "I had rather not tell him this. He would not accept your offer."

"Are you sure of that?"

"I shouldn't allow him."

"And why not, pray? Don't you, after all, like me well enough to suffer me to do you so small a service?"

She hesitated; then gave me her hand with magnificent frankness. "I like you too well to suffer you to do me just that service. We take that from *les indifférents*."

V

Before the month was out, Edgar had quarrelled with the healing waters of L——. His improvement had been most illusory; his old symptoms had returned in force, and though he now railed bitterly at the perfidious spring and roundly denounced the place, he was too ill to be moved away. He was altogether confined to his room. I made a conscience of offering him my company and assistance, but he would accept no nursing of mine. He would be tended by no one whom he could not pay for his trouble and enjoy a legal right to grumble at. "I expect a nurse to *be* a nurse," he said, "and not a fine gentleman, waiting on me in gloves. It would be fine work for me, lying here, to have to think twice whether I might bid you not to breathe so hard." Nothing had passed between us about John Guest, though the motive for silence was different on each side. For Edgar, I fancied, our interview with him was a matter too solemn for frequent allusion; for me it was a detestable thought. But wishing now to assure myself that, as I supposed, he had paid his ugly debt, I asked Edgar, on the evening I had extorted from Miss Guest those last recorded words of happy omen, whether he had heard from our friend

in New York. It was a very hot night; poor Edgar lay
sweltering under a sheet, with open windows. He looked
pitifully ill, and yet somehow more intensely himself than
ever. He drew a letter from under his pillow. "This
came to-day," he said. "Stevens writes me that Guest
yesterday paid down the twenty thousand dollars in full.
It's quick work. I hope he's not robbed Peter to pay Paul."

"Mr. Guest has a conscience," I said; and I thought bitterly of the reverse of the picture. "I'm afraid he has half
ruined himself to do it."

"Well, ruin for ruin, I prefer his. I've no doubt his
affairs have gone to the dogs. The affairs of such a man
must, sooner or later! I believe, by the way, you've been
cultivating the young lady. What does the papa say to
that?"

"Of course," I said, without heeding his question, "you've
already enclosed him the—the little paper."

Edgar turned in his bed. "Of course I've done no such
thing!"

"You mean to keep it?" I cried.

"Of course I mean to keep it. Where else would be his
punishment?"

There was something vastly grotesque in the sight of
this sickly little mortal erecting himself among his pillows
as a dispenser of justice, an appraiser of the wages of sin;
but I confess that his attitude struck me as more cruel even
than ludicrous. I was disappointed. I had certainly not
expected Edgar to be generous, but I had expected him to
be just, and in the heat of his present irritation he was
neither. He was angry with Guest for his excessive promptitude, which had given a sinister twist to his own conduct.
"Upon my word," I cried, "you're a veritable Shylock!"

"And you're a veritable fool! Is it set down in the
bond that I'm to give it up to him? The thing's mine, to
have and to hold forever. The scoundrel would be easily
let off indeed! This bit of paper in my hands is to keep
him in order and prevent his being too happy. The thought
will be wholesome company,—a *memento mori* to his
vanity."

"He's to go through life, then, with possible exposure staring him in the face?"

Edgar's great protuberant eyes expanded without blinking. "He has committed his fate to Providence."

I was revolted. "You may have the providential qualities, but you have not the gentlemanly ones, I formally protest. But, after a decent delay, he'll of course demand the document."

"Demand it? He shall have it then, with a vengeance!"

"Well, I wash my hands of further complicity! I shall inform Mr. Guest that I count for nothing in this base negation of his right."

Edgar paused a moment to stare at me in my unprecedented wrath. Then making me a little ironical gesture of congratulation, "Inform him of what you please. I hope you'll have a pleasant talk over it! You made rather a bad beginning, but who knows, if you put your heads together to abuse me, you may end as bosom friends! I've watched you, sir!" he suddenly added, propping himself forward among his pillows; "you're in love!" I may wrong the poor fellow, but it seemed to me that in these words he discharged the bitterness of a lifetime. He too would have hoped to please, and he had lived in acrid assent to the instinct which told him such hope was vain. In one way or another a man pays his tax to manhood. "Yes, sir, you're grossly in love! What do I know about love, you ask? I know a drivelling lover when I see him. You've made a clever choice. Do you expect John Guest to give the girl away? He's a good-natured man, I know; but really, considering your high standard of gentlemanly conduct, you ask a good deal."

Edgar had been guilty on this occasion of a kind of reckless moral self-exposure, which seemed to betray a sense that he should never need his reputation again. I felt as if I were standing by something very like a death-bed, and forbearingly, without rejoinder, I withdrew. He had simply expressed more brutally, however, my own oppressive belief that the father's aversion stood darkly massed in the rear of the daughter's indifference. I had, indeed, for the present, the consolation of believing that with Laura the day of pure indifference was over; and I tried hard to flatter myself that my position was tenable in spite of Mr. Guest. The next day as I was wandering on the hotel piazza, communing thus sadly with my hopes, I met Crawford, who, with his hands in his pockets and his hat on the bridge of his nose, seemed equally a sullen probationer of fate.

"I'm going down to join our friends," I said; "I expected to find you with them."

He gave a gloomy grin. "My nose is out of joint," he said; "Mr. Guest has come back." I turned pale, but he was too much engaged with his own trouble to observe it. "What do you suppose my cousin is up to? She had agreed to drive with me and I had determined to come home, once for all, engaged or rejected. As soon as she heard of Guest's arrival, she threw me overboard and tripped off to her room, to touch up her curls. Go down there now and you'll find her shaking them at Mr. Guest. By the Lord, sir, she can whistle for me now! If there was a decently good-looking woman in this house, I'd march straight up to her and offer myself. You're a happy man, my boy, not to have a d—d fool to interfere with you, and not to be in love with a d—d fool either."

I had no present leisure to smooth the turbid waters of poor Crawford's passion; but I remembered a clever remark in a French book, to the effect that even the best men —and Crawford was one of the best—are subject to a momentary need not to respect what they love. I repaired alone to the house by the river, and found Laura in the little parlor which she shared with Mrs. Beck. The room was flooded with the glow of a crimson sunset, and she was looking out of the long window at two persons in the garden. In my great desire to obtain some firm assurance from her before her father's interference should become a certainty, I lost no time. "I've been able to think of nothing," I said, "but your reply to that poor offer of mine. I've been flattering myself that it really means something,—means, possibly, that if I were to speak— here—now—all that I long to speak, you would listen to me more kindly. Laura," I cried, passionately, "I repent of all my follies and I love you!"

She looked at me from head to foot with a gaze almost strange in its intensity. It betrayed trouble, but, I fancied, a grateful trouble. Then, with a smile, "My father has come," she said. The words set my heart a beating, and I had a horrible fancy that they were maliciously uttered. But as she went on I was reassured. "I want him to see you, though he knows nothing of your offer."

Somehow, by her tone, my mind was suddenly illumined with a delicious apprehension of her motive. She had heard the early murmur of that sentiment whose tender essence resents compulsion. "Let me feel then," I said, "that I am not to stand or fall by *his* choice."

"He's sure to like you," she answered; "don't you remember my telling you so? He judges better of men than of women," she added sadly, turning away from the window.

Mr. Guest had been advancing toward the house, side by side with Mrs. Beck. Before they reached it the latter was met by two ladies who had been ushered into the garden from the front gate, and with whom, with an air of smothered petulance, perceptible even at a distance, she retraced her steps toward the summer-house. Her companion entered our little parlor alone from the piazza. He stepped jauntily and looked surprisingly little altered by his month's ordeal. Mrs. Beck might still have taken him for a duke, or, at least, for an earl. His daughter immediately introduced me. "Happy to make your acquaintance, sir," he exclaimed, in a voice which I was almost shocked to find how well I knew. He offered his hand. I met it with my own, and the next moment we were fairly face to face. I was prepared for anything. Recognition faltered for a mere instant in his eyes; then I felt it suddenly leap forth in the tremendous wrench of his hand, "Ah, you—*you*—you!"

"Why, you know him!" exclaimed Laura.

Guest continued to wring my hand, and I felt to my cost that he was shocked. He panted a moment for breath, and then burst into a monstrous laugh. I looked askance at Laura; her eyes were filled with wonder. I felt that for the moment anger had made her father reckless, and anything was better than that between us the edge of our secret should peep out. "We have been introduced," I said, trying to smile. Guest dropped my hand as if it burned him, and walked the length of the room.

"You should have told me!" Laura added, in a tone of almost familiar reproach.

"Miss Guest," I answered, hardly knowing what I said, "the world is so wide——"

"Upon my soul, I think it's damnably narrow!" cried Guest, who had turned very pale.

I determined then that he should know the worst. "I'm here with a purpose, Mr. Guest," I said; "I love your daughter."

He stopped short, fairly glaring at me. Laura stepped toward him and laid her two hands on his arm. "Something is wrong," she said, "very wrong! It's your horrible money-matters! Weren't you really then so generous?" and she turned to me.

Guest laid his other hand on hers as they rested on his arm and patted them gently. "My daughter," he said solemnly, "do your poor father a favor. Dismiss him forever. Turn him out of the house," he added, fiercely.

"You wrong your daughter," I cried, "by asking her to act so blindly and cruelly."

"My child," Guest went on, "I expect you to obey!"

There was a silence. At last Laura turned to me, excessively pale. "Will you do me the very great favor," she said, with a trembling voice, "to leave us?"

I reflected a moment. "I appreciate your generosity; but in the interest of your own happiness, I beg you not to listen to your father until I have had a word with him alone."

She hesitated and looked, as if for assent, at her father. "Great heavens, girl!" he cried, "you don't mean you love him!" She blushed to her hair and rapidly left the room.

Guest took up his hat and removed a speck of dust from

the ribbon by a fillip of his finger-nail. "Young man," he said, "you waste words!"

"Not, I hope, when, with my hand on my heart, I beg your pardon."

"Now that you have something to gain. If you respect me, you should have protested before. If you don't you've nothing to do with me or mine."

"I allow for your natural resentment, but you might keep it within bounds. I religiously forget, ignore, efface the past. Meet me half-way! When we met a month ago, I already loved your daughter. If I had dreamed of your being ever so remotely connected with her, I would have arrested that detestable scene even by force, brother of mine though your adversary was!"

Guest put on his hat with a gesture of implacable contempt. "That's all very well! You don't know me, sir, or you'd not waste your breath on *ifs!* The thing's done. Such as I stand here, I've been *dishonored!*" And two hot tears sprang into his eyes. "Such as I stand here, I carry in my poor, sore heart the vision of your great, brutal, staring, cruel presence. And now you ask me to accept that presence as perpetual! Upon my soul, I'm a precious fool to talk about it."

I made an immense effort to remain calm and courteous. "Is there nothing I can do to secure your good-will? I'll make any sacrifice."

"Nothing but to leave me at once and forever. Fancy my living with you for an hour! Fancy, whenever I met your eyes, my seeing in them the reflection of—of that piece of business! And your walking about looking wise and chuckling! My precious young man," he went on with a scorching smile, "if you knew how I hated you, you'd give me a wide berth."

I was silent for some moments, teaching myself the great patience which I foresaw I should need. "This is after all but the question of our personal relations, which we might fairly leave to time. Not only am I willing to pledge myself to the most explicit respect——"

"Explicit respect!" he broke out. "I should relish that vastly! Heaven deliver me from your explicit respect!"

"I can quite believe," I quietly continued, "that I should get to like you. Your daughter has done me the honor to say that she believed you would like me."

"Perfect! You've talked it all over with her?"

"At any rate," I declared roundly, "I love her, and I have reason to hope that I may render myself acceptable to her. I can only add, Mr. Guest, that much as I should value your approval of my suit, if you withhold it I shall try my fortune without it!"

"Gently, impetuous youth!" And Guest laid his hand on my arm and lowered his voice. "Do you dream that if my daughter ever so faintly suspected the truth, she would even look at you again?"

"The truth? Heaven forbid she should dream of it! I wonder that in your position you should allude to it so freely."

"I was prudent once; I shall treat myself to a little freedom now. Give it up, I advise you. She may have thought you a pretty young fellow; I took you for one myself at first; but she'll keep her affection for a man with the bowels of compassion. She'll never love a coward, sir. Upon my soul, I'd sooner she married your beautiful brother. *He*, at least, had a grievance. Don't talk to me about my own child. She and I have an older love than yours; and if she were to learn that I've been weak—Heaven help me!— she would only love me the more. She would feel only that I've been outraged."

I confess that privately I flinched, but I stood to it bravely. "Miss Guest, doubtless, is as perfect a daughter as she would be a wife. But allow me to say that a woman's heart is not so simple a mechanism. Your daughter is a person of a very fine sense of honor, and I can imagine nothing that would give her greater pain than to be reduced to an attitude of mere compassion for her father. She likes to believe that men are strong. The sense of respect is necessary to her happiness. We both wish to assure that happiness. Let us join hands to preserve her illusions."

I saw in his eye no concession except to angry perplexity. "I don't know what you mean," he cried, "and I don't want to know. If you wish to intimate that my daughter is so very superior a person that she'll despise me, you're mistaken! She's beyond any compliment you can pay her. You can't frighten me now; I don't care for things." He walked away a moment and then turned about with flushed face and trembling lip. "I'm broken, I'm ruined! I don't want my daughter's respect, nor any other woman's. It's a burden, a mockery, a snare! What's a woman worth who can be kind only while she believes? Ah, ah!" and he began to rub his hands with a sudden air of helpless senility, "I should never be so kissed and coddled and nursed. I can tell her what I please; I sha'n't mind what I say now. I've ceased to care,—all in a month! Reputation is a farce; a pair of tight boots, worn for vanity. I used to have a good foot, but I shall end my days in my slippers. I don't care for anything!"

This mood was piteous, but it was also formidable, for I was scantily disposed to face the imputation of having reduced an amiable gentleman, in however strictly just a cause, to this state of plaintive cynicism. I could only hope that time would repair both his vanity and his charity, seriously damaged as they were. "Well," I said, taking my hat, "a man in love, you know, is obstinate. Confess, yourself, that you'd not think the better of me for accepting dismissal philosophically. A single word of caution, keep cool; don't lose your head; don't speak recklessly to Laura. I protest that, for myself, I'd rather my mistress shouldn't doubt of her father."

Guest had seated himself on the sofa with his hat on, and remained staring absently at the carpet, as if he were deaf to my words. As I turned away, Mrs. Beck crossed the piazza and stood on the threshold of the long window. Her shadow fell at Mr. Guest's feet; she sent a searching glance from his face to mine. He started, stared, rose, stiffened himself up, and removed his hat   Suddenly he

colored to his temples, and after a second's delay there is-
used from behind this ruby curtain a wondrous imitation
of a smile. I turned away, reassured. "My case is not
hopeless," I said to myself. "You *do* care for something,
yet." Even had I deemed it hopeless, I might have made
my farewell. Laura met me near the gate, and I remember
thinking that trouble was vastly becoming to her.

"Is your quarrel too bad to speak of?" she asked.

"Allow me to make an urgent request. Your father for-
bids me to think of you, and you, of course, to think of me.
You see," I said, mustering a smile, "we're in a delightfully
romantic position, persecuted by a stern parent. He will
say hard things of me; I say nothing about your believing
them, I leave that to your own discretion. But don't contradict them. Let him call me cruel, pusillanimous, false,
whatever he will. Ask no questions; they will bring you
no comfort. Be patient, be a good daughter, and—wait!"

Her brow contracted painfully over her intensely lucid
eyes, and she shook her head impatiently. "Let me understand. Have you really done wrong?"

I felt that it was but a slender sacrifice to generosity to
say Yes, and to add that I had repented. I even felt gratefully that whatever it might be to have a crime to confess
to, it was not "boyish."

For a moment, I think, Laura was on the point of asking me a supreme question about her father, but she suppressed it and abruptly left me.

My step-brother's feeble remnant of health was now so
cruelly reduced that the end of his troubles seemed near.
He was in constant pain, and was kept alive only by stupe-
fying drugs. As his last hour might strike at any moment, I was careful to remain within call, and for several
days saw nothing of father or daughter. I learned from
Crawford that they had determined to prolong their stay
into the autumn, for Mr. Guest's "health." "I don't know
what's the matter with his health," Crawford grumbled.
"For a sick man he seems uncommonly hearty, able to sit
out of doors till midnight with Mrs. B., and always as spick
and span as a bridegroom. I'm the invalid of the lot,"

he declared; "the climate don't agree with me." Mrs. Beck, it appeared, was too fickle for patience; he would be made a fool of no more. If she wanted him, she must come and fetch him; and if she valued her chance, she must do it without delay. He departed for New York to try the virtue of missing and being missed.

On the evening he left us, the doctor told me that Edgar could not outlast the night. At midnight, I relieved the watcher and took my place by his bed. Edgar's soundless and motionless sleep was horribly like death. Sitting watchful by his pillow, I passed an oppressively solemn night. It seemed to me that a part of myself was dying, and that I was sitting in cold survival of youthful innocence and of the lavish self-surrender of youth. There is a certain comfort in an ancient grievance, and as I thought of having heard for the last time the strenuous quaver of Edgar's voice, I could have wept as for the effacement of some revered horizon-line of life. I heard his voice again, however; he was not even to die without approving the matter. With the first flash of dawn and the earliest broken bird-note, he opened his eyes and began to murmur disconnectedly. At length he recognized me, and, with me, his situation. "Don't go on tiptoe, and hold your breath, and pull a long face," he said; "speak up like a man. I'm doing the biggest job I ever did yet, you'll not interrupt me; I'm dying. One—two, three—four; I can almost count the ebbing waves. And to think that all these years they've been breaking on the strand of the universe! It's only when the world's din is shut out, at the last, that we hear them. I'll not pretend to say I'm not sorry; I've been a man of this world. It's a great one; there's a vast deal to do in it, for a man of sense. I've not been a fool, either. Write that for my epitaph, *He was no fool!*—except when he went to L. I'm not satisfied yet. I might have got better, and richer. I wanted to try galvanism, and to transfer that Pennsylvania stock. Well, I'm to be transferred myself. If dying's the end of it all, it's as well to die worse as to die better. At any rate, while time was mine, I didn't waste it. I went over my will, pen in hand, for the last time, only a week ago, crossed the *t*'s and dotted the *i*'s. I've left you—nothing. You need nothing for comfort, and of course you expect nothing for sentiment. I've left twenty thousand dollars to found an infirmary for twenty indigent persons suffering from tumor in the stomach. *There*'s sentiment! There will be no trouble about it, for my affairs are in perfect shape. Twenty snug little beds in my own little house in Philadelphia. They can get five in the dining-room." He was silent awhile, as if with a kind of ecstatic vision of the five little beds in a row. "I don't know that there is anything else," he said, at last, "except a few old papers to be burned. I hate leaving rubbish behind me; it's enough to leave one's mouldering carcass!"

At his direction I brought a large tin box from a closet and placed it on a chair by his bedside, where I drew from it a dozen useless papers and burned them one by one in the candle. At last, when but three or four were left, I laid my hand on a small sealed document labelled *Guest's Confession*. My hand trembled as I held it up to him, and as he recognized it a faint flush overspread his cadaverous pallor. He frowned, as if painfully confused. "How did it come there? I sent it back, I sent it back," he said. Then suddenly with a strangely erroneous recollection of our recent dispute, "I told you so the other day, you remember; and you said I was too generous. And what did you tell me about the daughter? You're in love with her? Ah, yes! What a muddle!"

I respected his confusion. "You say you've left me nothing," I answered. "Leave me this."

For all reply, he turned over with a groan, and relapsed into stupor. The nurse shortly afterwards came to relieve me; but though I lay down, I was unable to sleep. The personal possession of that little scrap of paper acted altogether too potently on my nerves and my imagination. In due contravention of the doctor, Edgar outlasted the night and lived into another day. But as high noon was clashing out from the village church, and I stood with the doctor by his bedside, the latter, who had lifted his wrist a little to test his pulse, released it, not with the tenderness we render to suffering, but with a more summary reverence. Suffering was over.

By the close of the day I had finished my preparations for attending my step-brother's remains to burial in Philadelphia, among those of his own people; but before my departure, I measured once more that well-trodden road to the house by the river, and requested a moment's conversation with Mr. Guest. In spite of my attention being otherwise engaged, I had felt strangely all day that I carried a sort of magic talisman, a mystic key to fortune. I was constantly fumbling in my waistcoat pocket to see whether the talisman was really there. I wondered that as yet Guest should not have demanded a surrender of his note; but I attributed his silence to shame, scorn, and defiance, and promised myself a sort of golden advantage by anticipating his claim with the cogent frankness of justice. But as soon as he entered the room I foresaw that Justice must show her sword as well as her scales. His resentment had deepened into a kind of preposterous arrogance, of a temper quite insensible to logic. He had more than recovered his native buoyancy and splendor; there was an air of feverish impudence in his stare, his light swagger, in the very hue and fashion of his crimson necktie. He had an evil genius with blond curls and innumerable flounces.

"I feel it to be a sort of duty," I said, "to inform you that my brother died this morning."

"Your brother? What's your brother to me? He's been dead to me these three days. Is that all you have to say?"

I was irritated by the man's stupid implacability, and my purpose received a check. "No," I answered, "I've several things more to touch upon."

"In so far as they concern my daughter, you may leave them unsaid. She tells me of your offer to—to *buy off* my opposition. Am I to understand that it was seriously made? You're a coarser young man than I fancied!"

"She told you of my offer?" I cried.

"O, you needn't build upon that. She hasn't mentioned your name since."

I was silent, thinking my own thoughts. I won't answer for it, that in spite of his caution, I did *not* lay an immaterial brick or two. "You're still irreconcilable?" I contented myself with asking.

He assumed an expression of absolutely jovial contempt. "My dear sir, I detest the sight of you!"

"Have you no question to ask, no demand to make?"

He looked at me a moment in silence, with just the least little twitch and tremor of mouth and eye. His vanity, I guessed on the instant, was determined stoutly to ignore that I held him at an advantage and to refuse me the satisfaction of extorting from him the least allusion to the evidence of his disgrace. He had known bitter compulsion once; he would not do it the honor to concede that it had not spent itself. "No demand but that you will excuse my further attendance."

My own vanity took a hand in the game. Justice herself was bound to go no more than half-way. If he was not afraid of his little paper, he might try a week or two more of bravery. I bowed to him in silence and let him depart. As I turned to go I found myself face to face with Mrs. Beck, whose pretty visage was flushed with curiosity. "You and Mr. Guest have quarrelled," she said roundly.

"As you see, madam."

"As I see, madam! But what is it all about?"

"About—his daughter."

"His daughter and his ducats! You're a very deep young man, in spite of those boyish looks of yours. Why did you never tell me you knew him? You've quarrelled about money matters."

"As you say," I answered, "I'm very deep. Don't tempt me to further subterfuge."

"He has lost money, I know. Is it much? Tell me that."

"It's an enormous sum!" I said, with mock solemnity.

"Provoking man!" And she gave a little stamp of disgust.

"He's in trouble," I said. "To a woman of your tender sympathies he ought to be more interesting than ever."

She mused a moment, fixing me with her keen blue eye. "It's a sad responsibility to have a heart!" she murmured.

"In that," I said, "we perfectly agree."

VI

It was a singular fact that Edgar's affairs turned out to be in by no means the exemplary order in which he had flattered himself he placed them. They were very much at sixes and sevens. The discovery, to me, was almost a shock. I might have drawn from it a pertinent lesson on the fallacy of human pretensions. The gentleman whom Edgar had supremely honored (as he seemed to assume in his will) by appointing his executor, responded to my innocent surprise by tapping his forehead with a peculiar smile. It was partly from curiosity as to the value of this explanation, that I helped him to look into the dense confusion which prevailed in my step-brother's estate. It revealed certainly an odd compound of madness and method. I learned with real regret that the twenty eleemosynary beds at Philadelphia must remain a superb conception. I was horrified at every step by the broad license with which his will had to be interpreted. All profitless as I was in the case, when I thought of the comfortable credit in which he had died, I felt like some greedy kinsman of tragedy making impious havoc with a sacred bequest. These matters detained me for a week in New York, where I had joined my brother's executor. At my earliest moment of leisure, I called upon Crawford at the office of a friend to whom he had addressed me, and learned that after three or four dismally restless days in town, he had taken a summary departure for L. A couple of days later, I was struck with a certain dramatic connection between his return and the following note from Mr. Guest, which I give verbally, in its pregnant brevity:—

SIR:—I possess a claim on your late brother's estate which it is needless to specify. You will either satisfy it by return of mail or forfeit forever the common respect of gentlemen.   J.G.

Things had happened with the poor man rather as I
hoped than as I expected. He had borrowed his recent exaggerated defiance from the transient smiles of Mrs. Beck.
They had gone to his head like the fumes of wine, and he
had dreamed for a day that he could afford to snap his
fingers at the past. What he really desired and hoped of
Mrs. Beck I was puzzled to say. In this woful disrepair of
his fortunes he could hardly have meant to hold her to a
pledge of matrimony extorted in brighter hours. He was
infatuated, I believed, partly by a weak, spasmodic optim-
ism which represented his troubles as momentary, and enjoined him to hold firm till something turned up, and partly
by a reckless and frivolous susceptibility to the lady's un-
scrupulous blandishments. While they prevailed, he lost
all notion of the wholesome truth of things, and would have
been capable of any egregious folly. Mrs. Beck was in love
with him, in so far as she was capable of being in love; his
gallantry, of all gallantries, suited her to a charm; but she
reproached herself angrily with this amiable weakness, and
prudence every day won back an inch of ground. Poor
Guest indeed had clumsily snuffed out his candle. He had
slept in the arms of Delilah, and he had waked to find that
Delilah had guessed, if not his secret, something uncomfort-
ably like it. Crawford's return had found Mrs. Beck with
but a scanty remnant of sentiment and a large accession
of prudence, which was graciously placed at his service.
Guest, hereupon, as I conjectured, utterly disillusioned by
the cynical frankness of her defection, had seen his horizon
grow ominously dark, and begun to fancy, as I remained
silent, that there was thunder in the air. His pompous
waiving, in his note, of allusion both to our last meeting
and to my own present claim, seemed to me equally characteristic of his weakness and of his distress. The bitter
after-taste of Mrs. Beck's coquetry had, at all events,
brought him back to reality. For myself, the real fact in
the matter was the image of Laura Guest, sitting pensive,
like an exiled pricess.

I sent him nothing by return of mail. On my arrival in
New York, I had enclosed the precious document in an

envelope, addressed it, and stamped it, and put it back in my pocket. I could not rid myself of a belief that by that sign I should conquer. Several times I drew it forth and laid it on the table before me, reflecting that I had but a word to say to have it dropped into the post. Cowardly, was it, to keep it? But what was it to give up one's mistress without a battle? Which was the uglier, my harshness or Guest's? In a holy cause,—and holy, you may be sure, I had dubbed mine,—were not all arms sanctified? Possession meant peril, and peril to a manly sense, of soul and conscience, as much as of person and fortune. Mine, at any rate, should share the danger. It was a sinister-looking talisman certainly; but when it had failed, it would be time enough to give it up.

In these thoughts I went back to L. I had taken the morning train; I arrived at noon, and with small delay proceeded to the quiet little house which harbored such world-vexed spirits. It was one of the first days of September, and the breath of autumn was in the air. Summer still met the casual glance; but the infinite light of summer had found its term; it was as if there were a leak in the crystal vault of the firmament through which the luminous ether of June was slowly stealing away.

Mr. Guest, I learned from the servant, had started on a walk,—to the mill, she thought, three miles away. I sent in my card to Laura, and went into the garden to await her appearance—or her answer. At the end of five minutes, I saw her descend from the piazza and advance down the long path. Her light black dress swept the little box-borders, and over her head she balanced a white parasol. I met her, and she stopped, silent and grave. "I've come to learn," I said, "that absence has not been fatal to me."

"You've hardly been absent. You left a—an influence behind,—a very painful one. In Heaven's name!" she cried, with vehemence, "what horrible wrong have you done?"

"I have done no horrible wrong. Do you believe me?" She scanned my face searchingly for a moment; then she gave a long, gentle, irrepressible sigh of relief. "Do you fancy that if I had, I could meet your eyes, feel the folds of your dress? I've done that which I have bitterly wished undone; I did it in ignorance, weakness, and folly; I've repented in passion and truth. Can a man do more?"

"I never was afraid of the truth," she answered slowly; "I don't see that I need fear it now. I'm not a child. Tell me the absolute truth!"

"The absolute truth," I said, "is that your father once saw me in a very undignified position. It made such an impression on him that he's unable to think of me in any other. You see I was rather cynically indifferent to his observation, for I didn't know him then as your father."

She gazed at me with the same adventurous candor, and blushed a little as I became silent, then turned away and strolled along the path. "It seems a miserable thing," she said, "that two gentle spirits like yours should have an irreparable difference. When good men hate each other, what are they to do to the bad men? You must excuse my want of romance, but I cannot listen to a suitor of whom my father complains. Make peace!"

"Shall peace with him be peace with you?"

"Let me see you frankly shake hands," she said, not directly answering. "Be very kind! You don't know what he has suffered here lately." She paused, as if to conceal a tremor in her voice.

Had she read between the lines of that brilliant improvisation of mine, or was she moved chiefly with pity for his recent sentimental tribulations,—pitying them the more that she respected them the less? "He has walked to the mill," I said; "I shall meet him, and we'll come back arm in arm." I turned away, so that I might not see her face pleading for a clemency which would make me too delicate. I went down beside the river and followed the old towing-path, now grassy with disuse. Reaching the shabby wooden bridge below the mill, I stopped midway across it and leaned against the railing. Below, the yellow water swirled past the crooked piers. I took my little sealed paper out of my pocket-book and held it over the stream, almost courting the temptation to drop it; but the temptation never came. I had just put it back in my pocket when I heard a footstep on the planks behind me. Turning round I beheld Mr. Guest. He looked tired and dusty with his walk, and had the air of a man who had been trying by violent exercise to shake off a moral incubus. Judging by his haggard brow and heavy eyes, he had hardly succeeded. As he recognized me, he started just perceptibly, as if he were too weary to be irritated. He was about to pass on without speaking, but I intercepted him. My movement provoked a flash in his sullen pupil. "I came on purpose to meet you," I said. "I have just left your daughter, and I feel more than ever how passionately I love her. Once more, I demand that you withdraw your opposition."

"Is that your answer to my letter?" he asked, eyeing me from under his brows.

"Your letter puts me in a position to make my demand with force. I refuse to submit to this absurd verdict of accident. I have just seen your daughter, and I have authority to bring you to reason."

"My daughter has received you?" he cried, flushing.

"Most kindly."

"You scoundrel!"

"Gently, gently. Shake hands with me here where we stand, and let me keep my promise to Laura of our coming back to her arm in arm, at peace, reconciled, mutually forgiving and forgetting, or I walk straight back and put a certain little paper into her hands."

He turned deadly pale, and a fierce oath broke from his lips. He had been beguiled, I think, by my neglect of his letter, into the belief that Edgar had not died without destroying his signature,—a belief rendered possible by an indefeasible faith he must have had in my step-brother's probity. "You've kept that thing!" he cried. "The Lord be praised! I'm as honest a man as either of you!"

"Say but two words,—'Take her!'—and we shall be honest together again. The paper's yours." He turned away and learned against the railing of the bridge, with his head in his hands, watching the river.

"Take your time," I continued; "I give you two hours.

Go home, look at your daughter, and choose. An hour hence I'll join you. If I find you've removed your veto, I undertake to make you forget you ever offered it: if I find you've maintained it, I expose you."

"In either case you lose your mistress. Whatever Laura may think of me, there can be no doubt as to what she will think of you."

"I shall be forgiven. Leave that to me! That's my last word. In a couple of hours I shall take the liberty of coming to learn yours."

"O Laura, Laura!" cried the poor man in his bitter trouble. But I left him and walked away. I turned as I reached the farther end of the bridge, and saw him slowly resume his course. I marched along the road to the mill, so excited with having uttered this brave *ultimatum* that I hardly knew whither I went. But at last I bethought me of a certain shady stream-side nook just hereabouts, which a little exploration soon discovered. A shallow cove, screened from the road by dense clumps of willows, stayed the current a moment in its grassy bend. I had noted it while boating, as a spot where a couple of lovers might aptly disembark and moor their idle skiff; and I was now tempted to try its influence in ardent solitude. I flung myself on the ground, and as I listened to the light gurgle of the tarrying stream and to the softer rustle of the cool gray leafage around me, I suddenly felt that I was exhausted and sickened. I lay motionless, watching the sky and resting from my anger. Little by little it melted away and left me horribly ashamed. How long I lay there I know not, nor what was the logic of my meditations, but an ineffable change stole over my spirit. There are fathomless depths in spiritual mood and motive. Opposite me, on the farther side of the stream, winding along a path through the bushes, three or four cows had come down to drink. I sat up and watched them. A young man followed them, in a red shirt, with his trousers in his boots. While they were comfortably nosing the water into ripples, he sat down on a stone and began to light his pipe. In a moment I fancied I saw the little blue thread of smoke curl up from the bowl. From beyond, just droning through the air, came the liquid rumble of the mill. There seemed to me something in this vision ineffably pastoral, peaceful, and innocent; it smote me to my heart of hearts. I felt a nameless wave of impulse start somewhere in the innermost vitals of conscience and fill me with passionate shame. I fell back on the grass and burst into tears.

The sun was low and the breeze had risen when I rose to my feet. I scrambled back to the road, crossed the bridge, and hurried home by the towing-path. My heart, however, beat faster than my footfalls. I passed into the garden and advanced to the house; as I stepped upon the piazza, I was met by Mrs. Beck. "Answer me a simple question," she cried, laying her hand on my arm.

"I should like to hear you ask one!" I retorted, impatiently.

"Has Mr. Guest lost his mind?"

"For an hour! I've brought it back to him."

"You've a pretty quarrel between you. He comes up an hour ago, as I was sitting in the garden with—with Mr. Crawford, requests a moment's interview, leads me apart and—offers himself. 'If you'll have me, take me now; you won't an hour hence,' he cried. 'Neither now nor an hour hence, thank you,' said I. 'My affections are fixed—elsewhere.' "

"You've not lost your head, at any rate," said I; and, releasing myself, I went into the parlor. I had a horrible fear of being too late. The candles stood lighted on the piano, and tea had been brought in, but the kettle was singing unheeded. On the divan facing the window sat Guest, lounging back on the cushions, his hat and stick flung down beside him, his hands grasping his knees, his head thrown back, and his eyes closed. That he should have remained so for an hour, unbrushed and unfurbished, spoke volumes as to his mental state. Near him sat Laura, looking at him askance in mute anxiety. What had passed between them? Laura's urgent glance as I entered was full of trouble, but I fancied without reproach. He had apparently chosen neither way; he had simply fallen there, weary, desperate, and dumb.

"I'm disappointed!" Laura said to me gravely.

Her father opened his eyes, stared at me a moment, and then closed them. I answered nothing; but after a moment's hesitation went and took my seat beside Guest. I laid my hand on his own with a grasp of which he felt, first the force, then, I think, the kindness; for, after a momentary spasm of repulsion, he remained coldly passive. He must have begun to wonder. "Be so good," I said to Laura, "as to bring me one of the candles." She looked surprised; but she complied and came toward me, holding the taper, like some pale priestess expecting a portent. I drew out the note and held it to the flame. "Your father and I have had a secret," I said, "which has been a burden to both of us. Here it goes." Laura's hand trembled as she held the candle, and mine as I held the paper; but between us the vile thing blazed and was consumed. I glanced askance at Guest; he was staring wide-eyed at the dropping cinders. When the last had dropped, I took the candle, rose, and carried it back to the piano. Laura dropped on her knees before her father, and, while my back was turned, something passed between them with which I was concerned only in its consequences.

When I looked round, Guest had risen and was passing his fingers through his hair. "Daughter," he said, "when I came in, what was it I said to you?"

She stood for an instant with her eyes on the floor. Then, "I've forgotten!" she said, simply.

Mrs. Beck had passed in by the window in time to hear these last words. "Do you know what you said to me when you came in?" she cried, mirthfully shaking a finger at Guest. He laughed nervously, picked up his hat, and stood looking, with an air of odd solemnity, at his boots. Suddenly it seemed to occur to him that he was dusty and dishevelled. He settled his shirt-collar and levelled a glance at the mirror, in which he caught my eye. He tried hard to look insensible; but it was the glance of a man who felt more comfortable than he had done in a month. He marched stiffly to the door.

"Are you going to dress?" said Mrs. Beck.

"From head to foot!" he cried, with violence.

"Be so good, then, if you see Mr. Crawford in the hall, as to ask him to come in and have a cup of tea."

Laura had passed out to the piazza, where I immediately joined her. "Your father accepts me," I said; "there is nothing left but for you——"

Five minutes later, I looked back through the window to see if we were being observed. But Mrs. Beck was busy adding another lump of sugar to Crawford's cup of tea. His eye met mine, however, and I fancied he looked sheepish.

ADINA

I

WE had been talking of Sam Scrope round the fire —mindful, such of us, of the rule *de mortuis*. Our host, however, had said nothing; rather to my surprise, as I knew he had been particularly intimate with our friend. But when our group had dispersed, and I remained alone with him, he brightened the fire, offered me another cigar, puffed his own awhile with a retrospective air, and told me the following tale:

Eighteen years ago Scrope and I were together in Rome. It was the beginning of my acquaintance with him, and I had grown fond of him, as a mild, meditative youth often does of an active, irreverent, caustic one. He had in those days the germs of the eccentricities,—not to call them by a hard name,—which made him afterwards the most intolerable of the friends we did not absolutely break with; he was already, as they say, a crooked stick. He was cynical, perverse, conceited, obstinate, brilliantly clever. But he was young, and youth, happily, makes many of our vices innocent. Scrope had his merits, or our friendship would not have ripened. He was not an amiable man, but he was an honest one—in spite of the odd caprice I have to relate; and half my kindness for him was based in a feeling that at bottom in spite of his vanity, he enjoyed his own irritability as little as other people. It was his fancy to pretend that he enjoyed nothing, and that what sentimental travelers call picturesqueness was a weariness to his spirit; but the world was new to him and the charm of fine things often took him by surprise and stole a march on his premature cynicism. He was an observer in spite of himself, and in his happy moods, thanks to his capital memory and ample information, an excellent critic and most profitable companion. He was a punctilious classical scholar. My boyish journal, kept in those days, is stuffed with learned allusions; they are all Scrope's. I brought to the service of my Roman experience much more loose sentiment than rigid science. It was indeed a jocular bargain between us that in our wanderings, picturesque and archæological, I should undertake the sentimental business—the raptures, the reflections, the sketching, the quoting from Byron. He considered me absurdly Byronic, and when, in the manner of tourists at that period, I breathed poetic sighs over the subjection of Italy to the foreign foe, he used to swear that Italy had got no more than she deserved, that she was a land of vagabonds and declaimers, and that he had yet to see an Italian whom he would call a man. I quoted to him from Alfieri that the "human plant" grew stronger in Italy than anywhere else, and he retorted, that nothing grew strong there but lying and cheating, laziness, beggary and vermin. Of course we each said more than we believed. If we met a shepherd on the Campagna, leaning on his crook and gazing at us darkly from under the shadow of his matted locks, I would proclaim that he was the handsomest fellow in the world, and demand of Scrope to stop and let me sketch him. Scrope would confound him for a filthy scare-crow and me for a drivelling album-poet. When I stopped in the street to stare up at some mouldering *palazzo* with a patched petticoat hanging to dry from the drawing-room window, and assured him that its haunted disrepair was dearer to my soul than the neat barred front of my Aunt Esther's model mansion in Mount Vernon street, he would seize me by the arm and march me off, pinching me till I shook myself free, and whelming me, my soul and my *palazzo* in a ludicrous torrent of abuse. The truth was that the picturesque of Italy, both in man and in nature, fretted him, depressed him, strangely. He was consciously a harsh note in the midst of so many mellow harmonies; everything seemed to say to him—"Don't you wish you were as easy, as loveable, as carelessly beautiful as we?" In the bottom of his heart he did wish it. To appreciate the bitterness of this dumb disrelish of the Italian atmosphere, you must remember how very ugly the poor fellow was. He was uglier at twenty than at forty, for as he grew older it became the fashion to say that his crooked features were "distinguished." But twenty years ago, in the infancy of modern æsthetics, he could not have passed for even a bizarre form of ornament. In a single word, poor Scrope looked *common:* that was where the shoe pinched. Now, you know that in Italy almost everything has, to the outer sense, what artists call style.

In spite of our clashing theories, our friendship *did* ripen, and we spent together many hours, deeply seasoned with the sense of youth and freedom. The best of these, perhaps, were those we passed on horseback, on the Campagna; you remember such hours; you remember those days of early winter, when the sun is as strong as that of a New England June, and the bare, purple-drawn slopes and hollows lie bathed in the yellow light of Italy. On such a day, Scrope and I mounted our horses in the grassy terrace before St. John Lateran, and rode away across the broad meadows over which the Claudian Aqueduct drags its slow length—stumbling and lapsing here and there, as it goes, beneath the burden of the centuries. We rode a long distance—well towards Albano, and at last stopped near a low fragment of ruin, which seemed to be all that was left of an ancient tower. Was it indeed ancient, or was it a relic of one of the numerous mediæval fortresses, with which the grassy desert of the Campagna is studded? This was one of the questions which Scrope, as a competent classicist, liked to ponder; though when I called his attention to the picturesque effect of the fringe of wild plants which crowned the ruin, and detached their clear filaments in the deep blue air, he shrugged his shoulders and said they only helped the brick-work to crumble. We tethered our horses to a wild fig tree hard by, and strolled around the tower. Suddenly, on the sunny side of it, we came upon a figure asleep on the grass. A young man lay there, all unconscious, with his head upon a pile of weed-smothcred stones. A rusty gun was on the ground beside him, and an empty game bag, lying near it, told of his being an unlucky sportsman. His heavy sleep seemed to point to a long morning's fruitless tramp. And yet he must have been either very unskilled, or very little in earnest, for the Campagna is alive with small game every month in the year—or was, at least, twenty years ago. It was no more than I owed to my reputation for Byronism, to discover a careless, youthful grace in the young fellow's attitude. One of his legs was flung over the other; one of his arms was thrust back under his head, and the other resting loosely on the grass; his head drooped backward, and exposed a strong, young throat; his hat was pulled over his eyes, so that we could see nothing but his mouth and chin. "An American rustic asleep is an ugly fellow," said I; "but this young Roman clodhopper, as he lies snoring there, is really statuesque;" "clodhopper," was for argument, for our rustic Endymion, judging by his garments, was something better than a mere peasant. He turned uneasily as we stood above him, and muttered something. "It's not fair to wake him," I said, and passed my arm into Scrope's, to lead him away; but he resisted, and I saw that something had struck him.

In his change of position, our picturesque friend had opened the hand which was resting on the grass. The palm, turned upward, contained a dull-colored oval object, of the size of a small snuff-box. "What has he got there?" I said to Scrope; but Scrope only answered by bending over and looking at it. "Really, we are taking great liberties with the poor fellow," I said. "Let him finish his nap in peace." And I was on the point of walking away. But my voice had aroused him; he lifted his hand, and, with the movement, the object I have compared to a snuff-box caught the light, and emitted a dull flash.

"It's a gem," said Scrope, "recently disinterred and encrusted with dirt."

The young man awoke in earnest, pushed back his hat, stared at us, and slowly sat up. He rubbed his eyes, to see if he were not still dreaming, then glanced at the gem, if gem it was, thrust his hand mechanically into his pocket,

and gave us a broad smile. "Gentle, serene Italian nature!"
I exclaimed. "A young New England farmer, whom we
should have disturbed in this fashion, would wake up with
an oath and a kick."

"I mean to test his gentleness," said Scrope. "I'm determined to see what he has got there." Scrope was very
fond of small *bric-a-brac*, and had ransacked every curiosity shop in Rome. It was an oddity among his many
oddities, but it agreed well enough with the rest of them.
What he looked for and relished in old prints and old china
was not, generally, beauty of form nor romantic association;
it was elaborate and patient workmanship, fine engraving,
skillful method.

"Good day," I said to our young man; "we didn't mean
to interrupt you."

He shook himself, got up, and stood before us, looking
out from under his thick curls, and still frankly smiling.
There was something very simple,—a trifle silly,—in his
smile, and I wondered whether he was not under-witted.
He was young, but he was not a mere lad. His eyes were
dark and heavy, but they gleamed with a friendly light,
and his parted lips showed the glitter of his strong, white
teeth. His complexion was of a fine, deep brown, just removed from coarseness by that vague suffused pallor common among Italians. He had the frame of a young Hercu-
les; he was altogether as handsome a vagabond as you
could wish for the foreground of a pastoral landscape.

"You've not earned your rest," said Scrope, pointing to
his empty game bag; "you've got no birds."

He looked at the bag and at Scrope, and then scratched
his head and laughed. "I don't want to kill them," he said.
"I bring out my gun because it's stupid to walk about pulling a straw! And then my uncle is always grumbling at
me for not doing something. When he sees me leave the
house with my gun, he thinks I may, at least, get my dinner. He didn't know the lock's broke; even if I had
powder and shot, the old blunderbuss wouldn't go off.
When I'm hungry I go to sleep." And he glanced, with
his handsome grin, at his recent couch. "The birds might

come and perch on my nose, and not wake me up. My uncle never thinks of asking me what I have brought home for supper. He is a holy man, and lives on black bread and beans."

"Who is your uncle?" I inquired.

"The Padre Girolamo at Lariceia."

He looked at our hats and whips, asked us a dozen questions about our ride, our horses, and what we paid for them, our nationality, and our way of life in Rome, and at last walked away to caress our browsing animals and scratch their noses. "He has got something precious there," Scrope said, as we strolled after him. "He has evidently found it in the ground. The Campagna is full of treasures yet." As we overtook our new acquaintance he thrust his indistinguishable prize behind him, and gave a foolish laugh, which tried my companion's patience. "The fellow's an idiot!" he cried. "Does he think I want to snatch the thing?"

"What is it you've got there?" I asked kindly.

"Which hand will you have?" he said, still laughing.

"The right."

"The left," said Scrope, as he hesitated.

He fumbled behind him a moment more, and then produced his treasure with a flourish. Scrope took it, wiped it off carefully with his handkerchief, and bent his near-sighted eyes over it. I left him to examine it. I was more interested in watching the Padre Girolamo's nephew. The latter stood looking at my friend gravely, while Scrope rubbed and scratched the little black stone, breathed upon it and held it up to the light. He frowned and scratched his head; he was evidently trying to concentrate his wits on the fine account he expected Scrope to give of it. When I glanced towards Scrope, I found he had flushed excitedly, and I immediately bent my nose over it too. It was of about the size of a small hen's-egg, of a dull brown color, stained and encrusted by long burial, and deeply corrugated on one surface. Scrope paid no heed to my questions, but continued to scrape and polish. At last—"How did you come by this thing?" he asked dryly.

"I found it in the earth, a couple of miles from here, this morning." And the young fellow put out his hand nervously, to take it back. Scrope resisted a moment, but thought better, and surrendered it. As an old mouser, he began instinctively to play at indifference. Our companion looked hard at the little stone, turned it over and over, then thrust it behind him again, with his simple-souled laugh.

"Here's a precious chance," murmured Scrope.

"But in Heaven's name, what is it?" I demanded, impatiently.

"Don't ask me. I don't care to phrase the conjecture audibly—it's immense—if it's what I think it is; and here stands this giggling lout with a prior claim to it. What shall I do with him? I should like to knock him in the head with the butt end of his blunderbuss."

"I suppose he'll sell you the thing, if you offer him enough."

"Enough? What does he know about enough? He don't know a topaz from a turnip."

"Is it a topaz, then?"

"Hold your tongue, and don't mentin names. He must sell it as a turnip. Make him tell you just where he found it."

He told us very frankly, still smiling from ear to ear. He had observed in a solitary ilex-tree, of great age, the traces of a recent lightning-stroke. (A week of unseasonably sultry weather had, in fact, some days before, culminated in a terrific thunder-storm.) The tree had been shivered and killed, and the earth turned up at its foot. The bolt, burying itself, had dug a deep, straight hole, in which one might have planted a stake. "I don't know why," said our friend, "but as I stood looking at it, I thrust the muzzle of my old gun into the aperture. It descended for some distance and stopped with a strange noise, as if it were striking a metallic surface. I rammed it up and down, and heard the same noise. Then I said to myself—'Something is hidden there—*quattrini*, perhaps; let us see.' I made a spade of one the shivered ilex-boughs, dug, and scraped and scratched; and, in twenty minutes, fished up a little, rotten, iron box. It was so rotten that the lid and sides were as thin as letter-paper. When I gave them a knock, they crumbled. It was filled with other bits of iron of the same sort, which seemed to have formed the compartments of a case; and with the damp earth, which had oozed in through the holes and crevices. In the middle lay this stone, embedded in earth and mold. There was nothing else. I broke the box to pieces and kept the stone. *Ecco!*"

Scrope, with a shrug, repossessed himself of the moldy treasure, and our friend, as he gave it up, declared it was a thousand years old. Julius Cæsar had worn it in his crown!

"Julius Cæsar wore no crown, my dear friend," said Scrope urbanely. "It may be a thousand years old, and it may be ten. It may be an—agate, and it may be a flint! I don't know. But if you will sell it on the chance?——" And he tossed it three times high into the air, and caught it as it fell.

"I have my idea it's precious," said the young man. "Precious things are found here every day—why shouldn't I stumble on something as well as another? Why should the lightning strike just that spot, and no other? It was sent there by my patron, the blessed Saint Angelo!"

He was not such a simpleton, after all; or rather he was a puzzling mixture of simplicity and sense. "If you really want the thing," I said to Scrope, "make him an offer, and have done with it."

" 'Have done with it,' is easily said. How little do you suppose he will take?"

"I haven't the smallest idea of its value."

"Its value has nothing to do with the matter. Estimate it at its value and we may as well put it back into its hole—of its probable value, he knows nothing; he need never know," and Scrope, musing an instant, counted, and fiung them down on the grass, ten silver *scudi*—the same number of dollars. Angelo,—he virtually told us his name, —watched them fall, one by one, but made no movement

to pick them up. But his eyes brightened; his simplicity
and his shrewdness were debating the question. The little
heap of silver was most agreeable; to make a poor bargain,
on the other hand, was not. He looked at Scrope with a
dumb appeal to his fairness which quite touched me. It
touched Scrope, too, a trifle; for, after a moment's hesitation, he flung down another *scudo*. Angelo gave a puzzled
sigh, and Scrope turned short about and began to mount.
In another moment we were both in the saddle. Angelo
stood looking at his money. "Are you satisfied?" said my
companion, curtly.

The young fellow gave a strange smile. "Have *you* a
good conscience?" he demanded.

"Hang your impudence!" cried Scrope, very red. "What's
my conscience to you?" And he thrust in his spurs and
galloped away. I waved my hand to our friend and followed more slowly. Before long I turned in the saddle
and looked back. Angelo was standing as we had left
him, staring after us, with his money evidently yet untouched. But, of course, he would pick it up!

I rode along with my friend in silence; I was wondering
over his off-hand justice. I was youthful enough to shrink
from being thought a Puritan or a casuist, but it seemed
to me that I scented sophistry in Scrope's double valuation
of Angelo's treasure. If it was a prize for him, it was a
prize for Angelo, and ten *scudi*,—and one over,—was meagre
payment for a prize. It cost me some discomfort to find
rigid Sam Scrope, of all men, capable of a piece of bargaining which needed to be ingeniously explained. Such
as it was, he offered his explanation at last—half angrily,
as if he knew his logic was rather grotesque. "Say it out;
say it, for Heaven's sake!" he cried. "I know what you're
thinking—I've played that pretty-faced simpleton a trick,
eh?—and I'm no better than a swindler, evidently! Let
me tell you, once for all, that I'm not ashamed of having
got my prize cheap. It was ten *scudi* or nothing! If I
had offered a farthing more I should have opened those
sleepy eyes of his. It was a case to pocket one's scruples
and *act*. That silly boy was not to be trusted with the

keeping of such a prize for another half hour; the deuce knows what might have become of it. I rescued it in the interest of art, of science, of taste. The proper price of the thing I couldn't have dreamed of offering; where was I to raise ten thousand dollars to buy a bauble? Say I had offered a hundred—forthwith our picturesque friend, thick-witted though he is, would have pricked up his ears and held fast! He would have asked time to reflect and take advice, and he would have hurried back to his village and to his uncle, the shrewd old priest, Padre Girolamo. The wise-heads of the place would have held a conclave, and decided—I don't know what; that they must go up to Rome and see Signor Castillani, or the director of the Papal excavations. Some knowing person would have got wind of the affair, and whispered to the Padre Girolamo that his handsome nephew had been guided by a miracle to a fortune, and might marry a *contessina*. And when all was done, where should I be for my pains? As it is, I discriminate; I look at the matter all round, and I decide. I get my prize; the ingenious Angelo gets a month's carouse, —he'll enjoy it,—and goes to sleep again. Pleasant dreams to him! What does he want of money? Money would have corrupted him! I've saved the *contessina*, too; I'm sure he would have beaten her. So, if we're all satisfied, is it for you to look black? My mind's at ease; I'm neither richer nor poorer. I'm not poorer, because against my eleven *scudi* may stand the sense of having given a harmless treat to an innocent lad; I'm not richer, because, —I hope you understand,—I mean never to turn my stone into money. There it is that delicacy comes in. It's a stone and nothing more; and all the income I shall derive from it will be enjoying the way people open their eyes and hold their breath when I make it sparkle under the lamp, and tell them just what stone it is."

"What stone is it, then, in the name of all that's demoralizing?" I asked, with ardor.

Scrope broke into a gleeful chuckle, and patted me on the arm. "*Pazrinza!* Wait till we get under the lamp, some evening, and then I'll make it sparkle and tell you. I must be sure first," he added, with sudden gravity.

But it was the feverish elation of his tone, and not its gravity, that struck me. I began to hate the stone; it seemed to have corrupted him. His ingenious account of his motives left something vaguely unexplained—almost inexplicable. There are dusky corners in the simplest natures; strange, moral involutions in the healthiest. Scrope was not simple, and, in virtue of his defiant self-consciousness, he might have been called morbid; so that I came to consider his injustice in this particular case as the fruit of a vicious seed which I find it hard to name. Everything in Italy seemed mutely to reproach him with his meager faculty of pleasing; the indefinable gracefulness of nature and man murmured forever in his ears that he was an angular cynic. This was the real motive of his intolerance of my sympathetic rhapsodies, and it prompted him now to regale himself, once for all, with the sense of an advantage wrested, if not by fair means, then by foul, from some sentient form of irritating Italian felicity. This is a rather metaphysical account of the matter; at the time I guessed the secret, without phrasing it.

Scrope carried his stone to no appraiser, and asked no archæological advice about it. He quietly informed himself, as if from general curiosity, as to the best methods of cleansing, polishing, and restoring antique gems, laid in a provision of delicate tools and acids, turned the key in his door, and took the measure of his prize. I asked him no questions, but I saw that he was intensely preoccupied, and was becoming daily better convinced that it was a rare one. He went about whistling and humming odd scraps of song, like a lover freshly accepted. Whenever I heard him I had a sudden vision of our friend Angelo staring blankly after us, as we rode away like a pair of ravishers in a German ballad. Scrope and I lodged in the same house, and one evening, at the end of a week, after I had gone to bed, he made his way into my room, and shook me out of my slumbers as if the house were on fire. I guessed his errand before he had told it, shuffled on my dressing-gown, and hurried to his own apartment. "I couldn't wait till morning," he said, "I've just given it the last touch; there it lies in its imperial beauty!"

There it lay, indeed, under the lamp, flashing back the light from its glowing heart—a splendid golden topaz on a cushion of white velvet. He thrust a magnifying glass into my hand, and pushed me into a chair by the table. I saw the surface of the stone was worked in elaborate intaglio, but I was not prepared for the portentous character of image and legend. In the center was a full-length naked figure, which I supposed at first to be a pagan deity. Then I saw the orb of sovereignty in one outstretched hand, the chiselled imperial scepter in the other, and the laurel-crown on the low-browed head. All round the face of the stone, near the edges, ran a chain of carven figures—warriors, and horses, and chariots, and young men and women interlaced in elaborate confusion. Over the head of the image, within this concave frieze, stood the inscription:

DIVUS TIBERIUS CÆSAR TOTIUS ORBIS IMPERATOR.

The workmanship was extraordinarily delicate; beneath the powerful glass I held in my hand, the figures revealed the perfection and finish of the most renowned of antique marbles. The color of the stone was superb, and, now that its purity had been restored, its size seemed prodigious. It was in every way a gem among gems, a priceless treasure.

"Don't you think it was worth while getting up to shake hands with the Emperor Tiberius?" cried Scrope, after observing my surprise. "Shabby Nineteenth Century Yankees, as we are, we are having our audience. Down on your knees, barbarian, we're in a tremendous presence! Haven't I worked all these days and nights, with my little rags and files, to some purpose? I've annulled the centuries—I've resuscitated a *totius orbis imperator*. Do you conceive, do you apprehend, does your heart thump against your ribs? Not as it should, evidently. This is where Cæsar wore it, dull modern—here, on his breast, near the shoulder, framed in chiselled gold, circled about with pearls as big as plums, clasping together the two sides of his gold-stiffened mantle. It was the agraffe of the imperial purple. Tremble, sir!" and he took up the splendid jewel, and held it against my breast. "No doubts —no objections—no reflections—or we're mortal enemies. How do I know it—where's my warrant? It simply must be! It's too precious to have been anything else. It's the finest intaglio in the world. It has told me its secret; it has lain whispering classic Latin to me by the hour all this week past."

"And has it told you how it came to be buried in its iron box?"

"It has told me everything—more than I can tell you now. Content yourself for the present with admiring it."

Admire it I did for a long time. Certainly, if Scrope's hypothesis was not sound, it ought to have been, and if the Emperor Tiberius had never worn the topaz in his mantle, he was by so much the less imperial. But the design, the legend, the shape of the stone, were all very cogent evidence that the gem had played a great part. "Yes, surely," I said, "it's the finest of known intaglios."

Scrope was silent a while. "Say of unknown," he answered at last. "No one shall ever know it. You I hereby hold pledged to secrecy. I shall show it to no one else— except to my mistress, if I ever have one. I paid for the chance of its turning out something great. I couldn't pay for the renown of possessing it. That only a princely fortune could have purchased. To be known as the owner of the finest intaglio in the world would make a great man of me, and that would hardly be fair to our friend Angelo. I shall sink the glory, and cherish my treasure for its simple artistic worth."

"And how would you express that simple artistic worth in Roman *scudi?*"

"It's impossible. Fix upon any sum you please."

I looked again at the golden topaz, gleaming in its velvet nest; and I felt that there could be no successful effort to conceal such a magnificent negation of obscurity. "I recommend you," I said at last, "to think twice before showing it to your mistress."

I had no idea, when I spoke, that my words were timely; for I had vaguely taken for granted that my friend was foredoomed to dispense with this graceful appendage, very much as Peter Schlemihl, in the tale, was condemned to have no shadow. Nevertheless, before a month had passed, he was in a fair way to become engaged to a charming girl. "Juxtaposition is much," says Clough; especially juxtaposition, he implies, in foreign countries; and in Scrope's case it had been particularly close. His cousin, Mrs. Waddington, arrived in Rome, and with her a young girl who, though really no relative, offered him all the opportunities of cousinship, added to the remoter charm of a young lady to whom he had to be introduced. Adina Waddington was her companion's stepdaughter, the elder lady having, some eight years before, married a widower with a little girl. Mr. Waddington had recently died, and the two ladies were just emerging from their deep mourning. These dusky emblems of a common grief helped them to seem united, as indeed they really were, although Mrs. Waddington was but ten years older than her stepdaughter. She was an excellent woman, without a fault that I know of, but that of thinking all the world as good as herself and keeping dinner waiting sometimes while she sketched the sunset. She was stout and fresh-colored, she laughed and talked rather loud, and generally, in galleries and temples, caused a good many stiff British necks to turn round.

She had a mania for excursions, and at Frascati and Tivoli she inflicted her good-humored ponderosity on diminutive donkeys with a relish which seemed to prove that a passion for scenery, like all our passions, is capable of making the best of us pitiless. I had often heard Scrope say that he detested boisterous women, but he forgave his cousin her fine spirits, and stepped into his place as her natural escort and adviser. In the vulgar sense he was not selfish; he had a very definite theory as to the sacrifices a gentleman should make to formal courtesy; but I was

nevertheless surprised at the easy terms on which the two
ladies secured his services. The key to the mystery was
the one which fits so many locks; he was in love with Miss
Waddington. There was a sweet stillness about her which
balanced the widow's exuberance. Her pretty name of
Adina seemed to me to have somehow a mystic fitness to
her personality. She was short and slight and blonde,
and her black dress gave a sort of infantine bloom to
her fairness. She wore her auburn hair twisted into a
thousand fantastic braids, like a coiffure in a Renaissance
drawing, and she looked out at you from grave blue eyes,
in which, behind a cold shyness, there seemed to lurk a
tremulous promise to be franker when she knew you better.
She never consented to know me well enough to be very
frank; she talked very little, and we hardly exchanged a
dozen words a day; but I confess that I found a perturbing
charm in those eyes. As it was all in silence, though, there
was no harm.

Scrope, however, ventured to tell his love—or, at least,
to hint at it eloquently enough. I was not so deeply
smitten as to be jealous, and I drew a breath of relief when
I guessed his secret. It made me think better of him again.
The stand he had taken about poor Angelo's gem, in spite
of my efforts to account for it philosophically, had given
an uncomfortable twist to our friendship. I asked myself
if he really had no heart; I even wondered whether there
was not a screw loose in his intellect. But here was a hearty,
healthy, natural passion, such as only an honest man could
feel—such as no man could feel without being the better
for it. I began to hope that the sunshine of his fine sentiment would melt away his aversion to giving Angelo his
dues. He was charmed, soul and sense, and for a couple
of months he really forgot himself, and ceased to send
forth his unsweetened wit to do battle for his ugly face.
His happiness rarely made him "gush," as they say; but I
could see that he was vastly contented with his prospects.
More than once, when we were together, he broke into a
kind of nervous, fantastic laugh, over his own thoughts;
and on his refusal to part with them for the penny which

one offers under those circumstances, I said to myself that this was humorous surprise at his good luck. How had *he* come to please that exquisite creature? Of course, I learned even less from the young girl about her own view of the case; but Mrs. Waddington and I, not being in love with each other, had nothing to do but to gossip about our companions whenever (which was very often) they consigned us to a *tête-à-tête*.

"She tells me nothing," the good-humored widow said; "and if I'm to know the answer to a riddle, I must have it in black and white. My cousin is not what is called 'attractive,' but I think Adina, nevertheless, is interested in him. How do you and I know how passion may transfigure and exalt him? And who shall say beforehand what a fanciful young girl shall do with that terrible little piece of machinery she calls her heart? Adina is a strange child; she is fanciful without being capricious. For all I know, she may admire my cousin for his very ugliness and queerness. She has decided, very likely, that she wants an 'intellectual' husband, and if Mr. Scrope is not handsome, nor frivolous, nor over-polite, there's a greater chance of his being wise." Why Adina should have listened to my friend, however, was her own business. Listen to him she did, and with a sweet attentiveness which may well have flattered and charmed him.

We rarely spoke of the imperial topaz; it seemed not a subject for light allusions. It might properly make a man feel solemn to possess it; the mere memory of its luster lay like a weight on my own conscience. I had felt, as we lost sight of our friend Angelo, that, in one way or another, we should hear of him again; but the weeks passed by without his re-appearing, and my conjectures as to the sequel, on his side, of his remarkable bargain remained quite unanswered. Christmas arrived, and with it the usual ceremonies. Scrope and I took the requisite vigorous measures,—it was a matter, you know, of fists and elbows and knees,—and obtained places for the two ladies at the Midnight Mass at the Sistine Chapel. Mrs. Waddington was my especial charge, and on coming out we found we had lost sight of our companions in the crowd. We waited awhile in the Colonnade, but they were not among the passers, and we supposed that they had gone home independently, and expected us to do likewise. But on reaching Mrs. Waddington's lodging we found they had not come in. As their prolonged absence demanded an explanation, it occurred to me that they had wandered into Saint Peter's, with many others of the attendants at the Mass, and were watching the tapers twinkle in its dusky immensity. It was not perfectly regular that a young lady should be wandering about at three o'clock in the morning with a very "unattractive" young man; but "after all," said Mrs. Waddington, "she's almost his cousin." By the time they returned she was much more. I went home, went to bed, and slept as late as the Christmas bells would allow me. On rising, I knocked at Scrope's door to wish him the compliments of the season, but on his coming to open it for me, perceived that such common-place greetings were quite below the mark. He was but half undressed, and had flung himself, on his return, on the outside of his bed. He had gone with Adina, as I supposed, into Saint Peter's, and they had found the twinkling tapers as picturesque as need be. He walked about the room for some time restlessly, and I saw that he had something to say. At last he brought it out. "I say, I'm accepted. I'm engaged. I'm what's called a happy man."

Of course I wished him joy on the news; and could assure him, with ardent conviction, that he had chosen well. Miss Waddington was the loveliest, the purest, the most interesting of young girls. I could see that he was grateful for my sympathy, but he disliked "expansion," and he contented himself, as he shook hands with me, with simply saying—"Oh yes; she's the right thing." He took two or three more turns about the room, and then suddenly stopped before his toilet-table, and pulled out a tray in his dressing-case. There lay the great intaglio; larger even than I should have dared to boast. "That would be a pretty thing to offer one's *fiancée*," he said, after gazing at it for some time. "How could she wear it—how could one have it set?"

"There could be but one way," I said; "as a massive medallion, depending from a necklace. It certainly would light up the world more, on the bosom of a beautiful woman, than thrust away here, among your brushes and razors. But, to my sense, only a beauty of a certain type could properly wear it—a splendid, dusky beauty, with the brow of a Roman Empress, and the shoulders of an antique statue. A fair, slender girl, with blue eyes, and sweet smile, would seem, somehow, to be overweighted by it, and if I were to see it hung, for instance, round Miss Waddington's white neck, I should feel as if it were pulling her down to the ground, and giving her a mysterious pain."

He was a trifle annoyed, I think, by this rather fine-spun objection; but he smiled as he closed the tray. "Adina may not have the shoulders of the Venus of Milo," he said, "but I hope it will take more than a bauble like this to make her stoop."

I don't always go to church on Christmas Day; but I have a life-long habit of taking a solitary walk, in all weathers, and harboring Christian thoughts if they come. This was a Southern Christmas, without snow on the ground, or sleigh-bells in the air, or the smoke of crowded firesides rising into a cold, blue sky. The day was mild, and almost warm, the sky gray and sunless. If I was disposed toward Christmas thoughts, I confess, I sought them among Pagan memories. I strolled about the forums, and then walked along to the Coliseum. It was empty, save for a single figure, sitting on the steps at the foot of the cross in the center—a young man, apparently, leaning forward, motionless, with his elbows on his knees, and his head buried in his hands. As he neither stirred nor observed me when I passed near him, I said to myself that, brooding there so intensely in the shadow of the sign of redemption, he might pass for an image of youthful remorse. Then, as he never moved, I wondered whether it was not a deeper passion even than repentance. Suddenly he looked up, and I recognized our friend Angelo—not immediately,

but in response to a gradual movement of recognition in
his own face. But seven weeks had passed since our meeting, and yet he looked three years older. It seemed to me
that he had lost flesh, and gained expression. His simple-
souled smile was gone; there was no trace of it in the shy
mistrust of his greeting. He looked graver, manlier, and
very much less rustic. He was equipped in new garments
of a pretentious pattern, though they were carelessly worn,
and bespattered with mud. I remember he had a flaming
orange necktie, which harmonized admirably with his picturesque coloring. Evidently he was greatly altered; as
much altered as if he had made a voyage round the world.
I offered him my hand, and asked if he remembered me.

"Per Dio!" he cried. "With good reason." Even his
voice seemed changed; it was fuller and harsher. He bore
us a grudge. I wondered how his eyes had been opened.
He fixed them on me with a dumb reproachfulness, which
was half appealing and half ominous. He had been brooding and brooding on his meager bargain till the sense of
wrong had become a kind of smothered fear. I observed
all this with poignant compassion, for it seemed to me that
he had parted with something more precious even than
his imperial intaglio. He had lost his boyish ignorance—
that pastoral peace of mind which had suffered him to
doze there so gracefully with his head among the flowers.
But even in his resentment he was simple still. "Where
is the other one—your friend?" he asked.

"He's at home—he's still in Rome."

"And the stone—what has he done with it?"

"Nothing. He has it still."

He shook his head dolefully. "Will he give it back to
me for twenty-five *scudi?*"

"I'm afraid not. He values it."

"I believe so. Will he let me see it?"

"That you must ask him. He shows it to no one."

"He's afraid of being robbed, eh? That proves its value!
He hasn't shown it to a jeweler—to a, what do they call
them?—a lapidary?"

"To no one. You must believe me."

"But he has cleaned it, and polished it, and discovered what it is?"

"It's very old. It's hard to say."

"Very old! Of course it's old. There are more years in it than it brought me *scudi*. What does it look like?. Is it red, blue, green, yellow?"

"Well, my friend," I said, after a moment's hesitation, "it's yellow."

He gave me a searching stare; then quickly—"it's what's called a topaz," he cried.

"Yes, it's what's called a topaz."

"And it's sculptured—that I could see! It's an intaglio. Oh, I know the names, and I've paid enough for my learning. What's the figure? A king's head—or a Pope's, perhaps, eh? Or the portrait of some beautiful woman that you read about?"

"It is the figure of an Emperor."

"What is his name?"

"Tiberius."

"*Corpo di Cristo!*" his face flushed, and his eyes filled with angry tears.

"Come," I said, "I see you're sorry to have parted with the stone. Some one has been talking to you, and making you discontented."

"Every one, *per Dio!* Like the finished fool I was, I couldn't keep my folly to myself. I went home with my eleven *scudi*, thinking I should never see the end of them. The first thing I did was to buy a gilt hair-pin from a peddler, and give it to Ninetta—a young girl of my village, with whom I had a friendship. She stuck it into her braids, and looked at herself in the glass, and then asked how I had suddenly got so rich! 'Oh, I'm richer than you suppose,' said I, and showed her my money, and told her the story of the stone. She is a very clever girl, and it would take a knowing fellow to have the last word with her. She laughed in my face, and told me I was an idiot, that the stone was surely worth five hundred *scudi;* that my *forestiere* was a pitiless rascal; that I ought to have brought it away, and shown it to my elders and

betters; in fine, that I might take her word for it, I had
held a fortune in my hand, and thrown it to the dogs.
And, to wind up this sweet speech, she took out her hairpin,
and tossed it into my face. She never wished to see me
again; she had as lief marry a blind beggar at a cross-
road. What was I to say? She had a sister who was
waiting-maid to a fine lady in Rome,—a *marchesa*,—who
had a priceless necklace made of fine old stones picked up
on the Campagna. I went away hanging my head, and
cursing my folly: I flung my money down in the dirt, and
spat upon it! At last, to ease my spirit, I went to drink a
foglietta at the wine-shop. There I found three or four
young fellows I knew; I treated them all round; I hated
my money, and wanted to get rid of it. Of course they
too wanted to know how I came by my full pockets. I
told them the truth. I hoped they would give me a better
account of things than that vixen of a Ninetta. But they
knocked their glasses on the table, and jeered at me in
chorus. Any donkey, out a-grazing, if he had turned up
such a treasure with his nose, would have taken it in his
teeth and brought it home to his master. This was cold
comfort; I drowned my rage in wine. I emptied one flask
after another; for the first time in my life I got drunk.
But I can't speak of that night! The next day I took
what was left of my money to my uncle, and told him
to give it to the poor, to buy new candlesticks for his
church, or to say masses for the redemption of my blasphem-
ing soul. He looked at it very hard, and hoped I had
come by it honestly. I was in for it; I told *him* too!
He listened to me in silence, looking at me over his specta-
cles. When I had done, he turned over the money in his
hands, and then sat for three minutes with his eyes closed.
Suddenly he thrust it back into my own hands. 'Keep it—
keep it, my son,' he said, 'your wits will never help you to
a supper, make the most of what you've got!' Since then,
do you see, I've been in a fever. I can think of nothing
else but the fortune I've lost."

"Oh, a fortune!" I said, deprecatingly. "You exagger-
ate."

"It would have been a fortune to me. A voice keeps ringing in my ear night and day, and telling me I could have got a thousand *scudi* for it."

I'm afraid I blushed; I turned away a moment; when I looked at the young man again, his face had kindled. "Tiberius, eh? A Roman emperor sculptured on a big topaz—that's fortune enough for me! Your friend's a rascal—do you know that? I don't say it for you; I like your face, and I believe that, if you can, you'll help me. But your friend is an ugly little monster. I don't know why the devil I trusted him; I saw he wished me no good. Yet, if ever there was a harmless fellow, I was. *Ecco!* it's my fate. That's very well to say; I say it and say it, but it helps me no more than an empty glass helps your thirst. I'm not harmless now. If I meet your friend, and he refuses me justice, I won't answer for these two hands. You see—they're strong; I could easily strangle him! Oh, at first, I shall speak him fair, but if he turns me off, and answers me with English oaths, I shall think only of my *revenge!*" And with a passionate gesture he pulled off his hat, and flung it on the ground, and stood wiping the perspiration from his forehead.

I answered him briefly but kindly enough. I told him to leave his case in my hands, go back to Lariceia and try and find some occupation which would divert him from his grievance. I confess that even as I gave this respectable advice, I but half believed in it. It was none of poor Angelo's mission to arrive at virtue through tribulation. His indolent nature, active only in immediate feeling, would have found my prescription of wholesome labor more intolerable even than his wrong. He stared gloomily and made no answer, but he saw that I had his interests at heart, and he promised me, at least, to leave Rome, and believe that I would fairly plead his cause. If I had good news for him I was to address him at Lariceia. It was thus I learned his full name,—a name, certainly, that ought to have been to its wearer a sort of talisman against trouble,—Angelo Beati.

PART II

Sam Scrope looked extremely annoyed when I began to tell him of my encounter with our friend, and I saw there was still a cantankerous something in the depths of his heart intensely hostile to fairness. It was characteristic of his peculiar temper that his happiness, as an accepted lover, had not disposed him to graceful concessions. He treated his bliss as his own private property, and was as little in the humor to diffuse its influence as he would have been to send out in charity a choice dish from an unfinished dinner. Nevertheless, I think he might have stiffly admitted that there was a grain of reason in Angelo's claim, if I had not been too indiscreetly accurate in my report of our interview. I had been impressed, indeed, with something picturesquely tragic in the poor boy's condition, and, to do perfect justice to the picture, I told him he had flung down his hat on the earth as a gauntlet of defiance and talked about his revenge. Scrope hereupon looked fiercely disgusted and pronounced him a theatrical jackanapes; but he authorized me to drop him a line saying that he would speak with him a couple of days later. I was surprised at Scrope's consenting to see him, but I perceived that he was making a conscientious effort to shirk none of the disagreeables of the matter. "I won't have him stamping and shouting in the house here," he said. "I'll also meet him at the Coliseum." He named his hour and I despatched to Lariceia three lines of incorrect but courteous Italian.

It was better,—far better,—that they should not have met. What passed between them Scrope requested me on his return to excuse him from repeating; suffice it that Angelo was an impudent puppy, and that he hoped never to hear of him again. Had Angelo, at last, I asked, received any compensation? "Not a farthing!" cried Scrope, and walked out of the room. Evidently the two young men had been a source of immitigable offense to each other. Angelo had promised to speak to him fair, and I inclined to believe had done so; but the very change in his appear-

ance, by seeming to challenge my companion's sympathy
in too peremptory a fashion, had had the irritating effect
of a menace. Scrope had been contemptuous, and his
awkward, ungracious Italian had doubtless made him seem
more so. One can't handle Italians with contempt; those
who know them have learned what may be done with a
moderate amount of superficial concession. Angelo had
replied in wrath, and, as I afterwards learned, had demanded, as a right, the restitution of the topaz in exchange
for the sum received for it. Scrope had rejoined that if
he took that tone he should get nothing at all, and the injured youth had retorted with reckless and insulting threats.
What had prevented them from coming to blows, I know
not, no sign of flinching, certainly, on my companion's part.
Face to face, he had not seemed to Angelo so easy to
strangle, and that saving grain of discretion which mingles
with all Italian passion had whispered to the young man to
postpone his revenge. Without taking a melodramatic view
of things, it seemed to me that Scrope had an evil chance
in waiting for him. I had, perhaps, no definite vision of
a cloaked assassin lurking under a dark archway, but I
thought it perfectly possible that Angelo might make
himself intolerably disagreeable. His simply telling his
story up and down Rome to whomsoever would listen to
him, might be a grave annoyance; though indeed Scrope had
the advantage that most people might refuse to believe in
the existence of a gem of which its owner was so little inclined to boast. The whole situation, at all events, made
me extremely nervous. I cursed my companion one day
for a hungrier Jew than Shylock, and pitied him the next
as the victim of a moral hallucination. If we gave him
time, he *would* come to his senses; he would repay poor
Angelo with interest. Meanwhile, however, I could do
nothing, for I felt that it was worse than useless to suggest
to Scrope that he was in danger. He would have scorned
the idea of a ranting Italian making him swerve an inch
from his chosen path.

I am unable to say whether Angelo's "imprudence" had
seemed to relieve him, generally, from his vow to conceal

the intaglio; a few words, at all events, from Miss Waddington, a couple of evenings later, reminded me of the original
reservation he had made to the vow. Mrs. Waddington
was at the piano, deciphering a new piece of music, and
Scrope, who was fond of a puzzle, as a puzzle, was pre-
tending, half jocosely, to superintend and correct her.
"I've seen it," Adina said to me, with grave, expanded eyes;
"I've seen the wonderful topaz. He says you are in the
secret. He won't tell me how he came by it. Honestly, I
hope."

I tried to laugh. "You mustn't investigate too closely
the honesty of hunters for antiquities. It's hardly dishonest in their code to treat loose cameos and snuff-boxes
as pickpockets treat purses."

She looked at me in shy surprise, as if I had made a
really cruel joke. "He says that I must wear it one of
these days as a medallion," she went on. "But I shall
not. The stone is beautiful, but I should feel most uncomfortable in carrying the Emperor Tiberius so near my
heart. Wasn't he one of the bad Emperors—one of the
worst? It is almost a pollution to have a thing that *he*
had looked at and touched coming to one in such direct
descent. His image almost spoils for me the beauty of the
stone and I'm very glad Mr. Scrope keeps it out of sight."
This seemed a very becoming state of mind in a blonde
angel of New England origin.

The days passed by and Angelo's "revenge" still hung
fire. Scrope never met his fate at a short turning of one
of the dusky Roman streets; he came in punctually every
evening at eleven o'clock. I wondered whether our brooding friend had already spent the sinister force of a nature
formed to be lazily contented. I hoped so, but I was
wrong. We had gone to walk one afternoon,—the ladies,
Scrope and I,—in the charming Villa Borghese, and, to
escape from the rattle of the fashionable world and its dis-
traction, we had wandered away to an unfrequented corner
where the old moldering wall and the slim black cypresses
and the untrodden grass made, beneath the splendid Roman
sky, the most harmonious of pictures. Of course there was

a mossy stone hemicycle not far off, and cracked benches
with griffin's feet, where one might sit and gossip and watch
the lizards scamper in the sun. We had done so for some
half an hour when Adina espied the first violet of the year
glimmering at the root of a cypress. She made haste to
rise and gather it, then wandered further, in the hope of
giving it a few companions. Scrope sat and watched her
as she moved slowly away, trailing her long shadow on the
grass and drooping her head from side to side in her charming quest. It was not, I know, that he felt no impulse to
join her; but that he was in love, for the moment, with
looking at her from where he sat. Her search carried her
some distance and at last she passed out of sight behind
a bend in the villa wall. Mrs. Waddington proposed in a
few moments that we should overtake her, and we moved
forward. We had not advanced many paces before she
re-appeared, glancing over her shoulder as she came towards
us with an air of suppressed perturbation. In an instant
I saw she was being followed; a man was close behind her
—a man in whom my second glance reconized Angelo Beati.
Adina was pale; something had evidently passed between
them. By the time she had met us, we were also face to
face with Angelo. He was pale, as well, and, between
these two pallors, Scrope had flushed crimson. I was
afraid of an explosion and stepped toward Angelo to avert
it. But to my surprise, he was evidently following another
line. He turned the cloudy brightness of his eyes upon
each of us and poised his hand in the air as if to say, in
answer to my unspoken charge—"Leave me alone, I know
what I am about." I exchanged a glance with Scrope,
urging him to pass on with the ladies and let me deal
with the intruder. Miss Waddington stopped; she was
gazing at Angelo with soft intentness. Her lover, to lead
her away, grasped her arm almost rudely, and as she went
with him I saw her faintly flushing. Mrs. Waddington,
unsuspicious of evil, saw nothing but a very handsome
young man. "What a beautiful creature for a sketch!"
I heard her exclaim, as she followed her step-daughter.

"I'm not going to make a noise," said Angelo, with

a somber smile; "don't be frightened! I know what good
manners are. These three weeks now that I've been hanging about Rome, I've learned to play the gentleman. Who
is that young lady?"

"My dear young man, it's none of your business. I
hope you had not the hardihood to speak to her."

He was silent a moment, looking after her as she retreated
on her companion's arm. "Yes, I spoke to her—and she
understood me. Keep quiet; I said nothing she mightn't
hear. But such as it was, she understood it. She's your
friend's *amica*; I know that. I've been watching you for
half an hour from behind those trees. She is wonderfully
beautiful. Farewell; I wish you no harm, but tell your
friend I've not forgotten *him*. I'm only awaiting my
chance; I think it will come. I don't want to kill him;
I want to give him some hurt that he'll survive and *feel*
—forever!" He was turning away, but he paused and
watched my companions till they disappeared. At last—
"He has more than his share of good luck," he said, with
a sort of forced coldness. "A topaz—and a pearl! both
at once! Eh, farewell!" And he walked rapidly away,
waving his hand. I let him go. I was unsatisfied, but his
unexpected sobriety left me nothing to say.

When a startling event comes to pass, we are apt to
waste a good deal of time in trying to recollect the correct
signs and portents which preceded it, and when they seem
fewer than they should be, we don't scruple to imagine them
—we invent them after the fact. Therefore it is that I
don't pretend to be sure that I was particularly struck,
from this time forward, with something strange in our quiet
Adina. She had always seemed to me vaguely, innocently
strange; it was part of her charm that in the daily noiseless movement of her life a mystic undertone seemed to
murmur—"You don't half know me!" Perhaps we three
prosaic mortals were not quite worthy to know her; yet
I believe that if a practised man of the world had whispered to me, one day, over his wine, after Miss Waddington
had rustled away from the table, that *there* was a young
lady, who, sooner or later, would treat her friends to a first

class surprise, I should have laid my finger on his sleeve and told him with a smile that he phrased my own thought. Was she more silent than usual, was she preoccupied, was she melancholy, was she restless? Picturesquely, she ought to have been all these things; but in fact, she was still to the illumined eye simply a very pretty blonde maiden, who smiled more than she spoke, and accepted her lover's devotion with a charming demureness which savored much more of humility than of condescension. It seemed to me useless to repeat to Scrope the young Italian's declaration that he had spoken to her, and poor Sam never intimated to me either that he had questioned her in suspicion of the fact, or that she had offered him any account of it. I was sure, however, that something must have passed between the young girl and her lover in the way of question and answer, and I privately wondered what the deuce Angelo had meant by saying she had understood him. What had she understood? Surely not the story of Scrope's acquisition of the gem; for granting—what was unlikely—that Angelo had had time to impart it, it was unnatural that Adina should not have frankly demanded an explanation. At last I broke the ice and asked Scrope if he supposed Miss Waddington had reason to connect the great intaglio with the picturesque young man she had met in the Villa Borghese.

My question caused him visible discomfort. "Picturesque?" he growled. "Did she tell you she thought him picturesque?"

"By no means. But he is! You must at least allow him that."

"He hadn't brushed his hair for a week—if that's what you mean. But it's a charm which I doubt that Adina appreciates. But she has certainly taken," he added in a moment, "an unaccountable dislike to the topaz. She says the Emperor Tiberius spoils it for her. It's carrying historical antipathies rather far: I supposed nothing could spoil a fine gem for a pretty woman. It appears," he finally said, "that that rascal spoke to her."

"What did he say?"

"He asked her if she was engaged to me."

"And what did she answer?"

"Nothing."

"I suppose she was frightened."

"She might have been; but she says she was not. He begged her not to be; he told her he was a poor harmless fellow looking for justice. She left him, without speaking. I told her he was crazy—it's not a lie."

"Possibly!" I rejoined. Then, as a last attempt—"You know it wouldn't be quite a lie," I added, "to say that *you* are not absolutely sane. You're very erratic, about the topaz; obstinacy, pushed under certain circumstances beyond a certain point, bears a dangerous likeness to craziness."

I suppose that if one could reason with a mule it would make him rather more mulish to know one called him stubborn. Scrope gave me a chilling grin. "I deny your circumstances. If I'm mad, I claim the madman's privilege of believing myself peculiarly sane. If you wish to preach to me, you must catch me in a lucid interval."

The breath of early spring in Rome, though magical, as you know, in its visible influence on the dark old city, is often rather trying to the foreign constitution. After a fortnight of uninterrupted sirocco, Mrs. Waddington's fine spirits confessed to depression. She was afraid, of course, that she was going to have "the fever," and made haste to consult a physician. He reassured her, told her she simply needed change of air, and recommended a month at Albano. To Albano, accordingly, the two ladies repaired, under Scrope's escort. Mrs. Waddington kindly urged my going with them; but I was detained in Rome by the arrival of some relations of my own, for whom I was obliged to play cicerone. I could only promise to make an occasional visit to Albano. My uncle and his three daughters were magnificent sight-seers, and gave me plenty to do; nevertheless, at the end of a week I was able to redeem my promise. I found my friends lodging at the inn, and the two ladies doing their best to merge the sense of dirty stone floors and crumpled yellow table-cloth in ecstatic contemplation, from their windows, of the great misty sea-like level of the Campagna. The view apart, they were passing delightful days. You remember the loveliness of the place and its picturesque neighborhood of strange old mountain towns. The country was blooming with early flowers and foliage, and my friends lived in the open air. Mrs. Waddington sketched in water colors. Adina gathered wild nosegays, and Scrope hovered contentedly between them—not without an occasional frank stricture on the elder lady's use of her pigments and Adina's combinations of narcissus and cyclamen. All seemed to me very happy and, without ill-nature, I felt almost tempted to wonder whether the most desirable gift of the gods is not a thick-and-thin conviction of one's own impeccability. Yet even a lover with a bad conscience might be cheated into a disbelief in retribution by the unbargained sweetness of such a presence in his life as Adina Waddington's.

I spent the night at Albano, but as I had pledged myself to go the next morning to a funzione with my fair cousins in Rome,—"fair" is for rhetoric; but they were excellent girls:—I was obliged to rise and start at dawn. Scrope had offered to go with me part of the way, and walk back to the inn before breakfast; but I declined to accept so onerous a favor, and departed alone, in the early twilight. A rickety diligence made the transit across the Campagna, and I had a five minutes' walk to the post-office, while it stood waiting for its freight. I made my way through the little garden of the inn, as this saved me some steps. At the sound of my tread on the gravel, a figure rose slowly from a bench at the foot of a crippled grim statue, and I found myself staring at Angelo Beati. I greeted him with an exclamation, which was virtually a challenge of his right to be there. He stood and looked at me fixedly, with a strangely defiant, unembarrassed smile, and at last, in answer to my repeated inquiry as to what the deuce he was about, he said he supposed he had a right to take a stroll in a neighbor's garden.

"A neighbor?" said I. "How——?"

"Eh, *per Dio!* don't I live at Lariceia?" And he laughed

in almost as simple a fashion as when we had awaked
him from his dreamless sleep in the meadows.

I had had so many other demands on my attention during my friend's absence that it never occurred to me that
Scrope had lodged himself in the very jaws of the enemy.
But I began to believe that, after all, the enemy was very
harmless. If Angelo confined his machinations to sitting
about in damp gardens at malarial hours, Scrope would not
be the first to suffer. I had fancied at first that his sense
of injury had made a man of him; but there seemed still
to hang about him a sort of a romantic ineffectiveness. His
painful impulsion toward maturity had lasted but a day
and he had become again an irresponsible lounger in Arcady.
But he must have had an Arcadian constitution to brave
the Roman dews at that rate. "And you came here for a
purpose," I said. "It ought to be a very good one to warrant your spending your nights out of doors in this silly
fashion. If you are not careful you'll get the fever and
die, and that will be the end of everything."

He seemed grateful for my interest in his health. "No,
no, *Signorino mio*, I'll not get the fever. I've a fever here"
—and he struck a blow on his breast—"that's a safeguard
against the other. I've had a purpose in coming here, but
you'll never guess it. Leave me alone; I shan't harm you!
But now, that day is beginning, I must go; I must not
be seen."

I grasped him by the arm, looked at him hard and tried
to penetrate his meaning. He met my eyes frankly and
gave a little contented laugh. Whatever his secret was,
he was not ashamed of it; I saw with some satisfaction
that it was teaching him patience. Something in his face,
in the impression it gave me of his nature, reassured
me, at the same time, that it contradicted my hypothesis
of a moment before. There was no evil in it and no
malignity, but a deep, insistent, natural desire which seemed
to be slumbering for the time in a mysterious prevision
of success. He thought, apparently, that his face was
telling too much. He gave another little laugh, and began
to whistle softly. "You are meant for something better,"

I said, "than to skulk about here like a burglar. How would you like to go to America and do some honest work?" I had an absurd momentary vision of helping him on his way, and giving him a letter of introduction to my brother-in-law, who was in the hardware business.

He took off his hat and passed his hand through his hair. "You think, then, I am meant for something good?"

"If you will! If you'll give up your idle idea of 're-venge' and trust to time to right your wrong."

"Give it up?—Impossible!" he said, grimly. "Ask me rather to chop off my arm. This is the same thing. It's part of my life. I *have* trusted to time—I've waited four long months, and yet here I stand as poor and helpless as at the beginning. No, no, I'm not to be treated like a dog. If he had been just, I would have done anything for him. I'm not a bad fellow; I never had an unkind thought. Very likely I was too simple, too stupid, too contented with being poor and shabby. The Lord does with us as he pleases; he thought I needed a little shaking up. I've got it, surely! But did your friend take counsel of the Lord? No, no! He took counsel of his own sel-fishness, and he thought himself clever enough to steal the sweet and never taste the bitter. But the bitter will come; and it will be my sweet."

"That's fine talk! Tell me in three words what it means."

"*Aspetti!*—If you are going to Rome by the coach, as I suppose, you should be moving. You may lose your place. I have an idea we shall meet again." He walked away, and in a moment I heard the great iron gate of the garden creaking on its iron hinges.

I was puzzled, and for a moment, I had a dozen minds to stop over with my friends. But on the one hand, I saw no definite way in which I could preserve them from annoyance; and on the other, I was confidently expected in Rome. Besides, might not the dusky cloud be the sooner dissipated by letting Angelo's project,—substance or shadow, whatever it was,—play itself out? To Rome accordingly I returned; but for several days I was haunted with a suspicion that something ugly, something sad, something strange, at any rate, was taking place at Albano. At last it became so oppressive that I hired a light carriage and drove back again. I reached the inn toward the close of the afternoon, and but half expected to find my friends at home. They had in fact gone out to walk, and the landlord had not noticed in what direction. I had nothing to do but to stroll about the dirty little town till their return. Do you remember the Capuchin convent at the edge of the Alban lake? I walked up to it and, seeing the door of the church still open, made my way in. The dusk had gathered in the corners, but the altar, for some pious reason, was glowing with an unusual number of candles. They twinkled picturesquely in the gloom; here and there a kneeling figure defined itself vaguely; it was a pretty piece of chiaroscuro, and I sat down to enjoy it. Presently I noticed the look of intense devotion of a young woman sitting near me. Her hands were clasped on her knees, her head thrown back and her eyes fixed in strange expansion on the shining altar. We make out pictures, you know, in the glow of the hearth at home; this young girl seemed to be reading an ecstatic vision in the light of the tapers. Her expression was so peculiar that for some moments it disguised her face and left me to perceive with a sudden shock that I was watching Adina Waddington. I looked round for her companions, but she was evidently alone. It seemed to me then that I had no right to watch her covertly, and yet I was indisposed either to disturb her or to retire and leave her. The evening was approaching; how came it that she was unaccompanied? I concluded that she was waiting for the others; Scrope, perhaps, had gone in to see the sunset from the terrace of the convent garden—a privilege denied to ladies; and Mrs. Waddington was lingering outside the church to take memoranda for a sketch. I turned away, walked round the church and approached the young girl on the other side. This time my nearness aroused her. She removed her eyes from the altar, looked at me, let them rest on my face, and yet gave no sign of recognition. But at last she slowly rose and I

saw that she knew me. Was she turning Catholic and preparing to give up her heretical friends? I greeted her,
but she continued to look at me with intense gravity, as if
her thoughts were urging her beyond frivolous civilities.
She seemed not in the least flurried—as I had feared she
would be—at having been observed; she was preoccupied,
excited, in a deeper fashion. In suspecting that something
strange was happening at Albano, apparently I was not far
wrong—"What are you doing, my dear young lady," I
asked brusquely, "in this lonely church?"

"I'm asking for light," she said.

"I hope you've found it!" I answered smiling.

"I think so!" and she moved toward the door. "I'm
alone," she added, "will you take me home?" She accepted my arm and we passed out; but in front of the
church she paused. "Tell me," she said suddenly, "are
you a very intimate friend of Mr. Scrope's?"

"You must ask him." I answered, "if he considers me so.
I at least aspire to the honor." The intensity of her manner embarrassed me, and I tried to take refuge in jocosity.

"Tell me then this: will he bear a disappointment—a keen
disappointment?"

She seemed to appeal to me to say yes! But I felt that
she had a project in hand, and I had no warrant to give
her a license. I looked at her a moment; her solemn
eyes seemed to grow and grow till they made her whole
face a mute entreaty. "No," I said resolutely, "decidedly
not!"

She gave a heavy sigh and we walked on. She seemed
buried in her thoughts! she gave no heed to my attempts
at conversation, and I had to wait till we reached the inn
for an explanation of her solitary visit to Capuccini. Her
companions had come in, and from them, after their welcome, I learned that the three had gone out together,
but that Adina had presently complained of fatigue, and
obtained leave to go home. "If I break down on the way,"
she had said, "I will go into a church to rest." They had
been surprised at not finding her at the inn, and were
grateful for my having met her. Evidently, they, too,

had discovered that the young girl was in a singular mood.
Mrs. Waddington had a forced smile, and Scrope had no
smile at all. Adina quietly sat down to her needlework,
and we confessed, even tacitly, to no suspicion of her being
"nervous." Common nervousness it certainly was not;
she bent her head calmly over her embroiderly, and drew
her stitches with a hand innocent of the slightest tremor.
At last we had dinner; it passed somewhat oppressively,
and I was thankful for Scrope's proposal, afterwards, to go
and smoke a cigar in the garden. Poor Scrope was unhappy;
I could see that, but I hardly ventured to hope that he
would tell me off-hand what was the matter with Adina.
It naturally occurred to me that she had shown a disposi-
tion to retract her engagement. I gave him a dozen chances
to say so, but he evidently could not trust himself to utter
his fears. To give an impetus to our conversation, I reminded him of his nearness to Lariceia, and asked whether
he had had a glimpse of Angelo Beati.

"Several," he said. "He has passed me in the village,
or on the roads, some half a dozen times. He gives me
an impudent stare and goes his way. He takes it out in
looking daggers from his dark eyes; you see how much
there is to be feared from him!"

"He doesn't quite take it out," I presently said, "in looking daggers. He hangs about the inn at night; he roams
about the garden while you're in bed, as if he thought that
he might give you bad dreams by staring at your windows."
And I described our recent interview at dawn.

Scrope stared in great surprise, then slowly flushed in
rising anger. "Curse the meddling idiot!" he cried. "If
he doesn't know where to stop, I'll show him."

"Buy him off!" I said sturdily.

"I'll buy him a horsewhip and give it to him over his
broad back!"

I put my hands in my pockets, I believe, and strolled
away, whistling. Come what might, I washed my hands
of mediation! But it was not irritation, for I felt a strange,
half-reasoned increase of pity for my friend's want of
pliancy. He stood puffing his cigar gloomily, and by

way of showing him that I didn't altogether give up, I asked him at last whether it had yet been settled when he should marry. He had told me shortly before that this was still an open question, and that Miss Waddington preferred to leave it so.

He made no immediate answer, but looked at me hard. "Why do you ask—just now?"

"Why, my dear fellow, friendly curiosity—" I began.

He tossed the end of his cigar nervously upon the ground. "No, no; it's not friendly curiosity!" he cried. "You've noticed something—you suspect something!"

Since he insisted, I confessed that I did. "That beautiful girl," I said, "seems to me agitated and preoccupied; I wondered whether you had been having a quarrel."

He seemed relieved at being pressed to speak.

"That beautiful girl is a puzzle. I don't know what's the matter with her; it's all very painful; she's a very strange creature. I never dreamed there was an obstacle to our happiness—to our union. She has never protested and promised; it's not her way, nor her nature; she is always humble, passive, gentle; but always extremely grateful for every sign of tenderness. Till within three or four days ago, she seemed to me more so than ever; her habitual gentleness took the form of a sort of shrinking, almost suffering, deprecation of my attentions, my *petits soins,* my lover's nonsense. It was as if they oppressed and mortified her—and she would have liked me to bear more lightly. I did not see directly that it was not the excess of my devotion, but my devotion itself—the very fact of my love and her engagement that pained her. When I did it was a blow in the face. I don't know what under heaven I've done! Women are fathomless creatures. And yet Adina is not capricious, in the common sense. Mrs. Waddington told me that it was a 'girl's mood,' that we must not seem to heed it—it would pass over. I've been waiting, but the situation don't mend; you've guessed at trouble without a hint. So these are *peines d'amour?*" he went on, after brooding a moment. "I didn't know how fiercely I was in love!"

I don't remember with what well-meaning foolishness I was going to attempt to console him; Mrs. Waddington suddenly appeared and drew him aside. After a moment's murmured talk with her, he went rapidly into the house. She remained with me and, as she seemed greatly perplexed, and we had, moreover, often discussed our companion's situation and prospects, I immediately told her that Scrope had just been relating his present troubles. "They are very unexpected," she cried. "It's thunder in a clear sky. Just now Adina laid down her work and told me solemnly that she would like to see Mr. Scrope alone; would I kindly call him? 'Would she kindly tell me,' I inquired, 'what in common sense was the matter with her, and what she proposed to say to him? She looked at me a moment as if I were a child of five years old interrupting family prayers; then came up gently and kissed me, and said I would know everything in good time. Does she mean to stand there in that same ghostly fashion and tell him that, on the whole, she has decided not to marry him? What has the poor man done?"

"She has ceased to love him," I suggested.

"Why ceased, all of a sudden?"

"Perhaps it's not so sudden as you suppose. Such things have happened, in young women's hearts, as a gradual revision of a first impression."

"Yes, but not without a particular motive—another fancy. Adina is fanciful, that I know; with all respect be it said, it was fanciful to accept poor Sam to begin with. But her choice deliberately made, what has put her out of humor with it?—in a word the only possible explanation would be that our young lady has transferred her affections. But it's impossible!"

"Absolutely so?" I asked.

"Absolutely. Judge for yourself. To whom, pray? She hasn't seen another man in a month. Who could have so mysteriously charmed her? The little hunchback who brings us mandarin oranges every morning? Perhaps she has lost her heart to Prince Doria! I believe he has been staying at his villa yonder."

I found no smile for this mild sarcasm. I was wondering—wondering. "Has she literally seen no one else?" I asked when my wonderings left me breath.

"I can't answer for whom she may have *seen*; she's not blind. But she has spoken to no one else, nor been spoken to; that's very certain. Love at sight—at sight only—used to be common in the novels I devoured when I was fifteen; but I doubt whether it exists anywhere else."

I had a question on my tongue's end, but I hesitated some time to risk it. I debated some time in silence and at last I uttered it, with a prefatory apology. "On which side of the house is Adina's room?"

"Pray, what are you coming to?" said my companion. "On this side."

"It looks into the garden?"

"There it is in the second story."

"Be so good ——— which one?

"The third window—the one with the shutters tied back with a handkerchief."

The shutters and the handkerchief suddenly acquired a mysterious fascination for me. I looked at them for some time, and when I glanced back at my companion our eyes met. I don't know what she thought—what she thought I thought. I thought it *might* be out of a novel—such a thing as love at sight; such a thing as an unspoken dialogue, between a handsome young Italian with a "wrong," in a starlit garden, and a fanciful western maid at a window. From her own sudden impression Mrs. Waddington seemed slowly to recoil. She gathered her shawl about her, shivered, and turned towards the house. "The thing to do," I said, offering her my arm, "is to leave Albano to-morrow."

On the inner staircase we paused; Mrs. Waddington was loath to interrupt Adina's interview with Scrope. While she was hesitating whither to turn, the door of her sitting-room opened, and the young girl passed out. Scrope stood behind her, very pale, his face distorted with an emotion he was determined to repress. She herself was pale, but her eyes were lighted up like two wind-blown torches. Meeting the elder lady, she stopped, stood for a moment, looking down and hesitating, and then took Mrs. Waddington's two hands and silently kissed her. She turned to me, put out her hand, and said "Good night!" I shook it, I imagine, with sensible ardor, for somehow, I was deeply impressed. There was a nameless force in the girl, before which one had to stand back. She lingered but an instant and rapidly disappeared towards her room, in the dusky corridor. Mrs. Waddington laid her hand kindly upon Scrope's arm and led him back into the parlor. He evidently was not going to be plaintive; his pride was rankling and burning, and it seasoned his self-control.

"Our engagement is at an end," he simply said.

Mrs. Waddington folded her hands. "And for what reason?"

"None."

It was cruel, certainly; but what could we say? Mrs. Waddington sank upon the sofa and gazed at the poor fellow in mute, motherly compassion. Her large, caressing pity irritated him; he took up a book and sat down with his back to her. I took up another, but I couldn't read; I sat noticing that he never turned his own page. Mrs. Waddington at last transferred her gaze uneasily, appealingly, to me; she moved about restlessly in her place; she was trying to shape my vague intimations in the garden into something palpable to common credulity. I could give her now no explanation that would not have been a gratuitous offense to Scrope. But I felt more and more nervous; my own vague previsions oppressed me. I flung down my book at last, and left the room. In the corridor Mrs. Waddington overtook me, and requested me to tell her what I meant by my extraordinary allusions to—"in plain English," she said, "to an intrigue."

"It would be needless, and it would be painful," I answered, "to tell you now and here. But promise me to return to Rome to-morrow. There we can take breath and talk."

"Oh, we shall bundle off, I promise!" she cried. And we separated. I mounted the stairs to go to my room; as I did so I heard her dress rustling in the corridor,

undecidedly. Then came the sound of a knock; she had
stopped at Adina's door. Involuntarily I paused and
listened. There was a silence, and then another knock;
another silence and a third knock; after this, despair-
ing, apparently, of obtaining admission, she moved away,
and I went to my room. It was useless going to bed;
I knew I should not sleep. I stood a long time at my
open window, wondering whether I had anything to say
to Scrope. At the end of half an hour I wandered down
into the garden again, and strolled through all the alleys.
They were empty, and there was a light in Adina's window. No; it seemed to me that there was nothing I could
bring myself to say to Scrope, but that he should leave
Albano the next day, and Rome and Italy as soon after
as possible, wait a year, and then try his fortune with Miss
Waddington again. Towards morning, I *did* sleep.

Breakfast was served in Mrs. Waddington's parlor, and
Scrope appeared punctually, as neatly shaved and brushed
as if he were still under tribute to a pair of blue eyes.
He really, of course, felt less serene than he looked. It
can never be comfortable to meet at breakfast the young
lady who has rejected you over night. Mrs. Waddington
kept us waiting some time, but at last she entered with
surprising energy. Her comely face was flushed from
brow to chin, and in her hand she clasped a crumpled note.
She flung herself upon the sofa and burst into tears; I
had only time to turn the grinning *cameriêra* out of the
room. "She's gone, gone, gone!" she cried, among her sobs.
"Oh, the crazy, wicked, ungrateful girl!"

Scrope, of course, knew no more than a tea-pot what
she meant; but I understood her more promptly—and yet
I believe I gave a long whistle. Scrope stood staring at
her as she thrust out the crumpled note: that she meant
that Adina—that Adina had left us in the night—was too
large a horror for his unprepared sense. His dumb amazement was an almost touching sign of the absence of a
thought which could have injured the girl. He saw by my
face that I knew something, and he let me draw the note
from Mrs. Waddington's hand and read it aloud:

*Good-by to everything! Think me crazy if you will.
I could never explain. Only forget me and believe that I
am happy, happy, happy!*   *Adina Beati.*

I laid my hand on his shoulder; even yet he seemed
powerless to apprehend. "Angelo Beati," I said gravely,
"has at last taken his revenge!"

"Angelo Beati!" he cried. "An Italian beggar! It's a
lie!"

I shook my head and patted his shoulder. "He has
insisted on payment. He's a clever fellow!"

He saw that I knew, and slowly, distractedly he answered
with a burning blush!

It was a most extraordinary occurrence; we had ample
time to say so, and to say so again, and yet never really
to understand it. Neither of my companions ever saw the
young girl again; Scrope never mentioned her but once.
He went about for a week in absolute silence; when at last
he spoke I saw that the fold was taken, that he was going
to be a professional cynic for the rest of his days. Mrs.
Waddington was a good-natured woman, as I have said,
and, better still, she was a just woman. But I assure you,
she never forgave her step-daughter. In after years, as I
grew older, I took an increasing satisfaction in having assisted, as they say, at this episode. As mere *action*, it
seemed to me really superb, and in judging of human nature I often weighed it mentally against the perpetual
spectacle of strong impulses frittered in weakness and per-
verted by prudence. There has been no prudence here,
certainly, but there has been ardent, full-blown, positive
passion. We see the one every day, the other once in five
years. More than once I ventured to ventilate this heresy
before the kindly widow, but she always stopped me short,
"The thing was odious," she said; "I thank heaven the
girl's father did not live to see it."

We didn't finish that dismal day at Albano, but returned
in the evening to Rome. Before our departure I had an
interview with the Padre Girolamo of Lariceia, who failed
to strike me as the holy man whom his nephew had de-

scribed. He was a swarthy, snuffy little old priest, with a dishonest eye—quite capable, I believed, of teaching his handsome nephew to play his cards. But I had no reproaches to waste upon him; I simply wished to know whither Angelo had taken the young girl. I obtained the information with difficulty and only after a solemn promise that if Adina should reiterate, *vivâ voce*, to a person delegated by her friends, the statement that she was happy, they would take no steps to recover possession of her. She was in Rome, and in that holy city they should leave her. "Remember," said the Padre, very softly, "that she is of age, and her own mistress, and can do what she likes with her money;—she has a good deal of it, eh?" She had less than he thought, but evidently the Padre knew his ground. It was he, he admitted, who had united the young couple in marriage, the day before; the ceremony had taken place in the little old circular church on the hill, at Albano, at five o'clock in the morning. "You see, Signor," he said, slowly rubbing his yellow hands, "she had taken a great fancy!" I gave him no chance, by any remark of my own, to remind me that Angelo had a grudge to satisfy, but he professed the assurance that his nephew was the sweetest fellow in the world. I heard and departed in silence; my curiosity, at least, had not yet done with Angelo.

Mrs. Waddington, also, had more of this sentiment than she confessed to; her kindness wondered, under protest of her indignation, how on earth the young girl was living, and whether the smells on her staircase were very bad indeed. It was, therefore, at her tacit request that I repaired to the lodging of the young pair, in the neighborhood of the Piazza Barberini. The quarters were modest, but they looked into the quaint old gardens of the Capuchin Friars; and in the way of smells, I observed nothing worse than the heavy breath of a great bunch of pinks in a green jug on the window sill. Angelo stood there, pulling one of the pinks to pieces, and looking quite the proper hero of his romance. He eyed me shyly and a trifle coldly at first, as if he were prepared to stand firm against a possible blowing up; but when he saw that I chose to make no allusions whatever to the past, he suffered his dark brow to betray his serene contentment. I was no more disposed than I had been a week before, to call him a bad fellow; but he was a mystery,—his character was as great an enigma as the method of his courtship. That he was in love I don't pretend to say; but I think he had already forgotten how his happiness had come to him, and that he was basking in a sort of primitive natural sensuous delight in being adored. It was like the warm sunshine, or like plenty of good wine. I don't believe his fortune in the least surprised him; at the bottom of every genuine Roman heart,—even if it beats beneath a beggar's rags,— you'll find an ineradicable belief that we are all barbarians, and made to pay them tribute. He was welcome to all his grotesque superstitions, but what sort of future did they promise for Adina? I asked leave to speak with her; he shrugged his shoulders, said she was free to choose, and went into an adjoining room with my proposal. Her choice apparently was difficult; I waited some time, wondering how she would look on the other side of the ugly chasm she had so audaciously leaped. She came in at last, and I immediately saw that she was vexed by my visit. She wished to utterly forget her past. She was pale and very grave; she seemed to wear a frigid mask of reserve. If she had seemed to me a singular creature before, it didn't help me to understand her to see her there, beside her extraordinary husband. My eyes went from one to the other and, I suppose, betrayed my reflections; she suddenly begged me to inform her of my errand.

"I have been asked," I said, "to inquire whether you are contented. Mrs. Waddington is unwilling to leave Rome while there is a chance of your——" I hesitated for a word, and she interrupted me.

"Of my repentance, is what you mean to say?" She fixed her eyes on the ground for a moment, then suddenly raised them. "Mrs. Waddington may leave Rome," she said softly. I turned in silence, but waited a moment for some slight message of farewell. "I only ask to be forgotten!" she added, seeing me stand.

Love is said to be *par excellence* the egotistical passion; if so Adina was far gone. "I can't promise to forget you," I said; "you and my friend here deserve to be remembered!"

She turned away; Angelo seemed relieved at the cessation of our English. He opened the door for me, and stood for a moment with a significant, conscious smile.

"She's happy, eh?" he asked.

"So she says!"

He laid his hand on my arm. "So am I!—She's better than the topaz!"

"You're a queer fellow!" I cried; and, pushing past him, I hurried away.

Mrs. Waddington gave her step-daughter another chance to repent, for she lingered in Rome a fortnight more. She was disappointed at my being able to bring her no information as to how Adina had eluded observation—how she had played her game and kept her secret. My own belief was that there had been a very small amount of courtship, and that until she stole out of the house the morning before her flight, to meet the Padre Girolamo and his nephew at the church, she had barely heard the sound of her lover's voice. There had been signs, and glances, and other unspoken vows, two or three notes, perhaps. Exactly who Angelo was, and what had originally secured for us the honor of his attentions, Mrs. Waddington never learned; it was enough for her that he was a friendless, picturesque Italian. Where everything was a painful puzzle, a shade or two, more or less, of obscurity hardly mattered. Scrope, of course, never attempted to account for his own blindness, though to his silent thoughts it must have seemed bitterly strange. He spoke of Adina, as I said, but once.

He knew by instinct, by divination,—for I had not told him,—that I had been to see her, and late on the evening following my visit, he proposed to me to take a stroll through the streets. It was a soft, damp night, with vague, scattered cloud masses, through which the moon was slowly drifting. A warm south wind had found its way into the dusky heart of the city. "Let us go to St. Peter's," he said, "and see the fountains play in the fitful moonshine." When we reached the bridge of St. Angelo, he paused and leaned some time on the parapet, looking over into the Tiber. At last, suddenly raising himself—"You've seen her?" he asked.

"Yes."

"What did she say?"

"She said she was happy."

He was silent, and we walked on. Half-way over the bridge he stopped again and gazed at the river. Then he drew a small velvet case from his pocket, opened it, and let something shine in the moonlight. It was the beautiful, the imperial, the baleful topaz. He looked at me and I knew what his look meant. It made my heart beat, but I did not say—no! It had been a curse, the golden gem, with its cruel emblems; let it return to the moldering underworld of the Roman past! I shook his hand firmly, he stretched out the other and, with a great flourish, tossed the glittering jewel into the dusky river. There it lies! Some day, I suppose, they will dredge the Tiber for treasures, and, possibly, disinter our topaz, and recognize it. But who will guess at this passionate human interlude to its burial of centuries?

DE GREY: A ROMANCE

IT was the year 1820, and Mrs. De Grey, by the same token, as they say in Ireland (and, for that matter, out of it), had reached her sixty-seventh spring. She was, nevertheless, still a handsome woman, and, what is better yet, still an amiable woman. The untroubled, unruffled course of her life had left as few wrinkles on her temper as on her face. She was tall and full of person, with dark eyes and abundant white hair, which she rolled back from her forehead over a cushion, or some such artifice. The freshness of youth and health had by no means faded out of her cheeks, nor had the smile of her imperturbable courtesy expired on her lips. She dressed, as became a woman of her age and a widow, in black garments, but relieved with a great deal of white, with a number of handsome rings on her fair hands. Frequently, in the spring, she wore a little flower or a sprig of green leaves in the bosom of her gown. She had been accused of receiving these little floral ornaments from the hands of Mr. Herbert (of whom I shall have more to say); but the charge is unfounded, inasmuch as they were very carefully selected from a handful cut in the garden by her maid.

That Mrs. De Grey should have been just the placid and elegant old lady that she was, remained, in the eyes of the world at large, in spite of an abundance of a certain sort of evidence in favor of such a result, more or less of a puzzle and a problem. It is true, that every one who knew anything about her knew that she had enjoyed great material prosperity, and had suffered no misfortunes. She was mistress in her own right of a handsome property and a handsome house; she had lost her husband, indeed, within a year after marriage; but, as the late George De Grey had been of a sullen and brooding humor,—to that degree, indeed, as to incur the suspicion of insanity,—her loss, leaving her well provided for, might in strictness have been acounted a gain. Her son, moreover, had never given her a moment's trouble; he had grown up a charming young man, handsome, witty, and wise; he was a model of filial devotion. The lady's health was good; she had half a dozen perfect servants; she had the perpetual company of the incomparable Mr. Herbert; she was as fine a figure of an elderly woman as any in town; she might, therefore, very well have been happy and have looked so. On the other hand, a dozen sensible women had been known to declare with emphasis, that not for all her treasures and her felicity would they have consented to be Mrs. De Grey. These ladies were, of course, unable to give a logical reason for so strong an aversion. But it is certain that there hung over Mrs. De Grey's history and circumstances a film, as it were, a shadow of mystery, which struck a chill upon imaginations which might easily have been kindled into envy of her good fortune. "She lives in the dark," some one had said of her. Close observers did her the honor to believe that there was a secret in her life, but of a wholly undefined character. Was she the victim of some lurking sorrow, or the mistress of some clandestine joy? These imputations, we may easily believe, are partially explained by the circumstance that she was a Catholic, and kept a priest in her house. The unexplained portion might very well, moreover, have been discredited by Mrs. De Grey's perfectly candid and complacent demeanor. It was certainly hard to conceive, in talking with her, to what part of her person one might pin a mystery,—whether on her clear, round eyes or her handsome, benevolent lips. Let us say, then, in defiance of the voice of society, that she was no tragedy queen. She was a fine woman, a dull woman, a perfect gentlewoman. She had taken life, as she liked a cup of tea,—weak, with an exquisite aroma and plenty of cream and sugar. She had never lost her temper, for the excellent reason that she had none to lose. She was troubled with no fears, no doubts, no scruples, and

blessed with no sacred certainties. She was fond of her
son, of the church, of her garden, and of her toilet. She
had the very best taste; but, morally, one may say that
she had had no history.

Mrs. De Grey had always lived in seclusion; for a couple
of years previous to the time of which I speak she had lived
in solitude. Her son, on reaching his twenty-third year,
had gone to Europe for a long visit, in pursuance of a plan
discussed at intervals between his mother and Mr. Herbert
during the whole course of his boyhood. They had made
no attempt to forecast his future career, or to prepare him
for a profession. Strictly, indeed, he was at liberty, like
his late father, to dispense with a profession. Not that
it was to be wished that he should take his father's life as
an example. It was understood by the world at large, and,
of course, by Mrs. De Grey and her companion in particular, that this gentleman's existence had been blighted, at an
early period, by an unhappy love-affair; and it was notorious
that, in consequence, he had spent the few years of his
maturity in gloomy idleness and dissipation. Mrs. De
Grey, whose own father was an Englishman, reduced to
poverty, but with claims to high gentility, professed herself unable to understand why Paul should not live decently
on his means. Mr. Herbert declared that in America, in
any walk of life, idleness was indecent; and that he hoped
the young man would—nominally at least—select a career.
It was agreed on both sides, however, that there was no
need for haste; and that it was proper, in the first place, he
should see the world. The world, to Mrs. De Grey, was
little more than a name; but to Mr. Herbert, priest as he
was, it was a vivid reality. Yet he felt that the generous
and intelligent youth upon whose education he had lavished
all the treasures of his tenderness and sagacity, was not
unfitted, either by nature or culture, to measure his sinews
against its trials and temptations; and that he should love
him the better for coming home at twenty-five an accomplished gentleman and a good Catholic, sobered and seasoned by experience, sceptical in small matters, confident in
great, and richly replete with good stories. When he came

of age, Paul received his walking-ticket, as they say, in the shape of a letter of credit for a handsome sum on certain London bankers. But the young man pocketed the letter, and remained at home, poring over books, lounging in the garden, and scribbling heroic verses. At the end of a year, he plucked up a little ambition, and took a turn through the country, travelling much of the way on horseback. He came back an ardent American, and felt that he might go abroad without danger. During his absence in Europe he had written home innumerable long letters,— compositions so elaborate (in the taste of that day, recent as it is, and so delightful) that, between their pride in his epistolary talent and their longing to see his face, his mother and his ex-tutor would have been at a loss to determine whether he gave them more satisfaction at home or abroad.

With his departure the household was plunged in unbroken repose. Mrs. De Grey neither went out nor entertained company. An occasional morning call was the only claim made upon her hospitality. Mr. Herbert, who was a great scholar, spent all his hours in study; and his patroness sat for the most part alone, arrayed with a perfection of neatness which there was no one to admire (unless it be her waiting-maid, to whom it remained a constant matter of awe), reading a pious book or knitting undergarments for the orthodox needy. At times, indeed, she wrote long letters to her son,—the contents of which Mr. Herbert found it hard to divine. This was accounted a dull life forty years ago; now, doubtless, it would be considered no life at all. It is no matter of wonder, therefore, that finally, one April morning, in her sixty-seventh year, as I have said, Mrs. De Grey suddenly began to suspect that she was lonely. Another long year, at least, was to come and go before Paul's return. After meditating for a while in silence, Mrs. De Grey resolved to take counsel with Father Herbert.

This gentleman, an Englishman by birth, had been an intimate friend of George De Grey, who had made his acquaintance during a visit to Europe, before his marriage.

Mr. Herbert was a younger son of an excellent Catholic family, and was at that time beginning, on small resources, the practice of the law. De Grey met him in London, and the two conceived a strong mutual sympathy. Herbert had neither taste for his profession nor apparent ambition of any sort. He was, moreover, in weak health; and his friend found no difficulty in persuading him to accept the place of travelling companion through France and Italy. De Grey carried a very long purse, and was a most liberal friend and patron; and the two young men accomplished their progress as far as Venice in the best spirits and on the best terms. But in Venice, for reasons best known to themselves, they bitterly and irretrievably quarrelled. Some persons said it was over a card-table, and some said it was about a woman. At all events, in consequence, De Grey returned to America, and Herbert repaired to Rome. He obtained admission into a monastery, studied theology, and finally was invested with priestly orders. In America, in his thirty-third year, De Grey married the lady whom I have described. A few weeks after his marriage he wrote to Herbert, expressing a vehement desire to be reconciled. Herbert felt that the letter was that of a most unhappy man; he had already forgiven him; he pitied him, and after a short delay succeeded in obtaining an ecclesiastical mission to the United States. He reached New York and presented himself at his friend's house, which from this moment became his home. Mrs. De Grey had recently given birth to a son; her husband was confined to his room by illness, reduced to a shadow of his former self by repeated sensual excesses. He survived Herbert's arrival but a couple of months; and after his death the rumor went abroad that he had by his last will settled a handsome income upon the priest, on condition that he would continue to reside with his widow, and take the entire charge of his boy's education.

This rumor was confirmed by the event. For twenty-five years, at the time of which I write, Herbert had lived under Mrs. De Grey's roof as her friend and companion and counsellor, and as her son's tutor. Once reconciled to his friend, he had gradually dropped his priestly character. He was of an essentially devout temperament, but he craved neither parish nor pulpit. On the other hand, he had become an indefatigable student. His late friend had bequeathed to him a valuable library, which he gradually enlarged. His passion for study, however, appeared singularly disinterested, inasmuch as, for many years, his little friend Paul was the sole witness and receptacle of his learning. It is true that he composed a large portion of a History of the Catholic Church in America, which, although the manuscript exists, has never seen, and, I suppose, is never destined to see, the light. It is in the very best keeping, for it contains an immense array of facts. The work is written, not from a sympathetic, but from a strictly respectful point of view; but it has a fatal defect,—it lacks unction.

The same complaint might have been made of Father Herbert's personal character. He was the soul of politeness, but it was a cold and formal courtesy. When he smiled, it was, as the French say, with the end of his lips, and when he took your hand, with the end of his fingers. He had had a charming face in his younger days, and when gentlemen dressed their hair with powder, his fine black eyes must must have produced the very best effect. But he had lost his hair, and he wore on his naked crown a little black silk cap. Round his neck he had a black cravat of many folds, without any collar. He was short and slight, with a stoop in his shoulders, and a handsome pair of hands.

"If it were not for a sad sign to the contrary," said Mrs. De Grey, in pursuance of her resolve to take counsel of her friend, "I should believe I am growing younger."

"What is the sign to the contrary?" asked Herbert.

"I'm losing my eyes. I can't see to read. Suppose I should become blind."

"And what makes you suspect that you are growing young again?"

"I feel lonely. I lack company. I miss Paul."

"You will have Paul back in a year."

"Yes; but in the mean while I shall be miserable. I wish I knew some nice person whom I might ask to stay with me."

"Why don't you take a companion,—some poor gentlewoman in search of a home? She would read to you, and talk to you."

"No; that would be dreadful. She would be sure to be old and ugly. I should like some one to take Paul's place,—some one young and fresh like him. We're all so terribly old, in the house. You're at least seventy; I'm sixty-five" (Mrs. De Grey was pleased to say); "Deborah is sixty, the cook and coachman are fifty-five apiece."

"You want a young girl then?"

"Yes, some nice, fresh young girl, who would laugh once in a while, and make a little music,—a little sound in the house."

"Well," said Herbert, after reflecting a moment, "you had better suit yourself before Paul comes home. You have only a year."

"Dear me," said Mrs. De Grey; "I shouldn't feel myself obliged to turn her out on Paul's account."

Father Herbert looked at his companion with a penetrating glance. "Nevertheless, my dear lady," he said, "you know what I mean."

"O yes, I know what you mean,—and you, Father Herbert, know what I think."

"Yes, madam, and, allow me to add, that I don't greatly care. Why should I? I hope with all my heart that you'll never find yourself compelled to think otherwise."

"It is certain," said Mrs. De Grey, "that Paul has had time to play out his little tragedy a dozen times over."

"His father," rejoined Herbert, gravely, "was twenty-six years old."

At these words Mrs. De Grey looked at the priest with a slight frown and a flushed cheek. But he took no pains to meet her eyes, and in a few moments she had recovered, in silence, her habitual calmness.

Within a week after this conversation Mrs. De Grey observed at church two persons who appeared to be strangers in the congregation: an elderly woman, meanly clad, and evidently in ill health, but with a great refinement of person and manner; and a young girl whom Mrs. De Grey took for her daughter. On the following Sunday she again found them at their devotions, and was forcibly struck by a look of sadness and trouble in their faces and attitude. On the third Sunday they were absent; but it happened that during the walk, going to confession, she met the young girl, pale, alone, and dressed in mourning, apparently just leaving the confessional. Something in her gait and aspect assured Mrs. De Grey that she was alone in the world, friendless and helpless; and the good lady, who at times was acutely sensible of her own isolation in society, felt a strong and sympathetic prompting to speak to the stranger, and ask the secret of her sorrow. She stopped her before she left the church, and, addressing her with the utmost kindness, succeeded so speedily in winning her confidence that in half an hour she was in possession of the young girl's entire history. She had just lost her mother, and she found herself in the great city penniless, and all but houseless. They were from the South; her father had been an officer in the navy, and had perished at sea, two years before. Her mother's health had failed, and they had come to New York, ill-advisedly enough, to consult an eminent physician. He had been very kind, he had taken no fees, but his skill had been applied in vain. Their money had melted away in other directions,—for food and lodging and clothing. There had been enough left to give the poor lady a decent burial; but no means of support save her own exertions remained for the young girl. She had no relatives to look to, but she professed herself abundantly willing to work. "I look weak," she said, "and pale, but I'm really strong. It's only that I'm tired, —and sad. I'm ready to do anything. But I don't know where to look." She had lost her color and the roundness and elasticity of youth; she was thin and ill-dressed; but Mrs. De Grey saw that at her best she must be properly a very pretty creature, and that she was evidently, by rights, a charming girl. She looked at the elder lady with lustrous, appealing blue eyes from under the hideous black bonnet in which her masses of soft light hair were tucked away. She assured her that she had received a very good education, and that she played on the piano-forte. Mrs. De Grey fancied her divested of her rusty weeds, and dressed in a white frock and a blue ribbon, reading aloud at an open window, or touching the keys of her old not unmelodious spinnet; for if she took her (as she mentally phrased it) Mrs. De Grey was resolved that she would not be harassed with the sight of her black garments. It was plain that, frightened and faint and nervous as she was, the poor child would take any service unconditionally. She kissed her then tenderly within the sacred precinct, and led her away to her carriage, quite forgetting her business with her confessor. On the following day Margaret Aldis (such was the young girl's name) was transferred in the same vehicle to Mrs. De Grey's own residence.

This edifice was demolished some years ago, and the place where it stood forms at the present moment the very center of a turbulent thoroughfare. But at the period of which I speak it stood on the outskirts of the town, with as vast a prospect of open country in one direction as in the other of close-built streets. It was an excellent old mansion, moreover, in the best taste of the time, with large square rooms and broad halls and deep windows, and, above all, a delightful great garden, hedged off from the road by walls of dense verdure. Here, steeped in repose and physical comfort, rescued from the turbid stream of common life, and placed apart in the glow of tempered sunshine, valued, esteemed, caressed, and yet feeling that she was not a mere passive object of charity, but that she was doing her simple utmost to requite her protectress, poor Miss Aldis bloomed and flowered afresh. With rest and luxury and leisure, her natural gayety and beauty came back to her. Her beauty was not dazzling, indeed, nor her gayety obtrusive; but, united, they were the flower of girlish grace. She still retained a certain tenuity and fragility of aspect, a lightness of tread, a softness of voice, a faintness of coloring, which suggested an intimate acquaintance with suffering. But there seemed to burn, nevertheless, in her deep blue eyes the light of an almost passionate vitality; and there sat on her firm, pale lips the utterance of a determined, devoted will. It seemed at times as if she gave herself up with a sensuous, reckless, half-thankless freedom to the mere consciousness of security. It was evident that she had an innate love of luxury. She would sometimes sit, motionless, for hours, with her head thrown back, and her eyes slowly wandering, in a silent ecstasy of content. At these times Father Herbert, who had observed her attentively from the moment of her arrival (for, scholar and recluse as he was, he had not lost the faculty of appreciating feminine grace),—at these times the old priest would watch her covertly and marvel at the fantastic, soulless creature whom Mrs. De Grey had taken to her side. One evening, after a prolonged stupor of this sort, in which the young girl had neither moved nor spoken, sitting like one whose soul had detached itself and was wandering through space, she rose, on Mrs. De Grey's at last giving her an order, and moved forward as if in compliance; and then, suddenly rushing toward the old woman, she fell on her knees, and buried her head in her lap and burst into a paroxysm of sobs. Herbert, who had been standing by, went and laid one hand on her head, and with the other made over it the sign of the cross, in the manner of a benediction,—a consecration of the passionate gratitude which had finally broken out into utterance. From this moment he loved her.

Margaret read aloud to Mrs. De Grey, and on Sunday evenings sang in a clear, sweet voice the chants of their Church, and occupied herself constantly with fine needlework, in which she possessed great skill. They spent the long summer mornings together, in reading and work and talk. Margaret told her companion the simple, sad details of the history of which she had already given her the outline; and Mrs. De Grey, who found it natural to look upon them as a kind of practical romance organized for her entertainment, made her repeat them over a dozen times. Mrs. De Grey, too, honored the young girl with a recital of her own biography, which, in its vast vacuity, produced upon Margaret's mind a vague impression of grandeur. The vacuity, indeed, was relieved by the figure of Paul, whom Mrs. De Grey never grew weary of describing, and of whom, finally, Margaret grew very fond of thinking. She listened most attentively to Mrs. De Grey's eulogies of her son, and thought it a great pity he was not at home. And then she began to long for his return, and then, suddenly, she began to fear it. Perhaps he would dislike her being in the house, and turn her out of doors. It was evident that his mother was not prepared to contradict him. Perhaps—worse still—he would marry some foreign woman, and bring her home, and she would turn wickedly jealous of Margaret (in the manner of foreign women). De Grey, roaming through Europe, took for granted, piously enough, that he was never absent from his good mother's thoughts; but he remained superbly unconscious of the dignity which he had usurped in the meditations of her humble companion. Truly, we know where our lives begin, but who shall say where they end? Here was a careless young gentleman whose existence enjoyed a perpetual echo in the soul of a poor girl utterly unknown to him. Mrs. De Grey had two portraits of her son, which, of course, she lost no time in exhibiting to Margaret,—one taken in his boyhood, with brilliant red hair and cheeks, the lad's body encased in a bright blue jacket, and his neck encircled in a frill, open very low; the other, executed just before his departure, a handsome young man in a buff waistcoat, clean shaven, with an animated countenance, dark, close-curling auburn hair, and very fine eyes. The former of these designs Margaret thought a very pretty child; but to the other the poor girl straightway lost her heart,—the more easily that Mrs. De Grey assured her, that, although the picture was handsome enough, it conveyed but the faintest idea of her boy's adorable flesh and blood. In a couple of months arrived a long-expected letter from Paul, and with it another portrait,—a miniature, painted in Paris by a famous artist. Here Paul appeared a far more elegant figure than in the work of the American painter. In what the change consisted it was hard to tell; but his mother declared that it was easy to see that he had spent two years in the best company in Europe.

"Oh, the best company!" said Father Herbert, who knew the force of this term. And, smiling a moment with inoffensive scorn, he relapsed into his wonted gravity.

"I think he looks very sad," said Margaret, timidly.

"Fiddlesticks!" cried Herbert, impatiently. "He looks like a coxcomb. Of course, it's the Frenchman's fault," he added, more gently. "Why on earth does he send us his picture at all? It's a great piece of impertinence. Does he think we've forgotten him? When I want to remember my boy, I have something better to look to than the flaunting bit of ivory."

At these words the two ladies went off, carrying the portrait with them, to read Paul's letter in private. It was in eight pages, and Margaret read it aloud. Then, when she had finished, she read it again; and in the evening she read it once more. The next day, Mrs. De Grey, taking the young girl quite into her confidence, brought out a large packet containing his earlier letters, and Margaret spent the whole morning in reading them over aloud. That evening she took a stroll in the garden alone,—the garden in which *he* had played as a boy, and lounged and dreamed as a young man. She found his name—his beautiful name—rudely cut on a wooden bench. Introduced, as it seemed to her that she had been by his letters, into the precincts of his personality, the mystery of his being, the magic circle of his feelings and opinions and fancies; wandering by his side, unseen, over Europe, and treading, unheard, the sounding pavements of famous churches and palaces, she felt that she tasted for the first time of the substance and sweetness of life. Margaret walked about for an hour in the starlight, among the dusky, perfumed alleys. Mrs. De Grey, feeling unwell, had gone to her room. The young girl heard the far-off hum of the city slowly decrease and expire, and then, when the stillness of the night was unbroken, she came back into the parlor across the long window, and lit one of the great silver candlesticks that decorated the ends of the mantel. She carried it to the wall where Mrs. De Grey had suspended her son's miniature, having first inserted it in an immense gold frame, from which she had expelled a less valued picture. Margaret felt that she must see the portrait before she went to bed. There was a certain charm and ravishment in beholding it privately by candlelight. The wind had risen,—a warm west wind,—and the long white curtains of the open windows swayed and bulged in the gloom in a spectral fashion. Margaret guarded the flame of the candle with her hand, and gazed at the polished surface of the portrait, warm in the light, beneath its glittering plate of glass. What an immensity of life and passion was concentrated into those few square inches of artificial color! The young man's eyes seemed to gaze at her with a look of profound recognition. They held her fascinated; she lingered on the spot, unable to move. Suddenly the clock on the chimney-piece rang out a single clear stroke. Margaret started and turned about, at the thought that it was already half past ten. She raised her candle aloft to look at the dial-plate; and perceived three things: that it was one o'clock in the morning, that her candle was half burnt out, and that some one was watching her from the other side of the room. Setting down her light, she recognized Father Herbert.

"Well, Miss Aldis," he said, coming into the light, "what do you think of it?"

Margaret was startled and confused, but not abashed. "How long have I been here?" she asked, simply.

"I have no idea. I myself have been here half an hour."

"It was very kind of you not to disturb me," said Margaret, less simply.

"It was a very pretty picture," said Herbert.

"Oh, it's beautiful!" cried the young girl, casting another glance at the portrait over her shoulder.

The old man smiled sadly, and turned away, and then,

coming back, "How do you like our young man, Miss Aldis?" he asked, apparently with a painful effort.

"I think he's very handsome," said Margaret, frankly.

"He's not so handsome as that," said Herbert.

"His mother says he's handsomer."

"A mother's testimony in such cases is worth very little. Paul is well enough, but he's no miracle."

"I think he looks sad," said Margaret. "His mother says he's very gay."

"He may have changed vastly within two years. Do you think," the old man added, after a pause, "that he looks like a man in love?"

"I don't know," said Margaret, in a low voice. "I never saw one."

"Never?" said the priest, with an earnestness which surprised the young girl.

She blushed a little. "Never, Father Herbert."

The priest's dark eyes were fixed on her with a strange intensity of expression. "I hope, my child, you never may," he said, solemnly.

The tone of his voice was not unkind, but it seemed to Margaret as if there were something cruel and chilling in the wish. "Why not I as well as another?" she asked.

The old man shrugged his shoulders. "O, it's a long story," he said.

The summer passed away and flushed into autumn, and the autumn slowly faded, and finally expired in the cold embrace of December. Mrs. De Grey had written to her son of her having taken Margaret into her service. At this time came a letter in which the young man was pleased to express his satisfaction at this measure. "Present my compliments to Miss Aldis," he wrote, "and assure her of my gratitude for the comfort she has given my dear mother, —of which, indeed, I hope before very long to inform her in person." In writing these good-natured words Paul De Grey little suspected the infinite reverberation they were to have in poor Margaret's heart. A month later arrived a letter, which was handed to Mrs. De Grey at breakfast. "You will have received my letter of December 3d," it began (a letter which had miscarried and failed to arrive), "and will have formed your respective opinions of its contents." As Mrs. De Grey read these words, Father Herbert looked at Margaret; she had turned pale. "Favorable or not," the letter continued, "I am sorry to be obliged to bid you undo them again. But my engagement to Miss L. is broken off. It had become impossible. As I made no attempt to give you a history of it, or to set forth my motives, so I shall not now attempt to go into the logic of the rupture. But it's broken clean off, I assure you. Amen." And the letter passed to other matters, leaving our friends sadly perplexed. They awaited the arrival of the missing letter; but all in vain; it never came. Mrs. De Grey immediately wrote to her son, urgently requesting an explanation of the events to which he had referred. His next letter, however, contained none of the desired information. Mrs. De Grey repeated her request. Whereupon Paul wrote that he would tell her the story when he had reached home. He hated to talk about it. "Don't be uneasy, dear mother," he added; "Heaven has insured me against a relapse. Miss L. died three weeks ago at Naples." As Mrs. De Grey read these words, she laid down the letter and looked at Father Herbert, who had been called to hear it. His pale face turned ghastly white, and he returned the old woman's gaze with compressed lips and a stony immobility in his eyes. Then, suddenly, a fierce, inarticulate cry broke from his throat, and, doubling up his fist, he brought it down with a terrible blow on the table. Margaret sat watching him, amazed. He rose to his feet, seized her in his arms, and pressed her on his neck.

"My child! my child!" he cried, in a broken voice, "I have always loved you! I have been harsh and cold and crabbed. I was fearful. The thunder has fallen! Forgive me, child. I'm myself again." Margaret, frightened, disengaged herself, but he kept her hand. "Poor boy!" he cried, with a tremulous sigh.

Mrs. De Grey sat smelling her vinaigrette, but not visibly discomposed. "Poor boy!" she repeated, but without a sigh,—which gave the words an ironical sound.—"He had ceased to care for her," she said.

"Ah, madam!" cried the priest, "don't blaspheme. Go down on your knees, and thank God that *we* have been spared that hideous sight!"

Mystified and horrified, Margaret drew her hand from his grasp, and looked with wondering eyes at Mrs. De Grey. She smiled faintly, touched her forefinger to her forehead, tapped it, raised her eyebrows, and shook her head.

From counting the months that were to elapse before Paul's return, our friends came to counting the weeks, and then the days. The month of May arrived; Paul had sailed from England. At this time Mrs. De Grey opened her son's room, and caused it to be prepared for occupation. The contents were just as he had left them; she bade Margaret come in and see it. Margaret looked at her face in his mirror, and sat down a moment on his sofa, and examined the books on his shelves. They seemed a prodigious array; they were in several languages, and gave a deep impression of their owner's attainments. Over the chimney hung a small sketch in pencil, which Margaret made haste to inspect,—a likeness of a young girl, skilfully enough drawn. The original had apparently been very handsome, in the dark style; and in the corner of the sketch was written the artist's name,—*De Grey*. Margaret looked at the portrait in silence, with quickened heartbeats.

"Is this Mr. Paul's?" she asked at last of her companion.

"It belongs to Paul," said Mrs. De Grey. "He used to be very fond of it, and insisted upon hanging it there. His father sketched it before our marriage."

Margaret drew a breath of relief. "And who is the lady?" she asked.

"I hardly know. Some foreign person, I think, that Mr. De Grey had been struck with. There's something about her in the other corner."

In effect, Margaret detected on the opposite side of the sketch, written in minute character, the word "*obiit*, 1786."

"You don't know Latin, I take it, my dear," said Mrs. De Grey, as Margaret read the inscription. "It means that she died thirty-four good years ago."

"Poor girl!" said Margaret, softly. As they were leaving the room, she lingered on the threshold and looked about her, wishing that she might leave some little memento of her visit. "If we knew just when he would arrive," she said, "I would put some flowers on his table. But they might fade."

As Mrs. De Grey assured her that the moment of his arrival was quite uncertain, she left her fancied nosegay uncut, and spent the rest of the day in a delightful tremor of anticipation, ready to see the dazzling figure of a young man, equipped with strange foreign splendor, start up before her and look at her in cold surprise, and hurry past her in search of his mother. At every sound of footsteps or of an opening door she laid down her work, and listened curiously. In the evening, as if by a common instinct of expectancy, Father Herbert met Mrs. De Grey in the front drawing-room,—an apartment devoted exclusively to those festivities which never occurred in the annals of this tranquil household.

"A year ago to-day, madam," said Margaret, as they all sat silent among the gathering shadows, "I came into your house. To-day ends a very happy year."

"Let us hope," said Father Herbert, sententiously, "that to-morrow will begin another."

"Ah, my dear lady!" cried Margaret, with emotion; "my good father,—my only friends,—what harm can come to me with you? It was you who rescued me from harm." Her heart was swollen with gratitude, and her eyes with rising tears. She gave a long shudder at the thought of the life that might have been her fate. But, feeling a natural indisposition to obtrude her peculiar sensations upon the attention of persons so devoutly absorbed in the thought of a coming joy, she left her place, and wandered away into the garden. Before many minutes, a little gate opened in the paling, not six yards from where she stood. A man came in, whom, in the dim light, she knew to be Paul De Grey. Approaching her rapidly, he made a movement as if to greet her, but stopped suddenly, and removed his hat.

"Ah, you're Miss—the young lady," he said.

He had forgotten her name. This was something other, something less felicitous, than the cold surprise of the figure in Margaret's vision. Nevertheless, she answered him, audibly enough: "They are in the drawing-room; they expect you."

He bounded along the path, and entered the house. She followed him slowly to the window, and stood without, listening. The silence of the young man's welcome told of its warmth.

Paul De Grey had made good use of his sojourn in Europe; he had lost none of his old merits, and had gained a number of new ones. He was by nature and culture an intelligent, amiable, accomplished fellow. It was his fortune to possess a peculiar, indefinable charm of person and manner. He was tall and slight of structure, but compact, firm, and active, with a clear, fair complexion, an open, prominent brow, crisp auburn hair, and eyes—a glance, a smile—radiant with youth and intellect. His address was frank, manly, and direct; and yet it seemed to Margaret that his bearing was marked by a certain dignity and elegance—at times even verging upon formalism—which distinguished it from that of other men. It was not, however, that she detected in his character any signs of that strange principle of melancholy which had exerted so powerful an action upon the other members of the household (and, from what she was able to gather, on his father). She fancied, on the contrary, that she had never known less levity associated with a more exquisite mirth. If Margaret had been of a more analytical turn of mind, she would have told herself that Paul De Grey's nature was eminently aristocratic. But the young girl contented herself with understanding it less, and secretly loving it more; and when she was in want of an epithet, she chose a simpler term. Paul was like a ray of splendid sunshine in the dull, colorless lives of the two women; he filled the house with light and heat and joy. He moved, to Margaret's fancy, in a circle of almost supernatural glory. His words, as they fell from his lips, seemed diamonds and pearls; and, in truth, his conversation, for a month after his return, was in the last degree delightful. Mrs. De Grey's house was *par excellence* the abode of leisure,—a castle of indolence; and Paul in talking, and his companions in listening, were conscious of no jealous stress of sordid duties. The summer days were long, and Paul's daily fund of loquacity was inexhaustible. A week after his arrival, after breakfast, Father Herbert contracted the habit of carrying him off to his study, and Margaret, passing the half-open door, would hear the changeful music of his voice. She begrudged the old man, at these times, the exclusive enjoyment of so much eloquence. She felt that with his tutor, Paul's talk was far wiser and richer than it was possible it should be with two simple-minded women; and the young girl had a pious longing to hear him, to see him, at his best. A brilliant best it was to Father Herbert's mind; for Paul had surpassed his fondest hopes. He had amassed such a store of knowledge; he had learned all the good that the old man had enjoined upon him; and, although he had not wholly ignored the evil against which the priest had warned him, he judged it so wisely and wittily! Women and priests, as a general thing, like a man none the less for not being utterly innocent. Father Herbert took an unutterable satisfaction in the happy development of Paul's character. He was more than the son of his loins: he was the child of his intellect, his patience, and devotion.

The afternoons and evenings Paul was free to devote to his mother, who, out of her own room, never dispensed for an hour with Margaret's attendance. This, thanks to the young girl's delicate tact and sympathy, had now become an absolute necessity. Margaret sat by with her work, while Paul talked, and marvelled at his inexhaustible stock of gossip and anecdote and forcible, vivid description. He made cities and churches and galleries and playhouses swarm and shine before her enchanted senses, and reproduced the people he had met and the scenery through which

he had travelled, until the young girl's head turned at the
rapid succession of images and pictures. And then, at
times, he would seem to grow weary, and would sink into
silence; and Margaret, looking up askance from her work,
would see his eyes absently fixed, and a faint smile on his
face, or else a cold gravity, and she would wonder what far-
off memory had called back his thoughts to that unknown
European world. Sometimes, less frequently, when she
raised her eyes, she found him watching her own figure, her
bent head, and the busy movement of her hands. But (as
yet, at least) he never turned away his glance in confusion; he let his eyes rest, and justified his scrutiny by
some simple and natural remark.

But as the weeks passed by, and the summer grew to its
fulness, Mrs. De Grey contracted the habit of going after
dinner to her own room, where, we may respectfully conjecture, she passed the afternoon in dishabille and slumber.
But De Grey and Miss Aldis tacitly agreed together that,
in the prime and springtime of life, it was stupid folly to
waste in any such fashion the longest and brightest hours
of the year; and so they, on their side, contracted the habit
of sitting in the darkened drawing-room, and gossiping
away the time until within an hour of tea. Sometimes, for a
change, they went across the garden into a sort of summer-
house, which occupied a central point in the enclosure, and
stood with its face averted from the mansion, and looking to
the north, and with its sides covered with dense, clustering
vines. Within, against the wall, was a deep garden bench,
and in the middle a table, upon which Margaret placed her
work-basket, and the young man the book, which, under the
pretence of meaning to read, he usually carried in his
hand. Within was coolness and deep shade and silence,
and without the broad glare of the immense summer sky.
When I say there was silence, I mean that there was nothing
to interrupt the conversation of these happy idlers. Their
talk speedily assumed that desultory, volatile character,
which is the sign of great intimacy. Margaret found occasion to ask Paul a great many questions which she had
not felt at liberty to ask in the presence of his mother,

and to demand additional light upon a variety of little points which Mrs. De Grey had been content to leave in obscurity. Paul was perfectly communicative. If Miss Aldis cared to hear, he was assuredly glad to talk. But suddenly it struck him that her attitude of mind was a singular provocation to egotism, and that for six weeks, in fact, he had done nothing but talk about himself,—his own adventures, sensations, and opinions.

"I declare, Miss Aldis," he cried, "you're making me a monstrous egotist. That's all you women are good for. I shall not say another word about Mr. Paul De Grey. Now it's your turn."

"To talk about Mr. Paul De Grey?" asked Margaret, with a smile.

"No, about Miss Margaret Aldis,—which, by the way, is a very pretty name."

"By the way, indeed!" said Margaret. "By the way for you, perhaps. But for me, my pretty name is all I have."

"If you mean, Miss Aldis," cried Paul, "that your beauty is all in your name——"

"I'm sadly mistaken. Well, then, I don't. The rest is in my imagination."

"Very likely. It's certainly not in mine."

Margaret was, in fact, at this time, extremely pretty; a little pale with the heat, but rounded and developed by rest and prosperity, and animated—half inspired, I may call it—with tender gratitude. Looking at her as he said these words, De Grey was forcibly struck with the interesting character of her face. Yes, most assuredly, her beauty was a potent reality. The charm of her face was forever refreshed and quickened by the deep loveliness of her soul.

"I mean literally, Miss Aldis," said the young man, "that I wish you to talk about yourself. I want to hear *your* adventures. I demand it,—— I need it."

"My adventures?" said Margaret. "I have never had any."

"Good!" cried Paul; "that in itself is an adventure."

In this way it was that Margaret came to relate to her companion the short story of her young life. The story was not all told, however, short as it was, in a single afternoon; that is, a whole week after she began, the young girl found herself setting Paul right with regard to a matter of which he had received a false impression.

"Nay, he is married," said Margaret; "I told you so."

"Oh, he is married?" said Paul.

"Yes; his wife's an immense fat woman."

"Oh, his wife's an immense fat woman?"

"Yes; and he thinks all the world of her."

"Oh, he thinks all the world of her!"

It was natural that, in this manner, with a running commentary supplied by Paul, the narrative should proceed slowly. But, in addition to the observations here quoted, the young man maintained another commentary, less audible and more profound. As he listened to this frank and fair-haired maiden, and reflected that in the wide world she might turn in confidence and sympathy to other minds than his,—as he found her resting her candid thoughts and memories on his judgment, as she might lay her white hand on his arm,—it seemed to him that the pure intentions with which she believed his soul to be peopled took in her glance a graver and higher cast. All the gorgeous color faded out of his recent European reminiscences and regrets, and he was sensible only of Margaret's presence, and of the tender rosy radiance in which she sat and moved, as in a sort of earthly halo. Could it be, he asked himself, that while he was roaming about Europe, in a vague, restless search for his future, his end, his aim, these things were quietly awaiting him at his own deserted hearth-stone, gathered together in the immaculate person of the sweetest and fairest of women? Finally, one day, this view of the case struck him so forcibly, that he cried out in an ecstasy of belief and joy.

"Margaret," he said, "my mother found you in church, and there, before the altar, she kissed you and took you into her arms. I have often thought of that scene. It makes it no common adoption."

"I'm sure I have often thought of it," said Margaret.

"It makes it sacred and everlasting," said Paul. "On that blessed day you came to us for ever and ever."

Margaret looked at him with a face tremulous between smiles and tears. "For as long as you will keep me," she said. "Ah, Paul!" For in an instant the young man had expressed all his longing and his passion.

With the greatest affection and esteem for his mother, Paul had always found it natural to give precedence to Father Herbert in matters of appeal and confidence. The old man possessed a delicacy of intellectual tact which made his sympathy and his counsel alike delightful. Some days after the conversation upon a few of the salient points of which I have lightly touched, Paul and Margaret renewed their mutual vows in the summer-house. They now possessed that deep faith in the sincerity of their own feelings, and that undoubting delight in each other's reiterated protests, which left them nothing to do but to take their elders into their confidence. They came through the garden together, and on reaching the threshold Margaret found that she had left her scissors in the garden hut; whereupon Paul went back in search of them. The young girl came into the house, reached the foot of the staircase, and waited for her lover. At this moment Father Herbert appeared in the open doorway of his study, and looked at Margaret with a melancholy smile. He stood, passing one hand slowly over another, and gazing at her with kindly, darksome looks.

"It seems to me, Mistress Margaret," he said, "that you keep all this a marvellous secret from your poor old Doctor Herbert."

In the presence of this gentle and venerable scholar, Margaret felt that she had no need of vulgar blushing and simpering and negation. "Dear Father Herbert," she said, with heavenly simpleness, "I have just been begging Paul to tell you."

"Ah, my daughter,"—and the old man but half stifled a sigh,—"it's all a strange and terrible mystery."

Paul came in and crossed the hall with the light step of a lover.

"Paul," said Margaret, "Father Herbert knows."

"Father Herbert knows!" repeated the priest,—"Father Herbert knows everything. You're very innocent for lovers."

"You're very wise, sir, for a priest," said Paul, blushing.

"I knew it a week ago," said the old man, gravely.

"Well, sir," said Paul, "we love you none the less for loving each other so much more. I hope you'll not love us the less."

"Father Herbert thinks it's 'terrible,' " said Margaret, smiling.

"O Lord!" cried Herbert, raising his hand to his head as if in pain. He turned about, and went into his room.

Paul drew Margaret's hand through his arm and followed the priest. "You suffer, sir," he said, "at the thought of losing us,—of our leaving you. That certainly needn't trouble you. Where should we go? As long as you live, as long as my mother lives, we shall all make but a single household."

The old man appeared to have recovered his composure. "Ah!" he said; "be happy, no matter where, and I shall be happy. You're very young."

"Not so young," said Paul, laughing, but with a natural disinclination to be placed in too boyish a light. "I'm six-and-twenty. *J'ai vécu,*—I've lived."

"He's been through everything," said Margaret, leaning on his arm.

"Not quite everything." And Paul, bending his eyes, with a sober smile, met her upward glance.

"Oh, he's modest," murmured Father Herbert.

"Paul's been all but married already," said Margaret.

The young man made a gesture of impatience. Herbert stood with his eyes fixed on his face.

"Why do you speak of that poor girl?" said Paul. Whatever satisfaction he may have given Margaret on the subject of his projected marriage in Europe, he had since his return declined, on the plea that it was extremely painful, to discuss the matter either with his mother or with his old tutor.

"Miss Aldis is perhaps jealous," said Herbert, cunningly.

"O Father Herbert!" cried Margaret.

"There is little enough to be jealous of," said Paul.

"There's a fine young man!" cried Herbert. "One would think he had never cared for her."

"It's perfectly true."

"Oh!" said Herbert, in a tone of deep reproach, laying his hand on the young man's arm. "Don't say that."

"Nay, sir, I shall say it. I never said anything less to her. She enchanted me, she entangled me, but, before Heaven, I never loved her!"

"Oh, God help you!" cried the priest. He sat down, and buried his face in his hands.

Margaret turned deadly pale, and recalled the scene which had occurred on the receipt of Paul's letter, announcing the rupture of his engagement. "Father Herbert," she cried, "what horrible, hideous mystery do you keep locked up in your bosom? If it concerns me,—if it concerns Paul, —I demand of you to tell us."

Moved apparently by the young girl's tone of agony to a sense of the needfulness of self-control, Herbert uncovered his face, and directed to Margaret a rapid glance of entreaty. She perceived that it meant that, at any cost, she should be silent. Then, with a sublime attempt at dissimulation, he put out his hands, and laid one on each of his companions' shoulders. "Excuse me, Paul," he said, "I'm a foolish old man. Old scholars are a sentimental, a superstitious race. We believe still that all women are angels, and that all men——"

"That all men are fools," said Paul, smiling.

"Exactly. Whereas, you see," whispered Father Herbert, "there are no fools but ourselves."

Margaret listened to this fantastic bit of dialogue with a beating heart, fully determined not to content herself with any such flimsy explanation of the old man's tragical allusions. Meanwhile, Herbert urgently besought Paul to defer for a few days making known his engagement to his mother.

The next day but one was Sunday, the last in August. The heat for a week had been oppressive, and the air was now sullen and brooding, as if with an approaching storm. As she left the breakfast-table, Margaret felt her arm touched by Father Herbert.

"Don't go to church," he said, in a low voice. "Make a pretext, and stay at home."

"A pretext?——"

"Say you've letters to write."

"Letters?" and Margaret smiled half bitterly. "To whom should I write letters?"

"Dear me, then say you're ill. I give you absolution. When they're gone, come to me."

At church-time, accordingly, Margaret feigned a slight indisposition; and Mrs. De Grey, taking her son's arm, mounted into her ancient deep-seated coach, and rolled away from the door. Margaret immediately betook herself to Father Herbert's apartment. She saw in the old man's face the portent of some dreadful avowal. His whole figure betrayed the weight of an inexorable necessity.

"My daughter," said the priest, "you are a brave, pious girl——"

"Ah!" cried Margaret, "it's something horrible, or you wouldn't say that. Tell me at once!"

"You need all your courage."

"Doesn't he love me?—Ah, in Heaven's name, speak!"

"If he didn't love you with a damning passion, I should have nothing to say."

"Oh, then, say what you please!" said Margaret.

"Well then,—you must leave this house."

"Why?—when?—where must I go?"

"This moment, if possible. You must go anywhere,— the further the better,—the further from *him*. Listen, my child," said the old man, his bosom wrung by the stunned, bewildered look of Margaret's face; "it's useless to protest, to weep, to resist. It's the voice of fate!"

"And pray, sir," said Margaret, "of what do you accuse me?"

"I accuse no one. I don't even accuse Heaven."

"But there's a reason,—there's a motive—"

Herbert laid his hand on his lips, pointed to a seat, and, turning to an ancient chest on the table, unlocked it, and drew from it a small volume, bound in vellum, apparently an old illuminated missal. "There's nothing for it," he said, "but to tell you the whole story."

He sat down before the young girl, who held herself rigid and expectant. The room grew dark with the gathering storm-clouds, and the distant thunder muttered.

"Let me read you ten words," said the priest, opening at a fly-leaf of the volume, on which a memorandum or register had been inscribed in a great variety of hands, all minute and some barely legible. "God be with you!" and the old man crossed himself. Involuntarily, Margaret did the same. " 'George De Grey,' " he read, " 'met and loved, September, 1786, Antonietta Gambini, of Milan. She died October 9th, same year. John De Grey married, April 4th, 1749, Henrietta Spencer. She died May 7th. George De Grey engaged himself October, 1710, to Mary Fortescue. She died October 31st. Paul De Grey, aged nineteen, betrothed June, 1672, at Bristol, England, to Lucretia Lefevre, aged thirty-one, of that place. She died July 27th. John De Grey, affianced January 10th, 1649, to Blanche Ferrars, of Castle Ferrars, Cumberland. She died, by her lover's hand, January 12th. Stephen De Grey offered his hand to Isabel Stirling, October, 1619. She died within the month. Paul De Grey exchanged pledges with Magdalen Scrope, August, 1586. She died in childbirth, September, 1587.' " Father Herbert paused. "Is it enough?" he asked, looking up with glowing eyes. "There are two pages more. The De Greys are an ancient line; they keep their records."

Margaret had listened with a look of deepening, fierce, passionate horror,—a look more of anger and of wounded pride than of terror. She sprang towards the priest with the lightness of a young cat, and dashed the hideous record from his hand.

"What abominable nonsense is this!" she cried. "What does it mean? I barely heard it; I despise it; I laugh at it!"

The old man seized her arm with a firm grasp. "Paul De Grey," he said, in an awful voice, "exchanged pledges with Margaret Aldis, August, 1821. She died—with the falling leaves."

Poor Margaret looked about her for help, inspiration, comfort of some kind. The room contained nothing but serried lines of old parchment-covered books, each seeming a grim repetition of the volume at her feet. A vast peal of thunder resounded through the noon-day stillness. Suddenly her strength deserted her; she felt her weakness and loneliness, the grasp of the hand of fate. Father Herbert put out his arms, she flung herself on his neck, and burst into tears.

"Do you still refuse to leave him?" asked the priest. "If you leave him, you're saved."

"Saved?" cried Margaret, raising her head; "and Paul?"

"Ah, there it is.—He'll forget you."

The young girl pondered a moment. "To have him do that," she said, "I should apparently have to die." Then wringing her hands with a fresh burst of grief, "Is it certain," she cried, "that there are no exceptions?"

"None, my child"; and he picked up the volume. "You see it's the first love, the first passion. After that, they're innocent. Look at Mrs. De Grey. The race is accursed. It's an awful, inscrutable mystery. I fancied that you were safe, my daughter, and that that poor Miss L. had borne the brunt. But Paul was at pains to undeceive me. I've searched his life, I've probed his conscience: it's a virgin heart. Ah, my child, I dreaded it from the first. I trembled when you came into the house. I wanted Mrs. De Grey to turn you off. But she laughs at it,—she calls it an old-wife's tale. *She* was safe enough; her husband didn't care two straws for her. But there's a little dark-eyed maiden buried in Italian soil who could tell her another story. She withered, my child. She was life itself,—an incarnate ray of her own Southern sun. She died of De Grey's kisses. Don't ask me how it began, it's always been so.

It goes back to the night of time. One of the race, they say, came home from the East, from the crusades, infected with the germs of the plague. He had pledged his love-faith to a young girl before his departure, and it had been arranged that the wedding should immediately succeed his return. Feeling unwell, he consulted an elder brother of the bride, a man versed in fantastic medical lore, and supposed to be gifted with magical skill. By him he was assured that he was plague-stricken, and that he was in duty bound to defer the marriage. The young knight refused to comply, and the physician, infuriated, pronounced a curse upon his race. The marriage took place; within a week the bride expired, in horrible agony; the young man, after a slight illness, recovered; the curse took effect."

Margaret took the quaint old missal into her hand, and turned to the grisly register of death. Her heart grew cold as she thought of her own sad sisterhood with all those miserable women of the past. Miserable women, but ah! tenfold more miserable men,—helpless victims of their own baleful hearts. She remained silent, with her eyes fixed on the book, abstractly; mechanically, as it were, she turned to another page, and read a familiar orison to the blessed Virgin. Then raising her head, with her deep-blue eyes shining with the cold light of an immense resolve,—a prodigious act of volition,—"Father Herbert," she said, in low, solemn accents, "I revoke the curse. I undo it. *I curse it!*"

From this moment, nothing would induce her to bestow a moment's thought on salvation by flight. It was too late, she declared. If she was destined to die, she had already imbibed the fatal contagion. But they should see. She cast no discredit on the existence or the potency of the dreadful charm; she simply assumed, with deep self-confidence which filled the old priest with mingled wonder and anguish, that it would vainly expend its mystic force once and forever upon her own devoted, impassioned life. Father Herbert folded his trembling hands resignedly. He had done his duty; the rest was with God. At times, living as he had done for years in dread of the moment which had now arrived, with his whole life darkened by its shadow, it seemed to him among the strange possibilities of nature that this frail and pure young girl might indeed have sprung, at the command of outraged love, to the rescue of the unhappy line to which he had dedicated his manhood. And then at other moments it seemed as if she were joyously casting herself into the dark gulf. At all events, the sense of peril had filled Margaret herself with fresh energy and charm. Paul, if he had not been too enchanted with her feverish gayety and grace to trouble himself about their motive and origin, would have been at loss to explain their sudden morbid intensity. Forthwith, at her request, he announced his engagement to his mother, who put on a very gracious face, and honored Margaret with a sort of official kiss.

"Ah me!" muttered Father Herbert, "and now she thinks she has bound them fast." And later, the next day, when Mrs. De Grey, talking of the matter, avowed that it really did cost her a little to accept as a daughter a girl to whom she had paid a salary,—"A salary, madam!" cried the priest with a bitter laugh; "upon my word, I think it was the least you could do."

"*Nous verrons,*" said Mrs. De Grey, composedly.

A week passed by, without ill omens. Paul was in a manly ecstasy of bliss. At moments he was almost bewildered by the fullness with which his love and faith had been requited. Margaret was transfigured, glorified, by the passion which burned in her heart. "Give a plain girl, a common girl, a lover," thought Paul, "and she grows pretty, charming. Give a charming girl a lover——" and if Margaret was present, his eloquent eyes uttered the conclusion; if she was absent, his restless steps wandered in search of her. Her beauty within the past ten days seemed to have acquired an unprecedented warmth and richness. Paul went so far as to fancy that her voice had grown more deep and mellow. She looked older; she seemed in an instant to have overleaped a year of her development, and to have arrived at the perfect maturity of her youth. One might have imagined that, instead of the further, she stood

just on the hither verge of marriage. Meanwhile Paul
grew conscious of he hardly knew what delicate change in
his own emotions. The exquisite feeling of pity, the sense
of her appealing weakness, her heavenly dependence, which
had lent its tender strain to swell the concert of his affections, had died away, and given place to a vague, profound instinct of respect. Margaret was, after all, no such
simple body; her nature, too, had its mysteries. In truth,
thought Paul, tenderness, gentleness, is its own reward. He
had bent to pluck this pallid flower of sunless household
growth; he had dipped its slender stem in the living waters
of his love, and lo! it had lifted its head, and spread its
petals, and brightened into splendid purple and green. This
glowing potency of loveliness filled him with a tremor which
was almost a foreboding. He longed to possess her; he
watched her with covetous eyes; he wished to call her
utterly his own.

"Margaret," he said to her, "you fill me with a dreadful
delight. You grow more beautiful every day. We must be
married immediately, or, at this rate, by our wedding-day,
I shall have grown mortally afraid of you. By the soul of
my father, I didn't bargain for this! Look at yourself
in that glass." And he turned her about to a long mirror;
it was in his mother's dressing-room; Mrs. De Grey had
gone into the adjoining chamber.

Margaret saw herself reflected from head to foot in the
glassy depths, and perceived the change in her appearance.
Her head rose with a sort of proud serenity from the full
curve of her shoulders; her eyes were brilliant, her lips
trembled, her bosom rose and fell with all the insolence of
her deep devotion. "Blanche Ferrars, of Castle Ferrars,"
she silently repeated, "Isabel Stirling, Magdalen Scrope,—
poor foolish women! You were not women, you were
children. It's your fault, Paul," she cried, aloud, "if I
look other than I should! Why is there such a love between us?" And then, seeing the young man's face beside
her own, she fancied he looked pale. "My Paul," she said,
taking his hands, "you're pale. What a face for a happy

lover! You're impatient. Well-a-day, sir! It shall be when you please."

The marriage was fixed for the last of September; and the two women immediately began to occupy themselves with the purchase of the bridal garments. Margaret, out of her salary, had saved a sufficient sum to buy a handsome wedding gown; but, for the other articles of her wardrobe, she was obliged to be indebted to the liberality of Mrs. De Grey. She made no scruple, indeed, of expending large sums of money, and, when they were expended, of asking for more. She took an active, violent delight in procuring quantities of the richest stuffs. It seemed to her that, for the time, she had parted with all flimsy dignity and conventional reticence and coyness, as if she had flung away her conscience to be picked up by vulgar, happy, unimperilled women. She gathered her marriage finery together in a sort of fierce defiance of impending calamity. She felt excited to outstrip it, to confound it, to stare it out of countenance.

One day she was crossing the hall, with a piece of stuff just sent from the shop. It was a long morsel of vivid pink satin, and, as she held it, a portion of it fell over her arm to her feet. Father Herbert's door stood ajar; she stopped, and went in.

"Excuse me, reverend sir," said Margaret; "but I thought it a pity not to show you this beautiful bit of satin. Isn't it a lovely pink?—it's almost red,—it's carnation. It's the color of our love,—of my death. Father Herbert," she cried, with a shrill, resounding laugh, "*it's my shroud!* Don't you think it would be a pretty shroud?—pink satin, and blond-lace, and pearls?"

The old man looked at her with a haggard face. "My daughter," he said, "Paul will have an incomparable wife."

"Most assuredly, if you compare me with those ladies in your prayer-book. Ah! Paul shall have a wife, at least. That's very certain."

"Well," said the old man, "you're braver than I. You frighten me."

"Dear Father Herbert, didn't you once frighten me?"

The old man looked at Margaret with mingled tenderness and horror. "Tell me, child," he said, "in the midst of all this, do you ever pray?"

"God forbid!" cried the poor creature. "I have no heart for prayer."

She had long talks with Paul about their future pleasures, and the happy life they should lead. He declared that he would set their habits to quite another tune, and that the family should no longer be buried in silence and gloom. It was an absurd state of things, and he marvelled that it should ever have come about. They should begin to live like other people, and occupy their proper place in society. They should entertain company, and travel, and go to the play of an evening. Margaret had never seen a play; after their marriage, if she wished, she should see one every week for a year. "Have no fears, my dear," cried Paul, "I don't mean to bury you alive; I'm not digging your grave. If I expected you to be content to live as my poor mother lives, we might as well be married by the funeral service."

When Paul talked with this buoyant energy, looking with a firm, undoubting gaze on the long, blissful future, Margaret drew from his words fortitude and joy, and scorn of all danger. Father Herbert's secret seemed a vision, a fantasy, a dream, until, after a while, she found herself again face to face with the old man, and read in his haggard features that to him, at least, it was a deep reality. Nevertheless, among all her feverish transitions from hope to fear, from exaltation to despair, she never, for a moment, ceased to keep a cunning watch upon her physical sensations, and to lie in wait for morbid symptoms. She wondered that, with this ghastly burden on her consciousness, she had not long since been goaded to insanity, or crushed into utter idiocy. She fancied that, sad as it would have been to rest in ignorance of the mystery in which her life had been involved, it was yet more terrible to know it. During the week after her interview with Father Herbert, she had not slept half an hour of the daily twenty-four; and yet, far from missing her sleep, she felt, as I have attempted to show, intoxicated, electrified, by the unbroken vigilance and tension of her will. But she well knew that this could not last forever. One afternoon, a couple of days after Paul had uttered those brilliant promises, he mounted his horse for a ride. Margaret stood at the gate, watching him regretfully, and, as he galloped away, he kissed her his hand. An hour before tea she came out of her room, and entered the parlor, where Mrs. De Grey had established herself for the evening. A moment later, Father Herbert, who was in the act of lighting his study-lamp, heard a piercing shriek resound through the house.

His heart stood still. "The hour is come," he said. "It would be a pity to miss it." He hurried to the drawing-room together with the servants, also startled by the cry. Margaret lay stretched on the sofa, pale, motionless, panting, with her eyes closed and her hand pressed to her side. Herbert exchanged a rapid glance with Mrs. De Grey, who was bending over the young girl, holding her other hand.

"Let us at least have no scandal," she said, with dignity, and straightway dismissed the servants. Margaret gradually revived, declared that it was nothing,—a mere sudden pain,—that she felt better, and begged her companions to make no commotion. Mrs. De Grey went to her room, in search of a phial of smelling-salts, leaving Herbert alone with Margaret. He was on his knees on the floor, holding her other hand. She raised herself to a sitting posture.

"I know what you are going to say," she cried, "but it's false. Where's Paul?"

"Do you mean to tell him?" asked Herbert.

"Tell him?" and Margaret started to her feet. "If I were to die, I should wring his heart; if I were to tell him, I should break it."

She started up, I say; she had heard and recognized her lover's rapid step in the passage. Paul opened the door and came in precipitately, out of breath and deadly pale. Margaret came towards him with her hand still pressed to her side, while Father Herbert mechanically rose from his kneeling posture. "What has happened?" cried the young man. "You've been ill!"

"Who told you that anything has happened?" said Margaret.

"What is Herbert doing on his knees?"

"I was praying, sir," said Herbert.

"Margaret," repeated Paul, "in Heaven's name, what *is* the matter?"

"What's the matter with you, Paul? It seems to me that I should ask the question."

De Grey fixed a dark, searching look on the young girl, and then closed his eyes, and grasped at the back of a chair, as if his head were turning. "Ten minutes ago," he said, speaking slowly, "I was riding along by the river-side; suddenly I heard in the air the sound of a distant cry, which I knew to be yours. I turned and galloped. I made three miles in eight minutes."

"A cry, dear Paul? what should I cry about? and to be heard three miles! A pretty compliment to my lungs."

"Well," said the young man, "I suppose, then, it was my fancy. But my horse heard it too; he lifted his ears, and plunged and started."

"It must have been his fancy too! It proves you an excellent rider,—you and your horse feeling as one man!"

"Ah, Margaret, don't trifle!"

"As one horse, then!"

"Well, whatever it may have been, I'm not ashamed to confess that I'm thoroughly shaken. I don't know what has become of my nerves."

"For pity's sake, then, don't stand there shivering and staggering like a man in an ague-fit. Come, sit down on the sofa." She took hold of his arm, and led him to the couch. He, in turn, clasped her arm in his own hand, and drew her down beside him. Father Herbert silently made his exit, unheeded. Outside of the door he met Mrs. De Grey, with her smelling-salts.

"I don't think she needs them now," he said. "She has Paul." And the two adjourned together to the tea-table. When the meal was half finished, Margaret came in with Paul.

"How do you feel, dear?" said Mrs. De Grey.

"He feels much better," said Margaret, hastily.

Mrs. De Grey smiled complacently. "Assuredly," she thought, "my future daughter-in-law has a very pretty way of saying things."

The next day, going into Mrs. De Grey's room, Margaret found Paul and his mother together. The latter's eyes were red, as if she had been weeping; and Paul's face wore an excited look, as if he had been making some painful confession. When Margaret came in, he walked to the window and looked out, without speaking to her. She feigned to have come in search of a piece of needle-work, obtained it, and retired. Nevertheless, she felt deeply wounded. What had Paul been doing, saying? Why had he not spoken to her? Why had he turned his back upon her? It was only the evening before, when they were alone in the drawing-room, that he had been so unutterably tender. It was a cruel mystery; she would have no rest until she learned it,—although, in truth, she had little enough as it was. In the afternoon, Paul again ordered his horse, and dressed himself for a ride. She waylaid him as he came down stairs, booted and spurred; and, as his horse was not yet at the door, she made him go with her into the garden.

"Paul," she said, suddenly, "what were you telling your mother this morning? Yes," she continued, trying to smile, but without success, "I confess it,—I'm jealous."

"O my soul!" cried the young man, wearily, putting both his hands to his face.

"Dear Paul," said Margaret, taking his arm, "that's very beautiful, but it's not an answer."

Paul stopped in the path, took the young girl's hands and looked steadfastly into her face, with an expression that was in truth a look of weariness,—of worse than weariness, of despair. "Jealous, you say?"

"Ah, not now!" she cried, pressing his hands.

"It's the first foolish thing I have heard you say."

"Well, it was foolish to be jealous of your mother; but I'm still jealous of your solitude,—of these pleasures in which I have no share,—of your horse,—your long rides."

"You wish me to give up my ride?"

"Dear Paul, where are your wits? To wish it is—to wish it. To say I wish it is to make a fool of myself."

"My wits are with—with something that's forever gone!" And he closed his eyes and contracted his forehead as if in pain. "My youth, my hope,—what shall I call it?—my happiness."

"Ah!" said Margaret, reproachfully, "you have to shut your eyes to say that."

"Nay, what is happiness without youth?"

"Upon my word, one would think I was forty," cried Margaret.

"Well, so long as I'm sixty!"

The young girl perceived that behind these light words there was something very grave. "Paul," she said, "the trouble simply is that you're unwell."

He nodded assent, and with his assent it seemed to her that an unseen hand had smitten the life out of her heart.

"That is what you told your mother?"

He nodded again.

"And what you were unwilling to tell me?"

He blushed deeply. "Naturally," he said.

She dropped his hands and sat down, for very faintness, on a garden bench. Then rising suddenly, "Go, and take your ride," she rejoined. "But, before you go, kiss me once."

And Paul kissed her, and mounted his horse. As she went into the house, she met Father Herbert, who had been watching the young man ride away, from beneath the porch, and who was returning to his study.

"My dear child," said the priest, "Paul is very ill. God grant that, if you manage not to die, it may not be at his expense!"

For all answer, Margaret turned on him, in her passage, a face so cold, ghastly, and agonized, that it seemed a vivid response to his heart-shaking fears. When she reached her room, she sat down on her little bed, and strove to think clearly and deliberately. The old man's words had aroused

a deep-sounding echo in the vast spiritual solitudes of her
being. She was to find, then, after her long passion, that
the curse was absolute, inevitable, eternal. It could be
shifted, but not eluded; in spite of the utmost strivings of
human agony, it insatiably claimed its victim. Her own
strength was exhausted; what was she to do? All her borrowed splendor of brilliancy and bravery suddenly deserted
her, and she sat alone, shivering in her weakness. De-
luded fool that she was, for a day, for an hour, to have
concealed her sorrow from her lover! The greater her
burden, the greater should have been her confidence. What
neither might endure alone, they might have surely endured
together. But she blindly, senselessly, remorselessly drained
the life from his being. As she bloomed and prospered, he
drooped and languished. While she was living for him, he
was dying for her. Execrable, infernal comedy! What
would help her now? She thought of suicide, and she
thought of flight;—they were about equivalent. If it were
certain that by the sudden extinction of her own life she
might liberate, exonerate Paul, it would cost her but an
instant's delay to plunge a knife into her heart. But who
should say that, enfeebled, undermined as he was, the shock
of her death might not give him his own quietus? Worse
than all was the suspicion that he had begun to dislike her,
and that a dim perception of her noxious influence had
already taken possession of his senses. He was cold and
distant. Why else, when he had begun really to feel ill,
had he not spoken first to her? She was distasteful, loath-
some. Nevertheless, Margaret still grasped, with all the
avidity of despair, at the idea that it was still not too•late
to take him into her counsels, and to reveal to him all the
horrors of her secret. Then at least, whatever came, death
or freedom, they should meet it together.

Now that the enchantment of her fancied triumph had
been taken from her, she felt utterly exhausted and overwhelmed. Her whole organism ached with the desire for
sleep and forgetfulness. She closed her eyes, and sank
into the very stupor of respose. When she came to her
senses, her room was dark. She rose, and went to her

window, and saw the stars. Lighting a candle, she found that her little clock indicated nine. She had slept five hours. She hastily dressed herself, and went down stairs.

In the drawing-room, by an open window, wrapped in a shawl, with a lighted candle, sat Mrs. De Grey.

"You're happy, my dear," she cried, "to be able to sleep so soundly, when we are all in such a state."

"What state, dear lady?"

"Paul has not come in."

Margaret made no reply; she was listening intently to the distant sound of a horse's steps. She hurried out of the room, to the front door, and across the court-yard to the gate. There, in the dark starlight, she saw a figure advancing, and the rapid ring of hoofs. The poor girl suffered but a moment's suspense. Paul's horse came dashing along the road—riderless. Margaret, with a cry, plunged forward, grasping at his bridle; but he swerved, with a loud neigh, and, scarcely slackening his pace, swept into the enclosure at a lower entrance, where Margaret heard him clattering over the stones on the road to the stable, greeted by shouts and ejaculations from the hostler.

Madly, precipitately, Margaret rushed out into the darkness, along the road, calling upon Paul's name. She had not gone a quarter of a mile, when she heard an answering voice. Repeating her cry, she recognized her lover's accents.

He was upright, leaning against a tree, and apparently uninjured, but with his face gleaming through the darkness like a mask of reproach, white with the phosphorescent dews of death. He had suddenly felt weak and dizzy, and in the effort to keep himself in the saddle had frightened his horse, who had fiercely plunged, and unseated him. He leaned on Margaret's shoulder for support, and spoke with a faltering voice.

"I have been riding," he said, "like a madman. I felt ill when I went out, but without the shadow of a cause. I was determined to work it off by motion and the open air." And he stopped, gasping.

"And you feel better, dearest?" murmured Margaret.

"No, I feel worse. I'm a dead man."

Margaret clasped her lover in her arms with a long, piercing moan, which resounded through the night.

"I'm yours no longer, dear unhappy soul,—I belong, by I don't know what fatal, inexorable ties, to darkness and death and nothingness. They stifle me. Do you hear my voice?"

"Ah, senseless clod that I am, I have killed you!"

"I believe it's true. But it's strange. What is it, Margaret?—you're enchanted, baleful, fatal!" He spoke barely above a whisper, as if his voice were leaving him; his breath was cold on her cheek, and his arm heavy on her neck.

"Nay," she cried, "in Heaven's name, go on! Say something that will kill me."

"Farewell, farewell!" said Paul, collapsing.

Margaret's cry had been, for the startled household she had left behind her, an index to her halting-place. Father Herbert drew near hastily, with servants and lights. They found Margaret sitting by the roadside, with her feet in a ditch, clasping her lover's inanimate head in her arms, and covering it with kisses, wildly moaning. The sense had left her mind as completely as his body, and it was likely to come back to one as little as to the other.

A great many months naturally elapsed before Mrs. De Grey found herself in the humor to allude directly to the immense calamity which had overwhelmed her house; and when she did so, Father Herbert was surprised to find that she still refused to accept the idea of a supernatural pressure upon her son's life, and that she quietly cherished the belief that he had died of the fall from his horse.

"And suppose Margaret had died? Would to Heaven she had!" said the priest.

"Ah, suppose!" said Mrs. De Grey. "Do you make that wish for the sake of your theory?"

"Suppose that Margaret had had a lover,—a passionate lover,—who had offered her his heart before Paul had ever seen her; and then that Paul had come, bearing love and death."

"Well, what then?"

"Which of the three, think you, would have had most cause for sadness?"

"It's always the survivors of a calamity who are to be pitied," said Mrs. De Grey.

"Yes, madam, it's the survivors,—even after fifty years."